THE BEWITCHING of AMORETTA IPSWICH

MARCIA LYNN McCLURE

Published by Distractions Ink
P.O. Box 15971
Rio Rancho, NM 87174

Published by Distractions Ink
©Copyright 2012 by M. Meyers
A.K.A. Marcia Lynn McClure
Cover Photography by
© Michael Shake/Dreamstime.com and Mark Perkes
Cover Design and Interior Graphics by Sandy Ann Allred/Timeless Allure

First Printed Edition: October 2012

McClure, Marcia Lynn, 1965—
The Bewitching of Amoretta Ipswich: a novel/by Marcia Lynn McClure.

ISBN: 978-0-9884276-2-4

Library of Congress Control Number: 2012950578

Printed in the United States of America

PREFACE

From the time I can remember (and I have memories that reach back to the cradle—or, more appropriately, the crib), my mom sang to me. My mom has a beautiful singing voice, and she sang me to sleep as she rocked me at night when I was very, very little. She sang to me when we were just doing things around the house. And she sang to me when we were traveling in the car. All the while my sister and I were growing up, it seemed Mom was always singing—and my favorite songs were those sweet, tender ones she sang to me when I was very little.

When I was seven years old, my little sister (and only sibling) was born, and although Mom didn't sing me to sleep every night anymore by then, she did begin singing my baby sister to sleep. Therefore, being that my sister and I shared a bed when she was baby, I was blessed with the gift of hearing Mom singing all my favorite lullabies again.

I could go on and on about how much I loved to hear my mom sing and how much I still cherish all the little songs she used to sing to my sister and me when we were little. Mom sang those same little songs to my daughter when she was born too, and they are just as much a part of my own daughter's memories of being little as they are of mine. Even now, if I sit in complete silence, close my eyes, and listen very hard, I can hear my mom's voice sweetly echoing through my mind. It's one of my very favorite sounds in all the world.

One of those precious lullabies Mom used to sing has always particularly lent scope to my imagination—inspiration to the fictional stories that bounce around in my head—and has at last led to my writing this book. That song is "Three Little Girls Dressed in Blue." That has echoed in my imagination as the premise for a romantic story for as long as I can remember. Sadly, it's nearly impossible to find—though I did (recently) find one Web site reference to give to you. It's a site that archives songs that have not had copyrights renewed:

http://archive.org/details/TexWilliams-ThreeLittleGirlsDressedInBlue

As far as I know, this is the only way you'll be able to hear the song that has inspired not only this book but also the two books to follow—the song that I can still hear my sweet mother singing to me if I find a quiet place, close my eyes, and listen very, very hard.

> There were three little girls dressed in blue.
> Then one married and left only two.
> Then one fell in love with a boy,
> Who loved her and gave her much joy.
> Then the last little girl had a dream,
> And she dreamed she was saying, "I do."
> And when she awoke it was true!
> Happy three little girls dressed in blue.
> —*Tex Williams*

And so, with the tender history of my most beloved childhood song in mind, I give you Book I of The Three Little Girls Dressed in Blue Trilogy, *The Bewitching of Amoretta Ipswich*.

To my beautiful mother...
You have the voice of an angel!
Thank you for singing to me all my life,
For filling my memories and dreams
with the sounds of a mother's selfless, perfect love.
I love you so much, Mom!
~ Your daughter, Marcia

CHAPTER ONE

"But it is what it is, Amoretta," Evangeline reiterated. "We're here now. We're not going back to Boston. And Daddy is *so* happy here…happier than he's been since Mama died."

Evangeline paused, and Amoretta mumbled, "I know."

"Calliope and I are finding things to like about the West," Evangeline continued. She wasn't nagging—only offering encouragement. Therefore, Amoretta wasn't at all perturbed with her older sister; she just wished she owned a bit of Evangeline's endurance and ability to make anything seem positive.

"Of course it's very different here, but linger on the beauty of the vistas, if nothing else, Retta," Evangeline buoyed with exuberance. "Just three steps out of town and the entire world seems to roll out before you!"

"And people are so kind and friendly," Calliope interjected. "Everyone has been so welcoming and helpful. I know you miss Boston, Amoretta, but out here…" Calliope paused to inhale a breath of fresh western air. Smiling, she continued, "Out here things seem so adventurous and new. And after all, you've got a more adventurous spirit than either Evangeline or I. Quite frankly, I'm surprised it's you who seems so unhappy with our move."

Amoretta shrugged, still disheartened and nursing an inescapable feeling of lonesomeness—even for the sweet, loving company of her beloved sisters.

"I don't know what's wrong with me," she admitted. "So many things flit around in my brain, things that worry me to near nausea. And yet they're all things I know shouldn't bother me at all."

"Such as?" Evangeline prodded.

But Amoretta shook her head. "You both will think I'm silly, petty, and just a plain old pouty baby."

"No, we won't," Calliope assured her. "We all have our secret strangenesses, Amoretta. All three of us."

"Exactly," Evangeline agreed. "Everyone in the whole world owns little idiosyncrasies. It's what individualizes us. So tells us, Amoretta…what kinds of things are bothering you so? What's keeping you from being happy here in Meadowlark Lake?"

Amoretta Ipswich looked from one of her sisters to the other. She wondered in that moment how miserable life may have been if she hadn't been blessed with such loving siblings. She wondered how she would've endured her mother's and baby brother's deaths when she was just ten years old. She wondered whom she would've played with, confided in, and loved if not for Evangeline and Calliope.

She felt a smile curl the corners of her mouth as she studied her older sister. Two years Amoretta's senior, Evangeline Ipswich owned the strongest, most persevering character of the three of Judge Lawson Ipswich's daughters—at least that's how Amoretta felt. Evangeline had been just twelve when their mother had died, and yet she had comforted and cared for Amoretta and Calliope nearly as perfectly as their mother had. Amoretta had always admired Evangeline's classic beauty as well—her raven hair and dark green eyes. She'd always thought that, other than their mother, there was no more beautiful woman ever born than Evangeline Ipswich.

Amoretta looked to her younger sister Calliope next. Instantly a giggle bubbled in Amoretta's throat, for there wasn't a person on earth that could keep from smiling once they'd gazed at Calliope Ipswich. There was something in her countenance—a sweetness and implication of constant mirth—that bred amusement in whomever looked at her. Her sunshine-colored hair flounced when she walked, and her bright blue eyes seemed to hold the same twinkle of starlight.

Calliope was exactly two years younger than Amoretta—to the day—and in that moment Amoretta grew anxious at the realization that she and her sisters were quite grown up. Calliope was already seventeen, officially a young woman, and somehow it caused a great melancholy to settle in Amoretta's bosom.

Looking from Evangeline to Calliope and back once more, Amoretta sighed, for there she sat—Amoretta Ipswich, with her plain brown hair and her plain green eyes. There she sat (plain old Amoretta Ipswich) right between the raven-haired beauty of Evangeline Ipswich and the golden-haired loveliness of Calliope Ipswich. She always mused how simply kaleidoscopic the three of them seemed, especially for sisters. Raven hair and emerald eyes—plain brown hair and plain green eyes—hair like spun sunshine and eyes as blue as the sky. Yes, it was how Amoretta perceived the physical appearances of herself and her sisters, like the varying patterns that appeared in the kaleidoscope her father had gifted their mother one Christmas.

Oh, Amoretta wasn't envious on any level. She just felt plain and simple in comparison with her sisters. She pondered a moment how different their personalities were as well, nearly as different as their physical appearances. Evangeline—strong, enduring, loving, and nurturing. Calliope—lighthearted and a bit silly-minded at times. Amoretta—adventurous, superstitious, and curious as a cat. She thought that if all three of Judge Ipswich's daughters were combined into one, they might well make the perfect woman.

Amoretta giggled at the thought, and Calliope urged, "What? What's so amusing? And you're supposed to be telling us your concerns."

"Yes," Evangeline confirmed. "What's bothering you? These things that are worrying you and keeping you from blooming where you're planted?"

Amoretta rolled her eyes with exasperation. "Evie…you *know* I hate that phrase," she sighed. "I've been hearing it from the moment we arrived here, and I'm tired of it."

But Evangeline was neither vexed nor impatient. As always she smiled with understanding.

"Just tell us your concerns, darling," she said. "Calliope and I will help you sort things out."

Exhaling a heavy sigh of resolve, Amoretta began. "Well, things like…like…and I know it's silly, for I know good and well Mama and baby Gilbert are in heaven and not here."

"But?" Calliope urged.

"But we just left them there!" Amoretta exclaimed. "We just left them there in their lonely grave, all alone, with no one to visit and no one to talk to! It haunts me…haunts my thoughts in the middle of the night." Amoretta wiped a sudden tear from her cheek. "I just think of them there all alone, cold when winter comes, no one to visit or talk to…no one to leave pretty flowers on their grave."

"But that's why Father had them buried together, Rettie," Calliope offered, "so that they wouldn't be alone there…even though they're truly in heaven and not even in the grave."

Amoretta nodded, brushing another insipid tear from her cheek. "I know that. But it haunts me all the same."

"And what else is haunting you, Rettie?" Evangeline asked.

"I'm not telling you the other things," Amoretta announced. "You'll think I belong in the lunatic asylum."

Evangeline giggled as Calliope said, "Oh, we already know you belong there, Rettie. That's not anything new."

Amoretta smiled, though she rolled her eyes with feigned disgust all the same.

"Come on now," Evangeline said. "Out with it. What else is keeping you from—"

"Blooming where I'm planted…I know, I know!" Amoretta interrupted.

"Besides Mama and baby Gilbert being left behind, what else is it?" Evangeline asked.

Amoretta shrugged. She knew she might as well confess—for she knew neither Evangeline nor Calliope would let her escape their interrogation and efforts to help until she did.

"It's the...well...it's the S in the peelings, if you must know," Amoretta purged.

"The Halloween apple peelings S?" Calliope exclaimed.

"Oh, heaven help us!" Evangeline sighed with exasperation.

"Four Halloweens running, Evangeline!" Amoretta reminded. "Four! You cannot deny the facts, Evie. Four Halloweens in a row, my apple peels laid out an S. Four!"

"I know, Rettie," Evangeline said. "Oh, believe me...Calliope and I both know. But it's only a Halloween game. You know that." Evangeline smiled, rolled her eyes with amusement, and recited, *"Pare an apple, miss or mister, and fling the peel behind you. The letter it shapes begins the name of your lover meant to find you."*

"Oh, wait!" Calliope giggled. "I like this one better. *Thrice around the apple go, with knife in paring whirl. Take the peel, and toss it back, whether you be boy or girl. Upon the ground the peel will shape the letter that begins your one true lover's given name, spelled out in apple skins."*

"I know it's just superstition," Amoretta interrupted, sighing with exasperation. "But some of us...some of us believe there may be a certain credibility to some superstitions."

"But even if that old superstition is true, which it's not," Calliope began, "your apple peelings shaping S does not mean you were meant to marry Sylvanus Tenney! There are hundreds of men in the world whose names begin with S. Sylvanus is only one."

Evangeline and Amoretta exchanged amused glances.

"I'm sure there are more than hundreds of men in the world with names that begin with S, Calliope," Evangeline teased.

Calliope rolled her eyes, shook her head, and corrected herself, "Thousands then...if you're going to pick nits, Evie." Sighing, she continued, "Regardless, Amoretta, your S apple peels do not mean you were meant to marry Sylvanus."

"And how can you be certain?" Amoretta asked rather daringly.

Calliope shrugged. "Well, it would make sense to me that if one superstition were true, then the others would follow with proof. And I don't remember you ever bobbing for an apple and retrieving one with an S carved into it...nor do I remember you ever confessing to us having seen Sylvanus appear behind you in a mirror on Halloween at midnight. Therefore, you can't convince me that the S your peelings have spelled out for four years running…you won't convince me it was Sylvanus Tenney's S, and there you have it." Calliope gestured with one hand that she'd proved her point. "You never, ever once saw Sylvanus Tenney's image appear behind you in a mirror held by candlelight at midnight on *any* Halloween past. Therefore, you cannot be sure it is Sylvanus's S that the apple peelings carved out."

"But I've always *felt* it was Sylvanus's S," Amoretta confessed.

"Of course you did," Calliope agreed. "Because Sylvanus Tenney was and still is the handsomest young man in all of Boston! Every one of us mooned about after him like a litter of hungry puppies. Add to that that none of us knew another young man of our family's acquaintance with a name that began with S, and of course you felt it was Sylvanus's S in your apple peelings."

Amoretta shook her head. "You've failed to convince me that the S of my apple peels—four Halloweens in a row, I might add—was not Sylvanus Tenney's S. And therefore, I worry that in leaving Boston and moving to this godforsaken West, my happiness has been obliterated before it had the chance to begin."

Evangeline puffed a sigh of frustration. "Amoretta…for pity's sake!" she exclaimed. Then, straightening her posture and seeming to find renewed resolve, she added, "Think of it this way, Rettie. If Sylvanus Tenney is meant to be your one true love and husband—if your Halloween apple peelings truly have been spelling out S for Sylvanus—then all will be well. Your paths will cross again when it is time. Don't you agree? After all, aren't you the one forever telling Calliope and me that true love always finds a way?"

Amoretta shrugged. "Well…well, yes, I suppose. But—"

"But nothing," Calliope interrupted. "You *are* always telling us that, and if you really believe it, then take heart and know that if you were meant to love Sylvanus and belong to him…then life will bring you together once more."

Amoretta shook her head, brushed one last tear from her cheek, and smiled. How could she linger in her dismal mood of loneliness with such wonderful companions as Evangeline and Calliope ever at hand?

"Fine," she sighed. "I'll make a better effort to bloom where I'm planted." Wagging an index finger at her elder sister and then her younger one, however, she added, "But please quit saying that! It makes me want to scream every time I hear it. 'Bloom where you're planted.' I'm not a tulip or daffodil. I'm a girl, a woman, and I was born in Boston, and it makes perfect sense I should feel...well, transplanted and under-watered if nothing else."

Evangeline and Calliope both laughed, and Calliope said, "All right! We won't think of you as a tulip...but rather as a snobbish, Bostonian woman who—"

"I'm not a snobbish Bostonian," Amoretta interrupted, giggling. "I'm a normal, Meadowlark Lake tulip, blooming where I'm planted."

"Or at least you will be one day," Evangeline offered.

"And besides, Rettie," Calliope began, "I've already seen several young men right here in Meadowlark Lake who are far better looking than Sylvanus Tenney."

"Well, I'll believe that when I see one for myself," Amoretta said, winking at her sister.

"You've got to meander around town a bit...actually get out of the house for a change, if you expect to see one for yourself, darling," Calliope added. "Maybe one will appear as we walk to Mrs. Montrose's house this afternoon for the sewing circle."

Amoretta forced a smile. In truth, Amoretta Ipswich felt no better about being dug up from her comfortable bed in Boston and plopped into the dusty, dry ground in Meadowlark Lake than she had before her sisters had endeavored to cheer her. But she would not allow Evangeline and Calliope to sense that all their efforts were once again in vain.

Thus, rising from the chair she'd been sitting in in the parlor, she said, "You're right, Calliope! It's time I got out and about...found some of these good-looking young men you're always telling me about. Perhaps even before we start for Mrs. Montrose's sewing circle this afternoon."

"Do you mean it?" Evangeline asked. "You're really going out? You haven't been out since we arrived last week. Well…for anything other than a visit to the outhouse anyway."

"Exactly," Amoretta said. "And it's time I changed my attitude, right?"

"Do you want us to go with you?" Calliope asked.

"Not at all," Amoretta answered. "I'm off on my very first, way-out-west, Meadowlark Lake adventure. After all, you two are always telling me I'm the adventurous Ipswich girl, right?"

"Right!" Calliope giggled.

The relief and joy were so plainly obvious on the faces of her sisters that Amoretta was glad she'd chosen to fib to them about having changed her perception of their move. She wanted them to be happy. They were both enjoying Meadowlark Lake, and it would only be selfish to continue to dampen their spirits the way Amoretta realized in those moments she had been doing—however unwittingly.

"And so, my darlings, I'm off for a stroll…off to linger in admiration of those beautiful vistas Evangeline loves so and those handsome young men Calliope admires." With a curtsy, and a secret satisfaction in the smiles on her sisters' faces, Amoretta hurried through the parlor, into the kitchen, and out the back door of the house.

Determined to be out of sight of her sisters before her true feelings erupted, Amoretta hastened past the old outhouse, through the line of fruit trees that backed her father's new property, and toward the wooded area she could see on the horizon. But being that the woods were more than a mile off, Amoretta knew her tears could not be withheld so long as it would take to reach the woods.

Suddenly, and without further warning, Amoretta burst into the bitter sobbing of disappointment, heartache, and unfamiliar loneliness. Oh, how she missed Boston! How she missed the plush, green grasses and flowering, fragrant shrubberies! Oh, how she longed to wander familiar byways. Meadowlark Lake only owned one major thoroughfare—a street that entered the small town at one end and exited at the other. All other streets and paths roundabout were simply wagon-rutted dirt roads or grassy trails that were more often than not hard to follow. Of course, her father saw things differently. Amoretta's father had told her the dirt roads and overgrown paths of Meadowlark Lake were wonderfully rural, picturesque, and simple adventures in themselves. But Amoretta's mind had known her father had seen what he wanted to see in Meadowlark Lake—a fresh start.

And it wasn't that she wasn't happy for her father. She was! It's why she had sworn Evangeline and Calliope to secrecy where their father's middle daughter's unhappiness was concerned. Judge Lawson Ipswich seemed so hopefully changed since the family had abandoned Boston for places west, and Amoretta truly wished her father happiness. She only quietly wished her own happiness could've accompanied his.

Brushing rivulets of tears from her cheeks and trying to catch something other than a ragged breath, Amoretta began to run. She didn't know whether her feet followed one of the rural, picturesque, and adventurous paths toward the woods; she didn't care. All she could think of was reaching the woods, hiding among the trees, and sobbing out her retched soul in peace.

Over and over the phrase she'd grown to despise echoed through her mind: *Bloom where you're planted. Bloom where you're planted.*

Oh, how she loathed that phrase! In those moments, Amoretta wished whoever had coined it in the first place had left well enough alone. She wondered who it was that spent his time making up such irritating metaphors. *Bloom where you're planted.* It made her want to scream!

She tripped then on a large root protruding from the ground. And when she found herself sprawled on the soft, fragrant grass, Amoretta Ipswich felt pure defeat. Not bothering to sit or stand—careless of whether she ever reached the woods and the privacy it offered—Amoretta folded her arms on the ground beneath her, placed her forehead on the protection they provided, and cried.

He'd seen the girl running—seen her trip and go tumbling forward into the grass. His powerful protective instinct caused him to rein his horse toward her. Yet when he heard her sobbing, heard her cry out, "Bloom where I'm planted? Never!" and realized no one was pursing her, he paused in offering assistance.

He figured she'd come from the new judge's house—figured she must be one of three daughters he'd heard tell the new judge had brought with him from Boston. And if there was one thing he didn't need, it was to attract the attention of a judge. Still, the girl seemed overwrought, and from the very marrow of his bones he wanted to make certain she was unharmed.

Still, his intuition whispered that this was one of those moments when a female just needed space and privacy in order to cry her heart out to the breeze—to purge her spirit of whatever was ailing it. Therefore, instead of descending on her unexpectedly and perhaps scaring the very life out of her in doing so, he simply lingered a moment and listened to the girl pouring her heart out to the grass (something about tulips). And when he was sure she was not in any sort of danger or experiencing truly life-threatening duress, he reined his horse to the left. He'd take the longer way to the woods. He'd have less chance of being seen that way anyhow.

As he rode toward the privacy of the tree line, he shook his head, realizing he'd best plan on taking the longer route to the woods from now on. Being that the new judge's house had a clear view of the woods and all those who might come and go into and out of them, it made better sense to take a little more time than to raise the suspicions of the new lawman.

Raising a curious brow, the man mumbled to his horse, "Looks like that new judge has his hands full if that's how all his daughters carry on." The horse whinnied as if agreeing with its rider.

The man chuckled. "Let's just get where we're goin', Gambler...before that girl sits up and sees us."

He urged Gambler into a trot, hoping the girl was still crying too hard to hear the rhythm of horse hooves.

Amoretta had no idea how long she'd been gone from the house—and part of her didn't care. Alone in the vast open field of grass between her father's house and the tree line of the woods, she'd somehow managed to cry herself to sleep. She'd awakened when she'd heard something—the unfamiliar, and yet beautifully serene, call of a songbird nearby. Her eyes opened slowly, and she was surprised by the sensation of delight that washed over her as the vision of the soft blue sky and white billowy clouds was what met her in those first waking moments.

She'd obviously rolled over during her out-of-doors nap, and there above her was pure wonderment in blue and white. She'd never seen clouds like these before—like giant kernels of the whitest of white popcorn, lazily drifting on a hue of bright blue she could have never imagined. The thought occurred to her that in Boston she would never have known such privacy—such quiet. Save the sound of the light breeze through the grass and the sweet song of the birds, there was not another sound—and she fancied her ears adored that fact.

The day was warm, and the air was light—not heavy and sticky the way it always was in Boston. And there were no unpleasant odors, it seemed. Amoretta inhaled several deep breaths, concentrating as she did so on discerning the scents in the air. There was no scent of rancid meat that often lingered in the marketplaces in Boston. There was only the fragrance of grass. There was no choking coal smell, only a freshness her vocabulary could not define.

An enormous yellow and black butterfly fluttered into her line of vision, and Amoretta smiled as it floated just above her. It seemed almost curious somehow, and when it did eventually land on the back of her hand for a moment, she smiled at the tickling sensation of its legs on her skin. She was astonished at how very long the butterfly lingered—several minutes actually—and she inwardly

11

admitted that the pretty thing could not have done so in the bustling city of Boston.

Eventually the butterfly took flight once more. Amoretta sat up as she watched it meander on its way. It looked just like a large yellow buttercup caught on the breeze, and she was disappointed when it disappeared into the grass somewhere, having found something else to be curious about.

"Where have you been, Amoretta Ipswich?" Calliope chirped as she rather romped through the grass toward Amoretta. "Evangeline and I are ready to walk down to Mrs. Montrose's house for the sewing circle gathering. You are coming, aren't you?"

Amoretta giggled, delighted by the sight of her sister skipping toward her. The manner in which bright sunshine glinted on the gold of Calliope's hair gave her the look of wearing a halo—just like an angel—and Amoretta did indeed feel better. Boston suddenly seemed very far away. And though she knew her anxieties would return—the strange loneliness she felt at the thought of never setting eyes on Sylvanus Tenney again—in that moment Amoretta wondered if perhaps she really could find a measure of happiness out west in the small town of Meadowlark Lake.

"Of course I'm coming," Amoretta chirped. Calliope offered her sister a hand, and Amoretta accepted, allowing her younger sister to help her to her feet. "I mean, after all…what's more exciting than a sewing circle?"

Calliope giggled, adding, "And we wouldn't want to miss it and make the sheriff's wife feel slighted, now would we?"

"No indeed!" Amoretta agreed.

"Then come on," Calliope said, linking her arm with Amoretta's. "Let's be off to our very first Meadowlark Lake sewing circle! There's bound to be gossip and thereby much to learn about the people of our new town." Calliope paused, winking at Amoretta. "Perhaps there'll even be a mother or two with a handsome son to marry off."

"A son more handsome than Sylvanus Tenney?" Amoretta teased.

"Oh, much more handsome, Rettie! Much more handsome!"

Amoretta's smile did not fade, and her heart remained lightened. She wondered if perhaps her wretched sobbing had purged some of her misery after all. Perhaps there was another man in the world whose name began with S—the S the apple peels had been spelling out for her every autumn for the past four years. Perhaps she could learn to *bloom where she was planted.* Though she still despised the phrase and determined that she always would, Amoretta looked up into the bright blue sky with its white popcorned clouds and smiled. Evangeline was right after all. Her mother and baby brother were in heaven, not in the cold Massachusetts ground. And if her apple peelings had spelled out S for Sylvanus, then true love would ensure that Sylvanus found his way back to her—somehow.

CHAPTER TWO

"And how is your mother faring, Prudence dear?"

Amoretta looked up from the handkerchief she'd been embroidering to see Mrs. Montrose looking at a pretty brunette girl who had introduced herself to Amoretta and her sisters as Prudence Mulholland.

Prudence sighed rather wistfully as a frown puckered her brow. "Not well, I'm afraid," she answered. "The doctors say she may have to remain away for quite some time yet."

"Oh dear," Mrs. Montrose sighed. "Consumption is such a mean, heartless illness."

"Yes, ma'am," Prudence agreed.

"Pru's mother has tuberculosis," the girl sitting next to Amoretta whispered. This young woman was Blanche Gardener. She and her mother were both in attendance at the sewing circle Dora Montrose was hostessing. Amoretta had been astonished at how similar Blanche and her mother, Judith, appeared—more like sisters separated by several years than mother and daughter.

"How sad," Amoretta whispered in return.

"Yes. It's very sad," Blanche added. "Mr. Mulholland, Pru's father, owns the mill. Her brother, Samuel, works there." Blanche smiled and winked at Amoretta. "Samuel Mulholland is as handsome as the day is long."

Amoretta bit her lip to stifle an amused giggle. She liked Blanche. Blanche was forthright and friendly and seemed to own a wonderful sense of humor.

Still, Amoretta's smile faded, however, as she studied Prudence a moment. It was obvious that the subject of her mother's illness had saddened her. Her brown eyes seemed to have lost the spark they held only a moment before.

"I feel so sorry for Pru and Samuel…for Mr. Mulholland too," Blanche added.

"And how are the Ipswich girls enjoyin' Meadowlark Lake?" Blanche's mother inquired.

Amoretta looked to Calliope, and Calliope looked to Evangeline.

"Why, it's lovely, Mrs. Gardener," Evangeline answered, smiling. "So much open space and serenity to linger in. So much fresh air…and such lovely people."

Amoretta sighed, relieved Evangeline had owned a quick answer.

"And your father?" a woman named Ellen Ackerman asked. Ellen's daughter, Sallie, was present as well.

Buoyed by Evangeline's courage in engaging conversation, Calliope exclaimed, "Oh, he quite adores it here! I think Boston had begun to close in on him somehow. Daddy seems to be thriving now that we've settled in a bit."

"He's quite a handsome man," Mrs. Montrose's daughter, Winnie, offered.

Amoretta, Evangeline, and Calliope giggled simultaneously as Mrs. Montrose gently scolded, "Winnie! What a thing to say!"

But Winnie shrugged. "Well, he is, Mother. I heard you tell Mrs. Ackerman yourself…just before the Ipswich girls arrived today."

Amoretta smiled as Dora Montrose blushed the color of summer radishes.

"He is quite handsome," Mrs. Gardener agreed. "And after all, there's no shame in noticin' it."

"I understand he lost your mother some years back," Prudence commented. Amoretta felt that Prudence was looking for some sort of emotional strength from the only other young women in the room without their mothers present—the Ipswich girls. Prudence was looking directly at Amoretta; thus Amoretta felt obligated to answer, though she would have much rather allowed Evangeline to do it.

"Y-yes," Amoretta managed. "She died shortly after our baby brother was born…and he was lost as well. Nearly seven years ago now."

"How terrible," Mrs. Montrose said, shaking her head. Her sincerity of sympathy was clear in her countenance. "I'm so sorry."

"How sad," Prudence added. "I'm sorry as well."

"And I suppose your father still mourns her fiercely," Mrs. Gardener put in. "It's not somethin' one ever truly recovers from…the loss of a spouse."

"But now you're all here!" Winnie offered with enthusiasm, gesturing to Amoretta and her sisters. "And everyone in Meadowlark Lake is delighted that you are…*and* very excited about havin' the county judge right here in town."

"I suppose you've already been introduced to just about everyone," Mrs. Ackerman mused.

"Other than Fox, of course," Winnie added.

Amoretta was amused, and her curiosity piqued, when every woman in the room, save her and her sisters, giggled and blushed a little.

Readily taking the bait, as she always did, Calliope asked, "Who's Fox?"

"Fox is my older brother," Winnie explained.

"And the very handsomest of young men," Blanche giggled.

"He's been away at university," Winnie continued. "And he's due to arrive home this very week!"

"Yes," Mrs. Montrose sighed. "It will be so good to have Fox home again."

"Mrs. Montrose has been worried that Fox would fall in love with some silly city girl and decide not to return to Meadowlark Lake," Blanche whispered to Amoretta.

"So you haven't quite met *everyone* in town yet," Prudence interjected, wearing a smile as broad as the Mississippi. "Not until you've met Winnie's brother, Fox."

The girls all giggled again, and Evangeline smiled. "Well, your son must be quite the handsome young man indeed, Mrs. Montrose. He's not even present, and it seems he has all our feminine hearts aflutter."

Mrs. Montrose smiled, offering a humble shrug in response.

"And you haven't met the witch yet either," Sallie Ackerman stated.

Instantly the room fell silent, and every smile that the mention of Fox Montrose had caused a moment before suddenly faded.

"The witch?" Amoretta asked. A shiver of delicious curiosity traveled over her spine, and she wondered if Meadowlark Lake might well turn out to be wildly interesting after all.

"Oh, for Pete's sake, Sallie," Mrs. Ackerman scolded. "She's not a witch."

"A gypsy woman then," Sallie offered. "You Ipswich girls need get a look at the wi...at the gypsy woman who lives in the woods before you truly know everyone in Meadowlark Lake."

"A gypsy?" Calliope inquired. Amoretta could see that Calliope's interest was nearly as heightened as her own.

"Yes...well, I guess that's what she is," Sallie answered, glancing guiltily at her mother.

"Her name is Kizzy, and she lives in a little cottage in the center of the woods," Mrs. Gardener offered.

"The woods just beyond your house a mile or so, Miss Ipswich," Prudence said, looking to Amoretta.

"Oh, please do call me Amoretta," Amoretta offered. Prudence smiled and nodded.

"And she's truly a gypsy?" Calliope asked.

"Oh, we don't know for certain," Mrs. Montrose answered. "She keeps quite to herself. She and her little girl very rarely venture into town. I think...I think they prefer the solitude the woods provides."

"But why do people think she's a witch?" Evangeline asked. "For that's what Sallie said she was at first." Amoretta was glad Evangeline had asked the question. She didn't want to appear too interested in the witch of Meadowlark Lake, lest all the ladies at Mrs. Montrose's sewing circle begin thinking she was too strange.

Mrs. Ackerman rather glared at her daughter with disapproval as she answered, "Kizzy is somewhat of...of an herbalist. She makes and sells certain remedies and tonics for common complaints."

"She deals in love potions and charms, as well," Sallie added.

"Oh now, Sallie Ackerman!" Mrs. Ackerman finally scolded severely. "Stop this gossip at once."

"And she doesn't have a husband," Blanche whispered to Amoretta. Amoretta looked to Blanche, and the girl added, "A little girl...but no husband."

"Perhaps he died," Prudence suggested, having heard Blanche's comment.

"Then why doesn't she just tell folks that?" Winnie asked.

"Maybe she feels it's not pertinent information for the townsfolk to know," Prudence answered.

"And she has no last name to speak of," Sallie added.

"Sallie!" Mrs. Ackerman exclaimed. "Stop this at once! We none of us know the circumstances that woman lives under...or what she may have endured in her life. I won't have you spreadin' rumors and causin' any more suspicion to follow that poor woman."

"Yes, Mother," Sallie agreed.

"Well, if any of you ladies are as intrigued with superstitions as you are with gypsies, you should have Amoretta tell you all about the book she's been studying of late," Calliope announced.

Amoretta felt the color fade from her face as fast as butter melted in a hot skillet. As every set of eyes in the room rested on her, Amoretta wondered whether she should reach out and wring Calliope's neck at that very moment or wait until they were in private.

"Calliope!" Amoretta scolded in a whisper.

"Oh, don't be shy, Amoretta," Calliope giggled, however. Looking out to the group of inquisitive women, she added, "It's a fascinating book! All about Halloween and the customs and superstitions that accompany it…so very informative and inspiring of the imagination."

"Do tell," Mrs. Montrose said, winking understandingly at Amoretta. "Tell us about it, dear," the hostess urged. "And don't worry. We're quite open-minded here in Meadowlark Lake."

"That's right!" Sallie assured her. "We won't lump you in with the likes of the gypsy woman in the woods."

"Sallie!" Mrs. Ackerman growled.

"Now," Mrs. Gardener began, "do tell us about this book of Halloween customs you're studying, Amoretta dear. It sounds deliciously intriguing!"

Amoretta gulped, glared at Calliope, and then looked to Evangeline for encouragement. Evangeline did encourage, with a smile and a nod.

"Well, it's mostly about the fun and games of Halloween," Amoretta began. "You know, things like the power of the lucky apple, the spell of the apple parings, seeing the image of your true lover in a mirror behind you at midnight…"

"Oh! Like chestnuts on the coals and things!" Mrs. Gardener exclaimed.

"And findin' the ring in the cake," Mrs. Montrose added. "That actually happened to me! It was the Halloween I was seventeen," she began.

Amoretta smiled, dazzled by what obviously promised to be a captivating yarn.

"Ooo, do tell them, Mama!" Winnie encouraged gleefully. "I love this story!"

"Well, I was seventeen that Halloween, and the Bradfords were havin' a barn dance," Mrs. Montrose explained. "Oh, I was so smitten with Dennison at the time! Fairly insane with admiration for him."

Winnie looked to Evangeline, Calliope, and Amoretta and explained, "Dennison is my daddy...the sheriff."

"Well, I went to the barn dance just wishing, hopin', and prayin' that Dennison Montrose would ask me for a dance," Mrs. Montrose said. "I tried to convince myself that I would be happy even with just a glance or a kind word from him...but what I really wanted was a dance."

Amoretta giggled along with all the other young women and mothers in the room. She adored such tellings of romance, of how a man and a woman first met and fell in love. She smiled when she noticed that not one female in the room was darning, stitching, or mending. All attention was glued to Mrs. Montrose.

"Naturally, as the night wore on and Dennison didn't ask me for a dance—didn't even smile at me—I began to wonder if I would ever manage to capture his attention...even for a moment." Mrs. Montrose paused, smiled, and continued, "And then it was time for the games. Oh, what fun we had! We bobbed for apples, ventured the bowls of fate, pared apples and tossed the peelings over our shoulders...every delightful Halloween custom you could name." Mrs. Montrose smiled and sighed with amused reminiscing. "At last came the time for the lucky cake—the cake with a ring, a dime, a thimble, and a key baked into it." She looked to Amoretta and asked, "And you know what that means?"

Amoretta nodded. "The cake is cut, and everyone takes a slice...and fortunes are told."

"Exactly!" Mrs. Montrose chimed. "Well, my mortal enemy, Eunice Frahmholtz, found the thimble in her piece of cake. The thimble—the token that meant she was to be a spinster! I was delighted."

"Mama! How mean!" Winnie teased.

"I was only seventeen, darling...and Eunice was as sour a pickle as any ever bottled," Mrs. Montrose explained. "My friend Thelma found the dime in her piece of cake."

"The token of wealth," Amoretta offered.

"Right!" Mrs. Montrose laughed.

"Ooo! I think we need a lucky cake at our Halloween festivities this year, Mama," Blanche suggested. Her mother nodded and winked at her.

"I don't remember who found the key in their piece of cake," Mrs. Montrose admitted. "But I...I found the ring in mine! A weddin' ring!"

"So you were to be the girl to marry next...to be a happy wife soon thereafter," Amoretta chirped. "Or so the customs says," Amoretta explained as the others looked at her inquisitively.

Mrs. Montrose nodded. "Yes. Oh, we all knew it was just fun and games, but it was wonderful to me...just wonderful!"

"And then *Daddy* did ask her for a dance that night!" Winnie revealed.

"Yes, he did," Mrs. Montrose affirmed. "And Dennison and I were married within a month...before Thanksgiving actually."

"Truly, Mrs. Montrose?" Prudence asked.

Amoretta giggled—for Prudence, Blanche, and Sallie all wore expressions of pure astonished wonderment and delight.

"Truly, Prudence," Mrs. Montrose answered. "So you see, Amoretta, I for one am sincerely interested in this book of Halloween customs you're studying. For I believe in them...or at least in their power of suggestion to the human mind."

"I pared an apple and tossed the peelings over my shoulder on the Halloween I was twenty," Mrs. Ackerman confessed.

"And?" Amoretta coaxed. "Did they spell out the first initial of your lover?"

Everyone giggled.

"Well, I thought they spelled out a W," Mrs. Ackerman answered.

"But Daddy's name begins with M, Mama. M for Martin," Sallie noted with disappointment.

But Mrs. Ackerman smiled. "Yet had I looked at the peelings from another vantage point—"

"They would have shaped M!" Prudence giggled, clapping her hands together.

Everyone laughed and begged Amoretta to share details of the book she was reading. And she did so with great enthusiasm for near to an hour, holding rapt the attention of every woman in sewing circle.

❧

"Thank you so very much for having us, Mrs. Montrose," Evangeline said. As she stepped out of the Montrose house and onto the front porch, she added, "We had such a wonderful time!"

"Yes," Amoretta offered, taking Mrs. Montrose's hand between her own and giving it a grateful squeeze. "Thank you so much! It did me a world of good to get to know some of the other ladies in town."

Mrs. Montrose smiled with understanding. "I thought that it might, dear. I'm glad you enjoyed yourself."

"I hope you'll come to our house one day for a sewing circle," Calliope chirped. "You must let us return your kindness."

"Of course, Calliope!" Mrs. Montrose assured with sincere enthusiasm. "I would love it!"

Once the young ladies had descended the front porch steps of the Montrose home, Winnie Montrose unexpectedly came skipping down behind the others. Mrs. Gardener and Mrs. Ackerman lingered behind in conversation with Mrs. Montrose.

"Do you girls want to do somethin' really interestin' now?" Winnie whispered.

"You mean *see* somethin' really interestin', don't you, Winnie?" Prudence giggled.

"Yep! That's exactly what I mean!" Winnie agreed. The smile Winnie wore gave her the look of knowing something entirely delicious, and Amoretta's curiosity was immediately piqued.

"What?" Amoretta couldn't keep from asking.

"I think Winnie plans on sharin' the secret of the mill with you Ipswich girls," Blanche guessed, her smile nearly as broad as Winnie's.

"Oh yes! The mill!" Sallie whispered. "You girls *must* come with us to the mill. If you want to see the most beautiful thing in Meadowlark Lake, then you just have to come with us."

"I've walked to the mill several times since we arrived," Evangeline said. "It is so very beautiful! Simply picturesque!"

But as Sallie, Winnie, Prudence, and Blanche exchanged mischievous glances, Amoretta felt there was something to do with the mill that Evangeline had missed.

"Well, there's more to it than what you saw, Evangeline...at least, most likely," Prudence offered. "Come with us, girls. I promise you that you'll never forget it as long as you live!"

"I'm game!" Calliope squealed instantly.

"Me too," Amoretta put in. She could feel the excitement rising within her already. She felt there was an adventure at hand—one swathed in mystery and mischief—and she couldn't wait to begin it!

"Well, I think I'll have to skip this particular outing," Evangeline sighed. "It's my night to cook, and I promised Daddy that I would have dinner on promptly. But you girls have fun, and I'll join you next time."

"Are you sure you won't come with us, Evangeline?" Blanche begged. "I promise it will be far more interestin' than puttin' supper on."

Evangeline smiled but shook her head. "No, I should be getting home. But Amoretta and Calliope will go."

"We can't go without you, Evie!" Amoretta exclaimed, however. "Not on such an excursion that sounds so mysterious and promising."

But Evangeline laughed. "I'm fine, Amoretta...truly. I want to go home. I'm fixing up something very special for dinner tonight. You and Calliope have fun." She paused a moment and then teasingly added, "But don't do anything that might find Sheriff Montrose dragging you home to Daddy by the scruff of your neck."

"Well, if you're sure," Calliope began.

"I am," Evangeline assured her.

"But you have to promise to come with us next time, Evangeline. All right?" Prudence begged.

"I will. I promise," Evangeline assured her. "Now you all run along and have fun. I'm off to cook."

Blanche sighed with disappointment. Recovering her enthusiasm quite quickly, however, she linked arms with Amoretta as Winnie linked arms with Calliope.

"Come on, Ipswich girls!" she giggled. "Let us take you on a tour of the true wonders of Meadowlark Lake!"

"Indeed!" Prudence giggled.

"I swear I'm so excited I'm near to flyin' apart at the seams!" Sallie rather panted.

"Ladies," Calliope began, "it's a gristmill, right? For making flour, cornmeal, and such?"

Blanche looked to Prudence, and Sallie looked to Winnie—all four wearing smiles that spread from ear to ear.

"Oh, it is a gristmill," Prudence confirmed. "But it turns out so much more than flour and cornmeal!"

All four girls giggled, and Amoretta's curiosity was too powerful to resist. With an ever-heightening sense of excitement, she said, "Let's go then! I can't wait to see what this magic mill grinds out!"

CHAPTER THREE

Meadowlark Lake's gristmill could not have been situated in a more perfect setting. Evangeline had not been exaggerating when she'd described it as very beautiful and picturesque.

Nestled near a large water-worn rock formation on the riverbank, Prudence's father's mill was beautifully embellished by a backdrop of lovely birch and maple trees. Upon seeing the tall, slender birches and wide, canopied maples, Amoretta's heart leapt with delight. No doubt this thick outcropping of trees would burn brilliant with crimson and gold once autumn arrived. Being that Amoretta had feared missing the colors of autumn that were so varied and prolific in Boston, a sudden hope sprang in her—a hope that all the colors she loved would be waiting at the old gristmill for her in keeping it company.

Save where the mill wheel worked its magic, groves of cattails lined the shallows of the river, and Amoretta could see the whirring of dragonfly wings as the dreamy insects flitted in and out of the velvet-brown cattail pods. The sun seemed to love dragonflies best, for it kept glinting on the slender green, violet, or blue iridescent bodies of the playful insects, just as if attempting to kiss them as they frolicked hither and thither.

The wooden walls of the mill stood weatherworn from decades of enduring seasons of rain, snow, and hot sun. Yet it looked sturdy enough—probably as sturdy as the day it was built.

There was something pleasantly inviting about the gristmill—at least to Amoretta—as if it were alive somehow and beaconing her closer. The whoosh-whoosh rhythm of the paddle in the water lent a rather tranquil feel to the already serene sensation of it all, and Amoretta was enchanted.

"Oh my goodness!" she exclaimed. "It's lovely. I don't know if I've ever laid eyes on such a lovely scene in all my life!"

Prudence smiled. "Yes, it is beautiful," she sighed. "I love it, and I'm so glad Daddy decided to move here and purchase the mill after Mother took ill. It's my haven of tranquility."

"I can surely understand that!" Calliope added, gazing at the river, the mill, and all nature's beauty with deep admiration.

"So you like the gristmill, hmmm?" Winnie asked Calliope. Winnie still wore an expression of mischief.

"Of course!" Calliope giggled. "Who wouldn't like it?"

"Then are you Ipswich girls ready to see the *real* beauty of the mill?" Sallie asked.

"The *real* beauty?" Amoretta asked. She looked from the picturesque scene of the mill and then back to Sallie and the others. "How could it be more beautiful than it looks from here?"

Blanche giggled. "Oh, you've got to see what's inside, Amoretta," she explained, albeit vaguely. "It's what's *inside* the mill that's so incredible."

"Inside?" Calliope asked, her brow wrinkling with curiosity. "I suspect it's only grain and stone and wood."

"Oh, it has all those things too," Prudence confirmed with a smile. "But let us show you what else is in there." Taking Amoretta's hand, she said, "Now come along…but be quiet. Don't make a sound. All right?"

"All right," Amoretta agreed.

The spirit of adventure and curiosity that dwelled within her bosom was passionate with excitement! It was obvious there was something wildly interesting inside the gristmill, and Amoretta silently swore to herself she would discover what it was no matter what. She promised herself that nothing short of torture could keep her from seeing what was inside now that her feet were set on the path.

"Is it frightening at all?" Calliope asked.

"Shh," Blanche kindly scolded.

But Winnie whispered, "I suppose it *could* be considered frightenin'…to some girls."

"Is it a ghost?" Calliope asked in a softer whisper.

"Oh heavens no!" Sallie giggled. "It's ever so much more wonderful than a ghost!"

"Now everyone hush," Prudence whispered as she began to rather creep toward the back outer wall of the mill. "If they hear us…well…we don't want anyone to hear us is all."

Slowly Amoretta and Calliope followed the others to a place where a board hung loosely from the rest of the wooden planks of the outer back wall of the gristmill. Blanche put a finger to her lips to remind everyone to be silent.

Winnie smiled as she took hold of Amoretta's shoulders. "Just kneel here in the grass," she whispered. Sallie knelt down in the grass and took Calliope's hand to guide her to follow.

Amoretta carefully knelt in the cool grass shaded by mill and trees. Once Prudence and Blanche had knelt down with the others, Prudence pointed to the low, loosely hanging board, indicating that Amoretta and Calliope should look through the open space it presented.

Amoretta's heart was pounding like the rapids of some raging river! What were they about to witness? Spirits roaming the old mill? Pirates? Outlaws? Her imagination couldn't list possibilities quickly enough.

And then, all at once—in the space of a moment and a short gasp—Amoretta Ipswich knew exactly why the young ladies of Meadowlark Lake liked to sneak out to the gristmill and peep through the loose siding board.

"Oh my—" Amoretta's exclamation of astonishment was silenced by Winnie's hand quickly covering her mouth.

"Hush!" Winnie scolded in a breathy giggle. "Do you want them to catch us?"

Amoretta shook her head, for she certainly did not want the men working inside the mill to become aware of her presence.

Inside the mill were four very brawny men. And of these four men, one in particular had arrested Amoretta's attention at once. Certainly he was the handsomest of the four—but it was beyond that. Amoretta knew full well which man every sneaky young woman peering through the gaps in the board was focused on. Not only was he, in truth, sinfully handsome, but he was also only half-clothed! All the other men wore shirts with their suspenders, pants, and boots. But the distressingly good-looking man wore only his pants and boots—his suspenders supported on broad, broad, broad and very bare shoulders.

"He's magnificent!" Calliope breathed.

"Isn't he though?" Prudence agreed in a sighed whisper.

Brown-haired, square-jawed, and tall, the handsome, shirtless stranger lifted one large flour sack after another as he moved them from one side of the room to the other. Each time he lifted a heavy flour sack, the muscles in his arms, shoulders, back, and stomach would harden to granite, giving him the appearance of having been sculpted from stone.

"Who is he?" Amoretta asked.

"Brake McClendon," Blanche answered, "every girl's daydream here in Meadowlark Lake."

"Every girl's daydream *anywhere*!" Winnie corrected with a sigh of longing.

"Shh," Sallie shushed. "He's comin' this way."

Amoretta held her breath as, indeed, the Greek sculpture of a man strode directly toward them. Pausing just before the loose wallboard, he seemed to be fiddling with something high up on the wall. However, none of the girls could see what he was working with—for they were on their knees in spying on the mill workers, which put their eyes exactly level with the man's muscular stomach.

Obviously the man was finally able to do whatever he'd walked over toward the back wall to do, for in a moment he'd turned around and strode back to his previous task.

Amoretta was grateful to be able to draw a breath once more.

"Who are the others?" she heard Calliope inquire.

Looking across the room to where the three other men were engaged in tasks similar to the shirtless man's, Amoretta listened as Prudence answered.

"The tall one with the lighter brown hair is my brother, Samuel," she began. Amoretta nodded, thinking she could well see the resemblance between Prudence and her brother. Both had light brown hair and were very attractive.

"I think Samuel Mulholland is so handsome!" Blanche whispered.

Prudence smiled. "Blanche has been sweet on Sam since the day we moved to Meadowlark Lake," she giggled.

"Who's the scruffy man there in the back? The one with the dark hair and wild beard?" Calliope asked. "He looks to have some ailment."

"That's Rowdy Gates," Prudence began. "He moved here last year…and I suppose he's handsome enough."

"Not that a girl could really see for herself," Sallie put in. "He wears far too much facial hair for my liking…and he's very quiet and secretive."

"And he limps," Winnie added. "I heard he's missin' part of his right foot."

"Oh, I see," Calliope said, frowning as she studied the rough-looking man.

"The other man is Dex Longfellow," Prudence said. "He's very handsome as well. That dark, dark hair and those blues…yum! In fact, I had quite an infatuation for him…until Brake McClendon came to town, that is."

"But now we all have eyes only for Brake," Blanche explained. "Though I suspect when Winnie's brother, Fox, returns…a few of us may find ourselves being Fickle Fannys."

31

"Even Fox isn't as handsome as Brake McClendon," Winnie offered.

"That's because he's your brother, and you see him differently than the rest of us do," Sallie giggled.

"I suppose," Winnie admitted. Then shaking her head with determination, she added, "But I don't think anyone could ever turn my head from Brake McClendon! He's too…too…"

"Naked?" Calliope offered with a playful grin.

All the girls snickered and clamped their hands over their mouths to keep from laughing too loudly.

"I was gonna say he's too delicious," Winnie giggled. "The naked part just makes him…well, sort of mildly scandalous."

"And thereby more attractive," Prudence added.

Amoretta didn't know whether to be amused, aghast, delighted, or disgusted. On one hand, the notion that the young ladies in Meadowlark Lake were mischievous, lighthearted, and as easily infatuated with a good-looking man as any of the friends she left in Boston elated her. Yet on the other hand, spying on a seminude man in such a manner was beyond any mischief she'd ever been involved in before. But then again, Amoretta's father had warned her and her sisters that life out west might seem a bit more rough and improper at times—especially at first. Judge Lawson Ipswich had explained that folks worked very hard in a new town, endeavoring to build it and its economy. And a rural life led to a more relaxed manner where some social interactions were concerned.

"What do you think, Amoretta?" Calliope asked. "And I mean truly…what do you truly think?"

Amoretta sighed, gazing through the opening in the mill's back wall a moment in studying the handsome, scandalously seminude Brake McClendon.

Then, as a smile spread over her lovely face, she answered, "I think I'm going to like Meadowlark Lake far more than I initially thought!" All the girls quietly giggled, and Amoretta added, "Thank you for sharing such a wondrous secret with us, ladies. Evangeline is going to regret making that prompt dinner for Daddy all the days of her life!"

As Calliope nodded in agreement, Amoretta looked back to the shamefully handsome mill worker in Prudence's father's gristmill. She felt better. A good cry, meeting nice women at the sewing circle, and finding that there was obviously enough mischief in the hearts of those who would be her friends seemed to give her worries a little competition. And as for Brake McClendon, he'd inspired her as well—inspired her to knowing that she never would have seen such a man in Boston.

Goose bumps inadvertently broke over her arms as again Brake McClendon returned to the place just on the other side of the loose board and began fiddling with something again. If she'd been ignorant enough to give into temptation, Amoretta could've easily slipped her fingers through the space provided by the loose board and touched the chiseled, male Grecian torso in front of her. But she was not that ignorant and simply stifled her snickering the way the other girls were doing.

The girls spent awhile longer in studying the men inside the mill—specifically Brake McClendon.

But then, far too soon for Amoretta's liking, Prudence said, "We best be gettin' back before we're missed."

"Must we?" Calliope asked.

"I think so," Prudence answered. "And besides, for all we know one of the men may come out here on his way to the outhouse. It's just back in the trees a ways behind us. And we don't want my daddy to catch us spyin' on his men, now do we?"

Everyone shook her head in firm agreement.

"He might fix this loose board if he did, and then our fun would be ruined," Prudence added playfully.

Everyone giggled and stood up to begin the walk back to town. There were many sighs of disappointment, and Amoretta thought perhaps hers was the heaviest.

It had been such an unexpected adventure—going to the mill with the other girls—and now it was finished. The September day would be at an end soon too. And although Amoretta loved this time of year when summer made way for autumn, evening still brought a certain anxiety to her heart where leaving Boston and moving to Meadowlark Lake was concerned. She loved autumn—hoped that cool evening breezes, harvesting in the fields, crisp mornings, and changing leaves would further assist her in learning to bloom where she'd been tossed.

As she followed behind Blanche and the others, Amoretta noted to herself that she would have to visit the gristmill often—to watch the leaves change in the trees, of course. She smiled, wondering if even the beauty of crimson and gold autumn leaves would ever drive the vision of the sinfully handsome Brake McClendon from her thoughts.

"Hello, ladies," a deep, masculine voice greeted.

Startled from her thoughts, Amoretta looked to her right to see none other than the seminude, heartbreakingly handsome Brake McClendon standing not five feet from her—from her and her friends.

"What are you all doin' out this way?" the intoxicatingly handsome man asked. He grinned a dangerously alluring grin, chuckled, and added, "If I didn't know better, I'd think you ladies were spyin' on us gristmill boys."

It was Prudence who found her composure first. "Oh, don't be silly, Brake McClendon," she said with an amused giggle. "We were walkin' out this way to see if any of the birch leaves had begun to turn yet."

Glancing around her, Amoretta discovered that every one of her companions wore red roses for cheeks. She felt hers must be the rosiest.

When she looked back to the man who had addressed them, it was to find his smoldering brown eyes fixated on her.

She gulped as he asked, "And are they?" He was speaking to Prudence, but his gaze lingered on Amoretta like a hungry fox might eye a mouse. "Are the birch leaves turnin' gold yet?"

Amoretta couldn't breathe, for the harmfully handsome man (and she was sure it was harmful to a woman to look at a man like him for too long) began to study her head to toe—not in any lewd manner really—more like a man who'd seen something in a shop window that he hadn't seen before.

"Yes," Prudence answered. "They're starting to."

Brake McClendon only continued to stare at Amoretta—even for the fact that five other young ladies were in her company.

"Looks like you have somethin' new of interest, Pru," the man said, his grin broadening into a smile that captured Amoretta's already enraptured attention. "I'm figurin' these must be a couple of that new judge's girls," he said. "Right?"

"Yes indeed," Prudence answered. "This is Calliope Ipswich."

Turning his attention to Calliope, Brake offered a hand to Amoretta's sister, saying, "Nice to meet you, Miss Calliope." Amoretta took the opportunity to breathe once more and attempted to regain a shred of her former composure.

"I assure you it's my pleasure entirely, Mr. McClendon," Calliope answered in her sweet, melodic voice. She smiled—giggled a little as she accepted his hand and he grasped it firmly a moment.

"And this is her sister…Amoretta Ipswich," Prudence continued.

Once more the wickedly attractive man's attention settled on Amoretta. As her heart leapt into her throat, Amoretta felt her hand slowly raise to grasp the one Brake McClendon was offering to her.

"A pleasure to meet you too, Miss Amoretta," he greeted. His smile was so dazzling, his eyes so very, very, very dark brown and enthralling, that Amoretta felt entirely bewitched somehow—exactly as if the seminude Brake McClendon were casting some sort of spell over her. Never in all her life had simply meeting a man for the first time affected her so intensely. Never in all her life had simply clasping hands with a man caused her to feel so suddenly discombobulated. And as his clasping of her hand seemed to linger, her never-in-all-her-life experience escalated to near rapture! His warm, strong, callused hand holding hers caused a ridiculous amount of goose bumps to erupt over her.

"The pleasure is mine, sir," Amoretta managed to respond.

Brake McClendon's eyebrows arched with simultaneous surprise and approval. "Well, your new friends sure are polite if nothin' else, Pru," he said.

Yet even though he was addressing Prudence, Brake McClendon continued to study Amoretta. She felt her blush deepen under his scrutiny.

"Well, of course, Brake," Prudence giggled. "Why do you seem so surprised? Don't I always choose the best friends?"

The man shrugged his broad shoulders, even as his gaze stayed on Amoretta.

"So your daddy's the new judge, hmm?" he unexpectedly asked her.

"Yes, sir," Amoretta answered, still blushing, still awash in goose bumps—for Brake McClendon had yet to release her hand.

"Hmmm," he seemed to muse. He released her hand then and looked to Calliope for a moment, then to Prudence.

"I guess you best stay out of mischief, Pru…now that you're keepin' company with the daughter of the sheriff here." He winked at Winnie, and Amoretta heard her sigh with delight. "And the daughters of the new judge," he added, winking at Calliope, "lest you find yourself in jail for somethin'."

Prudence laughed. "I never do anything bad enough that it would land me in jail, Brake. You know that," she said.

"I don't know about that," Brake teased, shaking his head. He chuckled, studied each girl a moment, and then said, "You girls be careful walkin' home. All right?"

"Yes, sir," Amoretta heard herself answer.

Again Brake McClendon's gaze settled on her, an amused and wildly charming grin curving his lips. "Hmm. You do sound like your daddy's a judge, now don't you?"

"Well…you have a nice afternoon, Brake," Sallie said, offering a hand to him.

Brake's brows arched with what resembled astonishment. Still, he clasped Sallie's hand and said, "You too, Miss Sallie."

"Mama says we'll have you for supper one night after Fox gets home...so you can meet him and all," Winnie said, holding out her hand toward the walking daydream.

Brake smiled and clasped Winnie's hand a moment as well, saying, "That'll be right nice."

"Tell Samuel I said hello...won't you, Brake?" Blanche asked, extending her hand in his direction.

"Of course," he assured her with a wink.

"Well, we'll be seein' you again," Prudence said, holding out her hand. "You keep an eye on Daddy and Samuel for me."

"Yes, ma'am," Brake chuckled, shaking Prudence's hand. "Now you ladies be on your way before dusk settles. All right?"

"Yes," all six girls answered in unison.

Brake McClendon smiled, nodded, and turned toward the grove of birch and maple trees.

"My stars and garters!" Blanche exclaimed. "You were right, Pru! We almost got found out by the man himself!"

Prudence nodded. "Yep. We need to be more careful next time," she suggested.

"Next time?" Amoretta asked.

"Of course, darlin'!" Winnie giggled as she linked one arm with Amoretta's and the other with Calliope's. "We come out here two or three times a week to get our fill of dreamin' after Brake McClendon." She laughed and winked at Amoretta, adding, "And don't worry, Amoretta...we all get numb tongues and go weak in the knees whenever Brake talks to one of us."

Amoretta shook her head, rolled her eyes, and blushed. "Was I that bad?"

"Not at all," Blanche answered, smiling.

Calliope laughed, looked to Amoretta, and said, "See, Rettie? Leaving Boston and Sylvanus Tenney isn't all bad."

"Who is Sylvanus Tenney?" Blanche asked as the group of girls began to meander along the path that led back to town.

"Amoretta thinks Sylvanus Tenney might be the man meant to be her lover," Calliope answered.

"Calliope Ipswich!" Amoretta scolded—although more out of being bashful than irritation that her sister was revealing secrets.

"Well, it's the truth," Calliope explained. She giggled. "But come Halloween this year, I bet you're going to be hoping your apple peels spell out a B, now aren't you?"

"Okay, girls...tell all," Sallie demanded with excitement. "Tell us all about this boy you left in Boston."

Amoretta smiled. "Well, first of all...Sylvanus is no boy. He's twenty-three years old and handsome near to a fault!"

Yet even as Amoretta continued to tell her newfound friends the tale of Sylvanus Tenney and her four Halloweens running of tossing apple peels over her shoulder to find them lying in the shape of an S, she felt something had changed. Just in those few moments she'd stood face to face with Brake McClendon, something in her had changed—and she began to wonder if he really had managed to cast some sort of enchantment or spell over her. For as she talked of Sylvanus, she found that there was not one thread of her being that missed him—not anymore. As she talked of Boston and Halloween customs and handsome Sylvanus Tenney, there in the forefront of her mind lingered fabulous, scandalous, bewitchingly handsome Brake McClendon.

Leave it to a judge to have a daughter the likes of that one, Brake thought as he rode toward town that evening. Goodness knew a man didn't dare to even look at a judge's daughter, lest he find himself at the business end of a Winchester rifle—or a noose.

Yet even for all his good sense in knowing a man best stay clear of any woman related to any judge, Brake hadn't been able to get that Ipswich girl out of his mind—not from the moment he'd left the mill and run into the girls from town on his way to the outhouse. There was something about her—something that drew him to her like a bee to pollen. Her sister was pretty enough—very pretty, in fact. Yellow hair and sparkling blue eyes, sure—the one with the name he couldn't remember right offhand was as pretty as a summer day. But it was that other one—the one with hair the color of soft, brown mink and eyes of peacock green that had wiggled her way under his skin the very moment he'd looked at her—she was the one he couldn't quit thinking about. And he knew how dangerous it was— what kind of trouble could follow if he allowed himself to keep thinking on her.

He needed distraction, and he knew where to find it. Therefore, instead of heading for home, he reined his horse toward the woods outside of town.

"Come on, Gambler," he mumbled. "Let's see how those pretty gypsy ladies of ours are doin' tonight. What do you say?"

The horse whinnied in favor of the new direction, and Brake tried to think of something besides that new judge's daughter—that Amoretta Ipswich. "Hell, even her name sounds like trouble," he grumbled as he rode toward the seclusion of the woods and the distraction he knew dwelled in it.

CHAPTER FOUR

Lawson Ipswich had not been born a man of means. Rather he'd been born to a hard-working farmer and his loving wife, English immigrants. Tall, brawny, and nurtured in a home where physical labor was required and camaraderie and fun with family were the reward, Lawson had not known the trial of wealth as he'd fought to gain an education, a law degree, and a position of respect as a young man. What had been important to Lawson, above all else, was family. And when he married the woman of his dreams, she and the three beautiful daughters they'd had together were what he cherished, not the wealth and position his profession allotted.

Lawson Ipswich was happy in life—as happy as any man ever had been. Yet when his beloved wife died in childbirth, Lawson found that though he enjoyed his occupation, he did not so much enjoy life any longer. As he watched his daughters grow—his three little girls so often dressed in blue the way their mother had always dressed them—and watched them hurry and scurry about the streets of Boston, Lawson Ipswich had feared his innocent darlings were being absorbed by the society of the city somehow. He didn't like it. He didn't want to see his girls swallowed up in fashion, socializing, and the constant search for entertainment. He wanted to see them relaxed, barefooted, and meandering through tall, endless meadows of green grass, just as he'd done as a boy. And as he began to think of such an existence for his three girls, he began to dream of it— began to obsess on it—until one day, he acted.

The judge's bench in Meadowlark Lake, a small western town a traveling colleague had discovered, became available, and Lawson Ipswich leapt at the opportunity to leave the hurry-scurry of Boston and escape with his three girls to open space and fresh air.

Though initially distressed by the prospect of leaving the only home they'd ever known, Evangeline and Calliope had accepted their father's decision—even come around to being excited at the adventure in moving. But to Lawson's great surprise, his middle daughter—the one with the most daring of natures—burst into hurt and fearful tears.

Amoretta had been distraught for days after Lawson's announcement of the move. And yet she'd buoyed her courage and even managed a smile as the wagon that had brought the family out to Meadowlark Lake from the train station rambled along the countryside. Lawson knew Amoretta would soldier on—even thrive once she admitted to herself that Meadowlark Lake was a far more lovely place than Boston. Still, he worried over her. She had such a strong spirit, and he did not want to be the cause of crushing it in the least. Yet the move had gone well, and the girls (even Amoretta) had begun to settle in.

But as Lawson Ipswich stood beneath a large maple tree, studying the pile of dead animals laid out beneath it, the first twinge of doubt in the decision to move his family west pricked at his mind.

"Two foxes, a dog, and three cats," Sheriff Dennison Montrose said as he hunkered down and studied the animals more closely. "It just doesn't make sense to me, Judge...and believe me, I tried thinkin' of every excuse that I could for this...this mess. But I cannot, for the life of me, come up with one."

"Fox fur is valuable," Lawson mused aloud. "Those pelts would've brought someone a nice sum. You're thinking, why were they left to rot?"

"Exactly," Sheriff Montrose agreed. "The dog...I recognized right off. It belongs to Dex Longfellow. Dex works out at the gristmill and rents a room at the boardin' house in town. And the cats, they just look like ol' barn cats to me...but you can bet somebody's missin' them. Who would do such a thing to a body's pets?"

Lawson inhaled a deep breath and exhaled it slowly. One week. He'd been in Meadowlark Lake just one week, and already he'd stepped in something he'd never expected to find in such a small town.

"The foxes look to have been trapped," he observed. "But the dog and the cats..."

"Slit throats," Sheriff Montrose finished. "That's why I brought you out here, Judge. This looks a bit beyond simple mischief to me. You ever seen anything like this in the city?"

Lawson nodded. "Unfortunately, yes. And it doesn't bode well."

"What kind of person does somethin' like this? And why?" Dennison asked.

"In my experience, it's usually an angry adolescent," Lawson began truthfully. "Perhaps some young man who's angry or...or a person mourning the loss of a loved one. There are other possibilities, of course. Does Meadowlark Lake have any...characters to speak of?"

"If by *characters* you mean strange folks with strange behavior...then yes," Dennison admitted.

"Will you tell me about them?"

"Sure. If you think it'll help us," Dennison answered. Exhaling a rather discouraged sigh, he began, "Rowdy Gates comes to mind. He doesn't like to be bothered. Keeps to himself...doesn't hardly talk to anybody. He works out at the gristmill, same as Dex. Lights the new gaslights in town every night. But I don't really think he's trouble."

"Who else came to mind when I inquired, Sheriff?" Lawson prompted. The heap of dead animals was disturbing, and Lawson did not want to doubt whether bringing his three girls out west to live were the right thing to do. He'd sleep somewhat better if he and the sheriff could determine who had killed the animals and why. If they could determine that the incident had just been some angry youth's way of acting up, he'd feel better.

"Well, I…uh…I don't like to be suspicious, Judge, but…well, I…" Dennison stammered.

"We're lawmen, Dennison," Lawson firmly reminded. "Suspicion is in our nature…and necessary for us to be successful in upholding the law and protecting the citizens of this town."

Dennison nodded. "I know it. It's just that…well, the poor young woman already has enough trouble."

"Young woman?" Lawson urged.

"Kizzy," Dennison answered.

"Kizzy who?"

Dennison shrugged. "Kizzy," he answered. "That's all any of us know. She showed up about a year ago…bought a run-down little house out in the woods behind your place. She and her daughter moved in…no man with them, mind you."

"I see," Lawson mumbled. And he did see. "A young woman with no husband, and yet a child, and seeking isolation—an unwed mother, the perfect target for prejudice and gossip."

Again Dennison shrugged. "Yep. She claims to be a gypsy, and she's real good with healin'…makes all sorts of tonics and such from herbs and plants. Folks aren't against purchasin' some of her concoctions and things, but they ain't at all acceptin'. Not that she's really tried to be accepted. She's a bit like Rowdy Gates…keeps to herself and don't want to be bothered." Dennison paused, a pleased grin spreading across his face. "But she's a mighty handsome young woman, Judge. Mighty handsome! And her little girl is just as sweet as any summer peach. I imagine one of our boys will eventually get up the gumption to go courtin' her…if she'll let him."

Lawson nodded. Neither of the "characters" Dennison had mentioned seemed to prick Lawson's mind with deep suspicion—not based on the information the sheriff had offered.

And so he offered, "Well, I think that the juveniles in town should be where we look first, Sheriff." He paused a moment and then continued, "Has anyone lost a parent or sibling of recent? Suffered a tragedy?"

Dennison sighed and was pensive for a time. "No. I mean, Mary Francis Newton died last summer. She's got three boys…and the oldest, Lucas, is about seventeen now. But they have a good man in their daddy, Granville." He shook his head. "Nope. I think Granville has a handle on his boys." He exhaled another heavy breath. "Benjamin Mulholland owns the gristmill, and his wife is away suffering from consumption, but she was away before Ben and his children moved here. His son, Sam, seems fine…works at the gristmill for his daddy. And his daughter, Prudence, is a sweetheart of a girl." Dennison's eyebrows arched then. He'd obviously thought of another possibility. "Now, Mrs. Peters…she and her sons moved here so she could teach at the schoolhouse. They moved to Meadowlark Lake just after her husband was killed in a railroad accident. She's got two boys, and they're a little bit of a handful. I mean, they're young. I can't imagine either of them could do somethin' like this," he said, gesturing toward the pile of dead animals. "But then again, I was huntin' rabbits and fox when I was six years old and skinnin' them myself…and both her boys are older than I was then."

Lawson nodded. "In truth, it sounds like you have quite a list, Sheriff," he noted. "Maybe I can help you out a bit…talk to a few of them…though they might be somewhat offended or perhaps think I'm interfering somehow, considering that I'm so newly arrived in town."

"I agree with you there," Dennison confirmed. "Why don't we do this? Since you live so near the woods, if you'd be willin', would you make a visit out to that gypsy girl's place and see what you think about her? I'm doubtful she's the type to do such a thing, but I also know how people often suspect and blame gypsies of every wrongdoin' they can."

"I'd be happy to do that," Lawson answered.

"Meanwhile, I'll talk to ol' Rowdy Gates tonight when he's lightin' the lamps and drop in on Mrs. Peters tomorrow." Sheriff Montrose paused, frowning. Looking to Lawson, he asked, "It *is* just somebody up to some ugly mischief, right?"

But Lawson didn't know any more than Sheriff Montrose did. In fact, he knew even less because he wasn't familiar with the townspeople the way their lawman was. Yet he sensed the sheriff's anxiety, for his own was heightened as well. He knew they both needed reassurance that nothing too dangerous or horrible was afoot—that the pile of slaughtered animals was an isolated incident.

Therefore, he answered, "I believe so. It's most likely just some angry young man needing to vent his pain and frustration."

Sheriff Montrose nodded. "All right then." He looked around and started toward his horse. "I'll go on ahead and dig a hole to put the carcasses in. It wouldn't do any good to have somebody else find them and start talkin' in town about it."

"Very wise thinking," Lawson affirmed. "I'll ride out and talk to this gypsy woman—this Kizzy—first thing in the morning." He strode to his horse and mounted. "Good evening, Sheriff. And please do keep me informed of what you discover."

"I will, Judge. Thank you."

Lawson exhaled a tired breath as he rode for home. Someone in Meadowlark Lake was angry—angry enough to slaughter the pets of his fellow townspeople. The knowledge tainted Lawson's newfound pleasure in the beauty of the place—tainted his feelings that his girls would be safe there. Still, he was determined not to allow it to frighten him. Most likely it truly was just some adolescent boy working out some pent-up frustration. After all, life was different in rural settings; things like this might not seem so unusual to farmers and ranchers. But Sheriff Montrose had truly been disturbed by what he'd found—disturbed enough to involve the county's new judge— and that fact did little to ease Lawson's mind.

There was nothing to do but investigate the situation and put an explanation and a close to the incident as soon as possible. He knew Sheriff Montrose would do his part, and Lawson would ride into the woods and check up on the gypsy woman himself in the morning. Eliminate the obvious suspects—that's what they'd do. No doubt one of them would turn out to be the culprit.

As he rode on, Lawson wondered how the girls had enjoyed their time at the sewing circle. He hoped they'd made friends—Amoretta especially. He wanted his girls to be happy as well as safe. He tried to press the knowledge of the slaughtered animals to the back of his mind. He needed to meet the girls with a pleasant, calmed countenance, lest he raise their anxieties.

The house came into view, and instantly Lawson's own anxieties settled a bit. He was almost certain he could see a lovely, beckoning radiance around the pretty house—a radiance he knew emanated from it for the fact that his girls were home. They'd be giggling when he entered the kitchen—they were always giggling, it seemed—and to Lawson Ipswich the melodic giggling of his three little girls was the most beautiful sound in all of earth and heaven.

"Oh, he's so handsome, Evangeline!" Calliope exclaimed. "I truly, truly have never seen anyone like him...not in all my life!"

Evangeline's smile broadened. "Well now, you two are making me even more regretful that I didn't accompany you out to the gristmill," she sighed. "If I had know you all were off to scout out the eligible bachelors in town...well, Daddy could've waited a little while for dinner."

"Oh, we'll make sure you don't miss it next time," Amoretta assured her sister. "Don't worry, darling. We'll make sure." Amoretta put a comforting arm around her sister's shoulders and offered a reassuring smile.

"I'm going to hold you to it," Evangeline giggled. Her brow wrinkled then. "Still, I thought that this brother of Winnie Montrose's was supposed to be the handsomest man in town...this Fox Montrose. But from what you say, it sounds like he'll have some heavy competition from this Brake fellow when he returns, hmmm?"

"Fox Montrose *is* supposed to be as handsome as Adonis," Calliope answered. "But truly, I can't imagine it...not after the mill today. And mind you that Amoretta and I were so distracted by Brake McClendon that we really didn't give any of the other men a second glance."

"That's true!" Amoretta exclaimed as the sudden realization struck her as well. "For all we know, the other men working at the mill might be even more handsome than Brake McClendon."

Calliope laughed. "Well, they were certainly more dressed," she mumbled, winking at Amoretta.

"What?" Evangeline exclaimed. "What do you mean the other men were more dressed?"

Amoretta shrugged. "Exactly what we said. The other men had more clothes on."

Evangeline tapped the large spoon she'd been using to stir her stew with on the side of the cooking pot. Placing it on the spoon rest on the counter, she put one hand on one hip and almost glared at Calliope and Amoretta as she demanded, "Okay, tell me everything I missed. And this time...I do mean everything."

"Well, we arrived to find that the man all the girls in town are simply gobbling geese over was not only as handsome as a dream...but rather scandalously unclad," Amoretta explained.

"How so?" Evangeline asked.

Amoretta shrugged. "He wasn't wearing a shirt," she answered. "He had his boots and britches on...suspenders too...but no shirt. It was quite scandalous."

But Evangeline shrugged then, shaking her head with a lack of astonishment. "So? Many a man working laboriously in Boston often discarded his shirt on hot, muggy days. Scandalous though it may be, it's not something we haven't seen before."

Amoretta exchanged amused glances with Calliope and then said, "Oh, believe me, Evangeline...it's something we haven't seen before." Amoretta and Calliope couldn't keep from bursting into giggles—giggles that quickly erupted into laughter of an uncontrollable nature.

"Oh, Evie!" Calliope laughed as tears of mirth filled her eyes. "You should've *seen* Amoretta's face when Brake McClendon spoke to us! It was...it was priceless!"

Evangeline began to giggle as well, captured by the contagion of wild laughter even though she hadn't seen Amoretta's reaction.

"What did she do?" Evangeline asked through a giggle.

Amoretta couldn't speak; she found it difficult to even draw breath for laughing so hard. Therefore, she simply waved a hand toward Calliope, gesturing that her little sister would have to explain.

"She…she looked like a baby with its nose pressed to the window of a candy shop!" Calliope managed. "Or maybe more like a preacher's wife who'd just stepped into a burlesque!"

At this description, Evangeline's laughter increased to the heightened manner of her sisters'. "Really?" she gasped.

Calliope nodded. "Like this," she breathed. Then gasping, as if suddenly astonished, and widening her pretty blue eyes to near the size of wagon wheels, Calliope sent Evangeline and Amoretta both into such a delirious round of laughter that any passersby would've thought it near maniacal.

"It's true!" Amoretta gasped, wiping tears of amusement from the corners of her eyes. "It's so true! I thought I might expire when he just stood there staring at me like he'd never seen a stranger before."

"And her cheeks were the color of radishes!" Calliope added. "Oh, it was so funny," Calliope sighed as her laughter finally subsided. "It was priceless, Evie!"

Evangeline's laughter lessened as well, and she breathed, "I'm so very sorry I missed it. I can just imagine Amoretta's expression." She giggled a little one last time.

Amoretta sighed with the relief of having once again been able to inhale a deep breath. "I'm sure he thinks I'm quite the brainless schoolgirl," she added.

But Calliope shook her head. "No, he did not. That much was painfully obvious."

"What do you mean?" Evangeline asked.

Calliope pointed to Amoretta, answering, "He couldn't quit staring at her! You would've thought she had three nostrils or something. It was delicious the way he stared." Calliope's eyes narrowed with mischief as she added, "Undressing her with his eyes!"

Amoretta gasped with chagrin. "Calliope Ipswich! What a thing to say!"

But Evangeline allowed another giggle to erupt from her throat as she said, "Why so defensive, Amoretta? It seems only fair to me that he would do so…after all the ogling you girls did without his knowledge."

"And we didn't even have to use our imaginations the way he did," Calliope added. Instantly all three girls were conquered with more delirious laughter. Mirthful tears streamed from their eyes as they attempted to gasp for breath and lessen their hilarity.

"What on earth is so amusing?" Judge Ipswich asked as he strode into the kitchen to find his daughter overcome with merriment. He chuckled as he watched them, all three, reach for the support of chairs and plop down in them as they continued to laugh.

He loved the scene playing out before him. As Amoretta laid her head on the table to try and slow her laughter—as Evangeline complained that her back hurt from laughing so hard and Calliope wiped tears from her eyes—Lawson Ipswich knew all would be well. He had his girls, and that was all that mattered—that and their happiness. And it was sorely obvious that they were all three happy in that moment, at least.

"Tell me," he playfully demanded. "What has you three so tickled?"

"Oh, Daddy," Amoretta sighed, drawing a deep breath, lifting her head from the table, and wiping tears from her eyes. "It's just silly girl talk…nothing you would understand."

But Lawson Ipswich smiled. "Oh, you're so certain are you?" He chuckled. "Must be about boys then, hmmm?"

When all three of his daughters blushed and broke into guilty giggles, Lawson Ipswich shook his head with his own amusement.

"Let's just say that Amoretta may be hoping her apple peels spell out B this Halloween, Daddy," Calliope offered.

Amoretta's eyes widened, and she mouthed, *Will you hush?* to her little sister.

"A B, is it?" Lawson mused. "That wouldn't happen to be a B for Brake McClendon, would it?"

"Daddy!" Amoretta exclaimed. "Why in the world would you think that? Why...why, I've hardly met anybody in town and—"

"Well, from what I hear tell, he's the best-looking fellow in Meadowlark Lake," Lawson teased. "I met him a few days ago, and I just guessed that there wouldn't be much that could change you from despairing this morning to giggling this evening...unless you'd met Mr. McClendon." Lawson paused and then added, "Though I do hear that Sheriff Montrose's son stands to give McClendon some competition when he returns next week."

But Amoretta was not distracted. "How did you know, Daddy?" she asked. "How did you know we'd met Brake McClendon...at least that Calliope and I did?"

Amoretta's eyes narrowed as she studied her father. It was uncanny, the manner in which he always seemed to know everything. She and Calliope hadn't been home more than forty-five minutes, so how did her father know?

"I have my ways, honey. That's all you need to know," her father teased.

"Daddy!" Amoretta demanded, stomping one foot on the floor. "You can't do that! You know it drives me nearly insane when you do that. You have to tell us how you knew."

Lawson Ipswich chuckled. "I saw all you young ladies coming from the direction of the gristmill when I was in town. The way you were all twittering away like excited little birds, I just guessed that you all must've bumped into McClendon one way or the other." Taking Amoretta's hand, he smiled at her and said, "It truly was just a guess...because I do know that nothing in all the world sets young ladies to blushing, giggling, and twittering like birds more than a good-looking man."

"Because it's the way young women always used to behave around you, isn't it?" Amoretta lovingly teased.

"Used to?" her father exclaimed, feigning a wounded ego.

"Still do!" Calliope offered, kissing her father on one cheek. "And we *did* meet Brake McClendon today, Daddy. And we made new friends at the sewing circle too."

Lawson sighed, and Amoretta could see his relief. As he smiled at her, his eyes twinkling with gladness, she smiled at him. She knew she'd caused him far too much grief and worry since he'd announced the move to Meadowlark Lake—and suddenly she was humbled and sorry for it.

Throwing her arms around his neck, Amoretta hugged her father and said, "I'm so sorry I'm your difficult daughter, Daddy. I don't mean to be. It's just that…that…"

"You're not difficult, darling," Lawson said. "But I am glad some young man managed to knock old Sylvanus Tenney off that pedestal a bit."

"Me too!" Evangeline and Calliope chimed in unison.

For a moment, Amoretta felt defensive—fought the impulse to defend Sylvanus. Yet she found that she couldn't—that she didn't even want to. Something had happened to her in those moments when Brake McClendon had stood studying her like he'd never seen a girl before. She couldn't explain it—because she didn't understand it herself. She couldn't put a word or phrase to the way she felt. All she knew was that, from the moment she'd first seen Brake McClendon through the space the loose board of the mill wall provided, something had happened to her. She wasn't sure what, but something had happened.

And as she lay in bed that night, listening to the soothing song of the crickets outside her open window—as she smiled when she heard Calliope giggle in her sleep from the bed across the room—Amoretta tried to decipher what exactly it was that had happened to her, what she was feeling. Surely it was simply the fact that Brake McClendon was so powerfully handsome, that he'd displayed an archetype of what the perfect male physique should look like. Surely it was just some sort of startling, lingering astonishment that caused her heart to flutter in her bosom each time she thought of him. After all, Amoretta had never been fickle; she'd never been shallow in her feelings or ways of thinking. Therefore, what was it churning inside her? What was it that kept the name "Brake McClendon" echoing in her mind?

Unable to settle her thoughts, Amoretta crept quietly out of bed and down the hall to the parlor. Plopping down on the soft, comfortable sofa, she picked up her book she'd left on its arm and began reading. She needed to distract her thoughts, needed to think of something else besides the handsome stranger she'd met only once—the handsome stranger that was haunting her thoughts in the strangest, most dominant way she could ever imagine.

Reading the chapter heading aloud, she whispered, *"How to Learn the Identity of One's True Love on Halloween—Mirrors."* Clearing her throat, she continued, *"Fortune-tellers and gypsies often use a crystal ball to tread the future paths of those inquiring for the identity of lovers. Still, one need not possess either a crystal ball or gifts of clairvoyance to discover one's own true love. All that it is required is a hand mirror and a lit candle on All Hallows' Eve."* Pausing in her reading, Amoretta sighed, "Is that so?" Naturally she already knew the custom of the mirror and candle on Halloween, but as she read on, she found that the book offered new insight into the ritual—even new ways of performing it.

Reading the book did not entirely chase thoughts of Brake McClendon from her mind, but it did cause her eyes to become dry and heavy. Eventually, Amoretta drifted off to sleep on the parlor sofa. And there she dreamed dreams of Brake McClendon—of his dazzling smile and sculpted muscles—of his dark brown eyes and voice as low and warm and alluring as maple syrup.

CHAPTER FIVE

No one else had wanted to watch the sun rise, but Amoretta did. Even though she'd slept somewhat fitfully on the parlor sofa, she awoke very early—and with a driven desire to breathe in the cool morning air, feel the dew on vast stretch of fragrant grass behind the new Ipswich home, and be alone with her thoughts—her confusion. Thus, she had risen and dressed, taken a shawl from the hook near the kitchen door, and quietly left the house while that early dark that really isn't so dark still cloaked her part of the world.

All the world seemed very still and quiet as Amoretta made her way deep into the stretch of grass between her home and the woods—the woods wherein the gypsy woman lived, she remembered as she studied the tree line on the horizon. Somewhere in the distance, she heard a calf bawl—heard its mother lowing in answer— and it made her smile. Robins and larks and other varieties of birds hopped and flittered here and there through the grass, and Amoretta could only imagine the big, fat worms these early birds were treating themselves to. She smiled as she closed her eyes and inhaled deeply of the oh-so-very-fresh morning air. She fancied she could smell bread baking—remembered she'd seen a bakery in town and silently promised herself that she must visit it very soon. But what her olfactory sense clung to was the sweet fragrance of grass and trees— of wildflowers and cattails—of clean, clear water and the comforting scent of burning cedar emanating, no doubt, from the cozy hearths of others who had risen early in Meadowlark Lake.

Naturally it was chilly. Amoretta hadn't expected it to be quite so very chilly. But the slight chatter of her teeth and shiver on her skin made her feel more alive than she had...well, since she could remember!

Opening her eyes, Amoretta frowned, for she wondered if it were truly the fresh western morning that was making her feel so suddenly aware and animate. Or was it him? Was it Brake McClendon and the fact that every thought of him caused her heart to flutter in her bosom, that every vision of him lingering in her head caused her to smile and inwardly sigh with a sort of delight she'd never before experienced?

The book of Halloween customs she'd taken to the night before in order to distract herself had helped her to finally fall asleep. But that didn't mean her unconscious mind hadn't continued to ponder the strangeness of it all.

The sun broke the horizon behind her, and Amoretta turned to face it. She smiled as the most beautiful amber color she had ever seen kissed the clouds as the sun peeked up at her. Slowly the amber brightened to a lovely honey color—sweet and inviting like the syrupy ambrosia of bees.

As Amoretta stood in the dew-dipped grass—as she watched the yellow sun ever so slowly overcome its seeming shyness and rise a bit more—she searched her feelings again. Where was her despair? Where was her disappointment in leaving Boston? Where was her resentment of the bitter phrase, *Bloom where you're planted*? Where was her sadness at leaving Sylvanus Tenney behind to never see him again? It was gone—all of it!—just as if God himself had reached into her body and blessedly stripped it from her soul.

Yet as thankful as Amoretta was for the absence of sorrow and misery, she was somewhat frightened at what had filled the space it left inside her—thoughts and visions of a man, a man who was nothing but a stranger to her! She wondered at how it could be. Was it simply the dream of true love and romance that resides in all young women? The dream of winning the heart of a handsome prince and a blissful happily ever after? And was she so shallow as to fall into instant infatuation with a man simply because he was beautiful? She liked to think she wasn't—was certain she wasn't (or at least almost certain). But what other explanation was there? Love at first sight? Surely the old cliché did not apply to Amoretta. And even if it did, what chance did she have of winning Brake McClendon's heart when every other marriageable woman in town owned the same desire?

"Pff!" Amoretta puffed with self-disgust. "You're an idiot, Amoretta. That's all there is to it."

And then she thought of something—an entirely ridiculous something—but a thoroughgoing intriguing something.

Turning back to look at the woods, she whispered, "The gypsy."

Gypsies were known for telling fortunes and reading the futures of others, especially in matters of the heart. If the woman in the woods truly were a gypsy, then perhaps she could help explain to Amoretta the strange sense of emotional transformation that had come over her so suddenly.

Amoretta smiled. She would do it! She would visit the gypsy woman! Hadn't Prudence mentioned that the woman in the woods sold herbal remedies and things to the townsfolk? Yes, she had. Amoretta remembered it clearly then. On their way home from the gristmill the day before, Prudence had begun talking about the gypsy in the woods and of how she sold herbal remedies to the townsfolk who were brave enough to venture into the woods to seek her out. Of course, at the time, Amoretta had still been whirling about in the cloud of blissful euphoria her encounter with Brake McClendon had created. But now that her head was a little more clear, she did remember Prudence talking of the gypsy. Therefore Amoretta reasoned that if the gypsy woman in the woods were willing enough to sell her remedies to people, then perhaps she'd be willing to tell a fortune or two—for compensation, of course.

Glancing up to the tree line ahead in thinking of the gypsy woman of the woods, Amoretta gasped, placing a hand to her bosom in awed astonishment. For just as her thoughts had turned to the gypsy woman and fortune telling, a handsome buckskin horse stepped out of the woods and into the grassy expanse—a horse with a rider—a man. As if by means of the supernatural, some enchantment or spell, none other than Brake McClendon himself was riding toward her through the morning mist that was quickly evaporating in the growing sunlight.

Brake frowned as Gambler ambled through the grass toward the young woman. His mistrustful suspicions told him to rein away—to go left or right (it didn't matter) and urge Gambler to a gallop and thereby avoidance. But something else inside him—something stronger—kept his gaze fixed on the woman, kept him moving toward her instead of away the way his defenses whispered that he should.

He knew who the girl was, of course. He'd seen her before—twice. Only the day before he'd seen her sobbing out her heart in the same grasses she now stood in. Then he'd seen her again outside the gristmill—seen her and been entirely bewitched by her. Amoretta Ipswich. The name had echoed over and over in his mind from the moment he'd heard it. Amoretta Ipswich—over and over in his thoughts like some repetitive song lyric that lingers in a body's mind for days on end. Amoretta Ipswich—it made his mouth water for reasons Brake didn't understand.

Certainly the girls was beautiful, even more so as she stood there in the dewy grass, with her hair unpinned and the wisp of a shawl she wore about her slight shoulders. But it was more than that—his instant attraction to her—and it rattled Brake to his very core. But still he slowed Gambler to a stop as he reached her. In truth, he was surprised at the way she just stood there, entirely still, staring at him as if she'd seen some haunting specter exit the woods and ride toward her.

"Good mornin', Miss Amoretta Ipswich," Brake said, touching the brim of his hat and offering what he hoped appeared to be a friendly smile and not the smile of the absolute pleasure he was feeling by just looking at her.

Amoretta gulped but forced a welcoming smile. "Good morning, Mr. McClendon," she managed. Oh, he was simply scrumptious! He wore a day or two's facial hair growth, a white shirt, suspenders, pants, boots, and a hat—and all of it only complemented his good looks and stunning smile.

"Out for your mornin' constitutional, I see," he said, still smiling at her.

"Yes," Amoretta affirmed. "I love mornings," she told him— though he hadn't asked for details of why she was out. "Mornings and early evenings. Those are the times of day I adore. I think life is more full and exciting at those times, don't you?" She gulped, trying to swallow the lump in her throat—disgusted at herself for babbling on about things she was sure a man like Brake McClendon didn't care about.

But to her astonishment, and delight, Brake nodded. "I'm a mornin' person myself," he said. "I like to be up long before the sun…take some time to appreciate the calm, quiet time of day."

"Me too," Amoretta said, feeling her smile broaden. "And I see you've been to the woods." She shouldn't have gone fishing the way she instantly had; she knew she shouldn't have tried to lure him into telling why he'd been in the woods. But to Amoretta, there could only be one reason anyone would go into the woods—the gypsy.

A strange sense of panic began to rise in her as Brake's smile did indeed fade somewhat. He seemed pensive for a moment—as if deciding whether he would continue talking to her or simply be on his way. Amoretta's heart was already beating like a hammer on an anvil, and now it added anxiety to the forging.

"Yep," he responded at last. "There's a woman who lives in the woods—her and her little girl—and once in a while I see to it that they have enough firewood chopped and split to keep their cookstove fed and their hearth warm."

Amoretta sighed with relief. He'd decided to tell her why he'd been in the woods instead of riding off in irritation at her poking into his private matters. "How kind," she said. "I'm glad to know someone is thoughtful of her."

Brake shrugged. "It's the neighborly thing to do," he mumbled. "Me and the other fellas out at the gristmill, we try to be helpful to folks when they need it."

Amoretta's heart leapt with approval and admiration. "Well, it's comforting to know that you all are so helpful."

Brake leaned on the pommel of his saddle, smiled, and said, "Yes, ma'am, we are. And I'm the *most* helpful of the bunch…just in case you ever need any…any neighborly assistance of your own, Miss Ipswich."

She'd only seen him once before—met him less than twenty-four hours ago. And yet somehow Amoretta recognized the inviting nature of his smile—as if he were daring her to flirt with him in return—as if he wanted her to.

"Well, you'll be the first one I turn to when I need some neighborly assistance then, Mr. McClendon," she ventured, accepting his unspoken dare. She bit the inside of her cheek to keep from giggling with delight as his smile broadened and one eyebrow arched with pleased approval.

"In fact," he began then, unexpectedly dismounting his horse, "why don't you let me see you back home?" He stepped forward to stand directly in front of Amoretta, and she thought her heart would beat itself right out of her chest. He was so close to her—even closer than he'd been the day before. As she paused—breathless and momentarily speechless with enraptured awe—Brake added, "If you're finished with your mornin' stroll, that is, Miss Ipswich."

"I-I-I am," Amoretta stammered, nodding her assurance.

"Well then, lead the way," he said, taking his horse's reins in one hand and gesturing that she should precede him with the other.

Amoretta smiled and started walking toward home. She sighed with delight as Brake stepped into a slower stride beside her. After all, his legs were much longer than hers; thus he had to walk more slowly to stay just next to her.

"That's a very handsome horse you have there," she commented, nervous and thinking that conversation was necessary to keep her from fainting with the joy of being in his company.

"Yep. Ol' Gambler...he's a good man," Brake said. Amoretta looked up to Brake, and he winked at her, adding, "And quite popular with the ladies."

Amoretta giggled. "Is that so?" she teased, thinking that it only made sense for Brake McClendon's horse to be popular as well. "You mean he's popular with the horse ladies, right?"

"Well, that too," Brake answered. "But he's popular with the human ladies as well."

Amoretta's eyebrows arched with being impressed. "Oh, is he now?"

Brake nodded. "Yep. And I'm man enough to admit that Gambler is more popular with the human ladies than I am."

Amoretta rolled her eyes and shook her head. "Oh, he is not," she giggled.

"I'm serious!" Brake playfully argued, however. "Want me to prove it to you?"

Amoretta stopped walking, turned, and looked up at Brake as he turned and looked down at her. "You're going to prove to me that your horse is more popular with the ladies than you are? Surely you can't be that naive." Realizing what she'd just implied—that being that Brake was, no doubt, popular with all ladies—Amoretta quickly stammered, "I-I mean, surely you can't think that *I'm* that naive...to think a horse would be better liked by humans than a human."

"Well, it's true," he said, smiling at her. "And now I'm gonna have to prove it to you, just to save my pride." Dropping his horse's reins, Brake smiled. "Are you up for it? Because you might be surprised at how charmin' my horse can be, Miss Amoretta."

Straightening her posture, Amoretta answered, "Of course I'm up for it."

Brake's smile broadened, sending goose bumps pouring over Amoretta's arms and legs with its quality of absolute enticement.

"All righty then," he chuckled. Then leveling an index finger at her, he added, "But remember...I warned you."

"I'll remember," Amoretta cheerfully assured him.

She watched then as Brake stroked the horse's jaw-line and, speaking to the animal in a low voice, said, "Gambler...this lady here is doubtin' your popularity with the womenfolk. Now you be a good boy and show her your charm. All right?"

Amoretta watched as Brake patted the horse behind one ear three times. With a quiet whinny, the horse nodded once and then moved toward Amoretta.

"Now stand still," Brake instructed. "He won't hurt you. He's just gonna flirt with you a bit."

Amoretta giggled as the horse nodded again and then used its nose to brush her long hair from her shoulder. Three more pats behind the ear from his owner and Amoretta squealed with surprised amusement when the horse began to carefully move its lips against her neck as if it were trying to kiss her there. The gesture tickled mercilessly, and Amoretta laughed.

"Now, Gambler," Brake said, taking the horse's ear with one hand and gently petting it, "show the lady your romantic gaze, boy." Aside to Amoretta, he whispered, "Hold still."

Smiling a smile that hurt her face it was so broad, Amoretta did as Brake instructed. Slowly, and obviously with great care, the horse lowered its head, placed its soft, velvety nose against Amoretta's for a moment, and then turned its head to one side, looking directly into her eyes with its deep brown one.

After a moment, Amoretta couldn't resist bursting into delighted laughter and reaching up to stroke the horse's soft muzzle. She heard Brake laugh and looked to see him smiling at her.

"I told you he was popular with the ladies," he said. Reaching into his pocket, he produced three sugar cubes and offered them to Amoretta. "Here," he said as he dropped them into her hand. "Give him those, and he'll do anything you ask for the rest of his life."

Amoretta held her open hand under the horse's mouth, giggling as his lips gathered them from her hand and into his mouth.

"Good boy, Gambler," Brake said, stroking the horse's long neck with approval and affection. "You ol' Romeo, you."

As they began walking again, Amoretta said, "So that's how you bewitch the ladies, is it, Mr. McClendon? You train your horse to charm them for you?"

Brake laughed, and the sound of his laughter again caused goose bumps to ripple over Amoretta's arms.

"So you're wise to me already?" he asked. "Dang!" Amoretta laughed—until Brake added, "Well…did it work for me this time? Did I get your attention?"

Amoretta had no idea from whence her response came, but she nearly gasped with bashful astonishment as she heard her own mouth answer, "You already had my attention, Mr. McClendon. You've had it since yesterday at the mill."

Amoretta felt the crimson of an embarrassed blush heat her cheeks—was certain she might drop dead of mortification at her own emboldened flirting.

But her blush lessened a little and her heart soared as Brake said, "Likewise, Miss Ipswich. Likewise."

Amoretta found that she couldn't look at him for long moments. Her heart was beating so fiercely—she could feel the blood coursing through her body—and she feared that if she looked directly at Brake McClendon in those first moments following their flirting, she might just abandon all reason and confess to him that he'd bewitched her somehow—that she'd thought of nothing else but him since meeting him the day before.

Thus they walked in silence for a moment, and then it was Brake who spoke first.

"Well, it's gettin' close to time for me to be at the mill, Miss Ipswich," he said as they neared the back of the Ipswich house.

She knew she had to acknowledge him then—had to thank him for seeing her home. Summoning her courage, she turned and looked up into his handsome, handsome, intoxicatingly handsome face.

"Well, I-I…thank you for seeing me home, Mr. McClendon," she managed.

He nodded, touched the brim of his hat, and smiled. "My pleasure, Miss Ipswich…and everybody just calls me Brake, darlin'."

Darling? Darling? She knew it was just a casual word to folks out west—like saying ma'am or miss. Yet it stirred her emotions up all over again, and she felt her hands begin to tremble.

"And everybody just calls me Amoretta," she countered at last.

"Well then, Amoretta," he began, still smiling at her, "you have yourself a nice day, all right?"

"You as well," she said as she watched him mount Gambler.

He nodded to her once more, for some reason mumbled, "Amoretta Ipswich," and chuckled before clicking his tongue in signaling Gambler into a trot toward Meadowlark Lake's main thoroughfare.

As Amoretta stood in the glow of the still-rising sun, she shook her head as she watched Brake McClendon ride his Romeo of a horse toward the mill road. "I'm going to die," she said aloud to herself. "I'm going to stand here, bathed in so much wonder and joy, that I'm going to literally die."

But she didn't die, of course. After several more moments of watching Brake ride away, Amoretta turned and hurried into the house. She was changed—eternally altered—and though she didn't understand how it had happened or why, she knew what had caused it. She'd never again be the same rather silly, sulky, selfish young woman she'd been only a day before—never. And though she had no idea whether Brake McClendon would even ever talk to her again, she knew it was because of him that she had changed. He'd altered her somehow—bewitched her—and Amoretta Ipswich knew she would never regret that he had.

CHAPTER SIX

Amoretta stepped through the kitchen door to find her father sitting at the table.

"You were up and out early, honey," Lawson noted, smiling at Amoretta. Laying down his pen on top of the paper he'd been writing on, Lawson's smile broadened. "Did you enjoy the sunrise?"

Amoretta's smile hadn't faded—not from the moment Brake McClendon had smiled at her that morning. "Oh, immensely!" she exclaimed in answering. "It's a beautiful morning, Daddy! The most beautiful morning I can ever remember waking to."

Lawson Ipswich's eyebrows arched with suspicion. "Well, that's certainly a change from yesterday morning, isn't it?" He chuckled. "If I recall, yesterday was the most miserable morning of your life...or at least so it appeared when I left to go into town."

Amoretta sighed, her smile dulling as her thoughts were again drawn back to the fact that she seemed to have changed, literally in the blink of an eye.

"Daddy?" she began. "Do you think I'm insane?"

Puffing a breath of amusement, Lawson shook his head. "Why in all the world would I think you're insane, Amoretta? I swear, your behavior does confound me so much of the time."

"But I'm serious, Daddy," Amoretta continued. "I mean, yesterday, just as you said, I felt so miserable and despairing in the morning. Then I went for a walk, cried myself nearly sick, and when

I came back I was beginning to feel differently…not so unhappy as I had just a short time before."

"And then?" Lawson prodded.

"And then I went to the sewing circle with Evangeline and Calliope, met some wonderful women and young ladies in the town, went for another walk with Calliope and our new friends, and by the time I returned home…" She paused—so thoroughly confused by the alteration in herself that she was nearly frightened.

"Go on, honey," Lawson urged.

"By the time I returned home, Daddy…I didn't even miss Boston!" she confessed. "By supper last night, it was if God himself had just reached into my heart and taken away all my heartaches and worries. I felt like…like I used to feel…like life was bright and hopeful again." She swallowed the lump that had gathered in her throat as her fear heightened. "I'm insane, aren't I, Daddy?"

But her father's sigh of understanding and compassion—his handsome smile of reassurance and amusement—began to instantly comfort her.

"Not at all, my sweet girl," Lawson said.

Pushing his chair out from the table, he patted his knee—a familiar indication that Amoretta should settle herself on his lap. Her smile returning, she happily did so, laying one arm across the breadth of his strong shoulders and placing a quick kiss to his warm forehead.

"I think you've just had a moment of maturation, honey," he explained simply. "I remember when I was not too much older than you girls are now…I'd had my eye on several fancy and quite pretty young ladies in town. But none of them turned my head enough to make me even think for one minute about settling down and having a family of my own."

Amoretta's smile broadened, and she felt warm and soothed inside. "And then you met Mama," she stated.

Lawson nodded—smiled even for the excess moisture Amoretta saw spring to his eyes at the memory of her mother.

"Yes," he confirmed. "Then I met your mother. And I swear to you, Amoretta, the moment just before I saw her, I was determined

I'd be a bachelor all my days...and excited at the prospect. But then...then your mother literally crossed by path—just walked across the path there in the park where I was strolling one morning. And just as if God had reached into my soul and planted her there himself...well, I couldn't think of anything else, not from that moment until I married her and took her home with me. I couldn't think of anything else but having your mother for my own, for my wife and the mother of my children. I wanted to build a life with her...to love her and provide for her like she deserved to be loved and provided for." He chuckled, shaking his head at the memory. "I remember wondering what in the world had happened to me. Had I gone mad?" He reached up, cupping Amoretta's chin in one hand. "But I hadn't. I'd just changed. All at once, I'd grown up. And remaining a bachelor held no excitement for me any longer."

Amoretta smiled, brushing a stray strand of hair from her father's forehead. "Well, I am nineteen, aren't I, Daddy?" she began. "I suppose it's time I grew up." She smiled at him and then frowned for one more moment as she asked, "So you're certain I'm not going insane or anything?"

Lawson shook his head as he chuckled. "No. Not at all. And I'm sure you'll find that all your worry and feelings of loss over our relocation...you'll probably find they're not entirely gone. Though I doubt that poor ol' Sylvanus Tenney's memory will ever have a chance of knocking that handsome Brake McClendon's image out of your mind, hmmm?"

Rolling her eyes, Amoretta playfully slapped her father on the chest and scolded, "Oh, Daddy. You don't really think I'm as fickle as all that, do you? And besides, my apple peelings spelled out S four years running...and Brake doesn't begin with S, you know."

"No," Lawson admitted. "But let's just wait and see what happens this Halloween, shall we? Maybe this Halloween those old apple peelings will give you a different letter than they have before. After all, we've made some enormous changes in our lives, and fate will just have to change along with them, won't it?"

Amoretta smiled. Oh, how she loved her father! He was the best of men, and she was so thankful for him.

"I guess we'll see, won't we?" she giggled, throwing her arms around her father's neck and hugging him tightly. "As long as you're sure I'm not a madwoman."

"I'm sure, honey," he said, embracing her in his powerful arms.

Amoretta felt safe with her father—safer than she did at any other time or with any other person. She'd felt that way for as long as she could remember. Since she was a toddler, the feeling of safety had been synonymous with thoughts of her father.

"I see Amoretta is up at the crack of dawn and as bright as a sunflower...as always," Calliope mumbled as she rather stumbled into the kitchen. She yawned, stretched, and collapsed into a chair at the table. Rather scowling at Amoretta, she grumbled, "Oh, I just resent you morning people to the ends of the earth."

Amoretta and her father both smiled. Calliope was not a person who enjoyed mornings. Although she was as radiant, happy, and bright as the summer sun once she'd had half an hour or so out of bed, her initial morning demeanor was more that of a badger.

"Good morning, Daddy!" Evangeline chirped as she stepped into the kitchen next. She kissed her father on the cheek. "Good morning, Amoretta."

"Good morning, Evie," Amoretta said, returning her elder sister's loving smile and embrace.

"I won't bother with you yet, Calliope," Evangeline sighed as Calliope slouched over, resting her forehead on the table.

"Thank you," she mumbled, and Evangeline and Amoretta exchanged amused glances with their father.

"What can we get you for breakfast, Daddy?" Amoretta asked, hopping up from her father's lap. She did feel much relieved—relieved in knowing that apparently there were leaps of maturity in life. And there was something comforting in knowing that not every growing experience dragged on and on for months like others sometimes did.

"Oh, I already had some toast," Lawson answered. "I've got quite a few things to tend to today…so I just thought I'd get an early start." Rising from his chair, he reached over, tousling Calliope's hair as if she were a schoolboy. She moaned, and he smiled. "But you girls go on and have a good, hearty breakfast for yourselves, and I'll be home for lunch. How's that sound?"

Amoretta and Evangeline nodded, even as Calliope made no sound or motion at all.

"Okay, Daddy," Evangeline said.

"Where are you off to first?" Amoretta asked.

"Oh, nowhere special," Lawson said.

But Amoretta's eyes narrowed with suspicion. Something had crossed her father's expression for just an instant; it almost looked like concern. Still, Amoretta decided she was just imagining things and nodded.

"Well, you have a pleasant day…wherever you're off to," she said.

"Thank you, honey," Lawson mumbled. "I'll see you girls at noon then."

Lawson made sure not to allow his gaze and Amoretta's to meet for too long, lest she suspect something were amiss. Amoretta was the watchful one in the family, and most of the time nothing snuck past her—no sadness, no worry, nothing that could be noticed by someone as observant as his middle daughter. Lawson didn't want Amoretta to look at him too long and figure out that he did indeed have some concerns.

He'd hardly slept a wink the night before. Every time he closed his eyes, all he could see was the pile of dead animals Sheriff Montrose had found outside of town. And the more he was kept awake by the vision, the more he began to worry that perhaps there was more to the incident than just some rambunctious, angry boy.

Still, worry did nothing but wear a person out. Therefore, Lawson had decided he wouldn't wait until late morning to start inquiring further into the incident the way he'd planned. He'd decided to ride out to the woods and interview the gypsy woman first thing. That way if Sheriff Montrose needed assistance checking into other folks, Lawson would be available to lend a hand.

Lawson saddled his horse, a handsome bay gelding he'd purchased from a local man, and rode through the stretch of grass between his own home and the woods. He had no notion of how the gypsy woman would react to him, so he'd determined to tread lightly. He didn't want to frighten her or irritate her into not cooperating and talking with him.

Thus as he rode into the trees of the woods, easily finding the path that no doubt led to the gypsy's abode, Lawson reasoned he would approach the gypsy on the pretense of being a new citizen of the town and offering his assistance in any way he could.

Lawson found the little house much more easily than he'd imagined. In fact, he wondered for a moment he if perhaps his horse had been to it before. Still, he quickly reasoned that it was not so hard a place to find. After all, the small path through the woods led him right to it. He noted as he dismounted and tied his reins to a tree a ways off from the house that the path was indeed well traveled. He figured that a great many more residents of Meadowlark Lake were well acquainted with the gypsy than he had been led to believe and, furthermore, that they visited her often. Otherwise the path would surely have had patches of new grass growing on it, and it didn't.

Quietly Lawson walked through the woods the remainder of the distance to the house. He wasn't sure why he'd felt the need to rather sneak up on the woman—but he did. And when he at last reached the open space in the woods where the gypsy's house was located, he was somewhat astonished at what a lovely little scene it was. Among a hidden grove of wild cherry trees sat the small house, which resembled something out of the imagination of a Grimm brother. Bright and white, with clean and shiny windows, the gypsy woman's house looked more like a dream than the den of evil it was rumored to be by some of the more intolerant citizens in Meadowlark Lake.

In fact, Lawson was so momentarily mesmerized by the ethereal setting of the house, it was several seconds before he noticed the child playing beneath one tree to the right of the house. Not until he heard the melodic voice of what seemed to be an angel did Lawson turn and glance over to see the little dark-haired girl. She appeared to be perhaps four years of age and was clad in the whitest little dress he'd ever seen on one so young.

He observed the child for a moment—smiled as he watched her busily serving pretend tea out of a tiny little porcelain teapot, carefully pouring the fantasy liquid into tiny little cups set on tiny little saucers positioned on top of an old quilt. A battered teddy bear and doll that looked to be well loved were the expected guests. Lawson smiled as the little girl poured tea into a cup set before a rather plump-looking marmalade cat, which was sitting on its haunches watching the little girl go about her pretend tea service.

For a moment, Lawson was awash in the sensation that he'd walked into someone else's dream. The very air was more fragrant where he stood; the colors of the forest seemed richer and the breeze more refreshing.

"And how are you feelin' today, Molly?" the little dark-haired girl asked as she gently stroked the cat's back a moment. "Mommy says it won't be long now and the house will be crawlin' with kittens! I can't wait. But you take care and drink your tea. Would you like some extra cream today?"

Lawson watched, mesmerized as the little girl hurriedly collected a tiny creamer pitcher and pretended to add cream to the cat's serving of tea.

"There you go, Molly," the child said. "We wanna make sure you're nice and strong when the babies come, now don't we?"

Lawson's breath caught in his chest as the little girl suddenly looked up, her attention instantly attached to him. He didn't want to frighten her by speaking too soon, yet he knew that not speaking might frighten her as well.

"Hello, mister," the child said, alleviating Lawson of the responsibility of the first verbal approach.

"Hello," he responded, smiling. "I see you're serving morning tea."

The child's face brightened. "Yes! Would you like some?" she asked. "We have an extra place." Lawson chuckled when the girl patted an empty spot on the quilt next to her.

"Well, perhaps we should ask your mother's permission first," Lawson suggested.

Tiny eyebrows puckered into a thoughtful frown a moment. "Hmm," the girl mused. "I think that would be a good idea." Lowering her voice, the girl added, "Mama is always worried that someone will take me away from her." She shook her head and smiled, adding, "Mamas can be so silly sometimes."

"I suppose they can," Lawson mumbled—though the child's inadvertently offered information troubled him. He knew all too well the fear every parent owned of losing a child. It was something that haunted the dreams of any adult with children.

"But I will go ask her for us," the little girl said, leaping to her feet as nimbly as a cat. Looking up to Lawson, she smiled. "You wait here, okay, mister?"

"Of course," Lawson agreed with a nod.

He watched the girl hurry to the front door of the house, delighted by the way her little dark curls bobbed up and down as she ran.

"Mama! There's another man outside," he heard the child's voice ring as she bolted through the front door. "Can he have some of my tea? Molly says she doesn't mind having him."

Lawson glanced back to the pregnancy-swollen marmalade cat. She didn't move—simply blinked her large green eyes slowly the way that cats do and looked away from him.

His attention was drawn back to the house when a voice greeted, "Hello?"

Judge Lawson Ipswich was struck entirely dumb for a moment. There, on the threshold of the small house—protectively pushing the little dark-haired girl to stand behind her—stood the most physically beautiful young woman Lawson Ipswich had ever seen.

The gypsy of the woods was small and slightly built, but her fitted bodice and belt revealed that her figure was curvaceous nonetheless.

Her colorful skirt looked more like a conglomeration of silk scarves rather than a typical piece of clothing. Bracelet after bracelet adorned her arms—some beaded, some appearing to be brass or silver—so many that her left arm was embellished nearly halfway to her elbow. Large hoop earrings adorned her ears, accentuating her slender neck, and though her dark hair hung unpinned and near to her waist, she wore a purple scarf covering the top of her head and tied in a knot to one side.

As for the features of her face, stunning did not go far enough to describe her. Her lips were as red as summer berries; her dark eyes shaded by heavy lashes stared at Lawson with fear and yet a warning. Lawson had seen gypsy women before but never one so strikingly beautiful as this.

For the first time since he could remember, Lawson struggled with speaking. "I-I…uh…um…I'm Judge Ipswich, ma'am," he managed at last. "My family and I are recently moved to Meadowlark Lake, and as judge, I would like to be certain that every citizen in the county knows I am here to serve them."

The gypsy's eyelashes fluttered as she quickly studied Lawson from head to toe with obvious suspicion, and Lawson found himself wishing he'd straightened his shoulders before she'd appeared.

"It would appear to me that you're terribly young to be a judge," she ventured.

Lawson nodded. "I suppose as most judges go…I am."

Her eyes narrowed, and she studied him again. "Ipswich," she said. "That's an unusual name."

"Yes," Lawson admitted. "My parents were immigrants from England."

"Mama? Can he have tea with me or not?" the child begged, tugging on her mother's colorful skirt.

"I suppose he may have tea with us if he truly wishes to, Shay," the woman answered.

"Oh, he does! He does!" the child giggled, snatching her mother's hand and tugging until the woman began to walk toward the laid-out quilt. "Come on, mister!" the girl giggled, gesturing to Lawson that he should join them.

Lawson saw the manner in which the beautiful woman arched one lovely, dark eyebrow in obvious wondering whether he was the sort of man who would appease a child. He was, of course, and he saw a slight smile curve the woman's berry-red lips as he nodded and took his seat on the quilt.

"So you're here to serve us. Is that it?" the young woman asked.

"Hush, Mama," the child scolded. "At least let the man have his tea first."

Lawson smiled as he watched the little girl pour her imaginary tea from her teapot into a tiny teacup and offer it to him. "Thank you," he said, accepting the cup and pretending to sip from it.

The little girl giggled with delight, and a warm tickling sensation spread through Lawson's chest at the sound.

"And how can you serve us, Judge Ipswich?" the child's mother asked. "Me and my daughter? A gypsy woman with a child and no man to speak of?"

Ah! There it was—the bitterness of heartbreak and ruination that some deviant male had left in her.

"I don't know, ma'am," Lawson answered, looking directly into her eyes. "That would be your determination, I suppose."

Her eyes were beautiful! Smoldering orbs of restrained emotion—curiosity, fear, heartache, and wariness. He had a sudden desire to know what her lips tasted like—to know if they tasted as sweet as they looked—and he called his thoughts to a harsh halt, wondering if the woman really did have some sort of gypsy power and was silently attempting to distract him somehow.

"Shay," the woman said, reaching out and twisting a strand of her daughter's hair around her index finger. Smiling at the child, she asked, "Would you please run in and fetch a jar of my best cherry preserves for our guest? Hmmm?"

The child—Shay, as she was obviously called—giggled with delight. "Yes, Mama!" Hopping to her feet once more, she skipped away and into the house.

The moment Shay was inside, the woman looked to Lawson once more and spoke. "My name is Kizzy, Judge Ipswich. And as you've no doubt been told, I am sinner…a loathsome sinner…a ruined woman with a child and no husband."

She paused, and Lawson saw the pain obvious in her eyes.

"We're all sinners, ma'am," Lawson responded. "Now tell me something about yourself and your daughter…something that would help me to better serve you as a member of this community."

Kizzy frowned, obviously puzzled. "Y-you don't think that what I just told you is…is…"

"If I told you that, as a boy, I once stole a basket of buttered rolls from a baker…would you think I didn't deserve to be a judge?" Lawson asked forthright.

"That's different," Kizzy answered. "You were a child. It's your past." She looked away from him a moment. "And anyway, people don't know you did that because the proof of it…it can't be seen."

Lawson knew full well her implication—that her child was evidence of her past mistake.

"I asked you if you thought I deserved to be a judge because of it…because I was once a thief," Lawson reminded her.

"I-I…I have no right to judge you for your past…and whether or not you should hold the position you do now because of it," she offered. "But it's so very different from—"

"Do I or do I not deserve to be a judge?" Lawson interrupted. "After all, I stole. I was once a thief, and now I sit here next to you claiming to have the right to judge people's crimes…whether or not they're guilty. So I'll ask you again, Miss…Miss Kizzy. Does my past make me unworthy to be a judge now?"

"A stolen basket of buttered rolls, stolen when you were a boy?" she asked. "It doesn't matter now. Obviously you've been a good enough man since to become a judge. But that's very different from what I—"

To Lawson's own surprise, he found that he'd reached out and firmly taken hold of the woman's wrist. "You're right. It doesn't matter now. All that matters now is who I became after I stole that basket." Releasing his grip on her, for he did not want to frighten her, Lawson sighed and repeated, "Now...tell me something about yourself and your daughter that will help me to better serve you."

"Here you go, mister!" Shay called as she bounded out of the house and to where Lawson sat.

He smiled as she handed him the small jar of preserves. "Thank you," he said.

"And you'll love those preserves, mister," the child prattled. "My mama makes the best preserves and...and...and well, she just makes the best everything!"

"I'm sure she does," Lawson chuckled.

Shay returned to her tea set, and Lawson watched as the chubby marmalade cat crawled into Kizzy's lap. The cat began purring, and Kizzy stroked its soft fur, kissing it squarely on the top of the head.

It seemed to Lawson that any woman who would nurture a pregnant cat would not be prone to slaughtering other people's pets.

"Shay and I have all that we need, Judge Ipswich," Kizzy said, looking up to him at last. He noted that some of the fear and anger were gone from her beautiful eyes—replaced by kindness. "Truly."

"Except real, live friends," Shay sighed with disappointment.

Lawson's heart hurt for the child, for it was obvious that she longed for companions near her own age. The isolation she and her mother lived in kept the child lonesome.

"Well, I'm your friend now, Miss Shay," Lawson offered. "And I have three daughters of my own that might like to come and have tea with you and your cat one day."

The child's eyes lit up. "Are they little like me?"

Lawson felt defeated as he answered, "No. They're grown up...like your mother. But they still love to play all the same." Shay smiled, and Lawson felt somewhat better.

"Three daughters?" Kizzy asked. "No sons?"

Lawson shook his head. "No sons." Then, for some reason he could not fathom, he added, "And my wife died over six years ago."

"Oh no!" Shay exclaimed then. "So your girls don't have a mama anymore?"

Lawson shook his head. "I'm afraid not."

He smiled, and every inch of his flesh warmed as the child patted the back of his hand and said, "Well, if they ever need a mama, you tell them I'll come and be their mama. I'm a good mama. Just ask Molly." Lawson watched as the girl snuggled down against the cat that sat purring in her own mother's lap. "Isn't that right, Molly? I'm a good mama too."

"Thank you, Shay," Lawson said. "I'll let my girls know that you're willing to help." Looking back to Kizzy—and once again awed by her beauty—Lawson said, "I'm sorry if I made you or your daughter uncomfortable. I'm sure that a strange man appearing from the woods isn't quite what you—"

"Oh, we always have men here," Shay interjected.

"Shay!" Kizzy scolded, her cheeks turning as red as summer roses. Looking to Lawson, she shook and stammered, "I-I...it's not what you think, Judge Ipswich. I-I sell herbal tonics to the men who work at the mill...the farmers...their wives. And once in a while, someone will come and split wood for our fire. That's all. I swear it."

Lawson could see the desperation in her—the desire that he not think the worst of her. No doubt she didn't want to have the county judge thinking she might be dragged into his court one day for...

"You have to believe me!" Kizzy nearly begged. "I'm no scarlet woman, Judge Ipswich. I-I—"

"I believe you," Lawson interrupted. And he did. There was nothing of a liar in her countenance—only the pain of a victimized woman. "I do."

Kizzy sighed with evident relief. "Thank you," she muttered. "People seldom do, you know."

"Unfortunately I do know," Lawson said.

Draining his tiny teacup of the remainder of his imaginary tea, he handed the cup to Shay and stood to take his leave.

"Thank you for the tea, Miss Shay," he said. "It was quite refreshing."

"You're welcome, mister," the child giggled.

"I-I hope you'll enjoy the preserves, Judge Ipswich," Kizzy said as she shooed the cat from her lap and stood as well. "And I promise you that Shay and I won't be any trouble to you."

Lawson smiled. "How could you ever be?" He offered a hand to her, and she tentatively accepted it. Of course, the moment she touched him, Lawson wished he hadn't offered to shake her hand, for the warmth of her small, tender grasp sent goose bumps racing over his back. "You ladies have a lovely day," he said, releasing Kizzy's hand, turning, and striding toward where he'd left his horse.

Once he'd mounted, Lawson couldn't resist the urge to turn and look upon the beautiful woman and her charming daughter once more. He smiled and returned Shay's wave before riding away into the woods.

As he rode toward town, Lawson Ipswich was certain the gypsy woman who lived in the woods was not the culprit who had killed the two foxes and miscellaneous pets of Meadowlark Lake. She was too tender with her daughter and her cat, and she certainly would never want to do anything to draw further attention or visitors to herself. No—Kizzy was innocent of the animal killings.

Yet something did bother Lawson about her, and that was the way he'd been so wildly attracted to her. He was, after all, a grown man with three grown daughters. For all he knew, and from his estimation, Kizzy was no older than Evangeline! Yet she seemed so much older—so much more weathered and broken down by life. Unlike Evangeline, Amoretta, and Calliope, Kizzy's innocence had been stolen years before. Thus she'd grown up much faster than his own girls. Lawson silently thanked God that his girls had been kept safe from the seductive ways of honorless men.

"She certainly is beautiful," he mumbled to himself as he neared town and the courthouse. Again he wondered if her lips tasted as sweet as summer berries the way they looked like they would. Then he scolded himself for even owning such thoughts—he, Lawson Ipswich, a widower with three grown daughters, a judge. Who was he to betray the wife who had died in birthing his child? Who was he to even think on kissing a woman as beautiful and exotic as the woman who lived in the woods? No doubt every other unmarried man in Meadowlark Lake wondered what her berry-red lips tasted like. Who was Lawson Ipswich to think he could daydream about tasting them?

And yet all through the remainder of the morning, he did daydream about it—about Kizzy the gypsy woman and her summer-berry lips.

CHAPTER SEVEN

"Well…looks like your competition has arrived, boys," Rowdy Gates mumbled.

"Damn!" Dex Longfellow cursed. "I've always hated Fox Montrose and his purty face."

"Oh now, boys," Sam Mulholland said in a lowered voice, "he's the new pup in town maybe…but once he's made his choice on which of them girls to court, then the others will fall off his trail and right back onto ours."

Brake laughed, frowned, and asked, "Hell, what's wrong with you boys? Ain't ya got no gumption?" He nodded toward the place across the street where people had gathered to meet and greet the newly returned Fox Montrose. "Hell, he's just all fancied up right now…shiny and bright like a new penny. Of course everyone is fawnin' all over him. He's the most excitin' thing that's come to town since the judge and his three girls. And folks just don't fawn over judges that way…and nobody's gonna tangle with his daughters." Brake nodded, even as he returned his attention to the gathering across the street. He frowned a little as he saw Winnie Montrose introduce her brother to Amoretta Ipswich. She accepted his offered hand and smiled as Fox greeted her. "I figure the new will wear off that penny soon enough."

"Well, that's easy for you to say, Brake," Sam began, "you bein' so purty yourself."

The men chuckled, and Brake shook his head. Then, as he continued to watch Fox Montrose speaking to Amoretta, he said, "And why are we all standin' around over here like whipped dogs anyhow? Best way to keep hold of our interests over there is to walk on over and meet the Fox fellow ourselves. Ain't that right?"

"Yeah, it is," Dex agreed. "Ol' Fox need to know he ain't the only rooster in the henhouse."

"Exactly," Sam agreed.

But Rowdy Gates only chuckled. "Well, you hotheaded mules go on over and claim your territory from the new lion in town…but it don't matter much to me at all." He nodded toward the gathering of people across the street—mostly the young women of the town. "Girls ain't nothin' but trouble and pain, boys. But you little cubs go on over and do what you gotta do. I'm headin' back to the mill."

Brake watched Rowdy turn and stride away. He wondered what had made the man so coldhearted and callused—wondered what injury had caused his limp. He was good fellow though, whether or not he thought women were worth the trouble.

Brake looked back to where Fox Montrose stood surrounded by a flock of smiling females, including his obviously very proud and delighted mother. He felt a smile spread across his face as, unexpectedly, he found that Amoretta Ipswich was looking directly at him and not at Fox. Some other girl had stepped into shaking hands in greeting Meadowlark Lake's newest and apparently most eligible bachelor. But Amoretta was looking at Brake—smiling at him, in truth.

"Well, I ain't standin' around while some peacock is flashin' his feathers," Brake said. "I got plenty of feathers of my own."

"Me too," Sam mumbled.

Brake continued to hold Amoretta's gaze as he strode across the street. He felt a triumphant grin curve his lips as her smile broadened the closer he got to her.

"Afternoon, Miss Ip…Amoretta," he greeted with a tug on the brim of his hat.

"Good afternoon, B-Brake," she responded.

Out of the corner of one eye, he saw Dex and Sam wriggle their way between the flock of womenfolk, with the intention of introducing themselves (and thereby their competition) to Fox Montrose. But Brake wasn't worried about intimidating Winnie's brother; he just wanted to see how long he could keep Amoretta Ipswich's attention.

Amoretta's heart was palpitating almost painfully! The way Brake McClendon had looked up to see her staring at him, and immediately stepped into striding across the street toward her, had taken her breath away. And now he stood still staring at her—smiling at her like a wolf that had cornered a rabbit—and the expression only made him that much more attractive.

For four days Amoretta had taken an early morning walk out into the grassy expanse between her home and the woods. Every day for four days she'd watched the sun rise, desperate with hoping that Brake McClendon would come riding out of the woods again. But he hadn't. She'd tried to find a reason to wander to the gristmill. For four days she tried—and failed. And by the time she and her sisters had arrived at the Montroses' house at Winnie's invitation to meet her brother, Amoretta had determined that, reason or not, she would take a walk by herself to the gristmill if she had to in order to see Brake again.

And yet now he stood directly in front of her—towering and handsome and staring at her with an alluring sort of smile on his handsome face. She could hardly breathe for the bliss coursing through her.

"H-how have you been?" she awkwardly asked, desperate to involve him in conversation—to keep his attention for as long as fate would allow.

"Just fine," he answered, his smile broadening with what she could only interpret as amusement because of her obvious agitation. "And you? You been doin' all right? You all settled in?"

Amoretta nodded, still smiling like a silly schoolgirl with a crush on her schoolmaster. "Yes. I think so...finally."

Brake's eyebrows arched. "Was it difficult to do for you?"

"At first," she admitted. "I was homesick...very homesick until...until recently."

"Well, I can understand that," he said, his eyes softening with—what was it? Compassion? "It's a mighty frightenin' thing to do...to leave everything you've always known and end up somewhere strange and unfamiliar."

"Yes, it is," she admitted. Then, feeling her smile broaden again, she added, "But it seems there's always something new and wonderful to win you over, isn't there?"

Again she watched as one suspicious eyebrow arched on the man before her. "Is there? And what kind of somethin' might that be?"

He took a step closer to her, and Amoretta's heart nearly leapt up into her throat and out of her mouth. There was something dangerously alluring about Brake McClendon—something almost supernatural—a tempting quality that rather unnerved her for a moment.

Still, she managed to answer, "Oh...oh, you know...the lovely open space...the fresh air...the serenity of the evenings."

"Hmm," he said, still gazing at her with an expression of amused suspicion. "Well, I'm glad to hear that." He paused a moment, rather slowly studying her from head to toe. "Sallie Ackerman was tellin' me just yesterday that you fancy Halloween. Is that true?"

Amoretta was mortified! Sallie Ackerman? She'd told Brake about Amoretta's silly infatuation with romantic Halloween customs?

"Well, y-yes. I do like Halloween," she admitted. After all, what more was there to do than to try to explain that it was just an interest she had? "I like all of autumn, in truth. It's my favorite time of year."

"Mine too," he said. "And if you like Halloween, you're gonna love it here. The town has all kinds of harvest and Halloween celebrations."

Amoretta felt somewhat relieved in that he seemed to be encouraging her, not making fun of her.

"Oh, how wonderful!" she exclaimed. "It's always nice to have something to look forward to, isn't it?"

"Yes, it is," he said.

"And this is Brake McClendon," Winnie said, startling Amoretta from whatever bewitchment Brake had again managed to lure her with.

Brake turned then, striking hands with Fox Montrose.

"Brake, this is my brother, Fox," Winnie introduced.

"We've heard a lot about you, Montrose," Brake greeted. "Winnie was near to bustin' her buttons with wantin' you home."

Fox Montrose chuckled. "Well, she's an angel...and I missed her too," he said.

Fox Montrose *was* handsome, but nothing as handsome as Brake McClendon—at least in Amoretta's opinion. She studied the two men as they stood talking for a moment. Fox was tall, raven-haired, blue-eyed, and with the overall look of a well-dressed city man. He was friendly, it seemed—charming—and Amoretta wondered if Calliope would ever stop staring at him and if Sallie Ackerman might start into panting any at any moment as she gazed at him like a lovesick puppy.

But as Amoretta studied Brake in comparison—the way his hat was rather battered and well broken in; his scuffed boots, worn from hard work; his somewhat tight-fitting shirt that did nothing to conceal the perfect sculpting of his arms, shoulders, and torso—she thought Fox Montrose looked a bit too soft to be causing such a stir among the young women of Meadowlark Lake.

It was at that moment that she glanced away to see that both Winnie Montrose and Prudence Mulholland were also staring at Brake—smiling as if they too owned the same opinion as Amoretta did where Brake's dominance in appearance was concerned. She felt her brow pucker a bit, disquieted by the knowledge. She'd secretly hoped that once Winnie's supposedly unequaled-in-attractiveness brother Fox returned, she might have less competition where her hopes of capturing Brake's notice and holding it were concerned.

But now she surmised that only Sallie and Blanche found Fox attractive enough to keep their attention from Brake. Calliope didn't appear to be as smitten by Fox as Sallie and Blanche did, and

Evangeline was too sensible to consider going up against so many rivals to perhaps win Fox's interest—or Brake's, for that matter.

Thus, Amoretta concluded that it would be Prudence and Winnie who remained loyal to their infatuation with Brake—Prudence and Winnie who would be her stumbling blocks where Brake was concerned.

She shook her head quickly, dispelling such ridiculous thoughts. *Brake McClendon—really?* she thought. Charming, handsome, mesmerizing Brake McClendon? She didn't have a hope in heaven of belonging to him! And why did she want to anyway? She barely knew him. And yet there it was: the quiet shouting in her mind, the demand from her soul that she accept the fact that Brake McClendon had somehow captured it, held it in his fist as surely as if Amoretta wore a bit and bridle owned by him.

Amoretta gasped as she felt someone take hold of her upper arm. Startled from her thoughts, she looked up to see it was Brake.

"Come here a minute, Amoretta, will you?" he asked—though it was obvious by the way he was pulling her along beside him that he'd only asked to let her know she would be going with him.

He released her arm quickly enough—though she was disappointed when he did—stopped walking, and turned to face her.

"I was wonderin' if I could ask you do to me a favor," he quietly began.

"A favor?" Amoretta asked in response. Mingled feelings of wild curiosity, delight, and trepidation were swirling in her stomach. What kind of a favor would Brake McClendon, whom she'd only seen twice before, ask of her?

"Yeah," he admitted. He grinned at her. "But first I had to get you away from that wily new Fox fellow…make sure you weren't caught in his trap of charm and good looks the way all the other girls are." He paused, frowned, and asked, "You're not, are you? You're not already swoonin' over him?"

Amoretta giggled, shook her head, and answered, "No." And it was true—for she was already caught in Brake McClendon's trap, whether or not he'd set it for her.

Brake smiled. "Well, good. I hope you can keep it that way?"

Amoretta blushed, wondering if she even had the right to blush. It could very well be that Brake hadn't singled her out from the other girls because he liked her more but simply because he was feeling a bit territorial with a new male in town.

"All right then," he said, lowering his voice. "Now you're a brave girl, aren't you?"

Amoretta shrugged. "Most of the time, I guess."

Brake chuckled. Reaching into his back pocket, he removed a folded envelope.

"I was supposed to give this to someone today…and I find that I can't get away from the gristmill in time to get it there before dark," he explained. "Would you be willin' to deliver it for me?"

"Of course," Amoretta agreed. She was so intent on pleasing the man she was quickly falling victim to that she didn't pause but accepted the task without further detail.

"Thank you," he said, smiling at her—and she decided the smile he'd bestowed on her was worth any inconvenience the task might require. "I need you to take this into the woods and give it to the gypsy woman who lives there."

Amoretta's eyes widened with astonishment. Oh, she was anxious enough, but her sense of adventure made certain that her curiosity overpowered any apprehension she might have.

"The gypsy?" she breathed.

Brake smiled. "She's a kind woman, Amoretta. You don't need to be afraid of her. All right?"

"I'm not," Amoretta slightly fibbed. "I've been thinking of going to meet her myself. I've never met a gypsy before."

"Well, here's your chance." Brake's smile faded, and his brow puckered a bit. "But…but don't tell anybody I'm sendin' you there, all right? It's just that I know she needs this today…and I can't get away."

Amoretta's smile spread nearly from ear to ear. Brake McClendon was entrusting her with a secret!

"I won't tell anyone," she assured him. "And I'll go as soon as my sisters and I return home from this little gathering to welcome Winnie's brother home."

"Thank you," Brake said. He inhaled a deep breath and exhaled a sigh as if some sort of great relief had washed over him. "I best be gettin' on back to the mill now...before Mr. Mulholland strings me up for bein' late back from lunch." He smiled, adding, "You have a good evenin', Amoretta Ipswich...and keep your distance from that wolf over there." He nodded toward Fox Montrose.

Amoretta giggled. "You mean that fox?"

But Brake shook his head. "I mean that wolf." He studied her from head to toe quickly and then quietly said, "Girls like you bring out the wolf in the best of men, darlin'."

He winked at her and then turned and sauntered away in the direction of the mill. As Amoretta watched him go, she realized she was quite breathless from being with him.

Once Brake had disappeared around the corner of the millinery shop, Amoretta looked at the envelope he'd placed in her hand. It was sealed, with one word written on the front—*Kizzy*.

"What was all that about?" Evangeline asked, smiling with intrigued delight as she approached. Calliope was with her, smiling with just as much delight.

"Nothing," Amoretta said, quickly stuffing the envelope into the waist of her skirt. "At least...I don't think it was anything."

"Brake McClendon had his hands on you, dragging you away from Fox Montrose as fast as he could!" Calliope exclaimed in a whisper. "What is going on between you? I didn't know you knew him that well!"

"Neither did I," Evangeline added.

"I don't," Amoretta said. "Not so well...not yet. But...but..."

"But what?" Calliope prodded.

Amoretta shook her head—felt an anxious nausea rise in her stomach unexpectedly. "But...I think I'm in love with him," she quietly confessed.

❦

"You can't be in love with him, Amoretta," Evangeline gently said as she sat with Amoretta and Calliope in the parlor of their home a short time later. "You've seen him, what, twice?"

"Three times," Amoretta mumbled. "We walked together for a while the other morning while I was out watching the sunrise."

Calliope smiled, putting a comforting arm around Amoretta's shoulders. "I think she *can* be in love with him," she said. "I absolutely believe in love at first sight."

"But every woman in town is in love with Brake McClendon!" Evangeline warned. "You've heard them talk, Rettie."

Amoretta nodded. "I-I know. But...I can't help it. I can't get him out of my mind...and every time I see him—"

"You mean all three times you've seen him?" Evangeline offered as kindly as possible.

"What don't you understand about falling in love the first time you see someone, Evie?" Calliope gently scolded.

"It doesn't matter. It doesn't matter what anyone thinks," Amoretta said, burying her face in her hands for a moment. "I shouldn't have told you. I don't want you to worry, Evie."

But Evangeline smiled. "I want you to always tell me everything, Amoretta. I'm sorry I take to acting like your mother sometimes. I can't seem to help it."

Amoretta smiled at her well-meaning older sister. "I know. And you probably think I'm simply stupid...after going on and on so as I did about Sylvanus Tenney." Amoretta shook her head and laughed. "I must've been mad!"

All three girls giggled together for a moment. Then Evangeline sighed.

"All right then...love at first sight it is," she said, smiling. "Not that I blame you, of course. In fact, I rather envy you. That Brake McClendon...he's some kind of dream, isn't he?"

"He is!" Calliope agreed.

"Now, why don't you just go on that walk you were wanting to take before Daddy gets home and it's time for supper?" Evangeline encouraged.

"Yes. It's my night to cook, Rettie, so enjoy your walk," Calliope chimed in.

Remembering the sealed envelope for the gypsy that was still tucked inside the waistband of her skirt, Amoretta nodded. "Yes. I think I will go for a walk. And I may be awhile, so don't worry about me. I just...I just need to gather my thoughts a bit."

"All right," Evangeline said, kissing Amoretta's cheek. "Enjoy your walk. It's a lovely September day, and I'm sure this pleasant weather won't last."

"Relax, Amoretta," Calliope cooed, kissing Amoretta's other cheek with tender affection. "Love at first sight...it's rare...but real."

Amoretta nodded, stood, and took her leave of the parlor. She would walk to the woods, find the gypsy's home, and deliver Brake's envelope. And as she did so, she would try to believe that the reason he'd entrusted it to her in the first place was that he felt the same spark that she did—that he'd singled her out for a reason other than simply needing an errand girl.

The September afternoon was warm and lovely, and as Amoretta meandered through the grass toward the woods, she thought about what Brake had said concerning harvest and Halloween in Meadowlark Lake. She imagined there would be wagonloads of vegetables and apples, of hay and wheat. She wondered what the air would feel like when autumn fully arrived and if there were any sort of Halloween carnival held in town.

But as Amoretta stepped out of the grass and onto easily found the dirt path that led through the woods, she wondered—if she were to pare an apple on Halloween and toss the peelings over her shoulder, would they again shape the letter S, or would this year bless her with a letter B as the initial of her lover? If she were to hold a hand mirror before her in candlelight on Halloween, would she see the faint image of Brake McClendon's face there beside her own?

These were all her thoughts as she walked. All her musings were of Brake and the unexpected, powerful feelings in her heart where he was concerned. In fact, thoughts of Halloween and Brake were all that was in Amoretta's mind as she hurried down the path Prudence had once mentioned led to the gypsy's house.

Yet the moment she stepped out of the thicker wooded area and into a clearing filled with wild cherry trees and an inviting little white house—the moment she stepped out of the woods and saw a little girl playing under a tree as her mother took bundles of herbs from a basket, tying them in bouquets for drying—the moment she saw the ethereal beauty of the young, young, very young gypsy woman—Amoretta's heart sank to the very pit of her stomach with a painful thud.

This was she? This was the witch of Meadowlark Lake? The gypsy who sold tonics to the townspeople? And most importantly, this was the woman Brake McClendon visited regularly to stock firewood for and sent sealed envelopes to?

But before Amoretta's stomach could vomit its contents for the sheer anxiety the woman's appearance had caused her, the little girl jumped to her feet, turned toward Amoretta, and said, "Hello! Have you come to see my mama?"

The child was beautiful! As beautiful as her mother, who looked up from her basket of herbs and smiled at Amoretta.

"Hello," the gypsy woman greeted. "I'm Kizzy." She was dressed in all reds and purples and lavenders—from the red scarf tied at the top of her head to the deep purple skirt she wore.

Amoretta felt drab and plain in the presence of such a woman. Her opal earrings—the ones that always made her feel more feminine because of their delicate, dangling craftsmanship—seemed nothing at all feminine compared with the dazzling gold hoops the gypsy wore at her ears. Her blue floral-print dress seemed dingy and colorless so near to the gypsy's lavender blouse and wide red belt.

"I-I…I'm Amoretta Ipswich," Amoretta stammered.

"Ipswich?" the little girl exclaimed with delight, racing to where Amoretta stood stunned. The child took Amoretta's hand and began pulling her toward her mother. "There was man here days ago. His name was Mr. Ipswich! Do you know him?"

"His name is Judge Ipswich, Shay," the gypsy kindly corrected.

"My father?" Amoretta asked, frowning. "My father was here?"

"He's your daddy?" the little girl squealed. "Oh, he is the kindest man! He had tea with us and everything!"

"My father…had tea with you?" Amoretta asked. She was flabbergasted—unable to fathom what business her father would have had with the gypsy.

"He said he wanted to know all the citizens of Meadowlark Lake," the gypsy offered, smiling. "I take it he is thorough at his job."

"He is," Amoretta confirmed.

"And why have you come into the woods, Amoretta Ipswich?" Kizzy asked.

"Oh!" Amoretta breathed, suddenly remembering why she had come. "I-I have a message for you."

"From you father?" Kizzy asked, her cheeks pinking and eyes seeming to spark.

"Um, no. It's actually an envelope from a man in town," Amoretta explained, taking Brake's envelope from its place at her waist. "Brake McClendon gave it to me and asked me if I would deliver it."

"Brake?" Kizzy asked. Her eyes narrowed with suspicion as she studied Amoretta a moment.

"Why didn't *he* bring it?" the little girl asked Amoretta.

Amoretta shook her head, still stunned by the fact that the gypsy woman Brake had sent a message to was a young, vibrant beauty and not a more mature woman. "I don't know," she answered at last.

Offering the envelope to Kizzy, she noticed that her own hand was trembling, and she could no longer keep the thought at bay that was screaming to be thought. Were the gypsy and Brake lovers?

Accepting the envelope, Kizzy very quickly tore it open. Amoretta watched as she read whatever was written on the paper inside. Amoretta watched as Kizzy bit her lip with obvious delight, pressed the note to her bosom, and giggled.

"Thank you," Kizzy said, smiling. "Thank you for bringing this to me, Amoretta."

"You're welcome," Amoretta managed—though the anxiety and nausea in her had grown to such a point she thought she might die.

"Will you share a piece of cake with us?" Kizzy asked. "As my thanks for delivering this?"

But Amoretta shook her head. She had no desire to sit down to eating cake with Brake's gypsy lover—if that's what she was. And what else could she be? She gazed at the child for a long moment, wondering if the beautiful little girl's brown eyes resembled Brake McClendon's at all.

"I-I better not linger," Amoretta politely declined. "I wouldn't want to get caught in the woods after sunset." She knew sunset was nearly three hours away, yet it was the only possibly gracious excuse she could think of.

"Very well," Kizzy said, her smile fading.

The corners of the little girl's mouth turned down so distinctly with disappointment that Amoretta nearly reconsidered.

"I hope to see you again," the gypsy said as Amoretta turned and began to flee into the woods. Her tears had already begun, and she didn't pause to turn back and offer a courteous response.

How could he be so cruel? Amoretta thought as she hurried through the woods toward home, angrily wiping the tears from her cheeks. How could he send *her* to deliver a letter to his lover? Couldn't he see she was smitten by him? Couldn't he see he'd trapped her with his charms, bewitched her with his beauty and flirting?

She tried to think of other reasons Brake might have sent her to deliver the note. She tried to convince herself that perhaps it hadn't been a love letter she'd delivered but perhaps simply a message bearing good news of some sort. Yet what good news could a man send to a gypsy woman who looked like Venus herself if it were not to do with amorous goings-on?

So distraught was Amoretta that, when she did finally break the tree line, stepping into the grassy space between the woods and her home, her tear-filled eyes failed to see the horse and rider trying to step into the woods as she stepped out.

Amoretta gasped as the horse reared in avoiding her, throwing its rider to the ground. She gasped again when she realized that she recognized the big buckskin—when she realized the man it had thrown was Brake McClendon.

Her sorrow, pain, and rage—the angry, hurt feelings and thoughts she'd been enduring the moment before—vanished in the wake of fear for Brake's safety. He'd fallen hard, that much she knew, and as the horse whinnied and stomped its hooves at the ground, Amoretta rushed to where Brake lay moaning in the grass.

"Brake!" she cried as she collapsed to her knees next to him. Tucking her hand beneath his head, her fear heightened, for he was as pale as a sheet, perspiring profusely and moaning in pain as he clutched his stomach.

"Amoretta?" he breathed, frowning and looking up at her through watery, reddened eyes.

"Brake! What's the matter?" she asked as panic owned her. His condition was not because of the horse throwing him. He looked like a man on the verge of death!

"Help me," he panted. "I-I have to get to Kizzy. She can help me."

A momentary feeling as if she could spit venom rose in Amoretta's mouth. He was on his way to the gypsy? Yet she could see he was seriously ill, perhaps near death, and she loved him. She loved him. Perhaps she could win him away from his beautiful gypsy lover. Amoretta shook her head for thinking such nonsense.

"I think I've been poisoned or somethin', Amoretta," Brake breathed. "I couldn't hardly mount Gambler before. Help me get to Kizzy. Please."

His beautiful brown eyes pleaded with her, and Amoretta brushed fresh tears from her cheeks as she said, "All right. All right."

Helping him to stand, she then reached out, taking hold of Gambler's reins. "Come on. I'll help you mount."

But Brake shook his head. "I-I can't. I'm not even sure I can walk."

Panic was quickly winning over hurt and anger in Amoretta's heart. Lifting Brake's heavy arm, she draped it around her shoulders and began helping him to walk as Gambler followed.

"A man can have too many muscles, Brake McClendon," she scolded. "Your arm is too heavy."

"Then run ahead and fetch her back to me," he growled. "I need her. I know she's the only one who can help me." When Amoretta did not release him, however, Brake used what little strength he had left to take hold of her face with his free hand. "I feel like I'm dyin', Amoretta," he growled, frowning at her as the perspiration continued to bead on his forehead. "Do you want me to die?"

"No! No, of course not," Amoretta breathed.

"Then leave me here, and fetch Kizzy for me," he demanded.

"All right," she agreed.

Brake squeezed his eyes closed for a moment and seemed to struggle for breath. He still hadn't released his hold on her face, and when Amoretta's hand went to his to urge him to do so, he opened his eyes once more, glaring at her as if his vision were not clear.

"And in case I'm dead before you get back," he mumbled—and Amoretta gasped as he placed a hot, moist, firmly driven kiss to her slightly open mouth.

He released her, dropping to his knees, and said, "Now go! Bring Kizzy to me."

Amoretta did not pause further. Brushing fresh tears from her face, she tried to ignore the hot, blissful tingle left on her lips by Brake's fevered kiss as she raced through the woods, calling the gypsy woman's name.

CHAPTER EIGHT

"What happened?" Kizzy asked, dropping to her knees next to Amoretta.

Amoretta shook her head and wiped the frightened tears from her cheeks with trembling hands.

"What's wrong with him, Mama?" Shay asked.

"I don't know, honey," Kizzy answered as she dropped the old leather satchel she'd brought with her to the ground next to him. "But I'm sure he'll be fine."

Shay sniffled, and Amoretta offered a shaky yet encouraging smile to the little girl.

"Brake! Brake!" Kizzy cried, endeavoring to roll Brake over onto his back. "What's happened?"

Brake was lying on his side, holding his stomach and moaning. Taking hold of his chin, Kizzy forced him to look at her.

"What's wrong? Are you sick? Did you eat somethin'?" she asked.

"H-he said he thought he'd been poisoned, I think," Amoretta offered, remembering what Brake had told her after Gambler had reared, throwing him.

Kizzy looked up to Amoretta, tears streaking her face and an expression of the same sort of panic Amoretta was experiencing. "Poisoned?" Looking back to Brake, she asked, "Did you eat somethin' you don't normally eat? Somethin' that had gone bad maybe?"

"No, no," Brake breathed. Amoretta covered her mouth to keep from screaming with fear, panic, and frustration. Brake was even more pallid than he had been when she'd left him to fetch Kizzy, and she'd only been gone a few minutes. "J-just a piece of the cake that Sallie Ackerman gave me."

"Sallie Ackerman?" Kizzy gasped. "She gave you a cake? D-did it taste like hazelnuts?"

"Well...yeah," Brake puffed. "But what does that have to do with..." He paused, staring at Kizzy. "What do you know about it?"

"Oh, that foolish girl," Kizzy mumbled, releasing Brake and reaching into her leather satchel. "That lyin', foolish girl!"

"What's wrong?" Amoretta asked, unable to keep silent any longer. "You know what's wrong, don't you?"

"Yes, I do," Kizzy said, retrieving a glass medicine bottle from the satchel. "Brake gets a rash if he fiddles with dandelions too much. I'm guessin' eatin' a cake with dandelions in it would...would probably just about...that cake had dandelion extract in it. "

"But how did you know that?" Amoretta asked.

She looked up to Amoretta a moment and said, "Because I made it! Here," Kizzy ordered, helping Brake to sit up. "Drink this...all of it, Brake. Drink it down quick."

"Oh, dammit to hell, Kizzy...not the ipecac!" he grumbled. "I'll be pukin' 'til the cows come home, girl!"

"Would you rather die?" Kizzy asked. "We best get as much of that out of your stomach as we can...and just hope it helps enough."

But Brake wrinkled his nose as Kizzy held the bottle to his lips. "Oh, hell," he mumbled.

"Please drink it, Uncle Brake!" Shay suddenly cried out. "Please! I need you to be all better!"

Amoretta looked down to Shay. The child was weeping and furiously wringing her hands.

"Uncle Brake?" Amoretta asked.

"Yes, Miss Ipswich," Kizzy answered, glancing up to Amoretta again. "Brake's my brother." She looked back to Brake, forced the rim of the bottle to his lips, and added, "Though I suspect you thought otherwise."

Amoretta watched as Kizzy rather bullied Brake into drinking the contents of the small bottle of ipecac.

"Dammit, Kizzy!" Brake bellowed once he'd finished. "That stuff tastes like shi—"

"Now we'll leave you here alone for about fifteen to twenty minutes," Kizzy interrupted. "We wouldn't want Miss Ipswich to see you at your worst, now would we, big brother?"

Brake glared at his sister. "You wait, Kizzy. You wait 'til I'm feelin' better. Then I'll deal with you and your conjurin'."

"Come along with Shay and me, Miss Ipswich," Kizzy said, taking Amoretta's hand. "Brake is gonna feel a whole lot worse if he's gonna feel any better."

"But I-I..." Amoretta stammered.

"You best bring Gambler along, Shay," Kizzy said. "We don't want him frettin' over your Uncle Brake any more than he already is."

Amoretta watched as Shay reached out, taking hold of Gambler's reins. "Come on, Gambler. Molly will be so glad to see you."

"But...we're just going to leave him here like this?" Amoretta argued, looking back to Brake.

"Unless you want to watch him writhe in misery and empty out anything and everything he's put in his stomach for the last two days, we are," Kizzy answered, brushing tears from her cheeks.

"Kizzy McClendon...I'm gonna tan your hide for this," Brake called after them.

Once they were back to the house—all three still crying tears of worry and horror over what Brake was enduring—Kizzy looked at Amoretta and asked, "Well, you might as well come in and have a chat wh-while we wait."

"Yes, please come in and give us some company, lady," Shay said, taking Amoretta's hand. Her large brown eyes pleaded with Amoretta so desperately that, even if she hadn't already planned to wait and see how Brake felt after the ipecac took hold of him, she would've stayed just for Shay's sake.

"Of course I'll stay," Amoretta said, squeezing the little girl's hand with reassurance.

Shay smiled and sighed with obvious relief. Then dropping the reins to Brake's horse, she said, "You wait here, Gambler. Uncle Brake will be back soon."

"Will he really wait?" Amoretta asked Kizzy.

Kizzy nodded, smiling a little. "That horse…he follows Brake around like a dog." Taking Amoretta's free hand, she added, "Now do come in. And I promise not to serve you any cake with dandelion extract in it."

A nervous giggle bubbled in Amoretta's throat as she nodded and stepped into Kizzy's house.

The very instant Amoretta crossed the threshold of the little white home, her spirits and hopes lifted. It was bright and lovely inside, all lace and doilies and canning jars filled with bouquets of fresh-cut mums—orange mums, yellow mums, and dazzling crimson mums.

"I like mums," Kizzy said. "I grow them out back just so Shay and I can bring them inside. Isn't that silly?"

"Not at all!" Amoretta assured her.

"Here, lady," Shay said, leading Amoretta to the worn sofa in the center of the little room. "Come and have a seat."

"I-I suppose you're wonderin' why no one in town knows that Shay and I are Brake's relations," Kizzy stammered.

"Well…yes, actually," Amoretta admitted.

"But you can't tell anybody that Brake is Mama's brother, lady!" Shay warned with pleading. "You have to promise not to tell!"

"I-I do," Amoretta said. "I won't tell a soul. I promise." And she meant it. In fact, it slightly delighted her—knowing that she would own information concerning Brake that no one else in all of Meadowlark Lake owned. Was it naughty to delight over such a thing? Amoretta figured that it was, but she delighted in it all the same.

"All right, Mama," Shay said with a contented sigh. "You can tell her now. She won't tell nobody else. She promised."

Yet Kizzy bit her lip with trepidation. Thus, Amoretta smiled and assured her, "I promise. I promise you that I won't tell anybody else. Not even my father."

At the mention of her father, Amoretta could've sworn she saw Kizzy's eyes flash with interest. But she decided it must've been her reiteration that she would keep Kizzy and Brake's secret.

"Why don't you go find Molly, Shay?" Kizzy said then. "She'd want to know about Uncle Brake."

"Oh yes, she would!" Shay exclaimed, leaping to her feet. Nodding at Amoretta, Shay added, "Molly will want to meet you too." And she was off like a little curly-haired rabbit.

Amoretta knew Kizzy had wanted to distract her daughter—wanted her to leave the room so that she could speak freely. Yet when she did, Amoretta found Kizzy felt saddened and uncomfortable.

"I'm a ruined woman, Miss Ipswich," Kizzy began as her tears returned. "Five years ago, I fell in love…and I thought I was loved in return. In a moment of weakness, I…I…"

Amoretta placed a hand on Kizzy's knee. "You don't have to tell me anything, Miss Kizzy. I'm not judging you for anything. Everyone owns—"

"But I want you to know," Kizzy interrupted. "And anyway, you need to know if you want to understand why I insist Brake keeps his relationship to me and Shay a secret."

"All right," Amoretta said. She smiled at Kizzy, hoping the woman understood that Amoretta felt only sympathy for her and the hardships she no doubt faced.

Kizzy inhaled a deep breath of courage and continued, "I-I was weak, and when I discovered I was gonna have Shay…the man I thought loved me…he left. He moved to another city, without even a word to me."

Amoretta felt her own tears trickle over her cheeks as she whispered, "I'm so sorry."

But Kizzy shook her head. "It was a long time ago, but it did leave me a ruined woman…in everyone's eyes but my brother's."

"And Shay's," Amoretta reminded her, smiling.

Kizzy smiled then, nodding. "And Shay's."

"Your parents? They…they didn't accept…things?" Amoretta ventured.

Kizzy shook her head. "Brake and I lost our parents before… several years before Shay came to me."

"Oh, I'm so sorry!" Amoretta breathed, for she knew the pain of losing one parent. How much worse it would've been had she lost her father as well!

"Anyway, Brake moved us to a different town," Kizzy continued, "but when folks discovered that I didn't have a husband, not only did they spurn me…but Brake as well."

"Well, if there's one thing in life that's true…it's that God forgets our shortcomings long before people do, right?" Amoretta offered.

Kizzy nodded. "I hope he forgets them…or at least forgives them," she mumbled.

"He does," Amoretta whispered.

Kizzy sighed. "Anyway, when Brake decided to move us to Meadowlark Lake, I made him swear to me that we would live apart, that no one could ever know he was my brother, because I was tired of Brake havin' to suffer for my weaknesses." She looked up from her wringing hands and smiled at Amoretta. "And it's worked out so much better this way! Brake has a good job down at the gristmill, and I find that people are more acceptin' of a gypsy who lives in the woods than they are of a woman who has a daughter and was never married."

Amoretta frowned with disappointment. "So you're really not a gypsy?"

Kizzy giggled with sudden amusement. "So I tell you my sinful history, and all you're worried about is whether or not I'm really a gypsy?"

Amoretta shrugged. "Well, Shay's a beautiful little girl. She's an angel…and there's nothing ever bad about an angel." She shrugged again. "And you...well, you're not the first young woman to fall prey to a wolf, and you surely won't be the last. Therefore, I will openly admit to you that my own selfish regret...is that you're not really a gypsy."

Kizzy laughed—wept with what appeared to be mingled amusement and despair. "Oh, Miss Ipswich! You're very good for my soul, I think."

Amoretta smiled. "I would like that, if it's true."

"Oh, it's true," Kizzy assured her. She sighed, adding, "And I'll tell you what else is true. My mother *was* a gypsy."

"Truly?" Amoretta exclaimed with renewed excitement.

"Yes," Kizzy affirmed. "Her parents were Romanian gypsies, born of true Romani gypsies. So, you see, I do have gypsy blood runnin' through my veins. Does that make you feel better?"

"Much better, actually!" Amoretta admitted. "Though you probably think I'm an idiot for being so delighted about it."

"Not at all!" Kizzy assured her. "You're the first person I ever met in all my life who didn't think badly of gypsies in one way or the other."

"Really?" Amoretta asked. Naturally she knew that many people thought badly of gypsies, though she'd never been able to fathom why. Yet everyone Kizzy had known thought badly of them? It was a terrible thing to be told.

"Yes," Kizzy confirmed. She tipped her head to one side with obvious curiosity. "But why is it that you would have been so disappointed...if I didn't have gypsy blood, I mean?"

Amoretta shrugged again. "I-I tend to like things that are out of the ordinary...customs, superstitions...unusual people and their traditions."

"That's right," Kizzy said, as if she already knew the information and had just forgotten it. "Sallie did say you were tellin' the ladies in town all about a book you're readin'. I think it's concernin' Halloween?"

"Do you think he's all right?" Amoretta asked, unable to keep from inquiring any longer. "Y-your brother, I mean? Do you think he'll recover?"

Kizzy smiled and nodded. "Oh, no doubt," she said. "He's had this happen before, and he would've endured it without the ipecac. But gettin' as much of what's left in him out…it'll help. He'll get over it a lot faster."

Amoretta sighed. She'd been trying to focus solely on the conversation she and Kizzy were having, but her thoughts were so fixed on Brake that she just had to ask, in the end. Yet with the slight relief at knowing he would be well, eventually, Amoretta's attention snapped back to what Kizzy had said just before Amoretta had asked about Brake.

"Sallie told you about the book I was reading?" she asked, entirely astonished. "But why?"

Kizzy shrugged. "She asked me how she could compensate for the cake…and…and I told her I just wanted news of town, that's all. She told me about you and your sisters…and your father…and about this Fox Montrose that's supposed to be so wildly handsome."

"Well, he is handsome…but not wildly," Amoretta mumbled. "She told you all that because of a cake you made? And why didn't she just make the cake herself?"

Amoretta startled as the front door burst open, revealing a very ill-looking Brake McClendon.

He was still, and as he stood before Kizzy and Amoretta, stripping off his shirt, he growled, "And why in the hell are you makin' cakes for Sallie Ackerman to give away, Kizzy?"

Brake wadded his shirt up, tossing it aside, only a moment before he stumbled forward and collapsed to his knees.

"Oh, Brake!" Kizzy exclaimed, quickly leaving her seat on the sofa and going to him. "Let me get you some water…or, better yet, milk."

"I had plenty of water," he rather panted. "I washed up in your rain barrel before I came in. Now answer my question."

Kizzy frowned as she began, "Well...Sallie came to me asking for a love potion."

"Oh, good hell," Brake grumbled.

Instantly, Kizzy began to defend herself. "I thought it was for this Fox Montrose! She was goin' on and on and on about him so that I didn't think to ask who the potion was for, Brake! I had no idea she intended it for you!"

"You can make a love potion?" Amoretta asked, intrigued even for her overwhelming concern for both Brake's well-being and the fact that Sallie Ackerman had tried to win him over with a gypsy love potion.

Kizzy shrugged. "If there's one thing I know, Miss Ipswich, it's that the way to a man's heart truly *is* through his stomach, and I bake the best cakes in all the world. It's worked before...one of my cakes. Several times in fact. My cakes do get a man's attention."

"And if they don't get his attention, they damn near kill him," Brake mumbled.

"Uncle Brake!" Shay exclaimed as she returned, lugging a very plump marmalade cat. "Are you feelin' better? Are you stayin' for supper?"

"He'll be stayin' the night, honey," Kizzy answered.

Stretching out on Kizzy's floor on his back, Brake sighed. "I feel like I've been run over by a train."

Giggling, Shay deposited the chubby cat in Amoretta's lap, whispered, "Her name's, Molly," and then hurried to where her uncle lay sprawled.

"Oh, I'm so glad you're better, Uncle Brake," the child said, gently caressing his whiskery face. "You wait here a minute...while I get somethin'."

Amoretta watched as Shay hurriedly snatched a decorative pillow from a nearby rocking chair and a quilt that had been folded and lying atop a trunk. Awkwardly racing back to her uncle, the child said, "Here, Uncle Brake. Lift up your head." Amoretta giggled as she watched the little girl struggling to shove the pillow under Brake's head. "And let's cover you up...since you're almost naked again," she mother-henned as she draped the quilt over Brake's torso. "Now you just go and get to sleep. You'll feel all better in the mornin'." Looking to her mother for reassurance, Shay asked, "Won't he, Mama?"

"Well, mostly…I think," Kizzy stammered.

"All right then, baby," Brake mumbled, taking Shay's hand a moment. "Then give me kisses, and I'll try to get some rest."

Shay smiled and bent down, placing a kiss to Brake's lips. "Green beans, Uncle Brake."

"Green beans, baby," Brake chuckled.

Kizzy must've noticed the curious pucker wrinkling Amoretta's brow because she explained, "When Shay was smaller, she always thought Brake was tellin' her 'green beans' instead of 'sweet dreams' when he tucked in at night." She shrugged. "So we've always said 'green beans' at night ever since."

Amoretta smiled. What a purely adorable and tenderhearted tradition. She watched as Shay gave her uncle a second kiss before tucking the quilt a little tighter around him.

"And Amoretta," she heard Brake say then, and she blushed when she saw that he was staring at her—when his smoldering gaze caused goose bumps to prickle her arms.

"Yes?" she asked.

"I-I'm sorry about…you know…what I did to you just before I sent you to fetch Kizzy," he explained.

Remembering the kiss he'd pressed to her mouth—bathing in the bliss of the memory—Amoretta breathed, "You are?" Her disappointment was nearly too deep to endure, but she tried to hide it as best she could. After all, she was sitting next to a gypsy—and gypsies could read people's thoughts, couldn't they? She didn't want Kizzy to know that she was already desperately in love with Brake. What would a sister think of a girl who fell in love so fast?

"Yeah," Brake answered. "It wasn't very gentlemanly of me, I reckon."

But Amoretta said nothing more concerning it. She simply forced a smile and, feeling frantic to escape before she burst into more tears (tears of disappointment over the fact Brake had apologized for kissing her), she gently prompted the cat to jump down from her lap, rather hopped up from her seat on the sofa, and said, "Well, I suppose I better be getting back home…before my family starts to worry."

Unexpectedly, Kizzy threw her arms around Amoretta's neck, embracing her tightly. "Thank you, Miss Ipswich!" she whispered. "Thank you so much! I don't know if Brake would've made it to the house in the condition he was in if you hadn't come along. Thank you." She pulled away, still smiling, however. "And thank you for your kindness…and for keepin' our secret."

It was more a lure for reassurance—an implied hope that Amoretta truly would keep Kizzy, Shay, and Brake's relationships a secret.

"Of course," Amoretta said. "You all have a wonderful evening," she offered. Then glancing to where Brake lay sick and sluggish on the floor, she added, "Well, as wonderful as you can have, considering the circumstances."

"Thank you," Kizzy said with a nod and a smile.

"And you'll come back someday to visit…won't you?" Shay asked.

"Of course," Amoretta answered, wondering if she truly ever would be able to find a believable excuse to return.

She studied Brake a moment. He was laid out directly in front of the door.

"Oh, just step over him," Kizzy sighed, shaking her head with lingering concern. "Pretend he's an old dog that found himself in a scrape with a porcupine or somethin'."

Amoretta smiled—thought she didn't want to leave him. What she truly wanted was to collapse to the floor next to him—stay with him all through the night or for however long it took to make sure he would recover completely. Yet who was she to stay with him? He had his sister there, his niece. Obviously Kizzy was very capable of taking care of him. But Amoretta's heart still ached with anxiety and longing.

She started to step over Brake's body, gasping, however, when she felt him suddenly take hold of both her ankles, pinning her feet to the floor on either side of his stomach.

"Thank you," he mumbled as he looked at her through narrowed, glassy eyes. "And I am sorry about—"

"Please don't be," Amoretta interrupted. His brow puckered in a puzzled frown, and she smiled down at him, saying, "Green beans, Brake."

He grinned a pale, wincing grin and mumbled, "Green beans, Amoretta."

At that moment, she knew she had to leave him, and she couldn't escape quickly enough! Racing through the woods toward home, Amoretta hoped that the farther away she was from Kizzy's house and Brake, the better she would feel.

Yet as she walked toward home, her mind began to boggle with the thoughts jumbled up inside it. Kizzy was Brake's sister. Then what had been written on the note that Brake had asked Amoretta to deliver to Kizzy? She'd assumed, by Kizzy's elated reaction, that it had been a love letter—but now that point was thoroughly moot.

Her mind leapt next to Sallie Ackerman, the fact that she'd gone to Kizzy, a gypsy woman, and requested a love potion—a love potion meant not for the newly returned Fox Montrose but for Brake! Naturally she knew every young woman in town found Brake lethally desirable, but she hadn't thought that any other young woman but herself was so in love—so desperately in love with him— that she'd put her hopes in a love potion!

Amoretta smiled as she thought of little Shay—of the way Brake treated her so sweetly, even as ill as he had been.

"Green beans," she whispered, giggling to herself. It was purely adorable!

She thought then of poor Kizzy—used and abandoned by a man she thought loved her. Kizzy McClendon was perhaps the most beautiful young woman Amoretta had ever seen (though it made sense, considering who her brother was), and it caused her heart to ache to think on her being so ill-treated and wounded to the core of her heart.

"And I can't tell a soul!" she breathed in misery. She couldn't! She'd given her word. Beyond that, she could well imagine the damage it would do to not only Brake but Kizzy and especially little Shay. Amoretta rarely, if ever, kept secrets from her sisters! How would she endure it, holding onto such a burden of knowledge?

And yet was it truly a burden? No! It was a gift! Amoretta thought of her feelings—the dread and pain, anxiety and nausea that had nearly overwhelmed her in the moments she thought perhaps Brake was in love with the beautiful gypsy woman. Suddenly, she felt so much joy in owning the truth—in knowing that it truly was Sallie Ackerman, Winnie Montrose, and the other girls in town who were her rivals for Brake's affections, instead of the beautiful Kizzy—that she felt her strength renewed!

The sun was low in the sky, and Amoretta didn't want her father or sisters to begin to wonder where she'd run off. And so she hurried her pace—hastened toward home, even faster than she had before. And as she broke the tree line, stepping into the wide expanse of grass, she could see the house. Moments more of walking and she could see her father there—sitting on the back porch watching the sunset.

Lawson sat on the back porch gazing out across the green expanse of grass to the tree line of the woods beyond. It seemed he couldn't get that beauty of a gypsy girl out of his mind, or her daughter either. The only thing that seemed to soothe him somewhat was to sit on the back porch at the end of the day, gaze out toward the woods, and think about her—about Kizzy and her little girl.

He'd spent many an hour since first meeting her scolding himself for being so intrigued with her—berating his mind and body for the way his heart had increased the rhythm of its beating when he'd been in her presence. She was no older than Evangeline, for pity's sake! Or at least he assumed. What right, what logical reason, would he have for allowing her to linger in his thoughts? What proper excuse could he offer to himself for the fact that she'd heated his blood like nothing he'd experienced in a very many, many years? There was none. Thus, Judge Lawson Ipswich sat attempting to convince himself that he'd only experienced a moment of mortal weakness—and that it would pass.

Lawson blinked as he saw someone step from the tree line and into the grassy expanse. His heart leapt for a moment in his chest—leapt with anxious hope. Was it she? It was a woman; he could tell that much by her manner of dress. Yet was it Kizzy? The woman at the tree line did not have a child with her, however. In fact, a moment later—as his good sense set in once more—her realized that he recognized the blue floral-print dress—the graceful, almost floating manner of the woman's walk.

"Amoretta?" he mumbled aloud. It was Amoretta who had stepped out of the woods. Had she been to meet Kizzy? If so, why? He could think of no other reason.

"Judge Ipswich?"

Lawson startled a bit at the sound of Sheriff Montrose's voice. He looked aside to see Dennison Montrose standing just to the right of the back porch.

"Good evening, Dennison," Lawson greeted. He studied the sheriff a moment—the frown on his face, the fatigue in his countenance. "I'm going to guess that you're not here just to pay a social call."

Dennison Montrose shook his head. "Nope. I'm afraid not, Judge." He exhaled a heavy sigh. "I just talked to Rowdy Gates in town. He's lightin' the lamps a bit early tonight." Dennison's eyes narrowed. "He asked me if I'd seen his dog, Dodger. He's a big ol' friendly mutt. And he's been missin' for three days."

Lawson stood up from his seat and descended the porch steps to meet Dennison. "Well, any chance the dog just ran off...or that it's off carousing?"

But Dennison shook his head. "Nope. Dodger...he's more loyal than Dex Longfellow's dog was. And besides..."

When Dennison paused too long, Lawson urged, "Besides what?"

"My daughter, Winnie? She hasn't been able to find her cat for two days either," he answered. "And that cat has slept with Winnie every night for ten years, Judge."

Lawson gazed out over the grass. Amoretta was almost home, and he didn't want her to see the worry on the sheriff's face—or on his.

"Well, Dennison…let's try not to think the worst of it," he said. "Let's see if any carcasses show up." He shrugged. "If we find the animals alive, or don't find them killed and piled up somewhere, then maybe all is well. But if we do find them…"

"I talked to Rowdy Gates and all the others, Judge," Dennison said. "And you saw the gypsy woman. I don't know where else to look."

Lawson nodded. "As I said, let's wait it out a bit. It might be just a coincidence."

"Beg your pardon, Judge Ipswich. But in my experience…there ain't no such thing," the sheriff said.

"Mine either," Lawson mumbled.

"Good evening, Daddy!" Amoretta greeted, rising on the tips of her toes and placing a loving kiss to Lawson's cheek.

"Good evening, honey," Lawson said. "Did you enjoy your walk?"

"I did," she answered. "For the most part, I guess anyway." Amoretta looked to Sheriff Montrose then. "I met your son today, Sheriff Montrose. He seems like a very fine and upstanding young man."

"Thank you, Miss Amoretta," Dennison said, beaming with pride.

"I'm going to go in and help with supper, Daddy." Looking to Sheriff Montrose once more, Amoretta added, "You tell Winnie and Mrs. Montrose I send my best regards, won't you, Sheriff?"

"I certainly will," Dennison assured her.

Once Amoretta was in the house and well out of hearing distance, Lawson lowered his voice and instructed, "Let's just keep this calm, Dennison. We still don't know enough to go announcing it to everyone in town and stirring up worry and fear."

"I agree," Dennison said with a nod. He sighed the sigh of a man with a great weight on his shoulders—and Lawson empathized with him. "Well, I'll see you in the mornin' then, Judge. Rest well."

"You too, Dennison."

As the sheriff of Meadowlark Lake strode away with drooping shoulders, the county judge looked back in the direction of the woods. It worried him—knowing Kizzy and her little girl were out there all alone. Especially when it appeared someone in town was up to such malicious nonsense.

CHAPTER NINE

Two days. It had been two days since Amoretta had seen Brake—since Sallie Ackerman had given him the cake laced with dandelion extract that had made him so grievously ill—since she'd met Kizzy and Shay and become a guardian of their secrets. Two days—two days that felt more like two weeks, or even two months!

Amoretta Ipswich wasn't used to keeping secrets from her family, especially her sisters. And the secret of being inexplicably in love with Brake was difficult enough not to share. But the secret concerning Kizzy and her relationship to Brake was almost impossible to keep to herself. Yet she did keep it to herself. Amoretta had promised Kizzy she would not tell anyone what she'd learned, and she had no intention of ever breaking that promise.

Still, for two days Amoretta felt agitated, nervous, and easily startled. She was worried for Brake. Had he recovered well enough? She hadn't seen him in town when she'd gone strolling with Calliope and Evangeline. She hadn't heard talk of him—though that was not so astonishing, considering that everyone in Meadowlark Lake was abuzz with talking of Fox Montrose's return, but it was still heavily worrisome.

Perhaps he was still writhing in agony! Perhaps he hadn't recovered and was near death! Yet what could Amoretta do? She couldn't simply wander out near the gristmill to where she'd heard Brake's house stood. She couldn't ask the folks in town about him, lest she give away the feelings of her heart—or make them all suspicious in the least. She couldn't simply impose on Kizzy and Shay just to inquire of his health, could she?

Therefore, she'd simply strolled with her sisters here and there, or with her father, cleaned house as if it were spring instead of late September, and cooked supper two nights in succession—anything to keep herself busy as her mind whirled with wondering how Brake was.

And she'd simply wanted to claw Sallie Ackerman's eyes out when she'd seen her in town the morning after Brake had taken so ill. The idiot! Amoretta and Calliope had walked to the general store to purchase some white thread. Winnie, Blanche, Prudence, and Sallie were all there (talking with Fox Montrose, of course), and the hot anger that had welled up inside Amoretta when she first set eyes on Sallie was not only unfamiliar but also nearly uncontrollable!

There Sallie stood, smiling and giggling as she talked with Fox Montrose and the other girls. A body would've never suspected that Sallie Ackerman wanted so badly to be loved by Brake McClendon that she would've bartered for a love potion with a gypsy. Nope— not the way she was smiling and batting her eyelashes at Fox.

And Amoretta's anger hadn't subsided yet, not for two days. Naturally, she hadn't confronted Sallie, but she'd remained angry— and, yes, jealous!

Therefore, the third morning after having met Kizzy and Shay, after having nearly been trampled by Gambler as she stepped out of the woods, and after having had to endure seeing Brake so sick because of stupid Sallie Ackerman—on that third morning, Amoretta could endure it not longer. She had to know! She had to know that Brake was well and safe. If she waited a moment longer, she'd end up nearly as ill as the dandelion extract cake had made Brake!

Informing her father and sisters that she was off for a leisurely, early autumn stroll, Amoretta set out for the gypsy's house, determined to learn of Brake's welfare. She'd intended to walk at a normal pace, in order to ensure that she would not arrive looking rumpled and breathless when Kizzy answered the door. But she found that as she drew closer to the woods that sheltered the little house, her desperation for news of Brake grew and grew to a near panic. She wanted to see him—not just know he was well but actually see he was well. As she stepped from the grassy expanse in her wake and into the woods, she again began to wonder if perhaps she were losing her wits. She was obsessed! Amoretta was obsessed with Brake McClendon. She laughed out loud at herself, thinking that the mild infatuation she'd carried for Sylvanus Tenney was like one drop of rainwater in comparison with the ocean! How could she have thought what she felt for Sylvanus was true love? How could she have spent four years thinking her annual Halloween apple peelings had spelled out S for Sylvanus? Spelled out S they had, but perhaps that was simply her fate before her father had moved the family from Boston to Meadowlark Lake. Perhaps in moving west, her fate had entirely changed. Perhaps loving Brake had always been her true destiny and S for Sylvanus had only been a distraction.

By the time Amoretta stumbled out of the woods and into the clearing among the wild cherry trees, she was breathless and so filled with anxiety she felt as if she might burst into tears. She quickly glanced about her and, seeing neither Shay nor Kizzy, assumed they must be in the house.

Hurrying to the front door of the quaint little place, Amoretta knocked several times. She stepped back, waiting for the door to open and nervously wringing her hands.

"Oh, please be home," she whispered. Again she knocked, and again she stepped back and waited, desperation pounding her heart like a butcher's meat mallet.

"They're out gathering the last of the berries in the woods."

Amoretta gasped, startled by the sound of his low, alluring voice. Looking to her left, she saw Brake turning the corner of the house and coming toward her. She breathed a heavy sigh of thankfulness when she noted how robust he looked—how handsome and healthy.

"Oh!" she breathed. "I-I wanted to…to say hello to them…and…and inquire after you…to find out if you were recovered from the…incident of a few days ago," she stammered.

115

Brake's presence had robbed Amoretta of her breath! Her heart beat wild and frantic, and again she wondered how it was possible that a man she'd known such a short time could have completely captured her.

"Well, that's mighty nice, Amoretta," he said, smiling. "You've been concerned about me then?" he asked. He strode to her—stopped just in front of her, standing so close that she had to tip her head back to look up at him in meeting his gaze.

"Yes," she answered in a whisper. "I-I was afraid...I was afraid that cake may have had worse ramifications than your sister initially thought."

"Oh, no worries, honey," he said. "I'm fine...and healthy as a horse once more."

Amoretta's smile broadened. "I'm glad to hear it. So glad."

"And I'm glad to see you again," he said.

"You are?" Amoretta asked. So many butterflies were flapping around in her stomach that she was sure they'd come flying right out of her mouth at any moment.

"Yep," he assured her. "I...uh...I wanted to make sure you weren't offended by my kissin' you the other day when I thought I was gonna die."

"Oh no! Not at all!" Amoretta answered far too excitedly. "I liked it!" Her hand flew up to cover her mouth, but what she'd said had already been said, and there was no stopping it now.

Brake chuckled. "Did you now?"

"I-I mean...well...I-I..."

"You know," he interrupted as his eyebrows puckered in a thoughtful expression, "Kizzy was tellin' me that you're pretty fond of Halloween and some of the customs that go along with it."

Grateful that he hadn't taken to teasing her about her confession of liking his kiss (and in truth, she was glad she hadn't told him that it was the most blissful thing she'd ever experienced in all her life), she was still vastly irritated with Sallie Ackerman, not only for poisoning Brake but also for revealing her secret fascination with Halloween customs to Kizzy. And now it was painfully obvious that Kizzy had revealed them to Brake. He must think she was an utter fool! First she'd plain and simple admitted to him she'd enjoyed his kissing her, and now she must surely appear childish because she so adored romantic Halloween customs.

"Oh…she was?" was all Amoretta could manage as a response, however—no matter how irritated she was with Sally "the Poisoner" Ackerman.

"Yes," he said. He was staring at her much like she imagined a tiger might stare down its prey. "She told me about the S thing…and that boy in Boston."

Amoretta's mind swirled! How could Kizzy have known about the S in the apple peelings? Amoretta was certain she hadn't told anyone about it—no one in Meadowlark Lake anyway.

"I guess Sallie Ackerman said your little sister mentioned it awhile back," Brake continued. "Somethin' about you gettin' Ss in apple peelin's four years runnin'."

"Calliope!" Amoretta mumbled through clenched teeth. Puffing a breath of frustration, she silently promised to give Calliope a piece of her mind when she got home.

"Oh, now don't be angry at your sister," Brake laughed. "I only brought it up because I think I can help you figure out whether this boy in Boston is the one meant for you is all."

Amoretta's emotions instantly leapt from anger with Calliope to intrigue with what Brake had just uttered. She stared at him a moment—studied his ridiculously attractive face. It was easy enough to read the mischief in him, and she bit at the bait.

"Oh really?" she asked. "And how can you do that, Mr. McClendon?"

He smiled, exhaled a breathy laugh, and, lowering his voice, answered, "Well, Kizzy ain't the only gypsy in Meadowlark Lake, now is she, Miss Ipswich?"

He was right! Brake was Kizzy's brother, which meant his mother and grandparents were gypsies as well. The sudden realization aroused Amoretta's intrigue to the point of near insanity.

"You're a gypsy?" she asked with a delighted giggle.

"Yes, ma'am," Brake assured her. "I've got the same…um, shall we say gifts?…that Kizzy does."

Amoretta arched one eyebrow and teased, "Are you saying you can make a better cake than the baker man in town?"

Brake laughed and shook his head. "Nope. I'm afraid if I were to make a cake, it'd pretty much taste like horse shi…well, let's just say it wouldn't taste too good. But I have some other talents she does."

"Such as?" Amoretta prodded. Oh, she adored his playful nature! He made life so much more exciting!

"Such as…I can get your soul to tell me who your lover really will be," he answered. "My grandmother taught me and Kizzy how to do it. It's called 'summonin' the soul.' And I can do it just as good as Kizzy." He shrugged broad shoulders. "I just don't do it all the time like she does."

Amoretta smiled, deliciously intrigued. At the thought of Brake summoning her soul, goose bumps raced over her arms and legs, causing a quick shiver to overtake her.

"See?" Brake chuckled. "You know I can do it. Someone just walked over your grave, as they say…made you shiver. It's a sign that you know I can summon your soul with my gypsy know-how."

"So you're telling me that your gypsy grandmother taught you how to—" Amoretta began.

"How to coax secrets from a person's soul," Brake finished for her. "Yep."

Amoretta's smile broadened. It was all too wonderfully enticing to resist! Oh, certainly she knew there was no such thing as gypsy magic—at least she thought she knew it. Yet in so many books she'd read—stories of how festively and traditionally gypsies lived, of how kind and willing they were to share their insights and talents—many excerpts placed more legitimacy to gypsy customs than to any other superstitious ways of gleaning information regarding what the future held.

And besides, Amoretta would welcome almost anything that allowed her to linger in the company of the unlawfully handsome, ridiculously muscular, and wholly alluring Brake McClendon.

"Then show me," she stated. "Draw out the secrets of my soul, Mr. McClendon…for I surely would like to know what they are."

Again Brake's beguiling grin appeared, and Amoretta could've sworn his smoldering brown eyes flashed with a brighter sparkle.

"All righty then," Brake agreed. "But you gotta do it right, Amoretta," he instructed, wagging an index finger at her. His smile faded, however, and he studied her a moment with an expression of somberness. "You gotta do just as I say, and you have to be patient. Patience is as important as anything else."

"Patience?" Amoretta asked, arching one brow. "Well…well, how long does it take?"

"Oh, five or ten minutes sometimes," he said as he began looking around as if searching for something. "Ten at the longest."

Amoretta shrugged. "Well, that's not so long," she noted. "So what do I do?"

"There it is," Brake mumbled, obviously having spied what he'd been looking for. "I knew it was close. Kizzy told me just the other day that a few were still hangin' on."

"A few what were hanging onto what?" Amoretta asked. But before answering, Brake took hold of Amoretta's forearm and began leading her away from the house and toward a wild cherry tree a short distance off.

"There for a minute I was afraid I wouldn't be able to perform the ritual," Brake said as he halted them beneath the tree.

"Ritual?" Amoretta squeaked. Suddenly, she was indeed a bit anxious. After all, *ritual*—it sounded so serious.

But Brake smiled and laughed. "Ritual. It's just a word," he said. "But if it bothers you, maybe *spell* will suit you better."

"Spell?" Amoretta squeaked once more.

Brake shook his head as he studied her a moment. "Worrisome little thing, ain't you?" His brow puckered a moment, and then he offered, "How about charm or…or just plain somethin' that we do to draw information outta your soul? That's all it is, darlin'. Just a game of sorts."

Amoretta sighed with renewed relief and delighted anticipation. A game—that's all it was. Just a game gypsy folks played—liked peeling apples and tossing the peel over one shoulder to learn the initial of one's true love.

"Okay. I like that. A game of sorts," she confessed.

Brake's smile returned, and he took hold of one tree limb, pulling it down and plucking several dark, late-season cherries from it.

"Now," he began, selecting the largest, juiciest-looking cherry Amoretta had ever seen and gently rubbing it on his shirt. Plopping the cherry in his shirt pocket, he continued, "Two bites to a cherry— that's part of how I'll summon your soul into tellin' me your future."

Amoretta's eyebrows arched with disbelief. "Two bites to a cherry?" she asked, doubtful. "It sounds more like a scandalous party game to me."

"Nope," he answered. "It's part of the ritual...I mean, the game. Now, let's see if I can remember the incantation."

"Incantation?" Amoretta exclaimed.

Brake exhaled a heavy sigh of impatience. Shaking his head, he chuckled, "For cryin' in the bucket, girl. It's just a word."

"But incantation...that implies sorcery or something," she explained.

Brake shook his head, still grinning. "All right then...how about poem? How about let's see if I can remember the *poem* that goes along with the *game*? Will that suit your sensitivities, sugar?"

Amoretta shrugged again. "Yes. But you do have to admit that incantation sounds a little—"

"Hush now, darlin'. Do you want to know who your lover will be or not?" Brake interrupted. "I have to get myself in the mood to perform the...to do the thing to you."

A delicious quiver of delight suddenly traveled through Amoretta's entire body. What was he going to do to her? Would it involve being touched by him somehow? Would he need to hold her hand? Her forearm was still tingling because he'd held it in leading her to the wild cherry tree. Thus, she couldn't imagine the effect his holding her hand might have on her. She felt her mouth warm and begin to water as she thought of the kiss he'd given her days before. Oh, what she wouldn't give for another kiss from him! But that was too much to hope for, she knew. At least she owned his attention for the time being. She'd be glad in that and try not to want him to kiss her again so badly.

"Now," Brake said, taking her shoulders and positioning her to face him straightforwardly. His touch was magnificent! The strength of his powerful hands holding her—the warmth of his palms seeping through the fabric of her shirtwaist—it rendered her breathless for a moment.

"The incan...the poem goes like this," he said. Staring directly into her eyes—the mesmerizing brown of his seeming to hold the green of her own with some commanding bewitchment—Brake recited, "Two bites to a cherry, two souls to be meet...the one of the gypsy and the one of the cheat."

"The cheat?" Amoretta exclaimed. "I'm a cheat?"

Brake sighed again and shook his head, grinning with further amusement. "Of course you're the cheat, baby. You're tryin' to pull secrets out of your soul, aren't you?"

"But how does that make me a cheat?" Amoretta frowned. "I don't like being called a cheat."

Brake laughed. "Will you just hush long enough for me to do this thing? I swear, you're more persnickety about words than any woman I ever met."

"I'm sorry," she apologized. "I-I do want you to do this...b-but...but..."

"But what?" he asked, smiling at her. His beautiful eyes fairly twinkled with amusement.

Amoretta frowned again. "But I don't like being called a cheat."

Brake raised his brows and shrugged. "Sorry, sunshine...but it's the price of gleanin' soul secrets."

"All right," Amoretta puffed defeatedly.

"Now, no matter what I say, don't interrupt me again. You're clutterin' up my spell...I mean, the game. Understand?"

Amoretta nodded. She wouldn't argue with him anymore. In truth, she wondered if she'd only been arguing with him over words simply to linger longer with him.

"All right. I'm startin' over," he mumbled.

Gazing into her eyes once more, he said, "Two bites to a cherry, two souls to be meet...the one of the gypsy and the one of the cheat." He paused, arching one reprimanding eyebrow. When Amoretta remained silent, he nodded and continued. "Two bites to a cherry." He stopped, however, grumbling, "Dammit!"

"What?" Amoretta asked. "I didn't say anything that time."

But Brake shook his head. "It wasn't you this time. It was me. I have to say it once in English and once in Romanian."

"Romanian?" Amoretta exclaimed. Now she was intrigued beyond endurance! The gorgeous man she'd fallen in love with at first sight—he spoke another language as well? And not just Spanish or French or anything somewhat common among second languages, but Romanian.

"Well, of course. My grandmother was Romani...a true gypsy. But she was raised up in Romania, so that became the language she spoke most."

"Oh, I remember. Kizzy did tell me that," Amoretta offered.

Sighing and shaking his head, Brake said, "I sure am rusty at this." Retrieving the wild cherry from his pocket, he dangled it by the stem. "I almost forgot the most important part—the cherry."

"What part does it play?" Amoretta inquired.

"Shhh," he ordered, holding the cherry by its stem. "Now hold onto this cherry with your teeth...just barely now. Don't bite into it yet."

As he pressed the cherry to her lips, Amoretta did as he'd instructed, gently holding the cherry between her teeth.

"And remember," he added, wagging an index finger in front of her nose, "do as I say...and don't talk. If you want to know your own secrets, you have to be patient, stay still, and do as I say. Otherwise the ritual—I mean, the game—won't work proper. All right?"

Amoretta nodded as she tried very hard not to bite the cherry. Already her mouth was watering simply from the taste of the ripened fruit at the tip of her tongue.

"Okay now, this time is it. It's the last time I'll try it…so neither one of us can mess it up," he mumbled.

Brake inhaled a deep breath, exhaling it slowly as he took Amoretta's shoulders again. With a smoldering gaze that caused Amoretta's arms to once again prickle with goose bumps, Brake began once more.

"Two bites to a cherry, two souls to be meet…the one of the gypsy and the one of the cheat," he said. "Two bites to a cherry and secrets revealed…when gypsy and cheat find cherry lips sealed."

"What?" Amoretta quietly gasped.

"Shhh," Brake growled. Then in a language Amoretta had never heard before, he began, "Cele două musca la o cireaşă, două suflete să se îndeplinească, de una din tigan si de unul de a trisa." It was as if Brake truly had poured some sort of witch's brew over her! Amoretta was intoxicated by the romantic sound of the foreign language. She didn't move—only watched his mouth as he finished the poem. "Două musca la o cireaşă, si dezvaluit secretele…când tigan si triseze găsiţi cherry buzele inchise."

"Now hold still," he demanded as his head began to descend toward hers. "When you feel me begin to bite it, you bite it too," he explained.

Amoretta knew there was no possible way that they could each bite the cherry without their lips touching. The knowledge of it, coupled with the sudden exhilaration rising in her, caused her body to begin trembling a little—and she hoped he didn't notice.

"Două musca la o cireaşă, si dezvaluit secretele…când tigan si triseze găsiţi cherry buzele inchise," Brake repeated an instant before Amoretta felt his lips lightly touch hers.

It was instinctive—the way her teeth broke the tender skin of the cherry, sinking into the sweet fruit beneath. But as sweet as the cherry juice and meat of the fruit were to her tongue, the light brush of Brake's lips to hers was far more delicious!

Once she'd bitten the cherry, Brake's lips pressed more firmly to hers as he captured the remains of the cherry in his mouth. As Brake pulled away from her slightly, Amoretta watched, mesmerized as he discarded the cherry stem, turned his head, and spit the cherry pit aside.

"Now tell me the secrets of your soul, Amoretta Ipswich," Brake demanded, his voice low and provocative—causing an overwhelming desire to take hold of his face and kiss him herself to rise in her. "Spune-mi secretele sufletului tau, Amoretta Ipswich," he repeated in Romanian.

Amoretta couldn't draw a sufficient breath. As Brake's hands rested at her waist a moment before sliding to her back and then up her back to rest at her shoulder blades, Amoretta's breathing became ragged and labored.

"What do you want to know? What does your soul want to reveal through me?" he mumbled. "Ce vrei să știi? Ce nu-ți sufletul vrea să dezvăluie prin mine?"

He grinned as he continued to gaze into her eyes—to pull her closer to him until her body was flush with his. "You want to know what every woman wants to know, don't you? Who will be your lover—the name or initials of your one true love?"

Amoretta began to shake her head and whispered, "No."

But Brake only smiled and spoke, "Vrei sa stii ce fiecare femeie vrea sa stie, nu-i asa? Care va fi iubita dvs....numele sau inițialele dvs. o adevarata dragoste."

As his head descended toward hers once more, Amoretta held her breath. She was certain of one thing and one thing only: that being, if Brake McClendon kissed her again, it would be the end of her!

"Tell me who your heart most desires," he said. His voice was low and alluring—as bewitching as any ancient sorceror's. "Spune-mi cine mai dorește inima ta," he repeated in the fascinating language of his grandmother. "Tell me the secrets of your soul. Spune-mi secretele sufletului dvs. Surrender all your secrets to me, Amoretta

Ipswich. Renunțarea toate secretele voastre pentru mine, Amoretta Ipswich."

And then Amoretta knew the bliss of the angels! Slowly Brake pressed his lips to hers—kissed her.

"Tell me the secrets of your soul. Spune-mi secretele sufletului dvs. Surrender all your secrets to me, Amoretta Ipswich. Renunțarea toate secretele voastre pentru mine, Amoretta Ipswich," Brake repeated as he paused in kissing her. He kissed her again, this time more firmly. "Renunțarea toate secretele voastre pentru mine, Amoretta," he mumbled against her mouth.

Suddenly, and forcefully, he took hold of her wrists, guiding her hands to rest on his shoulders before his own hands returned to her back. "Renunțarea toate secretele voastre pentru mine, Amoretta," he whispered. And when next he kissed her, Amoretta understood what his words meant. Wrapping her arms around his neck, she met Brake's next kiss with acceptance. Not just acceptance—with yearning desire!

He had beguiled her! Brake McClendon had captured her soul, enchanted her mind, and bewitched her will. Oh, she knew she'd been in love with him from the moment she'd seen him, but this was even more thoroughgoing! He owned every part of her—every part!

"VREAU să vă," he mumbled when there was a pause in their kiss. "Daca AS fi fost un om bun, MI-ar face eforturi pentru a vă câștiga."

Amoretta had no concept of what he was saying then—only that he was saying something in Romanian. She didn't care what it was. He could be telling her she was a dimwitted fool for all she knew. But she found that she didn't care; she only wanted another kiss from him—one more kiss from the bewitching Brake McClendon. "Surrender all your secrets to me, Amoretta. Renunțarea toate secretele voastre pentru mine, Amoretta," he repeated. And this time, Amoretta was sure she felt her soul submit to him as he kissed her.

Brake's kiss was an ethereal experience! Amoretta had never imagined a kiss could be so powerful, so controlling of a woman's senses. But then again, Brake's kiss was no simple kiss. It was tender and firm at the same time—a kiss applied to both Amoretta's lips at once, but then somehow moved to linger on her lower lip a moment and then her upper lip the next. She felt as if she were wrapped in the warmest, softest quilt ever crafted, sipping the nectar of the sweetest fruit ever ripened.

"Surrender all your secrets to me, Amoretta. Renunțarea toate secretele voastre pentru mine, Amoretta," Brake mumbled, and Amoretta felt her arms tighten around his neck as her body endeavored to press closer against his—even closer than the perfect press it already relished.

Suddenly, however, Brake's kiss changed, and Amoretta gasped, pulling away from him and stepping out of his embrace.

"Wh-what are you doing to me?" she asked, tightly folding her arms across her stomach in an effort to still the butterflies that had erupted inside her when Brake's kiss had become moist, heated, and very intimate. She'd felt his mouth open on hers—allowed her own mouth to match the approach—and it had caused such a quiver of bliss, such a swarm of butterflies in her stomach, that it frightened her. Had Brake McClendon merely bewitched her, or had he nearly seduced her?

"S," Brake answered. "S is the first initial of the man who will one day be your lover...your one true love."

"S?" Amoretta repeated as her heart sank to the pit of her stomach with painful disappointment. She hadn't wanted to hear that S was her lover's first initial. She wanted to hear it was B—B for Brake.

Brake nodded. "S is his first initial."

Amoretta frowned. "It's not S," she stated.

Brake shook his head. "But that's the letter your soul gave up to me." He frowned, seeming pensive. "Maybe it's Samuel Mulholland. He's about the right age to be your lover, isn't he?"

"Prudence's brother?" Amoretta squealed, feeling suddenly nauseated. He didn't want her? Brake didn't want her the way she wanted him? He hadn't felt what she felt? He couldn't have, or else he wouldn't have easily given over to S being her lover's initial.

"I could've misunderstood," he admitted. "It has been a long time since I practiced."

"Practiced?" Amoretta cried out in horror. "So you practice this, Mr. McClendon?" she snapped.

"No, Amoretta," he answered, smiling at her guiltily. He reached out, taking hold of her arm and pulling her into his embrace. "I just made that all up so I could kiss you again."

But lingering hurt was still forefront in her mind, and Amoretta whispered, "I don't believe you."

He laughed. "So it's more believable that I'm a gypsy and can get your soul to tell me who your lover will be than it is that I just wanted to trick you into kissing me?"

"Yes," she pouted. She looked up into his fiery brown eyes and melted against him.

"Why?" he chuckled.

"Because you didn't need to trick me into kissing you," she confessed in a whisper. "I would've gladly—"

Brake's mouth claiming hers silenced Amoretta's confession. And this time, as Brake kissed her—as his mouth opened against hers, warm, moist, demanding, and intimate—Amoretta succumbed to the passion of it. More than succumbed to it—she welcomed it, answered it, and bathed in the rapturous bliss of it.

His hands held her face as his mouth demanded a driven response to his affectionate endeavors, and she savored the sense of his palms against her skin. Brake's hands were in her hair—caressed her neck—and then she was in his arms again. Amoretta's hands traveled up and over his powerful arms to his shoulders, and when at last she found the courage to let her palms relish the feel of skin—of his neck and face—she was undone!

As his mouth left hers a moment to place long, moist kisses along her throat and neck, Amoretta gasped for breath—tried to capture a moment of clear thinking—but she found neither. She felt tears welling in her eyes as, at last, his kiss returned to her lips. How could she ever stop kissing him? How would she leave him for the remainder of the day, the night—for any period of time at all? She wouldn't! She wouldn't leave him! Amoretta determined she would simply kiss him forever—until she dropped dead from lack of water and food. And she wouldn't care—for what in all of life could be more sensational, marvelous, and miraculous than the feel of Brake's mouth blending with her own?

"Uncle Brake?"

Amoretta held her breath as Brake broke the seal of their lips, gazing down at her with eyes filled with desire.

"Um, Uncle Brake...I think maybe you should let the lady breathe for a minute," Shay suggested.

Amoretta blushed—for before she even looked away from Brake, she could feel Kizzy's and Shay's astonished gazes.

Taking her face between his strong, warm, callused hands, Brake breathed, "I-I suppose that's enough practice for today, Miss Ipswich." He smiled and winked at her—and there was nothing to do but turn and face Kizzy.

Gulping with trepidation, Amoretta turned to see Kizzy standing mouth agape, holding Shay's hand in one hand and a basket of wild berries in the other.

CHAPTER TEN

"I-I...uh...I...um..." Amoretta stammered. She could feel that her cheeks were as red as ripe Rome Beauty apples.

"Hey there, Kizzy...Shay," Brake greeted his sister and niece. "How was your berry-pickin' excursion?"

"Just fine," Kizzy managed.

"Oh, we found lots of berries, Uncle Brake!" Shay exclaimed with excitement. "Mama says she's gonna make a cobbler for us to eat after supper tonight!"

"Well, that *is* somethin' to look forward to, honey," Brake chuckled, obviously amused by Shay's utter adorableness.

Brake looked back to Kizzy as Amoretta continued to blush. "Well, I was just workin' on a little project of my own here while you were gone, Kizzy."

"I can see that," Kizzy said, winking at Amoretta and smiling at last. "And how's that goin' for you so far, big brother?"

Brake shrugged. He looked to Amoretta and asked, "How's that goin' for me so far, Amoretta?"

Amoretta was astonished at his casual manner. Brake didn't seem at all alarmed that Kizzy and her daughter had come upon her and Brake kissing one another.

Still blushing and using every ounce of her restraint to keep from bursting into tears of embarrassment and running off into the woods, Amoretta shrugged and stammered, "I-I...um..."

"Looks like it's goin' real well for you there, Brake," Kizzy said, smiling at Amoretta. "She's speechless…so I guess you must be as good a lover as you've always claimed to be." Kizzy giggled and winked at Amoretta with reassurance.

Rather scurrying over to Amoretta, Kizzy reached out and took one of her hands in her own. "Oh, don't be shy, Miss Ipswich. Please don't!" she pleaded. "The fact is I'm just glad Brake chose to lose control of himself right here in the woods…instead of out in the middle of town with your daddy, the judge, lookin' on!"

"But I-I…you must think…" Amoretta stammered again, still mortified that Kizzy and her daughter had caught her sparking out in broad daylight.

"I think you're wonderful, and I'm glad it was you who finally caught Brake's attention enough to make him—" Kizzy began.

"Does she taste good, Uncle Brake?" Shay giggled.

Brake hunkered down in front of the child, gently tucking one of her wild, raven curls behind her ear. "Oh my, yes, Shay!" he exclaimed.

"Better than berry cobbler?" Shay asked, her eyes widening with astonished curiosity.

"Better even than berry cobbler," Brake assured his niece.

Shay looked up to Amoretta then, smiling. "So that's why Uncle Brake took to kissin' you like that, lady. You taste better than berry cobbler even!"

"Oh, I'm sure I don't," Amoretta began.

It was Kizzy's dropping her berry basket and throwing her arms around Amoretta that silenced her.

"Oh, Miss Ipswich," Kizzy laughed, "you're so funny!" She pulled back from Amoretta, keeping hold of her shoulders, however. "Why are you so flabbergasted? Brake's my brother, after all. Why wouldn't I want him to go sparkin' with a pretty girl?"

Amoretta was somewhat consoled. Forcing a smile, she said, "Will you please call me Amoretta?"

"Me too?" Shay squealed.

Amoretta looked to Shay, nodding as she felt her own smile become more sincere. "Of course."

Shay squealed with delight and quickly gathered up her mother's abandoned berry basket. "I'll run these inside, Mama," she said. Looking up to Brake, she added, "Don't do anything else interestin' until I get back, Uncle Brake. Promise?"

Brake chuckled and tousled Shay's hair. "All right, baby. I promise."

Shay hurried into the house, lugging the basket of berries like it were a basketful of gold instead.

"Well, I'll just leave you two alone," Kizzy said, winking at her brother, "in case you need to finish up any...business or anything."

"Oh no, no, no," Amoretta breathed as an exhilarating sort of nervousness washed over her. "I need to be on my way home and..."

"Not just yet, you don't," Brake said, reaching out and taking hold of her arm. Nodding to his sister, he said, "You run on in with Shay, and I'll be in pretty quick." He winked at Kizzy, and her smile broadened with mischievous understanding.

"Of course," she giggled. "I hope we'll see you again very soon, Amoretta," she added with a wink. She hurried into the house then, leaving Amoretta alone with Brake once more.

"Don't get all bashful on me now, darlin'," Brake said as he gathered each of Amoretta's hands into his own.

But it was far too late for Amoretta not to be bashful, and she blushed to the tips of her toes. "She probably thinks I'm a loose woman."

Brake smiled. "She does not. She likes you." He laughed a moment. "And she likes the fact that you've wiggled your way into wrappin' me around your little finger."

Amoretta rolled her eyes, mumbling to herself, "I *wish* I had you wrapped around my..." Gasping when she realized what she'd begun to say, Amoretta could only stare at Brake as he continued to smile at her.

"Oh, believe me, precious…you do," he told her. "Now…I'm gonna let you leap off into the woods like a doe that's just been shot at. Because I can tell the moment between us was lost the moment you heard that little girl's voice…and you ain't about to kiss me the way you did before."

Amoretta didn't argue with him. She couldn't possibly kiss him again, not when Kizzy and Shay were probably watching them from the front window of the house.

He laughed when she didn't respond. "Hmmm. I can see I'm gonna have to drag you someplace very, very secluded if I ever hope to trick you into sparkin' with me again." Once more she didn't answer, and he said, "All right, all right. I'm lettin' you go. You get on home and do whatever it is you do all day long. I'm late gettin' over to the mill anyhow."

"The mill!" Amoretta exclaimed. She'd suddenly remembered that Prudence Mulholland was hostessing a sewing circle that morning. Furthermore, Amoretta and her sisters had agreed to go for a walk with the other young ladies in town directly following the gathering. Naturally, they'd already set the gristmill as their destination. After all, Fox Montrose was working there temporarily now as well, and being that the mill now offered even more delightful scenery within, the young ladies of Meadowlark Lake had decided a visit to the gristmill would be well worth their time.

"Oh! Prudence's sewing circle!" Amoretta said. She was discombobulated all at once—thinking that she needed to hurry home, freshen her hair, and meet up with Evangeline and Calliope. "I'll be late!"

But as she began to turn to leave, she found Brake still held fast to her arm.

"I ain't no kind of a scoundrel, Amoretta," he said. Amoretta looked up into his face to find his expression that of firm honesty. "I kissed you because I wanted to kiss *you*…not because I just wanted to get my jollies. All right? It's important to me that you know that."

Amoretta's heart suddenly swelled with a delicious warmth, and she smiled at him. "Really?" she asked with a sigh of happiness.

Brake grinned a little. "Really."

Taking hold of her other arm, he pulled her to him, pressing one last moist, lingering kiss to her mouth. "Really," he assured her. Releasing her then, she gasped when he reached around, smartly patting her once on her sitter. "Now on your way. You leap off into the woods, little doe…and have yourself a good day."

Amoretta smiled. She didn't want to leave him—of course she didn't. But what else was there to do? He had to work at the mill, and she was committed to Prudence's sewing circle. At least there was the walk out to the gristmill afterward. She smiled, thinking of the first time she'd seen Brake working there—wondering if he would be wearing his shirt later in the day as she stared at him through the mill wall's loose board. Or would he be wearing only suspenders over his broad, muscular chest?

Amoretta didn't say anything more to Brake, just turned and hurried into the woods. If she stayed—if she lingered any longer in remembering the bliss of being held and kissed by him—she wasn't sure she could ever leave him!

Quickly Amoretta darted through the woods toward home. But as she approached the tree line that separated the woods from the grassy expanse, she gasped when she saw none other than her own father riding toward her. Hiding herself behind a tree, Amoretta held her breath—waiting until her father had entered the woods and was beyond her before cautiously exiting the woods and running through the grass toward the Ipswich house.

As she ran, she briefly wondered what business her father had in the woods. But knowing she might well be late in meeting her sisters to walk to Prudence's sewing circle, she abandoned curiosity for promptness. She wasn't ready to tell Evangeline and Calliope about the depth of her feelings for Brake—or the fact she'd just been embroiled in passionate kissing with him. How would she explain it all anyway? She couldn't tell them about Kizzy and Shay being Brake's relatives; she'd promised not to tell a soul. Therefore, she determined that silence about the entire tangle was best—at least for now.

"Wherever have you been, Rettie?" Calliope called from the back porch as Amoretta neared the house. "We'll be late if you dillydally any longer."

"I know. I'm so sorry. I lost track of the time," Amoretta answered, huffing and puffing as she hurried up onto the porch.

But Calliope smiled. "Well, just freshen a bit, and we'll leave." She giggled, reaching out to tuck a stray strand of Amoretta's dark hair behind one ear. "You look like you've been mauled by a bear, darling! What *do* you do on your walks that rumples you up so much?"

Blushing as she thought of Brake's kisses—breaking out in goose bumps at the sensational memories of the feel of his mouth to hers—Amoretta simply shrugged, answering, "I just enjoy the exhilaration, I guess."

Calliope giggled, linking her arm with Amoretta's. "Oh, you're so amusing, Rettie. I swear there'd be no fun in life at all without you."

No fun in life? Amoretta smiled—for it was obvious Calliope had never been kissed the way Amoretta had been kissed that glorious, wondrous autumn morning.

Lawson frowned as he approached Kizzy's home. He hadn't gotten much sleep the past few nights—not since Sheriff Montrose had informed him there were more missing pets. He'd been sleepless, worrying about his daughters, worrying about the beautiful young woman living alone in the woods with her little girl.

Lawson lived in a house with his girls, and that house was in town. But Kizzy and her daughter lived alone in the woods—so isolated, so easily victimized by anyone having malicious intent. And Lawson was becoming more and more certain that there was someone in Meadowlark Lake with a malicious nature.

Killing wild animals for no apparent reason was worrisome enough. But when a fragile mind began slaughtering pets—domesticated animals that were loved and protected by their owners—that was something entirely different. Yet what could be done? Dennison Montrose had interviewed everyone he and Lawson could readily think of to suspect, and there was nothing amiss with any of them. Or so it seemed.

As if it weren't enough worry to have three young adult daughters who were capturing the attention of every bachelor in town, now Lawson had begun to feel quite protective toward Kizzy and her daughter. And what disturbed him most about the fact was that he did indeed own paternal instincts toward the little girl, Shay—but his protective instincts toward her lovely mother were everything but paternal.

The truth was he hadn't been able to get the vision of the lovely young gypsy out of his mind from the very moment he'd first met her. Oh, he'd tried everything. He'd tried guilt in reminding himself of his dearly and very beloved wife. He'd reminded himself in constant that Kizzy was no older than Evangeline. Yet she seemed so much older because her sad experience and continuing vulnerability. Each time Lawson thought of Kizzy, his heart would leap in his chest and begin to hammer. And he didn't know what to do to stop it.

However, with all his confusing emotions concerning the woman in the woods, there was one thing he didn't want to ignore: that was her isolation when someone with evil intent was roaming about. So wracked with escalating worry, Lawson had decided to ride into the woods and check up on Kizzy and her daughter himself.

But now—now as he dismounted, frowning as he noticed the big buckskin horse tethered to a tree in front of Kizzy's house—there was something more than worry rising in him. He felt angry and jealous, even before he knew who was visiting the young woman. He recognized the buckskin. It belonged to Brake McClendon—the man his own daughter Amoretta was infatuated with. Brake McClendon was arguably the most handsome young man in Meadowlark Lake, and Lawson could think of no reason for Brake McClendon to be visiting the beautiful Kizzy, unless…

Just then, the front door to Kizzy's house opened. Brake McClendon stepped out onto the front porch, slipping his arms into a shirt and beginning to button it as he turned and continued to talk to Kizzy. Lawson was furious—enraged! The man was clearly taking advantage of a woman who had already been victimized, and before Lawson could pause to think otherwise, he found himself storming up Kizzy's porch.

Taking hold of the back collar of Brake McClendon's newly buttoned shirt, Lawson pulled the man around and let go a powerful fist to his jaw, sending the rounder stumbling back to tumble off the porch.

Kizzy screamed, covered her mouth with both hands, and stood in horrified awe, staring down at Brake.

But Brake was powerful himself and was on his feet almost instantly.

"You bastard!" Lawson growled, and he tugged at his tie to remove it. Tossing his tie aside and then stripping off his vest and tossing it aside as well, he strode angrily toward McClendon—who was obviously a coward, for he was shaking his head and walking backward away from Lawson.

"You don't understand, Judge," McClendon said. "It ain't at all what you must be thinkin'."

"How dare you take advantage of this woman!" Lawson shouted, however. He was still seething with rage—trembling with jealousy. He knew he was out of his mind, but he couldn't stop himself.

McClendon ducked, avoiding Lawson's next swing, but Lawson was quick and swung with his other fist, hitting McClendon square in the jaw.

Lawson reeled, however, as a fist to his own jaw dazed him for a moment.

"Judge Ipswich!" McClendon shouted. "You're outta your mind! Listen to me!"

But Lawson was determined to knock the young buck to the ground and continue to beat the life out of him.

McClendon ducked, swung, and hit Lawson in the stomach. But Lawson Ipswich was still a man in his prime, and he landed a hard punch to McClendon's ribcage.

"Brake! No!" Lawson heard Kizzy shout. "He doesn't know, Brake!"

"Oh, I know all right," Lawson growled as he advanced on McClendon again.

"Judge! Wait! I don't want to hurt you," McClendon warned.

But Lawson chuckled. "Hurt me? Boy, I could wipe up this woods with you."

"He's my brother, Judge Ipswich!" Kizzy cried then. "Brake McClendon is my older brother!"

"What?" Lawson asked, whirling around to see Kizzy standing on her porch sobbing. Shay was with her, clinging to her skirt and crying as well. He looked back to Brake McClendon.

Brake held up one hand in a gesture that Lawson should settle down. "It's true," he said. "Kizzy is my sister...and Shay is my niece. I swear to that, Judge. She's my sister."

Lawson's frown deepened, even as he tried to regulate his breathing. His anger was quickly dissipating—replaced by self-loathing at how irrationally he'd acted.

Looking directly at Shay, Lawson asked, "Is this man your uncle, honey?"

Shay nodded and brushed tears from her cheeks. "He's my Uncle Brake."

Children as young as Shay didn't normally lie, and Lawson felt more the fool than he ever had in all his life.

His shoulders slumped with humiliation as he growled, "Well, why the hell doesn't anybody know this?"

"Kizzy didn't want anybody to know," Brake answered, wiping blood from the corner of his mouth. "She's always so worried about my reputation—always thinks that folks will spurn me the way they have her—that she insisted we keep it a secret when we moved to Meadowlark Lake." Lawson watched as Brake frowned at Kizzy and shook his head. "I told you no good would come from keepin' folks ignorant about it, Kizzy."

"I'm so sorry," Kizzy wept. "I'm so sorry, Judge Ipswich."

"I'm so sorry, Judge Ipswich?" Brake asked, obviously irritated. "Judge Ipswich ain't the one takin' the beatin', Kizz."

Kizzy wiped tears from her beautiful cheeks. "I'm sorry, Brake. Y-you were right...but..."

"I owe you an apology, McClendon," Lawson said. He was sick to his stomach—ill over it all. To make matters worse, he looked like a fool in front of Kizzy and had frightened her little girl. He offered a hand to Brake, adding, "I am sorry. I just thought...I thought...I mean, you were coming out of the house without your shirt. I just assumed...I am sorry."

He was surprised when Brake McClendon rather grinned at him as he accepted Lawson's apologetic handshake.

"It's all right, Judge," he said. "It sure ain't the first time a pretty woman got a man's temper riled up, now is it?"

Again Lawson felt the heat of humiliation rise to his face. The man knew—Brake knew exactly why Lawson had lost his good sense.

"In fact, I gotta get over to the mill before Mr. Mulholland gives my job to somebody else," Brake began. "So why don't you stay and Kizzy can explain everything to you? I mean, you are the new county judge, sir...and I have heard it said around town that you prefer to know folks as best you can."

Before Lawson could argue, Brake bent down, placing an affectionate kiss on Shay's forehead, and then said, "I'm off to the gristmill." Hurrying toward his horse, he called to Kizzy, "You see to it that the judge goes home knowin' what he needs to know." He mounted quickly, and as he walked his horse past the front porch, he looked to his sister, adding, "I told you it was a bad idea to keep this all a secret, Kizz."

Then he was off. Brake McClendon was gone, leaving Lawson standing there looking disheveled and feeling like an utter fool.

There was nothing to do but to take what he deserved. Lawson knew he had acted irrationally by assaulting Brake McClendon, but he knew he'd done something even worse to Kizzy. By assuming what he had—that Brake was having an inappropriate dalliance with

Kizzy—Lawson had as good as told her he thought she was a loose woman.

Inhaling a deep breath of self-loathing and regret, Lawson turned to face Kizzy. He was surprised to see that her tears had stopped and that she stood looking at him with an expression not of disgust or hurt but rather of something closer to amusement.

Shay had stopped crying too. She sniffled and looked up at him through big brown, softened eyes that pinched his heart with sympathy.

"Miss Kizzy," Lawson began—for what else could he do but offer his sincerest apologies? "I am truly sorry for…for all this." He shook his head, thoroughly revolted with himself for having lost his composure so completely. "I had no idea the man is your brother. I thought…I thought he had treated you badly somehow and…I-I…I—"

As Lawson struggled to find words to convey his regret, Kizzy interrupted. "Won't you come in, Judge Ipswich? I really would like the chance to explain everything to you…myself."

"We have fresh berries and some cream," Shay offered, obviously hopeful that Lawson would agree to join her mother in their house. "We're gonna make a cobbler for after supper, but there's plenty of berries for you to have some. Isn't there, Mama?"

Kizzy answered her daughter, "Of course there is," even though she was still smiling at Lawson.

How could he refuse her? As Lawson's heart seemed to melt into warm syrup in his chest, he wondered how he could ever refuse Kizzy anything. He also wondered how both she and her daughter could be so instantly forgiving of a man who'd threatened the well-being of their, no doubt, very beloved brother and uncle.

"Are you certain that I'm welcome?" Lawson asked. He felt he needed to offer every opportunity for the woman and her sweet daughter to just send him on his way, if that was what they truly desired. He didn't want them being nice to him just because he was the county judge.

"Of course, Judge Ipswich," Kizzy assured him, smiling her beautiful, captivating smile. "We wouldn't invite you in if we didn't truly want you."

With great humility and feeling like a dog who'd been caught in the smokehouse, Lawson lowered his head and climbed the porch steps to Kizzy's front door.

"After you, Miss Kizzy," he said, gesturing that she and Shay should precede him into their home. Kizzy's smile broadened, and Shay's melodic giggle of delight curved the corners of Lawson's mouth up ever so slightly.

Upon entering Kizzy and Shay's home, Lawson was instantly struck with a nearly overpowering sensation of comfort—sheer coziness and the desire to settle in for a long stay. Soft and colorful, comfortable and fragrant—it was like walking into a dream.

"If you would have a seat, Judge Ipswich," Kizzy said, gesturing to a chair at her small kitchen table. "Your hands need a little tendin' to."

"Hm?" Lawson asked as Shay tugged at his pant leg and nodded toward the same chair her mother had indicated.

Kizzy smiled and giggled. "Your hands, Judge...your knuckles. You hurt them while you were goin' after my brother."

Frowning, Lawson looked at his hands as he sat in the chair. His knuckles had split a little during the altercation. His frown deepened, for his first thought was that he was disgusted that perhaps his hands were softer than they should be.

"Oh," he said. He licked one thumb and began rubbing the blood from his knuckles on the opposing hand. Yep, he needed a bit more physical work than he'd been getting. He didn't want his hands to start looking soft.

"Oh no, no, no!" Kizzy kindly scolded.

Lawson looked up to see her standing at the sink, working the pump. Soon she'd wrung out a wet cloth and was sitting next to him at the table.

"Can I get the berries and cream, Mama?" Shay asked excitedly.

"Please do, sweetie," Kizzy answered, taking one of Lawson's hands in her own and gently dabbing at his knuckles with the cool, wet cloth.

"I'm so sorry, Miss Kizzy," Lawson apologized again. He was momentarily mesmerized at how large his hand looked in comparison with hers.

"It's fine, Judge Ipswich," Kizzy assured him. She smiled. "Brake is as tough as an old cowhide." She shrugged. "And anyway...I'm very flattered that you would defend my honor." She smiled up at him, adding, "Even though I suppose that I have don't really have any honor to defend."

"I find you to be very honorable," Lawson told her.

Kizzy shook her head, smiling with amusement. "Oh? And how's that?"

Without pause—for his thoughts on the matter were utterly sincere—Lawson answered, "When you were ill-treated by...by..." He glanced to Shay, to make certain the child was intent on gathering the bowl of berries and small creamer of cream, and then continued, "By Shay's father...you could've chosen many different paths. Many sad, destructive paths. Yet you didn't. You chose well—chose to keep your baby with you, to raise her in the best home with infinite love." He paused once more, almost fearful of what he wanted to say next. But he said it anyway. "You didn't allow a man you didn't care for or would be subject to in worldly ways to provide for you."

"But my brother provides for us," Kizzy put in, humbly.

"And that is as it should be," Lawson confirmed. "He's a good man as well...and he should take care of you both. It's a testament to his fine character."

Kizzy sighed, still pressing the soft, cool cloth against Lawson's knuckles. "So because I didn't allow myself to become a...a *kept woman*...a saloon girl or the like...you think I'm honorable?"

"Yes," Lawson answered plainly.

She looked up at him, the brown of her beautiful eyes simmering with barely restrained emotions—heartache, longing, regret. "It was my demand, you know," she said. "I made Brake promise me that he wouldn't tell anyone in town that I was his sister and Shay was his niece."

"Why?" Lawson asked.

Kizzy shrugged. "Because…because I didn't want him to be…to be…"

"Ostracized," Lawson offered.

Kizzy smiled. "Yes. I want Brake to be happy one day…to be married and have children of his own. I didn't want people here to find out that he was associated with—"

"A very beautiful sister with a very precious daughter?" Lawson asked. He immediately began to scold himself in silence. He'd flat out told the woman he thought she was beautiful!

But the softening in her eyes—the visible change of emotion from heartache and longing to gratitude and hope—told him that he had not made a mistake in what he'd said.

"Here you go, Mister Judge," Shay said, awkwardly placing a small bowl of berries in Lawson's lap. He chuckled as he watched her pour cream from the little pitcher in her hand directly into the bowl of berries. He hoped her hand stayed steady, or else he'd find his trousers covered in cream.

"Oh, Shay!" Kizzy gasped. "Be careful."

"You worry too much, Mama," Shay said as she finished pouring the cream. Setting the small creamer pitcher on the table, she exclaimed, "Oh! You need a spoon too!" And off she scurried to retrieve one.

Kizzy looked up, meeting Lawson's admiring gaze. "She…she likes to help so much," she whispered.

Lawson smiled. "She's an angel, that one." He looked over to the cute little girl busily digging through a kitchen drawer for just the right spoon. "She reminds me so much of my girls when they were little." Lawson felt his smile fade a bit. "I miss that…my girls being little like Shay."

"Oh, but Amoretta is such a beautiful young woman! Is it really so bad that she's grown up?" Kizzy said, drawing Lawson's attention back to her. She held his other hand now—pressed the cool cloth to the bruised knuckles there. "Or so I've heard, I mean. I've *heard* that Amoretta is a beautiful young woman."

"Amoretta?" Shay asked, returning with a spoon. "Oh, I think Amoretta Ipswich is the prettiest lady I've ever seen! Other than Mama, of course," she added, placing the spoon in Lawson's free hand.

"Is that right?" Lawson asked the girl. Yes—he was fishing. It was obvious both Kizzy and Shay were familiar with Amoretta. How involved was his daughter with Kizzy's brother that Kizzy and Shay already knew of her?

"Yes!" Shay affirmed. "She was here just this mornin'...right before you, Mr. Judge. Mama and I were out pickin' berries, and when we got back, there was Uncle Brake and Miss Ipswich—"

"Shay!" Kizzy gently scolded, interrupting the child's revealing prattle. Instantly, Kizzy's eyes revealed fear and panic. "Please, Judge Ipswich...I need you to believe me when I tell you that Brake is the best of men! He would never, never act in any way inappropriately toward your daughter. I swear it! He's a good man—the best of men! Please, please don't do anything to keep him from Amoretta. He's a good man. I swear it...on my life!"

She was panicking—desperate—and Lawson wanted nothing more than to reassure her. Turning the tables of reassurance, he placed the spoon in the bowl of berries and cream and clasped Kizzy's hands firmly in his.

"I have no doubt that he is a good man, Miss Kizzy," he assured her. "Not many men would stay off beating the tar out of a fool who started a fight over a misunderstanding. I have no doubt Brake could've knocked me cold if he'd wanted to this morning...but he didn't. Furthermore, he takes care of his family—honors his responsibilities—so I have no doubt he is a very good man."

Kizzy sighed, seeming somewhat relieved.

"But I do have to tell you that I'm disappointed in the fact that Amoretta hasn't mentioned to me that she knows you and Shay," he continued. "I've always taught my girls to confide in me about important things, and—"

"Mama made her promise not to tell anyone," Shay interrupted. "The day someone poisoned Uncle Brake, Miss Ipswich was here, and Mama told her that he's my uncle and things. And then Mama made her promise not to tell anyone."

"Poisoned?" Lawson asked, his concerns suddenly shifting from Amoretta's keeping secrets to an implication of maliciousness.

But Kizzy shook her head. "It was a misunderstandin'...a terrible misunderstandin'. The Ackerman girl, Sallie, she came to me for a love potion, and I just naturally assumed it was for this Fox Montrose, who is supposed to be the embodiment of Adonis himself. However, it turned out that it's Brake she has her heart set on...and I'd used dandelion extract in the love potion cake. And it made Brake so ill, and Amoretta came upon him and brought him here." Kizzy shook her head as tears began trailing over her cheeks. "It was just an accident. Brake has always been allergic to dandelions, and I didn't know the love potion was made for him...and...and..."

Lawson reached out, firmly cupping Kizzy's chin in one hand. "It's all right, Kizzy," he told her. "Please don't upset yourself."

The moment he'd taken hold of her, Kizzy had relaxed. He'd felt her relax. Now she sat before him, gazing up at him with those beautiful doe-brown eyes, and Lawson's mouth began to water for want of kissing her. She was so lovely—so vulnerable—so smart and capable. He could only imagine what it would feel like to kiss her— what it would taste like and how completely it would be his undoing.

Lawson wondered how long it had been since Kizzy had been kissed, since she'd known the protection of a man's arms around her—a man other than her brother. He heard Shay giggle next to him and thought that it had probably been as many years as Shay was aged since Kizzy had known any semblance of romantic affection.

Lawson felt his head begin to descend toward hers—saw her eyes flutter with longing. But he was twenty years her senior, old enough to be her father, and the thought interrupted his ambition to comfort her.

He released her chin—heard a quiet sigh of disappointment escape her lips—heard a not-so-quiet sigh of disappointment escape Shay's.

"Well, at least Amoretta won't have to bear our secrets alone now," Kizzy mumbled, quickly rising from her chair and going to the sink. She began to rinse out the cloth she'd used on Lawson's knuckles.

"No...she won't," Lawson said. "And I'll trust your brother, Kizzy. I'll trust your brother with Amoretta's tender heart."

Kizzy turned and looked to him then. "Why? Why would you trust Brake when you now know the secrets he keeps?"

Lawson gazed at her a moment and then answered, "Because I trust you."

"Try the berries, Mr. Judge," Shay urged then. "They're so delicious! You'll love them!"

Lawson smiled at Shay and nodded. Raising the bowl and spoon from his lap, he shoveled a bite of berries and cream into his mouth.

"Mmmm!" he hummed, smiling and winking at Shay. "Why, you do make a mean bowl of berries and cream, Miss Shay."

"Shay McClendon," Shay giggled. She looked to her mother. "It's all right if I tell him my whole name, right, Mama?"

Kizzy nodded. "Yes, darlin'. You can tell Judge Ipswich anything you want to."

Shay giggled and announced, "Molly had her kittens, Mr. Judge!"

"She did?" Lawson asked as he ate more berries and cream. They were very delicious.

"Yes! Seven baby kittens!" Shay confirmed. "They're too new to show them to you now, Mr. Judge. But maybe next time when you come, Molly will let you hold one, okay?"

Lawson nodded. "Okay. That'll give me something to look forward to."

"Shay, would you please run out and fetch Judge Ipswich's tie and vest for him?" Kizzy asked.

Lowering her voice to a whisper and putting one hand to one side of her mouth, Shay confided in Lawson, "She's just tryin' to get me to go outside so she can tell you somethin' she don't want me to hear."

Lawson chuckled as Shay rolled her eyes, said, "Yes, Mama," and skipped out the front door.

"I truly am sorry for all this, Judge Ipswich," Kizzy said, returning to the table and sitting down in the chair next to him once more. "I don't want you to think that Shay and I—or Brake, for that matter—none of us McClendons are troublemakers. I promise."

"I never thought that you were, Miss Kizzy," Lawson said, smiling at her with reassurance.

"Thank you," Kizzy whispered, her eyes filling with excess moisture again. "Your wife was a very fortunate woman in havin' you for a husband, Judge Ipswich." She stood and met Shay as the little girl raced back inside carrying Lawson's tie and vest. "And I expect she knew that with all her heart."

Lawson was at a loss for words. What was the woman trying to convey to him with such a remark?

"Here now," she said, handing his vest to him. "Let's make you presentable once more." She giggled. "We can't have the new judge ridin' into town lookin' like a schoolboy who's been climbin' trees, now can we?"

Lawson stood and put on his vest. He buttoned it up and then accepted the tie Shay held out to him.

As he tucked it under his collar and began to struggle with tying it, Lawson said, "I am sorry for the incident between your brother and me, Miss Kizzy. And I will keep the knowledge of your relationship to myself." He smiled and added, "Well, to myself and between Amoretta and me."

Kizzy smiled at him and reached out, taking the ends of the tie from him and working with them herself.

"Brake is mighty picky about women, Judge Ipswich," she said. "I can assure you…he's not the kind to toy with a woman's heart just for his own amusements. He truly cares for your daughter."

She was so close to him that he could smell the fragrance of her skin and hair—the ambrosial scents of her. Lawson clenched his teeth for a moment, trying to ignore the goose bumps that erupted on his arms when Kizzy inadvertently caressed his neck while managing his tie.

"I'll take you at your word, Miss Kizzy…and try not to be too much the concerned father," Lawson told her.

"There!" Kizzy said, smiling at him. She brushed the front of his vest, adjusted his collar, and sighed as she looked at him. "You're as handsome and pristine as the moment you arrived, Judge Ipswich." She looked down, taking one of his hands in hers. "Except for this," she said, caressing his bruising knuckles. She giggled. "But I suppose you could just say you were cleanin' out the barn and scraped them up or somethin'."

But Lawson didn't smile or laugh. He was too overcome with trying to restrain himself—to keep from taking the woman in his arms and ravaging her with kisses and caresses the like he knew she'd never known.

"You know what, Mama?" Shay asked then.

"What, darlin'?" Kizzy asked, running her fingers through her daughter's soft, dark curls.

"I think Judge Ipswich needs a hug, don't you?" Shay answered.

Lawson almost laughed out loud at the way Kizzy's face drained of color.

"Oh…well…I don't know if the judge is a huggin' man, Shay," Kizzy stammered.

"Oh, Mama!" Shay giggled. "You always say everyone needs at least three hugs every day. Now let's hug him. Don't be shy. After all, Uncle Brake did box him around a bit."

"But…but, Shay…" Kizzy stammered, her face growing paler by the moment.

"I think I could use a hug," Lawson said, smiling down at Shay then.

Reaching down and lifting the darling little girl, Lawson gathered her into a warm, strong embrace. The feel of her tiny arms around his neck nearly brought tears to his eyes. Oh, how he missed his girls being little, being innocent of the ugliness in the world, and depending on only him as their protector and hero figure.

After several long moments, Kizzy reached out, placing a hand on her daughter's back to indicate she should release Lawson, and said, "All right, Shay. Let's allow Judge Ipswich to be off on his day. I'm sure he has important things to tend to this mornin'."

Lawson gently set Shay back on her feet once more, tousling her hair as he smiled at her.

"Your turn then, Mama," Shay announced, looking to her mother expectantly. She nodded. "Give Mr. Judge a hug. Thank him for visitin' us and eatin' our berries and cream."

But Kizzy paused, obviously anxious. She began to fiddle with one of the brass buttons at her wide belt.

"Well, Shay…the fact is that—" she began.

But Lawson could not resist the need to hold her any longer and, reaching out, gathered Kizzy McClendon into his arms and against the firm protection of his body.

She melted to him at once, laying her cheek against his chest and allowing her arms to go around his waist—clinging to him with near desperation. He felt her gather the fabric of his vest and shirt in her small fists at his back as she began to tremble slightly.

He could love her! Lawson knew that he could love Kizzy McClendon—love her the way she deserved to be loved, to be cherished and respected. She was so beautiful—so simultaneously fragile and strong! His mouth burned with wanting to kiss her, but again he remembered his age—the fact that he had grown daughters.

Thus, slowly and carefully, as to offer no offense to her, Lawson lessened the possessiveness of his embrace of Kizzy. She paused in releasing him, however, and Lawson thought he might weaken and kiss her if he didn't escape soon.

Pulling away from him and stepping out of his arms then, Kizzy brushed tears from her cheeks. "I must be tired," she said, forcing a laugh. "I'm so weepy today."

"Thank you for the berries and cream, Miss Shay," Lawson said, smiling at Shay. He needed to escape—to mount his horse and ride like hell away from the temptation to seduce a woman half his age.

"You're welcome, Mr. Judge," Shay said, dipping a quick curtsy.

"And thank you, Miss Kizzy," he said, finally finding the courage to look at Kizzy again.

Kizzy simply brushed more tears from her cheeks and nodded as she folded her arms across her chest in a gesture that hinted at a feeling of sudden insecurity.

Lawson turned toward the door but paused a moment and looked back to Kizzy and Shay. "And, Shay," he began. The child gave him her full attention, and he said, "You keep Molly and her kittens inside at night, all right? We wouldn't want some mean old coyote to bother them, now would we?"

"No, sir," Shay agreed.

"Good day then, Miss Kizzy," Lawson said with a nod.

Kizzy brushed fresh tears from her cheeks, forced a smile, and nodded in return.

"I think Mr. Judge likes us, Mama!" Shay whispered once Judge Lawson Ipswich had ridden into the woods.

"He's a good man, Shay," Kizzy gasped as she tried to keep from collapsing into a fit of sobbing. "He's a good man."

But Kizzy McClendon thought Lawson Ipswich was far more than just a good man. He was a great man—a man who stood for justice and right and all things superior. Lawson Ipswich was superior himself in every way—in character, in strength, and, oh, how superior in appearance! Kizzy had never seen such a handsome man—such a broad-shouldered, perfectly built man! His dark hair and ruggedly square chin, his mesmerizing eyes and captivating smile—all combined to send her heart fluttering like a silly schoolgirl. Yet she knew that was exactly as he saw her—as a young schoolgirl. And worse, a young schoolgirl with a scarlet past. Kizzy knew she could never hope to win the heart of Judge Lawson Ipswich. Perhaps no one could. Perhaps his love for his wife had been such that he could never love another woman. Yes—that was it. That was what Kizzy would tell herself whenever her body ached to be held by Lawson Ipswich again—whenever she dreamt of kissing him, the way she had every night from the moment she'd met him. Lawson Ipswich had given his whole heart to another woman long before, and there was nothing left of that heart to give to another.

"I like him...that Mr. Judge," Shay sighed. "I would like it if he were my daddy someday."

And it was too much for Kizzy McClendon's broken, battered heart. Her little girl's dream of having a father was something Kizzy nearly bled over every day of her life. And Kizzy knew it could never be, and that only broke her heart into more pieces.

"Let's st-start that cobbler," Kizzy stammered, brushing more tears from her cheeks. "Goodness! Can you imagine how disappointed Uncle Brake would be if we didn't get that cobbler made for tonight?"

"That's right!" Shay giggled. "I'll get the rest of the berries washed up!"

As she watched Shay drag her little stool to the kitchen sink, Kizzy knew that the cobbler she and Shay would make that day would own an ingredient it wasn't meant to own—tears of sorrow and regret at what could never be—tears borne of knowing the arms of the honorable Judge Lawson Ipswich would never hold her again.

CHAPTER ELEVEN

"You hardly said a word while we were at Pru's, Amoretta," Evangeline whispered aside to her sister as they walked. "Are you feeling all right?"

Calliope giggled. "Oh, I think she's feeling more than all right."

Amoretta glanced to Calliope with curiosity. "Why would you say that?" she asked.

Calliope shrugged. "Because you keep smiling to yourself as if you have a delicious secret. And sometimes when you're smiling, your cheeks pink up like cherries, and you touch your lips with your fingers." Taking hold of Amoretta's arm, Calliope paused in walking with Prudence, Blanche, Winnie, and Sallie. "You've been kissed, haven't you?"

Instantly, Amoretta felt the heat of an intense blush rise to her cheeks. "Shhh!" she scolded Calliope in a whisper. "Do want the others to hear?"

Evangeline smiled then. "Who kissed you, Amoretta? Not Brake McClendon. You hardly know him!" But Amoretta couldn't keep from smiling at the memory of kissing Brake, and Evangeline gasped, "It *is* Brake! He kissed you?"

"Be quiet, Evie!" Amoretta scolded. "I don't want the others to hear."

"Why not?" Calliope asked.

"I-I don't know," Amoretta stammered. And she didn't. Of course there was the deep, dark secret of Kizzy and Shay and their

151

relationship to Brake—but it was more than that. Somehow Amoretta knew that if the other young women of Meadowlark Lake were to find out Brake McClendon had chosen Amoretta to flirt with and kiss, their animosity and jealousy toward her would outweigh their desire to keep her as a friend.

"I do," Evangeline whispered. She nodded toward the other girls, who were now a ways ahead of the three Ipswich daughters. "Every last one of them is in love with Brake McClendon. And we're too new in town for them to accept that Amoretta won him over so quickly…when they've been fawning after him since he moved here."

"Yes…that's it," Amoretta admitted.

"So what?" Calliope asked. "You like him, and he likes you. Who needs the friendship of other young ladies when you have Brake McClendon?"

"That's true too. But there's…there's more to it," Amoretta stammered. Oh, how desperately she wanted to confide in her sisters all her secrets of Kizzy and Shay. But she couldn't! She'd sworn she would keep their secret safe. Therefore, how could she explain to them all that had transpired? Sallie Ackerman's love potion and how Amoretta was there when Brake turned up poisoned by it, Kizzy's confessions of her relationship to Brake—she couldn't tell her sisters any of it! And without the explanation of it all, she knew it was astonishing to them—or at least to Evangeline.

"Are you girls comin'?" Winnie asked, drawing the Ipswich girls' attention to the rest of the young women.

"Of course," Amoretta answered, smiling. "We'll talk about this later," she whispered to Evangeline and Calliope.

"All right," Evangeline agreed.

Calliope giggled as they hurried to catch up with the others. "How delicious, Amoretta!" she said quietly. "I knew the minute I saw him looking at you the way he did that day we first met him that—"

"And so I went to the gypsy in the woods…and I asked her for a love potion."

Calliope silenced what she was saying, her attention now captured by what Sallie Ackerman had just said.

"You did what?" Calliope asked.

Sallie shrugged. "I went to the gypsy in the woods and asked her for a love potion to give to—"

"To Fox, of course," Winnie offered.

But Sallie shook her head. "No. I wanted it for Brake."

"What?" Winnie, Blanche, Prudence, and Calliope exclaimed in unison.

"I...I wanted to make him love me," Sallie confessed. She paused a moment, looking at each young woman in turn. "And don't look so surprised. Don't pretend that every one of you hasn't considered doin' the very same thing."

"Well?" Prudence urged. "What happened?"

"Did she give you a love potion, Sallie?" Blanche asked.

"Did you give it to Brake?" Winnie added.

Sallie nodded. "She gave me a cake with the potion baked into it...and told me to give it to the one my heart desired."

"Did it work?" Winnie asked, obviously very anxious. Winnie's expression alone told Amoretta that the minute these young women found out she had been the object of Brake's attention—well, she would be friendless, save the company of her sisters. Yet she sighed, for if Brake truly did care for her—if she could one day win his heart for her own—then she knew her sisters were all the female friends she would ever need.

Sallie shook her head. "I wasn't sure at first...because I didn't even set eyes on Brake for two days after I gave him the cake. But when I did see him again, he simply smiled and nodded at me when we passed in the street."

"So the gypsy is a fake," Winnie stated. "I knew it."

"No," Sallie corrected, however. "I went to her and told her that it hadn't worked...that Brake seemed no different toward me than before I gave him the cake. She explained that it was a sign, that Brake wasn't meant for me, because a love potion only works when a love is meant to blossom anyway. It just speeds up the process."

"She's a fake," Winnie mumbled again. "Love potions work no matter what."

"Oh really, Winnie?" Prudence asked. "And how would you know? Do you have such vast experience in love potions?"

"You're just glad it didn't work," Winnie teased. "Because if it did, Sallie would have Brake for her own, and you would never have another chance at him."

"Neither would you," Prudence responded rather haughtily.

"Oh, stop it, girls," Blanche interjected. "Brake McClendon will choose who Brake McClendon wants to choose. And no amount of gypsy love potions, or anything else, will sway him."

"And you know this because?" Winnie baited.

"Because I believe in true love…and obviously, Brake hasn't discovered who his true love is," Blanche answered.

Calliope and Evangeline both glanced to Amoretta quickly. Yes, they were beginning to understand exactly why Amoretta wasn't readily announcing the fact that Brake had kissed her to all the young ladies of Meadowlark Lake.

"What do you Ipswich girls think?" Winnie asked unexpectedly.

"Us?" Evangeline gulped.

"Yes," Winnie confirmed. "You've been here quite some time now, and you've had your own chances to observe Brake. Who will he choose?"

"But I thought all of you were dazzled by Fox Montrose now," Calliope said. "Well…with the exception of Winnie, of course. I thought every one of you had moved beyond Brake McClendon."

"Are you insane?" Sallie exclaimed. She exchanged glances with the others. "Every one of us knows that Fox Montrose is entirely smitten with you, Calliope Ipswich! Are you really not aware of that?"

Calliope gasped—shook her head with astonishment.

"And besides, Fox is as handsome as anything…but Brake is still more handsome," Blanche offered.

"Ooo! I just love when he walks through town…just the way he walks!" Sallie exclaimed, feigning a shiver of delight in thinking of

Brake. "I swear, I could just sit and watch Brake do nothin' for all the rest of my days."

"So you're not giving up?" Evangeline asked.

"Of course not," Sallie answered. "The gypsy woman can't know everything. If I want Brake, I can get him."

"Me too," Winnie chimed in.

"And me," Prudence giggled.

"Well, Samuel doesn't seem to know I'm alive," Blanche added. She smiled. "But Brake said hello to me yesterday in town, so don't think you girls don't have more competition than ever." She looked to Evangeline, Amoretta, and Calliope. "Right? You Ipswich girls have tossed your hats in for Brake's attention too, haven't you?"

"O-of course," Evangeline answered. "And between all of us Meadowlark Lake girls…one of us is bound to snatch him up eventually, right?"

"Right!" everyone chimed.

"And as long as it's me, everything will be just fine," Winnie added. All the girls exchanged glances of slight exasperation.

"Well, let's just go get ourselves an eyeful of that tall drink of water at the mill, before he really is snatched up and we can't daydream about him anymore," Prudence suggested, smiling.

The girls were quiet then, for they were approaching the mill. Winnie motioned to everyone to follow her around to the back of the building, and once there, everyone kneeled down to look through the space the loose board allotted.

The moment Amoretta saw Brake—working without his shirt on and looking more handsome than he had even that morning—her heart fluttered in her bosom, and butterflies began to swarm in her stomach. Goose bumps broke over her as the feel of his mouth pressed to hers returned to her lips.

"He's lookin' particularly scrumptious today, isn't he?" Winnie asked in a whisper.

"My yes!" Prudence added.

"And there's Fox, Calliope!" Sallie said, nodding to where Fox Montrose stood listening to Mr. Mulholland's instructions nearby.

"You're a lucky girl, Calliope. Fox Montrose is so handsome and charmin'!"

"Yes, he is," Calliope said, smiling.

"Good gravy, Amoretta!" Evangeline quietly exclaimed. "No wonder you've been blushing all morning." Evangeline smiled and winked at Amoretta with conspiratorial delight.

"Oh, Evie!" Amoretta sighed. "You have no idea!"

"Oh, look! Samuel's caught a rat!" Sallie exclaimed, pointing to one corner of the room.

"Ew!" Prudence whined. "And Sam hates rats!"

The girls all watched then as Samuel Mulholland proceeded not to toss the rat out but to pull a small knife from one pocket of his trousers. Holding the wriggling rodent by the back of the neck, all the girls gasped, covering their mouths with their hands in horror as Samuel plunged the knife into the rat's throat and proceeded to slice it open from throat to tail, as if he were no more than gutting a fish.

"Get that thing out of here, Samuel!" Mr. Mulholland bellowed. "And I told you before, just stomp on their heads. You don't need to go torturin' them and leavin' such a mess of blood in the mill. It just attracts more of 'em."

All the girls looked to Prudence for some silent explanation as to why her brother would do such a thing. But Prudence's expression was that of being more horrified than everyone else.

"Wh-why would he do that?" she whispered.

"Look!" Blanche said then, pointing to Samuel.

Samuel Mulholland was striding directly for the space the girls were peering through.

"Quick, girls!" Winnie ordered in a whisper.

Amoretta joined the others in quickly hiding behind some nearby wild shrubbery. And not a moment too soon, for an instant later, the dead, bleeding rat came hurling through the opening in the back wall of the mill, landing in the grass with a horridly effective thud.

"Why would he do that?" Prudence asked in a whisper. Amoretta glanced over to see tears welling in Prudence's eyes.

"Well…you did say he hates rats, Pru," Calliope offered in an attempt to console her.

"But…but that was so cruel," Prudence breathed.

Winnie sighed and put an arm around Prudence's shoulders. "Come on, Pru. Let's just go home for today. We can come back next week and have our fill of oglin' Brake, all right?"

"Yes, Pru," Sallie added. "I need to get home anyhow. I'm supposed to be helpin' Mama with supper."

"We should be getting home as well," Evangeline said, looking to Calliope and Amoretta for reassurance.

"Oh yes!" Amoretta exclaimed. "It's my night to fix supper, isn't it?"

"Y-yes it is," Calliope stammered. Clearly every young woman was unsettled by Samuel's cruelty to the rat—even if it were a dirty, pesky rodent. And Amoretta, for one, couldn't wait to escape the gruesome evidence of it.

There hung in the air among the young ladies of Meadowlark Lake an unspoken discomfort as they hastened back to town. Prudence, though not sobbing by any means, continued to brush tears from her cheeks as they walked, barely conversing at all.

Polite smiles and biddings of farewell were exchanged once they'd all stepped foot on Meadowlark Lake's main thoroughfare, but the afternoon had been spoiled by Samuel Mulholland's inexplicable cruelty.

As Amoretta, Evangeline, and Calliope headed for home, Calliope exhaled a heavy sigh and began to prattle, "All right, *that* was not an enjoyable excursion…and therefore, I've decided we will simply put it behind us and go back to the happy thing we were discussing amongst us sisters before it happened."

Evangeline and Amoretta nodded, and Evangeline said, "That's right. So, Amoretta, tell Calliope and I more about your affair with Brake McClendon."

Amoretta blushed and felt a smile return to her face at the mention of Brake. "Well…it's hardly an affair of any sort, Evie," she began. "It's more like…oh, I don't know…a secret, accidental trysting."

"There's no such thing as an accidental tryst, Amoretta," Evangeline giggled. "You either meant to meet him or you didn't."

"Oh, don't be so particular, Evie," Calliope sighed with impatience. "Tell us, Amoretta. Tell us all about it! How in the world did you manage to find yourself kissed by Brake McClendon?"

But she couldn't tell them all about it! She'd come upon Brake while going back to Kizzy's to check on his well-being. How could she tell her sisters that when she couldn't even tell them she'd been to Kizzy's? It was purely maddening to keep secrets, and she swore to herself she would try with all her might to avoid the necessity of ever having to do so again.

"I-I…well…" she stammered. "Remember when we first met him, Calliope?" she sighed at last. She may have found an anchor of avoidance. Calliope nodded. "And remember how you told Evangeline…about how Brake kept staring at me?"

Again Calliope nodded and said, "The way he was undressing you with his eyes."

Amoretta blushed, sighed with exasperation, and continued, "Well, it seems we have a common attraction to one another. For me, it was instantaneous…and not just because he's so handsome."

"And it was the same for him then?" Evangeline asked, smiling.

Amoretta shrugged. "I-I guess so…because he…I was there, and he…he tricked me into letting him kiss me…and then I wanted him to continue, of course…and then…I didn't want him ever to stop kissing me and—"

"Delicious!" Calliope squealed, clapping her hands together with delight. "And how did he kiss you, Rettie? Soft and tender…or with passion?"

Remembering the first kiss she'd been blessed with from Brake—the powerful, forced kiss he'd given her the day he thought he'd been poisoned—Amoretta answered, "It was rather desperate the first time he kissed me. But the next time…he began carefully, as if he were afraid I'd run from him. But then…then…" Amoretta shook her head, rendered suddenly breathless at the mere memory of kissing Brake. "Then it rather erupted into something I'd never dreamed of! I mean...I never knew a man could kiss a woman so that her bones felt as if they were melting!"

"Melting bones, Rettie?" Evangeline giggled. "Really?"

"Really," Amoretta confirmed.

"Oh, how wonderful!" Calliope exclaimed. Her shoulders suddenly drooped, however, and she exhaled a sigh of disappointment. "I hope the right man kisses me like that someday."

"We all hope for that," Evangeline admitted. She smiled at Amoretta and took her hand, squeezing it with reassurance. "And I'm glad you may have found it, Rettie." Evangeline smiled. "He is quite the specimen, isn't he?"

"Oh, he's not a two-headed calf stuffed in a jar at a dime museum, Evie," Calliope said, scowling at her elder sister. "This is Brake McClendon we're talking about! Brake McClendon! And he has a passion for our sister." She laughed, adding, "And I can't wait to see Winnie Montrose's face the first time she sees..." Calliope paused, her thoughts obviously popping about like a grasshopper on a hot skillet. "How long do you think it will be before he asks Daddy if he can court you?"

"I-I don't know that he ever will," Amoretta mumbled as her joy vanished.

"He better ask!" Evangeline said. "If he's already melting your bones with his kisses, then it would be the next logical step."

"In Boston, it would've been the first step," Amoretta said.

Evangeline smiled, realizing Calliope's question had innocently caused Amoretta anxiety. "But as I've told you so many times since we moved here, Amoretta...we're not in Boston anymore. And aren't you glad now?"

Amoretta's smile returned, and she giggled. "Yes. Though I never thought it would be Brake McClendon who convinced me of it."

"Ooo, I do hope he keeps *convincing* you, Amoretta," Calliope chirped. Stepping between Amoretta and Evangeline, Calliope linked her arms with theirs. "And no more secrets, Rettie. Next time that dashing Brake McClendon melts your bones, you have to tell us! All right?"

Amoretta laughed, amused by Calliope's endless thirst for tales of romance. "All right," she agreed. Yet the secrets she held safe concerning Brake and his family still haunted her. They would be forever hard to keep, simply because it was often accidentally that secrets were revealed. She would have to be wary.

"Well...if it ain't the lovely Ipswich sisters."

Amoretta gasped at the sound of his voice, as she, Evangeline, and Calliope all turned to see Brake McClendon himself astride his horse behind them. He winked at Amoretta, and she felt a blush of delight rise to her cheeks.

"Looks like you young ladies are on your way home," he said.

"Yes," Evangeline answered. "We...we've been at Prudence's house for sewing and then out for a stroll."

"And now we're off to start supper," Calliope nervously interjected.

"Well, I'm off to supper myself," Brake said, still staring at Amoretta. "You ladies have a good evenin' now, you hear?" he said. Then, smiling at Amoretta, he touched the brim of his hat and nodded. "Tell your daddy I said hello...won't you, darlin'?"

"Of course," Amoretta managed, smiling at him and wishing she could simply hop up onto the back of his horse and ride away with him.

Brake nodded once more and then turned Gambler in the direction of the woods. Amoretta watched him go—missed him the instant he was out of sight with an aching she'd never known before.

"And to think," Calliope began, "to think those very lips were pressed up against yours, Amoretta. Oooo! It gives me goose bumps!"

"Me too," Amoretta sighed. "Me too."

❧

"Did you enjoy supper, Daddy?" Amoretta asked as she cleared her father's plate from the table later that evening.

"Of course, honey," Lawson Ipswich answered. "All three of you girls spoil me rotten with good food. I don't deserve it."

"Yes, you do, Daddy," Amoretta said, placing a loving kiss on his forehead. "You deserve everything good and wonderful."

Do I? Lawson wondered. Did he deserve the good and comfortable life he owned? Did he deserve to have three beautiful, loving, loyal, and good daughters? Did he deserve the chance to love again—to love the pretty gypsy woman in the woods?

"May I talk to you a minute about something, Amoretta?" Lawson asked bluntly.

"Well...of course, Daddy. Is something wrong?"

Lawson could see by the concern on Amoretta's face that his voice had revealed his concerns—his guilt over what had happened that morning between him and Brake McClendon—his guilt over his rapidly growing attraction and feelings toward Kizzy McClendon.

Evangeline and Calliope were out on the back porch enjoying the evening breeze. Thus, as Amoretta took a seat in the chair next to Lawson's at the table, he lowered his voice and began, "I know about Kizzy, her daughter, and Brake, Amoretta. I know that they're family."

The astonishment apparent on Amoretta's face, instantly followed by obvious relief, settled Lawson's anxieties a bit.

"Oh, Daddy!" Amoretta sighed. "Oh, Daddy! It's been so hard for me...to keep their secrets. I haven't been able to confide in anyone about it—not even Evangeline and Calliope...not you!" She buried her face in her hands a moment, overwhelmed with relief.

Yet Lawson knew that it would only take a moment for her mind to begin questioning him. Her relief was great, but he knew his daughter, and her curiosity would soon be greater.

Slowly she raised her head and looked at him. "But...but how did you discover their relationships?" Lawson watched as Amoretta's eyes widened with anxiety. "And how did you know that I already knew it?"

Lawson smiled at Amoretta. She was so lovely. He knew exactly why she had captured Brake McClendon's attention.

161

"I met Kizzy and her daughter not so short a time back…but not so long either," Lawson began to explain. "I-I couldn't keep from worrying about them…owning a constant concern for their safety and well-being. And so this morning, I rode out to check in on them…to make sure they were faring well." He paused.

"And?" Amoretta prodded.

Lawson swallowed the lump of regret in his throat—regret at having acted so irrationally at seeing Brake exiting Kizzy's house.

"And as I rode up to the house, I saw a man coming out of it. He wasn't wearing a shirt. In fact…he was putting his shirt on."

"Was it Brake?" Amoretta asked—though Lawson knew she more than merely suspected it had been Brake.

"Yes, it was," Lawson admitted. "And not knowing that Brake and Kizzy are siblings, I assumed…well, I assumed the worst. And I…I'm afraid that I hit Brake McClendon…punched him square in the jaw…knocked him off the porch, actually."

"Daddy! You didn't!" Amoretta exclaimed, fairly leaping up from her chair.

"I did," Lawson assured his horrified daughter. "And he hit me back…all the while trying to explain to me that Kizzy is his sister."

"Oh, Daddy! Daddy!" Amoretta moaned, shaking her head. Lawson was almost amused by her agony—for he knew it was borne of fear that his altercation with Brake had changed the man's mind about Amoretta.

"There's nothing to worry about, Amoretta," Lawson said, taking her hands in his and directing her to sit down once more. "I'm sure our little fist-to-cuffs misunderstanding won't change his mind about you."

"What do you mean?" Amoretta asked.

Lawson smiled. It was entertaining, watching Amoretta squirm as she tried to guess how much he knew about her and Brake McClendon.

"Kizzy tells me he favors you," he answered. "And I know you've been infatuated with him from the moment you first set eyes on the man." Lawson shrugged. "Therefore, I want to reassure you that my incident this morning with Brake…well, let's just say we worked it all out, and once I understood things—"

"I think I'm already in love with him, Daddy," Amoretta interrupted in a whisper. She looked up at him, gazing at him with frightened eyes that pleaded for reassurance. "And I know that you think it's impossible, but I—"

"A month ago I may have, honey," Lawson admitted. "But not anymore." He thought of Kizzy and the fire she'd lit in him both emotionally and physically. He'd not set eyes on Kizzy any more often than Amoretta had set eyes on Brake, but he knew he was in love with her already—whether it made sense or not, whether it was appropriate or not.

He reached out, taking Amoretta's face in his hands. Smiling at her, he said, "I truly do believe you. Though I cannot promise you all your dreams will come true where Brake is concerned…I do believe you."

Amoretta frowned. "But why? Why would you believe me now?"

"Because I've seen changes in you of late," Lawson answered. It wasn't the only reason, of course—it wasn't even the biggest reason—but it was true. Furthermore, he wasn't about to admit to his daughter that he believed her because he'd begun falling in love with Kizzy the moment he'd seen her. Amoretta would think her father had gone utterly mad!

"There's a different sort of light in your eyes, Amoretta," Lawson added, "a light I'm guessing Brake McClendon put there."

"He only kissed me twice, Daddy," Amoretta began to needlessly confess. "I swear…he was a true gentlemen both times and—"

"So he's kissed you already, has he?" Lawson chuckled. "The little devil."

"K-Kizzy didn't tell you that? She didn't tell you that this morning when she and Shay returned from picking berries—"

"Nope," Lawson answered with an amused grin. "I wouldn't have known Brake McClendon was already stealing your kisses if you hadn't told me just now."

Amoretta's cheeks were crimson! Lawson laughed and gathered his daughter into his strong, protective embrace. He owned a moment of melancholy—of sadness in knowing that he would no longer be the first protector she looked to from now on. Another man had stepped into that role.

"Amoretta!" Calliope called from the back porch. "For Pete's sake, you're missing the most refreshing autumn breeze! Hurry up and come out with us."

"Kizzy assures me that her brother is a trustworthy man, Amoretta," Lawson said, releasing his daughter at last. "I'm taking her at her word…trusting him with one of my precious daughters."

But Amoretta giggled. "Oh, Daddy, don't be so dramatic. I said I was in love with him. Please don't assume he's in love with me."

And there it was: the doubt. Lawson reasoned that any woman would doubt that a man like Brake McClendon—handsome, strong, and sought after by nearly every woman in the county—could ever love her. Yet men like Brake McClendon did love, just as women like Kizzy McClendon loved.

"Run along and join your sisters before Calliope explodes with apoplexy," he laughed in an effort to clear the air of such a serious matter.

Amoretta leaned forward and kissed him on one cheek. "All right, Daddy. I love you," she said. She smiled, rose from her chair, and hurried out the kitchen door to join her sisters on the back porch.

Lawson exhaled a heavy sigh of weariness—weariness of mind, not body. He felt in his very soul that he would soon be watching his girls marry and leave home to begin families of their own. Evangeline, Amoretta, and Calliope would leave him—and it was as it should be. Yet the thought caused a sudden and nearly overwhelming loneliness to wash over him. After all, he was still a youngish man—still a man with much to offer a woman. He thought of Kizzy and her darling little Shay. Kizzy needed a man in her life other than her brother. She needed a protector, a companion, a father for her child; she needed a lover. Shay needed a father and a sibling or two. Therefore, Lawson mused, what was wrong in allowing his mind to wander to such dreams as holding Kizzy in his arms through long, dark winter nights, or rocking Shay to sleep in the evenings as he'd done with his three grown girls? Nothing was wrong with it. Nothing! Or at least so he tried to convince himself all through the night—another restless night when his waking moments were filled with visions of the beautiful gypsy in the woods and his sleeping moments filled with visions of slaughtered dogs, cats, and foxes morbidly heaped in a rotting pile beneath an old maple tree.

CHAPTER TWELVE

"Well, Judge," Dennison Montrose began, exhaling a heavy sigh, "looks like we found Rowdy Gates's dog."

Lawson hunkered down to inspect the pile of animals more closely. "Who found this?" he asked.

"Rowdy Gates himself...last night when he was lightin' the lamps," Dennison answered. "It hadn't been here long when he found it though. Otherwise someone woulda smelled it, right?"

Lawson nodded, for the stench of the rotting dog and cat carcasses was overpowering. "And I supposed that's your daughter's cat there too?" Lawson said, shoving the large stick he'd picked up into the pile and pushing several of the slaughtered rats aside.

"Yep. As near as I can tell anyhow," the sheriff confirmed. "Still, them rats...they're fresh. And I'll tell you, Judge, I'm more disturbed than ever. Someone kept Rowdy's dog and the cat for a few days...after they were dead. Then it looks like the rats were maybe killed yesterday—maybe even last night right before Rowdy came by to light the lamps."

Lawson stood straight once more, rubbed at his tired eyes, and groaned. "Dennison, we've got to find out who is doing this and put a stop to it right now."

"Yes, Judge," Dennison agreed. "But I just don't know where else to look. I really can't imagine anybody in Meadowlark Lake would do somethin' like this. And I sure as hell can't imagine why."

But Lawson could well imagine why. Someone in Meadowlark Lake was slowly going mad.

"I'm afraid to say this out loud, Dennison," Lawson began. Lowering his voice, he continued, "But I really do think someone's mind is slowly fracturing here. This isn't normal behavior, not for an angry adolescent or even a man who hunts purely for sport. This kind of thing…I mean, there are ten rats here. This kind of thing was thought out…planned."

"A fractured mind?" Dennison repeated. "You're talkin' insanity, aren't you, Judge?"

"I am," Lawson confirmed. His frown deepened, and he asked, "Who else has seen this, other than Rowdy Gates?"

"Nobody to my knowledge," Dennison answered. "In fact, Rowdy tossed an old flour sack, a burlap bag, and some other things over this the moment he found it, in hopes no one else would notice this gruesome sight."

"That's good," Lawson mumbled. "But let's get it cleaned up before someone else does."

"I've got an old barrel out back of the jailhouse. I'll just shovel this mess in there, cover it, and haul it out of town," Dennison said. "But how in tarnation are we gonna figure out who's doin' this? I've talked to everybody I can think of to talk to, Judge."

"Well, let's do this. Let's get rid of this," Lawson said, nodding toward the heinous pile of rotting animals. "And then I think we better start talking to everyone in town—not just those we think might be struggling somewhat but everyone."

"And I say we tell them about this…about what we've found a couple of times now," Dennison added. "We'll put it as casually as possible and try not to frighten folks. But I do feel everyone needs to be wary."

"Agreed," Lawson said. "Have them keep their pets inside at night as well."

"All right."

"I'm going to return home and clean up a bit," Lawson began, "but I certainly am glad you came and got me before the sunrise and folks began milling around town. Thank Rowdy Gates for me too. And since I highly doubt he would do this to his own dog, I think he's free and clear of any further suspicion."

"Absolutely," Dennison agreed. "Rowdy had that dog for somethin' like seven years. He was pretty angry and rattled when he come to fetch me."

"I imagine that he was," Lawson mumbled. He exhaled a worried sigh, adding, "I'll be at the courthouse within the hour. I think we should meet and decide which of us will interview whom. Does that suit you, Sheriff?"

"Yes, it does, Judge," Dennison agreed.

Lawson watched as Dennison covered the mound of carcasses with the burlap and flour sacks Rowdy Gates had initially used to hide it. Then he turned and stormed back toward the house. He'd talk to his girls—tell them everything so that they would be wary and watchful. He knew Kizzy ought to be told as well. She and Shay were too vulnerable out in the woods alone. Maybe it had been safe enough before—and that was a big maybe—but now it wasn't, not with a fractured mind residing somewhere in Meadowlark Lake. But Lawson didn't want to frighten Kizzy, not when she was already so vulnerable and wary of people, and it wasn't his place to make the decision for her. Maybe he could persuade Brake to convince his sister to move into town, no matter what people thought. Lawson would find a time to speak with Brake about Kizzy's safety.

Lawson was surprised when he entered the house to find his girls already up and sitting at the kitchen table. Usually it was only Amoretta who rose as early as he did. But on this morning, the beaming faces of all three of his lovely daughters greeted him.

"Good morning, Daddy!" Calliope chirped. "You've already been out today?"

"Yes," Lawson answered. He quickly kissed each daughter on the forehead and then joined them at the table. He knew they sensed his dark mood; therefore, he saw no reason to delay.

"Girls," he began, "I need you to be wary."

"Of what, Daddy?" Evangeline asked.

"There's some…some rather unpleasant mischief going on in town, it seems," Lawson sighed. "And it quite disturbs me."

"What's going on, Daddy?" Amoretta put forth. "Just tell us."

Swallowing the lump of trepidation in his throat (for he again began to wonder whether he'd done the right thing in bringing his precious darlings to Meadowlark Lake), he ventured, "Someone has been killing animals…for no reason. Several pets are included."

"Killing animals? Pets?" Evangeline asked.

Lawson nodded. "The first incident…well, the sheriff happened upon a pile of foxes, dogs, and cats, just outside of town. They were not killed kindly, I'm afraid. And then last night, it seems the man who lights the gas lamps, Rowdy Gates…he found his dog, the Montroses' housecat, and several rats slaughtered and piled up near the north side of town."

"Rats?" all three girls exclaimed in unison.

"Yes, rats," Lawson affirmed. "Does that mean something to you girls?" As his daughters exchanged unsettled glances, he knew that the rats did mean something to them. "Tell me why the mention of the rats is important."

Amoretta shrugged. "Well, it's just that…and I'm sure it's nothing, Daddy," she began.

"Tell me what you need to, and then let me decide if it's important, honey," Lawson urged.

It was Calliope who spoke next. "Well, Daddy, after the sewing circle Prudence held yesterday, we all…well…all of us young ladies…we…we…"

"You what?" Lawson asked. He was growing worrisome, and it caused impatience to rise in him.

"We all walked over the gristmill to spy on the good-looking men Mr. Mulholland employs there," Evangeline answered plainly.

Lawson almost chuckled, for it seemed that when bluntness was required, it was always Evangeline who managed it.

"Yes? And?" Lawson prodded.

"Well, as we were, you know, observing the men in the mill…" Calliope stammered. She looked to Amoretta, and Lawson noted the deep frown that instantly furrowed both lovely brows.

Amoretta looked to her father then and said, "Samuel Mulholland…he caught a rat, and holding it at the throat in one hand, he killed it with a small knife by…by…"

"He slit it open from its throat to its end, Daddy," Evangeline finished. "It was such a cruel act that it deeply disturbed every one of us…and we left."

"Prudence wept all the way home," Calliope offered. "But none of the rest of us wanted to think about it any longer." She shrugged. "So we just pushed it from our thoughts."

Amoretta was still frowning. "And Mr. Mulholland harshly scolded Samuel for doing it. Apparently Samuel had done it before, from what we heard Mr. Mulholland saying."

Lawson frowned and nodded. "Samuel Mulholland," he muttered. "I think what you've told me should be carefully considered. It's a fracturing mind that does things like this. I've seen it before, several times in Boston."

"Daddy?" Calliope asked. "How frightened should we be?"

Lawson knew it was time for reassurance then. Forcing a relaxed and comforting smile, he answered, "Oh, not so frightened as you would think. But just be wary…watchful. You know, be sure you walk with someone when you're going to town." He looked at Amoretta, adding, "And you be sure Brake sees you all the way home after your little trysts."

Amoretta blushed but nodded.

"I'm sure it's not so terrible a thing as perhaps I'm thinking," Lawson said—though he thought it was probably just as terrible a thing as he was thinking. Splintering minds may begin by harming only animals, but Lawson had seen them escalate to hurting their fellowman. Still, he didn't want the girls to be entirely terrified every minute of every day. They'd grown up in Boston, for pity's sake—a city fraught with splintering minds and crime.

171

"Just be wary," he added at last. Then, exhaling a sigh and smiling, he asked, "What's for breakfast then? Any bacon on the menu for your dear old daddy this morning?"

Instantly the girls perked up. "Of course, Daddy!" Amoretta giggled.

He watched as all three of his beautiful daughters hopped up from their seats and began busily preparing breakfast. Lawson savored the way his girls seemed to delight in doing things for him. It was proof of their sweet, serving souls.

He maintained his smile and offered light, worriless conversation as he enjoyed a hearty breakfast with his girls. He'd warned them, and though their countenances were once again happy and bright, Lawson knew his daughters always took him at his word—that they would be wary while they were out and about—and it gave him a measure of comfort.

He would talk with Brake about Kizzy's safety later that day. Just in thinking of the pretty gypsy, Lawson found his flesh warmed and tingled, as if he were no more than a schoolboy with a heavy crush on the new teacher.

"Daddy is more worried than he wants us to think," Evangeline said, tossing a pebble into the creek.

"I know," Amoretta agreed. She sat in the cool grass of the creek bank, studying the soft, velvet-brown cattail she'd broken from its stem at the water's edge. "And if I know Daddy and how he worries, he's thinking, 'I never should've moved the girls here,' and such."

"It is a very disturbing thing," Calliope noted. She was hunkered down at the water's edge watching the last of the season's water skeeters striding hither and yon over the calm surface of water pooled in a small outcropping by the creek. "I feel sorry for Winnie, about her cat…and for that man who lights the lamps at night." Calliope looked up to Evangeline and Amoretta. "Do you really think it's Samuel Mulholland who did it?"

Amoretta shrugged. "I don't know. But after what we witnessed yesterday at the mill…I admit to being very suspicious of him."

"What did you witness yesterday at the mill, ladies?"

Amoretta's entire body warmed at the sound of Brake's voice. She turned and looked up the creek bank a ways to see him making his way toward her and her sisters. Exhaling an audible sigh of pleasure upon seeing him, she smiled—owning a sudden sensation that nothing at all in the world could be worrisome as long as Brake were near her.

"Good afternoon, Mr. McClendon," Evangeline greeted as Brake approached.

"And a good afternoon to you as well, Miss Ipswich," he said, smiling at Evangeline. "What brings you ladies out to this rather isolated spot today?"

It was Calliope who answered. She smiled at Brake as well, saying, "We needed a walk, Mr. McClendon. It's such a lovely day, and considering how beautiful the turning leaves were out by the mill yesterday on our amble, we thought we might try this lovely area near the creek."

"Hmm," Brake hummed with an understanding nod. He looked to Amoretta then. "And you lovely ladies...you say you were out by the gristmill yesterday...ambling?"

"Well...yes," Amoretta admitted at last. "We, all of us girls, took a walk yesterday. After all, we'd been so cooped up during the sewing circle at Pru's house that we just needed to stretch our legs. And lo and behold...somehow we ended up at the gristmill."

"And you didn't come in to say hello to me?" Brake asked, feigning dramatic disappointment.

As Brake stepped forward to stand directly in front of Amoretta, staring down at her with the smoldering allure of his syrupy brown eyes, Amoretta could only stammer, "I...well we...we...there were so many of us. And I'm sure Pru's father wouldn't have approved of our interrupting your work."

"Do you mind if I take her?" Brake asked, still staring at Amoretta. When no one answered—for neither Amoretta nor her sisters were certain of what his question actually meant—he turned, looking to Evangeline and then Calliope. "Do you mind if I steal your sister away from you?" Evangeline and Calliope both smiled, and Brake added, "Will you lend her to me for a few hours so I can take her for a little amble of my own?"

"Oh, you can have her! Right this minute you can have her!" Calliope chirped with delight. "Evie and I, we were getting bored anyway...and Amoretta never gets bored."

Brake chuckled, visibly amused by Calliope's obvious delight in his appearance and request to take Amoretta for a walk.

"Well, thank you, Miss Calliope," Brake said, still smiling. "I'll take good care of her and see that she gets home all safe and sound later on this evenin'. How's that?"

"That'll be fine, Mr. McClendon," Evangeline agreed. "Calliope and I will...well, we'll just be on our way then." Evangeline winked at Amoretta and added, "Have fun, Amoretta." Her smile broadened. "And I'm sure Mr. McClendon will see that you do." Looking to Brake with understanding, she added, "Isn't that right, Mr. McClendon?"

Brake's smile broadened as he said, "Oh, you can be sure of it, Miss Evangeline."

"Let's go then, Evie," Calliope giggled, taking hold of Evangeline's hand. "Right now."

They were gone in a matter of seconds, leaving a blushing Amoretta alone with the man of her dreams.

Still smiling, Brake gazed down into Amoretta's face and said, "Well, that was a might easier than I thought it was gonna be." He reached out, taking her hands in his and raising one of them to his lips. Kissing the back of her hand, he exhaled a pleased sigh, adding, "After all this fuss in town, I wasn't sure they'd leave you alone with me."

Amoretta frowned. "What fuss? Do you mean...do you mean you know about the dead animals?" she asked.

Brake nodded as his smile faded. "Yep. The sheriff come out to the mill and talked to us boys that work out there," he explained. "All he said was that some animals had shown up killed under mysterious circumstances and did any of us know anythin' about it." He shrugged. "Of course, Rowdy Gates told me a bit more once the sheriff was gone. It sounds like somebody around here is a bit off their hinge."

"Yes, it does. And I know Daddy is more worried about it than he's letting on," Amoretta told him. "He talked to us girls about it this morning...told us to stay together or to at least have a companion of some sort when we were away from the house."

"I was thinkin' I better ride out and tell Kizzy about it," Brake said. He shook his head, adding, "I wish she'd just move into town with me. I worry myself sick most nights about her and Shay livin' out there alone."

Amoretta paused a moment, uncertain as to whether she should say what she was thinking of saying. In the end, however, she said it anyway. "I think my daddy...I think he might be sweet on Kizzy," she told him in conspiratorial whisper.

But Brake didn't seem at all surprised. In fact, Amoretta was greatly relieved when he laughed and asked, "And what gave you that idea, darlin'? The fact that he almost knocked me out cold when he found me comin' outta her house?" Amoretta giggled and nodded. "I figured he would tell you about that," he said. "He's a good man, your daddy. He wouldn't keep that from you, considerin'..."

"Considering what?" she prodded.

"Considerin' Kizzy told him a bit about me likin' you so much."

Amoretta smiled—for he'd actually admitted it, right out loud! Brake McClendon had said he liked her! Oh, certainly she knew he did. Just by the kisses they'd shared she knew it. But to hear him say it—it was wonderful!

"I told him a bit more about how much I like you too," she bravely confessed.

Brake's eyes narrowed with being greatly pleased. "Well, that makes me feel better...because Judge Ipswich hasn't come gunnin' for me yet, so I figure he must be somewhat approvin'."

Amoretta smiled and nodded. But then—then she thought of something else, and it caused her expression to grow serious.

"Wh-why *do* you like me?" she asked.

"Why do *you* like *me*?" he playfully countered.

"I asked you first," she countered.

Brake moved closer to her, still holding her hands in his. "Well, do you really want the truth?" he asked. His smile had faded, and Amoretta's anxieties in insecurity began to well in her.

"Y-yes," she answered. "At least...I think I do."

"Then I'll tell you," Brake sighed. He looked away a moment. "I bewitched you, Amoretta Ipswich," he said. "I used an ancient gypsy spell—a love spell—and I bewitched you into liking me."

Amoretta growled, pulled her hands out of his grasp, and playfully smacked him on his broad, muscular chest. "Oh, don't try that 'I'm a gypsy' fiddle-faddle on me, Brake McClendon!" she scolded.

But Brake shrugged. "Why not? It worked wonders last time, remember?"

And indeed Amoretta did remember! How well and marvelously she remembered his playing at being a gifted gypsy who could discern her future with "two bites to a cherry."

"But I mean it, Brake," she somewhat pleaded. "It...it all seems very strange to me—that the moment I saw you through the space in the broken board of the mill—"

"Ah ha!" Brake exclaimed. "I knew it! I knew you girls were up to no good out there that day." He shook his head with amusement. "You girls were out there spyin' on us mill boys, weren't you?"

"That's beside the point," Amoretta answered, attempting to skirt the issue. She started to turn from him, trying to hide her guilty blush, but he took hold of her arms, making certain she could do nothing but look directly up at him.

"Tell me the truth, Amoretta," he demanded. He was firm, but she could see the emotion in his eyes. He simply wanted her to confess. "Tell me you felt it too...that first day we met at the mill. Tell me that when I stopped you outside the mill—when I couldn't quit starin' at you—tell me you were wonderin' where you'd known me before too."

"Actually," she began, suddenly breathless in his presence, "I was too busy wondering how in all the wide, wide world I could ever manage to capture even a moment of your attention when every girl in town was wanting you."

Brake grinned, pleased with what she'd said. "You've had my attention from that very instant, Amoretta," he mumbled. Even though he smiled, his brow puckered a little then. "But...but I can't quite understand it. You all moved here from Boston, and I heard the new judge had three beautiful daughters. I even knew you weren't too happy about bein' in Meadowlark Lake."

Amoretta felt her eyebrows arch in astonishment. "How? How did you know I didn't want to be here...at first?"

"I saw you out in the grass between your house and the woods, the very mornin' of the day we met," he explained. "And you weren't none too happy. I'm just guessin' really...that it was because you didn't want to be here."

"I didn't," she admitted. "In fact, I was miserable about it...until we went to the mill that day."

Again Brake grinned with understanding. He didn't say anything—not one more word—not for long moments. All he did was stare at her with an expression of mischievous gladness.

Then, quite unexpectedly, he took her hand and began leading her along the creek bank. "Come on, Amoretta Ipswich," he mumbled. "Let's me and you take a walk over to Mr. Ackerman's fields."

Amoretta giggled as she followed him. "Why?" she asked. She didn't really care where Brake was taking her. She'd follow him to the ends of the earth if he asked her. But she felt an obligation to inquire.

"You'll see when we get there," he said. "Meanwhile, let me ask you somethin'."

"Yes?"

"How would you feel if...well, if your daddy became sweet enough on my sister to wanna marry her?"

It was an entirely unexpected question, but Amoretta found that the mere idea caused her spirit to soar with delight. "Do you really think he's that sweet on her already?"

Brake chuckled. "From the way he wanted to rip my head clean off when he thought I was a man meanin' to...when he didn't know I was her brother? Absolutely!"

Amoretta sighed. "Then I would think it was a dream come true."

Brake stopped, turned, and looked at her. "I'm glad...because my gypsy instincts are tellin' me—"

"Oh, enough of that, Brake!" Amoretta laughed. "I won't fall for it again. Once was enough to teach me well."

A playful breeze sent several strands of Amoretta's hair streaming across her face, and she smiled as Brake reached out, gently tucking them behind her ear.

"You smell that?" he asked.

Amoretta closed her eyes and inhaled deeply. "Mmmm! The bakery, right?"

"Yep. And fresh-cut crops, autumn leaves. Someone's already got their fire goin' for the night." He paused, inhaling deeply himself. "Whoever it is...they're burnin' pine."

An evening bird called somewhere nearby, and the crickets were beginning their song, even though the sun had barely begun to set. As Amoretta stood with Brake on the banks of the creek, she could hear the breeze through the cattails—the frogs nestled in among them softly croaking. Overhead the colorful leaves of crimson and gold and orange rustled in the same breeze, and Amoretta was certain she caught the scent of cooking pumpkin—of spice and sugar.

"I swear...I think I smell pumpkin," she whispered.

"You do," Brake affirmed. "I was walkin' past the bakery earlier and saw pumpkin pie in the window."

Amoretta sighed as Brake gathered her into his arms and against the warm strength of his body. Gazing up into his unspeakably handsome face, she asked, "Why *do* you like me, Brake? When you could have any girl in town, any girl you set your mind to wanting…why is it you give me your attention?"

But Brake shrugged. "I-I can't explain it…not exactly," he answered. "The best I can do right this minute is to tell you…that you're the only girl I want to give my attention to…the only girl whose attention I want."

Amoretta wasn't elated with his answer, but she wasn't disappointed so much either. She understood what he meant, in truth. She knew she was in love with Brake, but if someone—anyone, including Brake himself—had asked her to explain why, she was quite certain that she wouldn't be able to put it into words either. She saw him, and her heart and soul fell in love with him. It was as simple as that.

"Are you gonna let me kiss you, darlin'?" he asked, smiling down at her. "Or do I need to use one of my gypsy bewitchin' ways again?"

Amoretta's heart fluttered with the wild, delicious anticipation of kissing Brake again. In fact, the sensations of rising desire and passion were so quickly overwhelming her that she was somewhat frightened. She needed a moment—just a moment more to gather herself—or else she feared she'd take to confessing her love to him right then and there!

"Of course I'm going to let you kiss me again, Mr. McClendon," she flirted. "In fact, I want you to."

But as Brake smiled, leaning forward as his head descended toward hers, Amoretta quickly snatched the hat from his head, hitched up her skirt, and bolted off at a dead run in the direction of the Ackerman fields.

"But you have to catch me first!" she called over her shoulder.

Figuring she could burn off some of her desire to kiss Brake all through the night by running a bit, she nearly panicked a moment when the thought crossed her mind that perhaps he wouldn't chase her! Perhaps he'd think she was being too juvenile—snatching his hat and running off like a silly schoolgirl.

But as she paused to glance back, she squealed with delight as she saw Brake right at her heels. He reached out, lunging for her, and Amoretta barely evaded his grasp.

She was a quick little thing—he'd certainly give her that. Brake smiled as he held off catching Amoretta—slowed his stride a bit to ensure that she stayed just out of his reach. He'd let her reach Ackerman fields before overtaking her, but then—well, the chase had caused his blood to run hotter than it had already been running! And he wasn't about to see Amoretta home until he'd had a good, long drink or two of her sweet, impassioned kisses.

Amoretta was breathless as she rather stumbled into Mr. Ackerman's field. She paused a moment, rather astonished to see the haystacks and cornstalks scattered in piles everywhere. Obviously Mr. Ackerman had been harvesting, and now all that was left of the massive fields were piles of cornstalks and haystacks.

"Give me my hat, girl!" Brake growled from behind her.

With one last squeal of delight, Amoretta tried to avoid him once more, but he was fast—faster than he'd been pretending to be—and in the next moment she gasped for breath as he caught her around the waist from behind.

Giggling with pure felicity, Amoretta turned in his arms when he stopped their forward motion. Panting for breath, she smiled at him as she plopped his hat back onto his head, tapping it firmly with one palm.

"So you caught me," she breathed as his eyes narrowed, their smolder warming her heart. "Now what?"

Brake grinned. "Well, I did have a purpose in comin' here, you know."

"Really?" she giggled. "And what would that be?"

Brake smiled and leaned forward, kissing her quickly on the mouth. "You ever been for a tumble in the hay, Amoretta Ipswich?"

"What?" Amoretta asked.

She squealed, giggling uncontrollably as Brake suddenly took her waist between his powerful hands, lifted her off her feet, and pushed her back into a nearby haystack.

"Now kiss me," he growled demandingly. He placed a long, moist, heated kiss to Amoretta's neck. "I caught you, girl...so kiss me."

Again his mouth lingered at her neck. Amoretta was vaguely aware of sweet-smelling, dry hay showering over her, but only vaguely aware—for Brake's hands still gripped her waist as his mouth toyed with her neck, her chin, her cheeks.

Somehow he'd managed to maneuver her body so that she sat back in the haystack, as he stood lavishing her with worshipping kisses.

Taking his face between her small hands and holding him away from her a moment, Amoretta studied the deep brown of Brake's eyes. Her heart leapt at the desire she saw flaming there—the desire for *her*! Slowly she caressed his lips with her thumbs, her hands trembling for want of having his kiss—for want of owning his heart!

Almost frantically, Amoretta pulled Brake's face to hers, kissing him with a confidence and ravenous wanting she would never have imagined lay hidden in her mere months before! The hay continued to sift down over them both, but Amoretta didn't care. As Brake's mouth melded to hers, demanding impassioned reciprocation, Amoretta melted against him—surrendered in his arms to his strong, powerful embrace.

Over and over he kissed her, sometimes softly with a teasing sort of gentleness as his hands caressed her throat or his fingers wove through her hair. Yet mostly his kisses were driven, hot, and moist—ambitious—sending Amoretta's senses racing with a blissful euphoria.

Brake and Amoretta lingered in the haystack in Ackerman fields—between whispers and laughter—between questions and not caring for answers—between light caresses, desperate embraces, and ripe, impassioned kisses. And as the sun set and the silver moon rose in the clear night sky—as a million stars winked overhead and every scent of harvest and autumn drifted through the air like an ambrosia sent from heaven—Amoretta Ipswich knew that either by chance or by means of gypsy magic, Brake McClendon had bewitched her—and he would own her forever.

CHAPTER THIRTEEN

Lawson yawned, stretched, and yawned again. He was tired. He'd been "visiting" with people in Meadowlark Lake all day long—just trying to stumble across something that might give him and Dennison Montrose some clue as to who was killing animals and leaving them in morbid piles to be found.

Evangeline and Calliope had returned from their walk about an hour before—but without Amoretta. Still, Lawson wasn't too worried about Amoretta walking with Brake McClendon after sundown. Lawson was an excellent judge of character, and he knew Brake was a good man. He even mused that Amoretta was probably safer in Brake's company than in the company of any other man. After all, Brake knew how a man could ruin a woman's life. He knew it firsthand because of Kizzy and Shay.

Thus, Lawson decided that he wouldn't allow himself to become too worried about Amoretta, at least until the hour grew much later or until Evangeline and Calliope returned from playing whist over at the Montrose home. And when Brake escorted Amoretta back home, Lawson would have an opportunity to discuss Kizzy and Shay's safety with him—the danger posed by the recent animal slaughterings and Lawson's worry over Kizzy's vulnerability living in the woods alone.

Raking one hand through his dark hair, Lawson pulled the suspenders from his shoulders and began unbuttoning his shirt. Everything he'd learned from every person he talked to in town that day was bouncing around in his head like a swarm of startled grasshoppers. He knew if he didn't relax and settle his mind soon, he'd end up with a throbbing headache and another sleepless night.

He tossed his shirt onto the chair in one corner of his bedroom and began to unbutton his trousers. But a sudden and frantic knocking at the front door caused him to groan and refasten the button at his waist.

"What the hell is it now?" he grumbled as he strode through the parlor and toward the front door. Had Dennison found another heap of slaughtered animals? It was his first thought—and why shouldn't it be? He and Dennison had spent nearly twelve hours with the citizens of Meadowlark Lake that day.

Consequently, when he pulled open the front door to find none other than Kizzy and Shay McClendon standing on his front porch trembling and weeping, his mouth gaped open a moment in astonishment.

"Kizzy?" he asked. It was obvious who was at the door, but Lawson was so astonished to find the beautiful young woman and her daughter standing before him instead of Dennison Montrose that he wondered (for just an instant) if he had perhaps fallen asleep already and was dreaming.

"J-Judge Ipswich," Kizzy stammered through her tears, "I-I'm so very sorry to bother you…to intrude on your evenin' like this. B-but Brake isn't at home…and I didn't know where else to go!"

The woman was obviously distraught. In truth, she owned an expression of being terrified.

Without pause, he reached out, taking hold of her arm and pulling her into the house, with Shay desperately clinging to her skirts. "Come in at once," he said, closing the door behind them. A deep frown furrowed his brow as he asked, "What's happened?"

"Well, I-I…we returned home this evenin'," Kizzy began, wringing her hands. "Shay and I were stargazing just after sunset, and when we returned home…"

"Yes?" Lawson prodded when she paused. He was battling the urge to gather the woman and her child into his arms to offer reassurance. Yet he knew that patience was of the utmost importance in those moments, and so he folded his arms across his broad chest and listened.

"Well, when we returned home…" Kizzy began, tears filling her eyes once more.

"Somebody stoled our kittens, Mr. Judge!" Shay cried out as sobbing overtook her.

"What?" Lawson asked. A cold shiver of trepidation traveled up his spine as he envisioned the piles of dead animals he and the sheriff had observed.

Shay nodded as Kizzy brushed tears from her cheeks. "It's true!" the child sobbed. "Someone took them right outta their bed! Mama can smell that somebody has been in our house—somebody that shouldn't be in it!" Shay sobbed and rubbed at her eyes. "And we can't find 'em…not one kitty…not even Molly!"

As little Shay's lower lip extended into a pout that would've won over the devil himself, Lawson felt exactly as if some powerful fist had reached into his chest, had taken hold of his heart, and was squeezing with a vise's grip.

"Come here, baby," he said then, unable to bridle his protective nature any longer. Reaching down and picking up the distraught little girl, Lawson felt a long-absent but very familiar warmth wash over him: the emotional warmth that holding a small child offered an adult. Shay hadn't paused when he'd taken her from her mother but rather wrapped her arms around Lawson's neck and her legs around his waist in a desperate sort of clinging.

"I'm sorry about your kitties, sweetie," Lawson soothed, stroking the girl's hair a moment as she cried on his shoulder. "Maybe they just went off for a stroll with their mama."

Shay sniffled, raised her head from Lawson's shoulders, and looked at him. "You mean…maybe they went stargazing too?"

Lawson forced a reassuring smile. "Maybe that's it exactly."

Shay nodded and sniffled again. A slight smile began to curve her sweet little lips.

"Yep. I'll bet that's just it. Your mama cat—"

"Molly," the child interrupted instructively.

Lawson chuckled and then began again. "Yes…Molly. Maybe Molly took her kitties on a walk just like your mama did you." Broadening his smile and wondering if offering false hope to the child were the right thing to do, Lawson added, "We'll sort it all out in the morning."

"Okeydokey," Shay said. She sighed and laid her head on Lawson's shoulder once more. He could feel her rigid little body begin to relax against him.

"Meanwhile, you and your mama can stay here with me and my little girls tonight," Lawson announced—surprising even himself.

"Oh no! No, no, Judge Ipswich!" Kizzy argued, shaking her head emphatically as she brushed more tears from her cheeks.

Lawson turned to see an expression akin to panic on her pretty face.

"We couldn't possibly do that!" she assured him. "Brake will be home soon, and…and anyway, I would never risk soiling your reputation in any manner. I know it was dangerous for me to even come here…but I didn't know where else to go. No one else would've—"

"Nonsense," Lawson interrupted. "That's what friends are for, Miss Kizzy—to offer assistance to one another when assistance is needed."

"But, Judge, Shay and I…we can't possibly—" Kizzy began to argue again, wringing her hands with anxiety.

"My name is Lawson, and I'll not see you two young ladies traipsing through the dark at night when kittens are missing," Lawson interrupted. He smiled at Shay and bounced her once, asking, "Isn't that right?"

Shay nodded, repeating, "No traipsin' around in the dark when kitties are missin'."

He smiled as Shay snuggled against him once more. Looking directly at Kizzy with an expression that conveyed that it was pointless for her to argue, he continued, "You and Shay can sleep in

Evangeline's room. Evangeline and Amoretta can share a bed tonight. All will be well with it."

"B-but...I can't possibly..." Kizzy began.

Ignoring her attempt at dispute, however, Lawson simply turned, carrying Shay as he strode to the rocking chair sitting across from the sofa in the parlor.

Sitting down, he nodded toward the sofa and said, "Have a seat, Kizzy. The girls will be home soon...and no doubt will take to codling you like you were a toddler." Kizzy paused, obviously still uncertain as to what to do. But Lawson smiled at her, nodded toward the sofa once more, and said, "Go on. Sit down and try to relax a bit. All right?"

Still wringing her hands, however, Kizzy still paused.

"Do you know any songs, Mr. Judge?" Shay asked as she maneuvered to cuddle up in Lawson's lap.

"Some," Lawson answered, smiling and awkwardly tucking a strand of stray hair behind her ear.

"Will you sing one to me?" the child asked, snuggling against him.

"Of course," Lawson agreed with a chuckle. "As soon as your mother has a seat on my sofa there." Lawson nodded toward the sofa a third time.

"B-but—" Kizzy continued to argue.

"Oh, sit down, Mama," Shay sighed with impatience. "We'll sort it all out in the mornin' like Mr. Judge says."

Lawson looked to Kizzy and smiled with reassurance. He watched as Kizzy exhaled a heavy sigh of defeat and stiffly took a seat on comfortable piece of furniture.

"Thank you, Miss Kizzy," Lawson said, smiling at her.

"And now for my song," Shay reminded, squirming in Lawson's lap until she was perfectly comfortable.

Lawson smiled as Shay's dark, springy curls tickled his chest just over his heart. The child was so sweet and trusting. He couldn't abide the thought of her ever being unhappy or frightened.

"Ah yes, your song," he said with a chuckle.

He looked to Kizzy again, winking with reassurance as the woman mouthed, *I'm so sorry*, to him.

"There's one song in particular that my own little girls used to favor. I used to sing it to them when they were your age, sweetie," Lawson told Shay.

Shay giggled. "I like the way your voice sounds in your chest, Mr. Judge."

Lawson chuckled once more and began rocking the chair ever so slightly as he cleared his throat.

"Now, I'm not sure how this will sound, Shay," he warned the little girl. "I haven't sung it in a while."

"It will sound perfect, Mr. Judge," Shay sighed. "If your own little girls liked it, then I know I will too."

The confidence and faith of a child—it was always something encouraging.

Inhaling a deep breath to boost his confidence (for Lawson had only just realized that Kizzy would hear him singing as well), Lawson began singing the simple song that all three of his own daughters still loved to hear him sing.

There were three little girls dressed in blue.
Then one married and left only two.
Then one fell in love with a boy,
Who loved her and gave her much joy.
Then the last little girl had a dream,
And she dreamed she was saying, "I do."
And when she awoke it was true!
Happy three little girls dressed in blue.

"Well, honey?" Lawson asked once he'd finished. "Did you like that song?"

Shay looked up at him—gazed at him through her mother's beautiful eyes. "I loved it!" she sighed with delight. "Will you sing it again? At least five times?"

"Shay!" Kizzy exclaimed, visibly embarrassed by Shay's forthrightness.

But Lawson only winked at Kizzy again as he answered Shay, "Of course, sweetie. I'll sing it as many times as you like."

Shay sighed, nestled against Lawson again, and said, "Thank you, Mr. Judge. And just in case I fall asleep or somethin' while you're singin', good night, Mr. Judge...and green beans."

Lawson frowned with puzzled curiosity. *Green beans?* he mouthed to Kizzy.

Smiling, she mouthed, *She means sweet dreams*, in return.

Lawson laughed, and Shay repeated, "Green beans, Mr. Judge."

"Green beans, honey," Lawson answered. He'd forgotten how entirely amusing little children were with their misunderstanding of words and phrases. Shay McClendon was simply enchanting.

"You can start singin' whenever you're ready, Mr. Judge," Shay hinted.

Again Lawson chuckled, as Kizzy shook her head and blushed with humiliation.

"All right then...at least five times, you say?" Lawson asked.

"At least," Shay confirmed.

Clearing his throat once more, Lawson sang:

There were three little girls dressed in blue.
Then one married and left only two.
Then one fell in love with a boy,
Who loved her and gave her much joy.
Then the last little girl had a dream,
And she dreamed she was saying, "I do."
And when she awoke it was true!
Happy three little girls dressed in blue.

Kizzy stared at the honorable county judge, Lawson Ipswich, sitting in a rocking chair, his suspenders hanging down from his waist and his marvelously chiseled torso bare for all the world to see—just sitting in a rocking chair, rocking her daughter and singing the sweetest little song Kizzy had ever heard.

The tears brimming in her eyes—the tears spilling over her cheeks—were no longer borne of fear and distress but of wonder, tender feelings, and amazement. There he sat, just rocking Shay as if it were the most natural thing in the world. Judge Ipswich—the illegally handsome man, whose physical strength and sculpted muscles had seemingly only improved with maturity.

As ever when she found herself in Judge Ipswich's company, Kizzy's stomach was rolling with waves of butterflies—the mad fluttering in her bosom causing her to be slightly breathless. He was so very handsome—the most handsome man Kizzy had ever known! And beyond being physically attractive, he owned a beautiful, magnificent, wise, kind, and heroic soul.

Kizzy wondered again if Lawson Ipswich had never remarried because his heart never healed from the loss of his wife. Certainly Kizzy was not worthy of the heart of a man like Lawson Ipswich—though in truth, Lawson was just the sort of man she'd always dreamt of belonging to. It went beyond that even. Kizzy knew that Lawson Ipswich was *just* the man she'd always dreamt of belonging to.

Still, she was no fool. Even if the judge could see past her seeming youthfulness, her past was scarlet.

Of course, Brake had chided Kizzy to near madness over the years about the fact that God had forgiven her long ago, but she could not forgive herself. Such conversations with Brake—or, rather, lectures from Brake—always ended with Kizzy rolling her eyes and telling him that she knew it was true (even though she could never quite believe it).

But as she sat on Judge Ipswich's comfortable sofa—as she listened to him singing to Shay, watched him raise Shay's tiny hand to his lips and kiss her fingers as she clung to his thumb—Kizzy began to dream that perhaps one day she could capture his attention, his heart.

She quickly shook her head in an effort to dispel such ridiculous notions, however. Lawson Ipswich—handsome, strong, a judge, for pity's sake! Sighing with discouragement, she looked from Lawson and Shay and their tender moment to the interior of the Ipswich home.

Cozy, welcoming, warm—those were the first words to pop into Kizzy's mind as she glanced about the parlor, peering into the kitchen. She could feel it was a happy home; she could actually feel the love Lawson owned for his daughters and the love and respect they owned for him. The warm feelings of love, comfort, and security only made more tears well in Kizzy's eyes.

"*There were three little girls dressed in blue,*" Judge Ipswich began once more. The fact that he'd lowered his singing to a near whisper instantly drew her attention back to him. Kizzy's mouth gaped open a little as she saw that Shay's eyes were already closed, a tender grin of pure respite donning her sweet little lips.

"*Then one married and left only two,*" he continued. The sound of his low, masculine, entirely beguiling voice caused goose bumps to break over Kizzy's arms. She listened as Judge Ipswich continued to rock Shay as his voice grew softer and softer—until he'd finished the song at last.

"We'll put her in Evangeline's room," he whispered to Kizzy. "Would you mind helping me turn the bed down for her?"

"Oh!" Kizzy startled, nervously hopping to her feet. "N-not at all."

Judge Ipswich stood and began striding out of the parlor and down the hall. He nodded, indicating a door on his left, and Kizzy hurried to open it.

"Why don't you light the lamp and turn it low…just in case she stirs and wakes up?" the judge suggested in a whisper.

"Oh! Yes…of course," Kizzy mumbled.

The lace curtains at the window were parted, allowing the moonlight into the room. Quickly, and with trembling hands, Kizzy went to the little table next to the bed, fumbling with the tin of stick matches there and lighting the lamp. She turned to see the judge standing in the doorway, smiling at her. He seemed amused—or pleased. Kizzy wasn't sure which, but he seemed to be waiting for something.

"Oh!" she gasped, remembering that he'd asked her to turn down the bed for Shay. "I'm so sorry. I'm just so terribly rattled about all this!" she exclaimed in a whisper.

Kizzy's hands were trembling even more violently as she turned down the lovely pink and cream nine-patch quilt and soft white sheets. Judge Ipswich strode to the bed and gently laid Shay there. He smiled as a soft snore escaped Shay's little nose and smoothed her hair from her face as he studied her a moment.

"She's a beautiful little girl, Miss Kizzy," he whispered. He looked to Kizzy then, and her heart leapt in her bosom as his eyes narrowed with an expression of something akin to desire. "Just like her mother."

Kizzy gulped the lump of nervousness in her throat. Forcing a smile, she turned her attention to Shay—to unlacing her little shoes. Certainly she would never put her daughter to bed with her shoes on. Carefully, so as to disturb Shay as little as possible, Kizzy removed her shoes and stockings and then tucked her neatly beneath the sheets and quilt.

She smiled herself as she studied Shay a moment. For all that had happened, all the pain and judgment Kizzy had endured, she truly couldn't imagine a life without Shay—wouldn't want a life without her.

Kizzy startled when she felt the judge take hold of her arm.

She turned to look at him, and he smiled at her. "Come on," he whispered. "Come and have a seat and tell me more about what happened."

Even if she'd wanted to run (but she didn't) or to deny his command, she couldn't have. She was entirely at his mercy, entirely under some spell he'd cast over her. She shouldn't be in his house—not alone. She shouldn't have come to him at all, but she had. And now—now she felt as if she would never be able to leave! In that moment, all Kizzy wanted was to stay with Lawson Ipswich, to stare at him for the rest of her life and pretend he could love her.

As Kizzy followed the judge back to the parlor, she wondered if she and Brake were both losing their wits! Who in his right mind fell in love at first sight? No one! Yet Brake had. He'd told her so himself—that the moment he'd seen Amoretta Ipswich, he wanted nothing to do with any other woman ever again. Kizzy had felt the same when she'd first met Judge Ipswich. She'd wanted him instantly—wanted his affections, his love—to marry him, live with him, sleep in his arms, and bear his children.

Kizzy rolled her eyes as she returned to her seat on the sofa. Bear his children—how ridiculous of her to even think it. Lawson Ipswich already had three children—three grown-up children. And why in all the world would he want any more?

"Tell me," the judge said then, astonishing Kizzy as he sat not in the rocking chair across from the sofa but right next to her. He leaned back, stretching one strong, muscular arm across the back of the sofa—all the while looking at her, a sturdy frown at his handsome brow.

Kizzy gulped, wishing he'd at least take the time to put on a shirt. His nearness while being so half-dressed was far too affecting on her sense of attraction to him. She wondered what his skin felt like—whether it were warm and soft or...

"Tell me exactly what happened...exactly what you found when you returned home this evening," Judge Ipswich kindly demanded, snapping Kizzy's attention back to the issue at hand.

"W-well," she began, "as I said, Shay and I had gone stargazin'. We'd gone for a stroll and watched the stars beginnin' to wink in the night sky."

Lawson grinned. She was lovely—absolutely lovely! Everything about her, even the way she described stars.

Kizzy's tears had stopped for the moment, but the lingering fear was still obvious in the way she sat on the edge of the sofa, nervously wringing her hands. Lawson wished he could soothe her as easily as he was able to soothe her daughter. He wished he could take pretty Kizzy McClendon in his arms, hold her, kiss her forehead, her cheeks, her lips, and tell her that all would be well as long as she stayed with him.

"And when we returned to the house," Kizzy continued, "the door was open. We'd left it closed. We never leave it open when we're away…not even in summer when it's hot out."

"And Shay said you could tell someone had been inside," Lawson prodded.

"Yes," Kizzy affirmed. "In fact, I was afraid to go in at first. But Shay wanted to check on Molly and the kittens, so I just went on in, prayin' that no one was there." She paused a moment and then went on. "I could smell something odd…the instant I stepped further into the house. It was a smell like…" She paused, looking at him with a frown puckering her pretty eyebrows. "Have you had a mouse die in your house or somethin' like that? It smelled like that…like a dead mouse."

Immediately, Lawson's sense of alarm leapt back to the forefront of his mind. A smell like a dead mouse? Or perhaps a dead rat—dead rats?"

"I began lookin' around for any evidence of someone havin' been inside," Kizzy added. "And that was when Shay came runnin' back into the kitchen, cryin' her eyes out, because Molly and the kittens were gone." Tears spilled from her eyes once more as she asked, "Who would steal a mama cat and seven kittens?"

Lawson exhaled a heavy sigh. Silently he scolded himself for not having gone out to see Kizzy himself earlier in the day. He didn't suspect her of anything to do with the dead animals, of course, and since she rarely talked to any of the people in town, he rather assumed she wouldn't know anything pertinent to the situation. Now, however, he was angry that he hadn't gone out and told her what was going on.

"I was frightened, and I didn't know what to do," she continued. "So Shay and I hurried over to Brake's house…but he wasn't home."

"He's with Amoretta," Lawson explained.

He was pleased when Kizzy smiled for a moment, saying, "Oh, good! That makes me feel so much better. That lightens my heart greatly."

Lawson smiled, nodded, and then said, "So you came here because you know Amoretta...and you know me."

Kizzy blushed and bit her lip, suddenly seeming quite bashful. "Well, I didn't really think about Amoretta," she confessed. "I was frightened, and with Brake unavailable...I...I...thought of you." She paused and then hurried on. "You did say if there was ever anythin' you could do for Shay and me—"

"I did say that," Lawson affirmed. "And I meant it. Furthermore, I'm very pleased that you felt you could come to me, Miss Kizzy." Lawson leaned forward then—closer to her. "And...and I hope that after what I feel I need to tell you...you won't be too angry with me. I just didn't realize that—"

"What is it?" Kizzy interrupted, her face draining of color—as if she were afraid of what he was going to say.

What did he mean to tell her? That he could see how she felt for him, that he could read it in her eyes, and that he could never feel the same for her? Kizzy held her breath as Judge Ipswich inhaled a deep breath.

"There have been two incidents in town of recent, Miss Kizzy," he began. She still couldn't breathe. "Sheriff Montrose and I haven't really mentioned them to people...not in detail. But I see now that perhaps I should've told you sooner about them, considering the isolation you and Shay live in."

"Incidents? What happened?" Kizzy asked, realizing with relief that the judge was referring to something other than the fact he could never reciprocate her feelings toward him. Kizzy waited, her hands beginning to tremble once more.

"Someone has been slaughtering small animals—wild and domesticated animals—and seemingly for no good reason," he told her. "Sheriff Montrose found the first heap of them—foxes, cats, a dog—not too long ago. In fact..." He looked up to her, his mesmerizing eyes narrowed with concern. "He found them the day before I met you and Shay," he said, as if confessing a dark secret. "That was why I came to introduce myself that morning. Sherriff Montrose thought one of us should speak to you because...well, because..."

"Because he suspected the gypsy woman in the woods might have somethin' to do with it," Kizzy finished for him.

"Yes," Judge Ipswich admitted. He exhaled a heavy sigh of discouragement.

"It's all right, Judge Ipswich," Kizzy whispered. "I'm not offended. In fact, I'm used to such things."

But Judge Ipswich shook his head. "Whether or not you're used to it doesn't make the fact that people instantly suspect those who are different as soon as something—"

"You said 'incidents,'" she interrupted. He was uncomfortable— owning guilt for something he shouldn't own guilt about. And she didn't want him to linger in inwardly scolding himself.

"Yes," the judge said. "Just this morning...well, last night, in truth. Rowdy Gates found another heap of dead animals—his own dog, the Montroses' cat...and a hoard of rats."

"Rats?" Kizzy exclaimed, suddenly jumping up from the sofa. "Rats? That's what I smelled in my house this evenin'!"

"And that's why I'm concerned," Judge Ipswich confirmed.

"And Shay's cat and kittens are gone!" Kizzy continued to exclaim. Remembering Shay was asleep in another room, she lowered her voice, adding, "You think whoever it was came into our house, took Shay's kittens, and..." But Kizzy found she couldn't speak her thoughts aloud; they were too horrifying.

"I don't know anything for certain," Judge Ipswich said. Rising to his feet, he took hold of Kizzy's shoulders. Looking directly into her eyes, he spoke earnestly. "I just think that it's a bit too coincidental that your cat and kittens have turned up missing...and that whomever was in your home left the stench of dead rats in his wake."

Closing her eyes and covering her mouth with both hands to keep from sobbing, Kizzy wept. *Poor Molly! Her poor babies*, she thought.

"Kizzy," the judge said. At the sound of him addressing her by her first name, Kizzy opened her eyes and looked at him. "You and Shay...you need to move into town."

Instantly, however, Kizzy began shaking her head. "No! No, I won't do that. I won't have Brake's reputation spoiled. Especially now that he and Amoretta—"

"It's not safe for you alone in the woods right now," the judge interrupted. "Just move into town. And if you're worried about Brake...first of all, he's a big boy, and I'm fairly positive he can handle anything that comes along. But second, if you just can't risk his reputation, then move into town and don't tell anybody Brake's your brother. I can't have you and Shay out there when someone's mind may be fracturing."

Kizzy frowned as understanding rinsed over her with nauseating force. "You think whoever this is...you think animals are just where they've started, don't you? You're afraid they may harm people next!" She was frantic—frantic about Brake—frantic about poor Molly and her kittens. "I have to go," she said. "Can Shay stay here with you while I go find Brake...or...or look for poor Molly? I can't just sit here waitin'. I—"

"You're not going anywhere, Kizzy," Judge Ipswich rather growled at her. "You'll stay right here where I'm sure you're safe...at least until morning, until Brake can be with you."

"I'm not good for your reputation either, Judge," she said, straightening her posture and forcing her tears to cease. "If anyone ever finds out that I've been here with you...alone..."

"We're not alone," he interrupted. "Your daughter is in the other room. And besides, I don't care what people think. I never have."

"Just please stay with Shay until I can find Brake," Kizzy said, starting for the door. She would not be responsible for ruining Lawson Ipswich's reputation. "I'll find him, and he can come and help me take Shay home. He can stay the night with us and then—"

But as she reached out, taking hold of the door latch, intending to open it, leave, and go out in search of her brother, Lawson Ipswich's powerful hands slammed down against the door on either side of her head.

"I said you're staying the night, Kizzy," he firmly reiterated.

Slowly—ever so slowly, for her heart was pounding like a hammer—Kizzy turned to face Judge Ipswich. He stood before her, leaning forward as his hands remained on the door at either side of her. His eyes were smoldering with a sort of angry determination—or some sort of primal protective instinct she couldn't quite discern. He was so close she could smell him—the scent of soap and wood smoke on his skin. He was so close to her that she could feel the heat coming off his body—feel his breath on her forehead and in her hair.

Oh, why had he been brought to Meadowlark Lake to tempt her, to break her heart without even trying or knowing?

"A-all right," Kizzy stammered in a whisper. She was not frightened of him in those moments. In fact, she was grateful for his dominant strength. But she was trembling—trembling from the warm desire that being so near to him was causing in her.

"All right," he repeated. He sighed, seeming satisfied with her answer. Yet he did not move, as she'd expected he would. He didn't ask her to sit on the sofa or whether she wanted to retire to the room where Shay was sleeping. He simply stood there—oh, so close to her—his hands still on the door, as if he meant to keep her there.

Judge Ipswich's eyes narrowed again as he studied her slowly from head to toe. "Do you know…" he began. His voice was low and somehow provocative. "Do you know that you're the most beautiful woman I've ever seen in all my life?"

Kizzy blushed, glancing away a moment. "A face can be deceivin', you know."

"I'm not just referring to your face, Kizzy," he said. "I mean *you*…all of you. You're the most beautiful woman I've seen in all my life—your face, your form, your smile, your spirit, your strength."

Kizzy was sure she was dreaming—she had to be! Or else she was imagining the desire she saw smoldering in Judge Lawson Ipswich's eyes, the adoring admiration as he looked at her.

"You feel sorry for me," she told him, for she did not dare to believe him. "It's your pity for me that—"

"I don't feel sorry for you," he interrupted, however. "I worry about you. I fear for you, for you and Shay. And I fear for myself…constantly dreading the day when one of the handsome young men in this town wins your heart."

Kizzy shook her head a little, whispering, "You can't mean to say—"

"I know. I know that to you, I'm old…more near to being a father figure than—"

The judge fell silent when Kizzy reached up, taking his handsome, whiskery face between her small hands. "No! No! I don't think that way about you at all. I swear it!"

One corner of the judge's delicious-looking mouth quirked in a hopeful but disbelieving grin. "Are you sure?"

Kizzy's knees grew weak as she gently caressed his face with her fingers. This was it; she felt it in the very depths of her soul! This was her one chance to be happy—the one chance to convince Judge Lawson Ipswich that she was *not* too young for him, that she could love him the way he'd never been loved before! Somehow heaven had helped her to capture his attention, and she knew that if she weren't brave in that moment, the most beautiful happiness she could ever hope for in this life or the next might be lost.

Gathering all the courage left in her, Kizzy gazed into the alluring eyes of the county judge and began, "I'm…I'm not…I'm very…I know that in your eyes I'm very young and naive, that my past is not as it should be, and that I should never even hope you would ever…"

Potent, passionate, perfect! It was how the judge's first kiss felt to Kizzy McClendon. She wasn't even sure how he'd managed it, but somehow, between her ridiculous babbling and caressing his face, Lawson Ipswich had gathered her into the incredible strength of his arms, pulling her body flush with his and claiming her mouth with his own! There was no tender, careful approach—no timidity or fear of rejection. Judge Ipswich was a powerful man, and his kiss was just as powerful!

Tears streamed over Kizzy's temples and cheeks as she met him with her own wanting kiss. She would not be bashful—not now—not when she was wrapped in his arms. Her arms were around him as well, holding him as tightly, as desperately as she could—meeting his ravenous mouth kiss for kiss with her own appetite for his affection.

The skin of his shoulders and back was soft, smooth, and warm. The sense of it comforted her in the same moment it exhilarated every sense she owned! His arms released her, his hands going to her waist as he lifted her off her feet. Quickly carrying her to the kitchen table, Kizzy smiled as she kissed the judge, for he plopped her down promptly, continuing then to kiss her madly as her face was now at the level of his.

The judge broke the seal of their lips a moment, scattering moist, hot kisses along Kizzy's neck and throat. Was it real? she wondered. Was she really sitting on Judge Ipswich's kitchen table as he rained passion over her? Did he truly care that much for her—enough to want her for more than just one night of seduction? Surely he did not.

But then he paused and took her face between his hands, gazing into her eyes for long moments.

"You don't think I'm too old for you?" he mumbled, staring at her mouth.

"You don't think I'm too young for *you*?" she asked, smiling at him as she stared at his mouth.

He smiled, his beautiful eyes sparkling with desire. "Age is irrelevant in matters such as these...or so I've always been told."

Kizzy smiled and buried her fingers in his soft, dark hair the way she'd wanted to since the moment she first saw him. "Then kiss me, Judge Ipswich...because I've never felt the way I did the moment you just kissed—"

But Kizzy's words were lost, silenced by Lawson's claiming her mouth again. She was beautiful—and she tasted it! Her berry lips were sweeter than anything he'd ever tasted, and suddenly, he didn't care that he was old enough to be her father—for he was old enough and experienced enough to be her lover, and that's what he meant to be. As Kizzy's arms encircled his neck—as she snuggled against him, meeting him mouth claim for claim in kissing—Lawson swore to himself he would have her! He'd be her lover, her husband, the father of her little girl, and whatever else she wanted from him. Lawson would own Kizzy's heart in the end—or in the very least, he'd die trying.

CHAPTER FOURTEEN

The cheerful sound of Evangeline, Amoretta, and Calliope chattering and giggling as they noisily bounded up the front porch steps and through the front door made Lawson chuckle. He sat on the sofa in the parlor (fully dressed, for he knew it would not be a good thing for his daughters to return home to find their father only half-clothed with the beautiful gypsy from the woods in his company), softly conversing with Kizzy, sitting in the rocking chair across from him.

Certainly Lawson had wanted nothing more than to continue kissing Kizzy, but he'd managed to find enough sense to think clearly for a moment and separate from her in preparation for his daughters' return. He winked at her as the girls came bursting into the parlor, pulling themselves up short the moment they saw Kizzy sitting in the rocking chair.

Evangeline and Calliope stood, mouths gaping for a moment as they simply stared at Kizzy. Amoretta, however, squealed with delight and raced forward.

"Kizzy!" she exclaimed, bending down to throw her arms around Kizzy's neck in an affectionate embrace. "What are you doing here?"

"W-well...it's a long story," Kizzy stammered.

Amoretta gasped with realization then. "Where's Shay? She's with you, isn't she?"

Kizzy nodded, and Lawson noted the manner in which she began wringing her hands with anxiety as she glanced beyond Amoretta for a moment to Evangeline and Calliope.

"She's...she's actually asleep—" Kizzy began.

"In Evangeline's room, Amoretta," Lawson finished. "There's been a disturbing incident out at Miss Kizzy's home, and she and her daughter will be staying the night with us."

"What?" Amoretta asked, obviously horrified.

"What happened, Daddy?" Evangeline asked, stepping forward at last.

Calliope strode to Kizzy, smiled, and breathed, "Oh my! You're beautiful, ma'am!"

Kizzy blushed and instantly began to apologize. "I'm so sorry for inconveniencin' all of you like this...but I-I didn't know where else to go. The only other person I know in town wasn't home."

Kizzy knowingly looked to Amoretta, and Amoretta blushed, whispering, "I'm so sorry, Kizzy!"

Lawson explained then, for he knew it was his place. Furthermore, Kizzy was far too anxious in the company of his daughters—at the moment.

"Evangeline, Calliope...this is Miss Kizzy," he began. "She and her daughter, Shay, live in the house in the woods. And tonight, she and her daughter were out for a stroll—stargazing and what have you. When they returned home, it was to find that their house had been intruded upon...and their cat and kittens missing."

Amoretta gasped, "Molly and the kittens?"

Evangeline's brow puckered as she looked to Amoretta. "And how is it you know so much about all this, and we don't?"

Kizzy could not endure it any longer! She loved Lawson Ipswich, and because she loved him, she did not want to keep his daughters from the truth.

Therefore, she rather unexpectedly (even to herself) blurted out, "Brake McClendon is my brother...though no one in all of Meadowlark Lake knows anything about it, except for your father and Amoretta."

Evangeline's eyebrows arched with astonishment, but Calliope giggled with delight.

"Oh, how positively delicious!" Calliope exclaimed. "A secret...a wonderful, delicious secret that I'm part of now!"

Kizzy couldn't help but smile as Calliope quickly sat down at her feet and, smiling up at her, added, "And I won't tell a living soul...not as long as you tell me not to."

"Me neither," Evangeline added with a smile. Her smile faded quickly, however, as she added, "But...but this business about someone taking your cats? Intruding in your home? Oh! You must've been terrified!" Evangeline reached down, taking one of Kizzy's hands in her own. "You did the best thing you could've under those horrible, frightening circumstances. You came to us. You came to Daddy."

"Yes," Amoretta agreed, smiling. "I'm so glad you came here, Kizzy."

Kizzy McClendon was overwhelmed! She'd never been treated with such kindness, welcomed with such willing and open arms. At least not in some years—not since Shay had been born.

Tears welled in her eyes again, and she whispered, "Thank you, Amoretta." Looking to Calliope and Evangeline, she added, "Thank you so much. But I must confess to you girls that...I am not the kind of woman people look kindly on. I have a little girl, and she doesn't have a father and—"

"Oh yes, Shay!" Amoretta exclaimed. "Can we sneak in and see her? Oh, Evie and Calliope will just die of adoration when they see her! Oh, please, Kizzy...we'll be very quiet."

"Oh yes! May we? How old is she?" Evangeline asked.

"F-four years old," Kizzy stammered, confused at the reaction the Ipswich girls were having to her confession of having a child out of wedlock. They didn't seem to give the fact a second thought—only wanted to see Shay.

"Oh please, Miss Kizzy!" Calliope begged. "We won't wake her, I promise."

Lawson chuckled, and Kizzy looked up to him once more. "You better let them peek in on her, or they won't let you have a moment's peace."

"Well...of course you can see her," Kizzy answered. "But...I don't understand..."

With giggles and quiet squeals of delight, however, Lawson's daughters were quietly racing down the hallway toward Evangeline's room.

Kizzy looked to Lawson—stared at him in confused disbelief. "Are they this acceptin' of everyone they meet?"

"Only when they sense a person's goodness instantly," he answered, grinning at her with understanding. "And all three of them are simply wild about little children. Like me, Kizzy, they won't judge Shay's origins. But I guarantee you that they will spoil her rotten if you allow it." Lawson smiled, adding, "And so will I."

Kizzy brushed tears from her cheeks. She wouldn't have thought she had any more tears in her body to shed, but she did.

Lawson nodded toward the hallway. "See for yourself, Kizzy," he told her. "You'll be lucky if they haven't awakened her with their cooing."

Kizzy rose from the rocking chair and quietly strode down the hallway to Evangeline's room. What she saw there caused even more tears escape her tired eyes. All three Ipswich girls were kneeled down on one side of the bed, cooing over Shay as she slept.

"Isn't she simple perfect?" Amoretta whispered.

"She's beautiful!" Calliope breathed.

"Oh, she's just an angel!" Evangeline said. "Look at her hair. Those curls! I could just die of envy!"

"Oh, look at her little hands!" Calliope said. "Those little fingers!"

"And her little dress!" Evangeline added. "It's so lovely."

"She looks just like Brake and Kizzy," Amoretta giggled.

"Oh, Amoretta!" Calliope sighed. "You have got to find a way to make Brake McClendon fall in love with you! Then you could marry him, and between the two of you being so good looking, all your babies will be just beautiful!"

"Don't tease me so, Calliope," Amoretta said, however.

Kizzy understood Amoretta—her fear that Brake did not feel for her the same way she did for him. Kizzy understood because even after the glorious, wonderful hour she'd spent in Lawson's arms in the kitchen, still she worried that he'd only been attracted to her for that moment—only physically attracted and nothing else. Yet she knew in the depths of her soul somewhere that Lawson Ipswich was no kind of scoundrel. Amoretta would begin to understand, if she didn't already, that neither was Brake.

"Look at those rosy cheeks!" Calliope exclaimed quietly. "Oh, I wish she weren't asleep! I'm sure she'd love to play with us or let us read a book to her or brush her hair."

"Maybe in the morning," Amoretta suggested. "If Kizzy doesn't hurry off too fast, maybe we can pamper Shay a bit in the morning."

Kizzy stepped back, turned, and quietly trod up the hall toward the parlor. Brushing the last few tears from her eyes, she returned to her seat in the rocking chair, looked to Lawson, and said, "They're angels...all three of them. You should hear them in there goin' on and on about Shay...about how lovely she is and how they wish they could play games and things with her."

Lawson smiled, nodding. "Oh yes," he said. "You'll be lucky if you get away before noon tomorrow. My girls will, no doubt, have Shay playing dolls, dressing up like a princess, or dancing around the room with them. They all three adore children. And your little Shay...well, she's a jewel."

Lawson stood then, stretching his long, muscular arms out at his sides. "However, I best reel them in a bit, before they wake her. You need to sleep as well. We'll sort all this out in the morning...with Brake."

Unexpectedly then, Lawson reached out, cupping Kizzy's chin in one hand, pressing his mouth to hers in a long, impassioned kiss. She gasped with wonder as he stood and strode down the hall toward the room where Shay lay sleeping entirely unaware of her admirers. He'd kissed her again! And with his daughters in the house! Kizzy smiled as her heart swelled with hope—hope in love and happiness.

"You girls need to let that baby rest," Lawson whispered as he entered Evangeline's room to see his daughters hovering over Shay.

All three girls sighed with disappointment, looking at him with the same pouty expressions they'd each owned since birth. Lawson grinned, adding, "Furthermore, her mother has had a very trying day. She would probably like to join Shay for the night."

"Oh, all right, Daddy," Calliope sighed, halfheartedly getting to her feet. Evangeline and Amoretta followed suit, and the girls and their father left the room—left Shay to her peaceful slumber.

"That is the most beautiful little girl I have ever seen in my life, Miss Kizzy!" Evangeline quietly exclaimed as she entered the parlor.

"Oh, absolutely!" Calliope agreed.

Lawson smiled as all three of his girls settled themselves on the sofa across from Kizzy.

"I suppose you'd probably like to get to bed, Kizzy," Amoretta suggested.

"Well…I-I am a little worn out," Kizzy admitted.

"Will you stay for breakfast at least?" Evangeline asked. "You and your little girl…we couldn't possibly send you home without a good breakfast."

There was a quiet yet determined knock on the door, and Lawson said, "That would probably be Brake now."

"Oh, he's probably worried sick!" Kizzy exclaimed. "I left that note on his door and…"

But Lawson simply strode to the door and opened it.

Amoretta's heart leapt as she saw her father usher Brake into the parlor. She could've sworn he looked more handsome every time she saw him! This time, however, a worried frown wrinkled his brow as he hurried to Kizzy.

"For cryin' in the bucket, Kizzy!" he grumbled, taking her hands in his.

"Oh, and, Brake," Calliope interrupted, "we all know that Miss Kizzy's your sister. She told us."

"Did she now?" he asked, winking at Amoretta. She smiled, knowing he understood her relief in being able to share the McClendons' secret with her family. Turning back to Kizzy, Brake asked, "What happened?"

Quickly Kizzy explained the events that had led her into town. All the while Kizzy was relating the story—all the while Evangeline and Calliope sat in rapt intrigue as they listened—Amoretta watched her father. Oh, her attention lingered on Brake alternately, but it was her father's countenance that she kept studying. Lawson Ipswich was more than just sweet on Kizzy McClendon. To Amoretta, it was plain obvious that he was entirely smitten! His eyes sparkled in a manner she'd never seen them sparkle, and the corners of his mouth were perpetually curved upward as he stared at Kizzy.

Looking to Kizzy, Amoretta thought that perhaps the slightly swollen appearance of her lips wasn't so much to do with crying as it was something else. Amoretta grinned and bit her lip in trying not to burst into overjoyed smiling. Her father was in love with Kizzy! And she was fairly certain Kizzy's feelings were the same toward her father. Why else would she have sought him out in her hour of need?

"Well, you and Shay are movin' into town with me, and that's that, Kizz," Brake grumbled, drawing Amoretta's attention back to the conversation he was having with Kizzy.

"No! No, Brake. I won't do it, especially not now when..." Kizzy began. But she glanced quickly at Lawson and then stammered, "Not yet. I'm not ready for you take on that...to have to endure that."

"May I intercede a moment?" Lawson ventured.

"Of course, Judge," Brake said, still glaring at his sister with concern, however.

Amoretta watched her father very closely. He was a wise and patient man—always able to handle any situation with the utmost care.

"Being that Shay is still asleep, and we certainly don't want to disturb her after all she's endured tonight," Lawson began. Amoretta hung on her father's every word—as did Evangeline and Calliope. "Might I suggest that Miss Kizzy stay with her here for the remainder of the night? And then, when morning finds us all fresh and rested, you and your sister may come to terms about what's best for her safety and Shay's."

"Excellent plan there, Judge Ipswich," Brake said with a firm nod. "That way Shay won't have to be disturbed, and Kizzy can get some sleep knowin' she's safe and sound. Meanwhile, I'll haul my fanny home and get to bed too and then, if it's all right, be back about—"

"Seven o'clock to have breakfast with all of us," Calliope interrupted.

Lawson nodded. "Yes. Let's do have breakfast all together, and then things can be decided upon."

He looked to Kizzy then, and Amoretta's smile broadened as her father said, "I respect your independence, Miss Kizzy. However, I cannot allow you and your daughter to remain in the woods alone, at least until this matter with the slaughtered animals…" He paused and then began again, "Or missing animals is resolved. You and your brother can work out the details in the morning."

Amoretta smiled, for her father wasn't bossing Kizzy; he wasn't taking away her freedom or choice. It was his concerned voice everyone in the room heard. Lawson Ipswich was telling Kizzy that he would be sure she and Shay were taken care of and safe.

Kizzy must've felt his intent as well, for she smiled at him and nodded.

"Come on, Miss Kizzy," Evangeline said, rising from the sofa and taking Kizzy's hand. "Let's get you a nightdress and allow you to get some sleep. You've got to be worn to the bone after all this."

"Good night, Kizz," Brake said, leaning forward as Kizzy stood up from the rocking chair. He kissed her cheek, cupped her chin a moment, and said, "Everything will be fine. Sleep well…because we'll work it all out in the mornin'."

"All right," Kizzy mumbled. She looked to Amoretta, Calliope, and then Lawson. "Good night, everyone. And thank you so much. I can't begin to tell you—"

"Then don't," Evangeline giggled. "Just come with me, and we'll get you all tucked in with your daughter. Okeydokey?"

Amoretta could see it then. She could visibly see Kizzy relax—see the great fatigue wash over her as she accepted the fact she and Shay would be safe for the night.

Lawson watched Kizzy and Evangeline until they disappeared into Calliope and Amoretta's room. Then he turned to Brake and in a lowered voice said, "And now…you and I both know Kizzy and Shay cannot stay out in the woods alone any longer."

"Damn right!" Brake growled. "She's so stubborn."

"Well, we'll just have to figure out how to make her understand that she needs to step into the world once more."

"Let's go help, Calliope," Amoretta said, realizing that her father and Brake needed to discuss Kizzy's situation alone.

Calliope no doubt understood it too, for she didn't pause in following Amoretta to their room.

"Let's have seat at the table, Brake," Lawson suggested.

Brake nodded and tried not to smile. Judge Ipswich was as tied around Kizzy's finger as he was around Amoretta's. Brake had read it in his eyes—in Kizzy's eyes—the moment he'd seen them in the same room. It gave his heart a measure of happiness and relief. The judge would take good care of Kizzy—love her like she'd never been loved—liked she'd never even hoped of being loved. He'd love Shay too, just as deeply as he loved his own grown daughters.

"She can't stay out there alone anymore," Lawson began as they each took a seat in chairs at the kitchen table. "I know you've been trying to convince her of that for a long time, and this time…you're going to succeed."

"You bet I am," Brake agreed. "Even if I have to stay out there every night until I can convince her to come into town and live with me…I'm not backin' off anymore."

Lawson nodded, but Brake could see he was concerned.

"What is it, Judge Ipswich? I can see somethin's eatin' at you."

"Well, I just feel she's got to be in town…that people need to know she's your sister," he answered. "I don't think the people in this town are going to be as hateful as she thinks they are—at least not all of them. But if you're spending the nights out there and someone gets wind of it somehow…"

Brake's eyes narrowed. He smiled and said, "You're thinkin' they'll start assumin' the same thing you did that mornin' you found me comin' out of the house."

Lawson chuckled. "Yes," he admitted. "And that won't do Kizzy or Shay any good at all. Or you, for that matter. Or…"

"Or Amoretta," Brake finished. The judge nodded, still smiling. Brake inhaled a deep breath, trying to muster his courage. And then, before his courage could skitter away, he boldly pushed forward. "I've been meanin' to come and talk to you about somethin', Judge…about Amoretta."

"Yes?" Lawson prodded.

"I know I'm not a wealthy man, and I'm not a city-born, university man either. But I'm a good man. And your daughter…she…the moment I saw her…it's so hard to explain…but I—"

"I'll make you a deal, Brake," Lawson interrupted.

"A deal?" Brake asked. For a moment, he wondered if the judge were going to offer to pay him off to stay away from Amoretta.

"I'm assuming, and maybe I'm wrong," Lawson began, "but I think you're getting ready to ask my permission to court my daughter Amoretta…officially."

"Yes, sir, I am," Brake said firmly.

"Then I'm glad to grant you that permission, Brake," Lawson continued. "You're a good man…a great man. I knew it the moment I met you, and I want you to know I have no qualms about allowing you to see Amoretta."

"But?" Brake prodded—for he felt the question hanging in the air.

"But do you have any qualms, worries, or concerns…may I have your permission, Brake, to pay court to your sister, Kizzy…officially?" the judge asked.

Brake had been so exhilarated over owning permission to officially court Amoretta, however, that Judge Ipswich's request caught him completely unexpecting.

"I have to say it, Judge," he said, shaking his head with amusement at the situation, "I didn't see that comin'…not this soon."

"You saw it coming?" Lawson asked, apparently astonished.

Brake chuckled. "Yep! The minute you tried to knock my head off for bein' at Kizzy's that mornin'," he admitted. "And absolutely, Judge. You absolutely have my permission to court my sister. And I thank you for askin'. You're a good man…but you may have some trouble convincin' Kizzy she's good enough for you."

Brake watched as Lawson Ipswich grinned. "Oh, I worked on that a bit tonight before the girls got home." He winked, and Brake chuckled as he added, "And I think groundwork is well laid now, Brake."

Brake laughed, lowered his voice, and said, "Why, you little devil, Judge Ipswich."

Lawson's grin spread into a full smile as he said, "And as you know, Brake…it takes one to know one."

Again Brake laughed. "Indeed it does. Indeed it does."

"Does everyone want to hear me count to a hundred?" Shay asked, pausing in consuming her flapjacks the next morning.

"Oh, Shay, honey, that'll take much too long," Kizzy gently explained. "We all have so much to do today and—"

"Please, Mama," the child begged, however.

"There's nothing so important that we need to rush, Miss Kizzy," Calliope said. Amoretta smiled and exchanged amused glances with Evangeline.

The women had begun to enjoy their breakfast, even though Lawson had not returned from his morning ride and Brake had yet to arrive. Amoretta thought it was delightful—just sitting in the kitchen, eating flapjacks and bacon and enjoying the company of other women. Shay had woken up as fresh as a dandelion and was obviously enjoying the company as well.

"Please, Mama," Shay begged again. "They don't any of them mind."

Kizzy sighed with anxiety. Amoretta was sure she was uncomfortable—no matter how Evangeline, Calliope, and Amoretta assured her they loved having her. Amoretta just wanted Kizzy to enjoy herself. Reaching across the table and putting a reassuring hand over Kizzy's, Amoretta smiled and nodded encouragement.

"Oh, all right, Shay," Kizzy relented. "But don't drag it out too long."

"Oh, I won't, Mama," Shay giggled. She looked to Amoretta and then to Evangeline and Calliope. "Are you all ready to hear me count to a hundred?" she asked.

"Of course!" Calliope exclaimed.

"Yes, let's have it," Evangeline encouraged.

"All right then," Shay said, straightening her posture and tossing her head to send her lovely dark curls bouncing in every direction. "Here I go. One, two, skip a few…ninety-nine…a hundred!"

Amoretta and her sisters burst into laughter. Shay McClendon was the most adorable child Amoretta had ever known! Evangeline and Calliope laughed and laughed, and Amoretta was laughing so hard, she couldn't catch her breath.

Naturally, with all the Ipswich girls reeling, even Kizzy was stricken with the merriment bug and began laughing. Shay was delighted with the reaction and clapped her small hands with excitement and triumph.

Once the women were able to settle themselves once more, sighing and wiping tears of glee from their eyes, Shay smiled with pride. "Uncle Brake taught me how to count to a hundred, but I had no idea that countin' was so funny!"

Again Amoretta, her sisters, and Kizzy erupted into laughter. They were able to settle themselves much more quickly this time, however, and Amoretta smiled as she watched Shay return to enjoying her flapjacks.

"Bacon is my favoritest meat," Shay told Amoretta in a whisper.

"Mine too," Amoretta said with an understanding wink.

"She is too adorable for her own good," Evangeline told Kizzy as she nodded toward Shay.

"Most of the time, yes," Kizzy agreed.

The kitchen door opened then, and Amoretta watched Kizzy's eyes light up as her father stepped into the house.

"Where have you been, Daddy?" Calliope asked. "We were simply starving, so we started without you."

Lawson kissed Calliope's cheek and then Evangeline's. He was carrying an old crate covered in burlap as he rounded the table to kiss Amoretta's forehead.

"Me too! Me too!" Shay begged.

Amoretta saw her father look to Kizzy—saw Kizzy shrug her shoulders with embarrassment at her daughter's forthrightness but nod all the same. She watched as her father bent, placing a tender kiss on Shay's cheek.

"He gave me a kiss too," Shay whispered with delight to Amoretta.

"I know!" Amoretta giggled in response.

"Good morning, Kizzy," Lawson greeted Kizzy.

Amoretta smiled when Kizzy blushed and said, "Good mornin', Judge."

Evangeline and Calliope exchanged understanding glances with Amoretta. After all, Amoretta had sat up half the night with her sisters filling in the details of what she suspected—of what she knew was kindling between her father and the beautiful gypsy from the woods.

"And," Lawson continued, setting the crate down on the kitchen floor next to Shay, "I have something for you, little Shay McClendon...something I think you might really like."

"What is it, Mr. Judge?" the child inquired.

Amoretta watched her father remove the burlap from the crate and gasped, feeling tears fill her eyes as she saw what was inside.

"Molly!" Shay squealed. "Oh, Molly! Molly, Molly, Molly!" Reaching into the crate, Shay awkwardly gathered her beloved mama cat into her arms. Instantly the cat began purring and licking Shay's ear. "Oh, Molly, we've been so worried!"

Amoretta looked to Kizzy to see tears of joy filling her eyes. She covered her mouth with one hand as she kept looking back and forth between Lawson and Shay.

"Did you find her babies too, Mr. Judge?" Shay asked, obviously overwhelmed with joy.

But Amoretta's smile faded as she watched her father hunker down next to Shay. "I found four of them, honey," he answered. "And, well, I think the other three have a new home now…in heaven."

Sadness mingled with despair in everyone's eyes as they watched the little girl gently place Molly back in the crate and begin counting the kittens.

"So three of them are in heaven," Shay mumbled. Amoretta held her breath. She could see Calliope and Evangeline tearing up.

"Yes, sweetie," Lawson said.

"With Jesus?" Shay asked Lawson.

Lawson Ipswich grinned, brushed a tender curl from Shay's forehead, and answered, "Yes. Of course."

Shay sighed and smiled once more. "Well, I guess if I have Molly and four kitties…I can be happy that Jesus has the other three. They'll be happy with him in heaven, won't they, Mr. Judge?"

"Yes. They most certainly will," Lawson assured the child.

"May I be excused from the table, Mama?" Shay asked Kizzy. "I want to spend some time with Molly and her babies."

"Yes, you may, Shay," Kizzy managed to answer.

Once Lawson had taken the crateful of cats into the parlor and settled Shay into cuddling them, he returned to the kitchen.

"You went to the house?" Kizzy asked in a whisper. "To see if…"

"I went to see if I could find Molly and the kittens for Shay," he interrupted.

Kizzy sighed with seeming relief and whispered, "Thank you, Judge Ipswich."

But Lawson Ipswich didn't smile. In fact, a tremor of fear traveled over Amoretta's spine as her father frowned.

"I did find *all* the kittens," he said quietly. "Molly managed to get those four out of the house and behind a wild berry bush out back, Kizzy."

"But?" Evangeline prodded.

Lawson glanced into the parlor to make certain Shay was not listening and then answered, "But the other three...I found...well, they had been killed."

"How?" Amoretta asked.

Lawson paused, obviously not wanting to answer. But Amoretta knew her father. Lawson Ipswich had answered every question his daughters had ever asked him from the moment they could each talk—and always truthfully.

"They'd been hung from a tree by their necks and...and cut down the middle the way the rats had been that Rowdy Gates found," he answered.

Kizzy gasped and began to weep, and Amoretta and her sisters had tears brimming in their eyes as well.

There was no time to linger in horror or mourning over the poor murdered kittens, however, for in the next moment, Brake McClendon stepped through the still open kitchen door. He was frowning—looked pale and angry.

Without pausing, he announced, "It's Sam Mulholland that did it. I saw Sheriff Montrose on my way over, and he told me to tell you, Judge Ipswich...that Sam Mulholland is the one who's been killin' animals."

CHAPTER FIFTEEN

Samuel Mulholland was gone. Sheriff Montrose arrived at the jailhouse the morning Lawson Ipswich had recovered Molly and four of her kittens to find a note nailed to the door. It was a confession— a written confession from Samuel Mulholland. In his letter to Sheriff Montrose, Samuel explained that something had suddenly overcome him weeks before—a terrible anger, rage at the fact that his father had moved the family so far from the tuberculosis sanitarium where their mother was convalescing. Samuel had admitted to killing Dex Longfellow's dog, Rowdy Gates's dog, the Montrose cat, and the other animals Sheriff Montrose had discovered. He'd written that his rage had caused him to begin slaughtering the animals and that he knew everyone in Meadowlark Lake would be forever wary of him if he were ever found out. Therefore, he'd left town—headed up north to the city where his mother was convalescing in order to spend more time with her. He could no longer endure the guilt he owned at not being with her—could no longer hide the rage he felt toward his father for abandoning his mother simply because she'd been stricken ill.

Sheriff Montrose and Judge Ipswich decided that with Samuel gone, there was no need to tell everyone in town exactly what had transpired. Privately they spoke with Rowdy Gates, Brake, Kizzy, the Ipswich girls, and the very few others who had known about the slaughtered animals.

Surprisingly, those who owned any knowledge of the thing must've kept very mum—kept the information to themselves entirely—for nearly a month later, when the morning of All Hallows' Eve dawned cool and crisp and colorful, the citizens of Meadowlark Lake were as calm and friendly with one another as ever they were. As preparations were made for the community Halloween gathering, there was no talk of Samuel Mulholland and what he'd done. Naturally, many people inquired of Samuel's father and sister, Prudence, as to his whereabouts, being that he hadn't been seen. But Mr. Mulholland and Prudence simply answered with smiles and a simple explanation that Sam had gone to visit his ailing mother.

Thus, everyone in Meadowlark Lake went about their daily routines, looked forward to the Halloween gathering with happy anticipation, and prepared for the onset of winter. Not another thought was given to Samuel Mulholland by those who knew nothing of the evidences of his rage, and very little thought was given to him by those who did know of it.

For one thing, four of the townsfolk who did know of poor Sam's wrongdoings were far too distracted bathing in the blisses of true love. Much had transpired in the weeks since Kizzy and Shay McClendon had appeared on Judge Ipswich's doorstep that frightening night.

Amoretta was delighted when her father and Brake finally convinced Kizzy to allow the folks of Meadowlark Lake to know she was Brake's sister and Shay, his niece. Though Kizzy and Shay still lived in the little house in the woods, Brake and Lawson Ipswich slowly eased her into visiting town, purchasing necessities from the general store, and speaking with people openly. Happily, the people in Meadowlark Lake proved to be far less judgmental than Kizzy had assumed they would be. Of course, Amoretta and her sisters often wondered if perhaps Meadowlark Lake's offering of kindness (and lack of self-righteousness) initially had to do with the fact that Judge Lawson Ipswich had fairly announced to all that he intended to court Kizzy and that Brake McClendon was her brother. Still, they were good citizens, those townsfolk who welcomed Kizzy McClendon and her daughter, Shay, with open arms and smiling lips. Therefore, Amoretta determined to not think so much on why everyone was so good to her and just be happy in the knowledge that they were.

Amoretta was also greatly relieved to find that she did not receive the distain of every young woman in town when she began appearing with Brake in public. She'd feared that Winnie, Blanche, Prudence, and especially Sallie would spurn her—envy and hate her for having won Brake's attentions. And so Amoretta was delighted when, instead of scowls and harsh words from her friends, she received only encouragement and well-wishes.

Thus, on the morning of All Hallows' Eve, as Amoretta, her sisters, and Kizzy busily prepared pumpkin pie in Ipswich kitchen, there was no thought of Sam Mulholland and slaughtered kittens. There was only laughter and the soothing, aromatic fragrance of blended pumpkin and spices wafting through the house.

Brake and Lawson had taken Shay with them to the Ackermans' barn to help decorate and set up for the games and other festivities. And though Kizzy constantly worried about her little girl (for she wasn't at all used to being without her, even for a minute), Amoretta and her sisters just as constantly reassured her that all would be well. After all, Shay was in the care of the two most capable men in all the world.

So as the day wore on, not only did the warm aroma of baking breads and sweet things emanate from the bakery, but they also mingled with the scent of spiced pumpkin, apples, and berries to sweeten the air throughout Meadowlark Lake. Autumn was nearly over, and the celebration that it had lingered would be the last community event until Christmastime. Amoretta had never been happier—not in all her life. She was in love with Brake McClendon, enveloped in everything about him. She couldn't wait to see him each day when he'd finished working at the gristmill—thought she might die of impatience by the time he was finished and they could take their evening walk or sit on the back porch and talk—or step off the porch into the darkness and share impassioned kisses.

Amoretta was nearly delirious with excitement in anticipation of the Halloween festivities to be held that night, as Brake had promised her that the annual jack-o'-lantern pumpkin parade of Meadowlark Lake would be something she'd never forget. But she found herself almost regretful that she'd be forced to share Brake's company with others. Secretly, Amoretta wanted Brake's attention all to herself all of the time. She could see by the light in her father's eyes whenever he looked at Kizzy that Lawson Ipswich felt the same about the beautiful gypsy from the woods.

Still, Amoretta had always loved Halloween—the traditions, the treats, the parties, and of course the superstitious customs.

"Well?" Calliope asked as she began peeling the first apple of many she would need in order to fill the piecrust waiting to be baked into a sweet, cinnamoned apple pie.

"Well, what?" Amoretta asked—though she already suspected to what Calliope was alluding.

"Are you going to toss the parings?" Evangeline asked.

Amoretta sighed with nonchalance. "I don't know," she answered. "It doesn't quite intrigue me the way it used to...tossing apple peels over my shoulder."

"That's just because you're afraid you won't get a B spelled out as your lover's initial," Calliope giggled.

Amoretta playfully glared at her sister, feigning indifference—even though Calliope had hit the proverbial nail exactly on the proverbial nail's head. "Oh, it's not that," she lied.

"Of course it is," Evangeline giggled.

But it was Kizzy who stepped in for Amoretta's defense. "Don't worry, Amoretta," she began. "Toss the apple peels. It won't matter what initial comes up. You'll find yourself in Brake's arms tonight no matter what the apple predicts."

"That's right!" Calliope exclaimed. Sighing with dramatics, she said, "You'll be wrapped in Brake's arms as the sun sets on All Hallows' Eve. And as the moon rises like a ghostly orb, as the jack-o'-lanterns wink with their frightening faces and flaming innards, Brake will slather you with warm, wet kisses and...ouch!" Calliope giggled as she pulled the apple peelings from her hair that Evangeline had tossed at her.

"It sounds very romantic, doesn't it?" Kizzy asked, winking at Amoretta.

"Yes, it does," Amoretta admitted.

"And then," Evangeline began, "just a ways down the road—perhaps under some lovely elderly maple tree that owns perhaps a few last crimson leaves of autumn—Kizzy and Daddy will be wrapped in each other's arms. And Daddy will kiss Kizzy's berry-red lips and say…" Evangeline giggled as winged apple peelings gently slapped her in the face as well.

Kizzy was smiling and continued to peel the apple she'd been working on. "You Ipswich girls…you lighten my heart like you'll never know."

"Okay, this one is it," Amoretta said then, picking up another apple. "I'll peel this one, all in one peeling length, and then I'll toss it…just for fun."

"I'll do one too," Calliope said, reaching for a new apple.

"And me!" Evangeline added, snatching up a fresh apple.

Kizzy finished peeling the apple she'd been holding and, taking a new one from the pile in the sink, said, "I can't be left out, you know. One length of peelin', huh?"

"Yes," Amoretta confirmed. "The book I've read is very specific about this. One apple…its peel pared in one length. If you break it, you'll have to do another one before you can toss it."

For the first time in hours, the Ipswich kitchen fell silent as all three Ipswich girls and Kizzy concentrated on paring their individual apples.

Calliope finished first. "All right. I'm ready," she said. Inhaling a deep breath, she exhaled and smiled.

"Hoping for an F for Fox Montrose, I'm assumin'?" Kizzy giggled.

But Calliope arched one eyebrow. "I'm not telling," she said. "It might not come true if I tell."

"Oh, that's birthday cake candle wishes, Calliope," Evangeline teased.

Inhaling another breath, Calliope tossed the apple parings over her left shoulder. Instantly, Amoretta, Evangeline, and Kizzy scurried to where the parings had landed.

"Oh, I can't look!" Calliope giggled. "You tell me, Amoretta. What letter is it?"

Amoretta studied the apple parings where they lay on the floor. Looking to Kizzy, she shrugged, however. Evangeline also shook her head.

All three women shifted their positions, looking at the parings from different venues than they had previously.

"D?" Evangeline suggested.

"Or maybe P?" Kizzy offered.

"Oh, for pity's sake," Calliope grumbled. Going to look at the peelings herself, she frowned, however. "Well, it's not an F. I think we can agree on that," she sighed with disappointment.

Amoretta put an arm around her little sister's shoulders. "It's just for fun, Calliope…right?"

Calliope sighed, resilient as ever. "Right," she cheerfully agreed. "Now you, Evangeline. You go next."

Evangeline straightened her posture, inhaled a breath of bravery, and tossed her apple parings over her left shoulder. They landed with a light whisper, and Amoretta, Calliope, and Kizzy hurried to them. Evangeline hurried as well.

"Hmmm," Calliope mused. "Maybe an M, I think."

"I agree," Kizzy said.

"I do think it's an M too," Amoretta agreed. She looked to Evangeline. "What do you see, Evie?"

"M," Evangeline said without pause. "Hmmm…M. I can't think of anyone we know here with the first name that begins with M."

"Ooo, then you must not have met your true love yet, Evangeline," Kizzy guessed. "How mysterious!"

"You next, Kizzy," Calliope pressed. "And I know what letter it will be. L…for Lawson Ipswich!"

Kizzy blushed crimson and giggled. But then her smile faded, and she paused.

"What if it isn't an L?" she asked Amoretta.

Amoretta shrugged. "It's just a game, Kizzy. No worries. We all know you've captured Daddy's heart."

Kizzy smiled, seeming somewhat relieved. "All right then…it's just a game, right?" Biting her lip with nervous anticipation, Kizzy tossed her apple parings over her left shoulder.

Amoretta, Calliope, and Evangeline all gasped in unison as they saw there on the floor Kizzy's apple parings shaping out a perfect letter L.

"L!" Evangeline exclaimed as Kizzy looked at the parings and smiled with delight. "L for Lawson!"

Every woman in the room began laughing with delirium. Quickly they were all sharing an embrace, circled around the magical apple parings.

"Maybe it's because you're a gypsy, Kizzy," Calliope suggested. "Maybe that's why your parings are so perfectly formed. There's no question they spelled out Daddy's first initial!"

Amoretta smiled and felt her heart warm in her bosom as she gazed upon the resplendence radiating from Kizzy's lovely face. Oh, how she hoped her father wouldn't tarry in asking Kizzy to be his bride!

"Now you, Amoretta," Kizzy urged at last. "It's your turn."

Amoretta tried not to feel anxious about the parings custom. After all, as she'd just told Kizzy it was only for fun—wasn't it?

Inhaling a breath of resolve not to be rattled no matter what letter her apple peels spelled out, Amoretta held her breath and tossed her own apple parings over her left shoulder.

"S? S again?" she heard Calliope whisper.

Turning and hurrying to where her parings had landed, Amoretta looked down with sore disappointment. Indeed, her Halloween apple parings had once again formed a very identifiable letter S.

"Well, I'm not going to let it bother me," Amoretta said—though she knew that it would to some extent.

"That's right. It's all in fun, Rettie, so just shrug it off," Calliope said.

"What are you ladies up to?" Brake asked, suddenly entering by way of the kitchen door. Evangeline had propped it open in order to keep the kitchen cooler while there was a fire in the cookstove. "What is it? A big ol' spider or somethin'?" Brake asked as he strode toward the circle of young ladies staring down at the floor.

"Oh, nothing important," Amoretta answered as she began to bend over to retrieve her tossed parings.

"Nope…just Amoretta's apple peelings for this year," Calliope intentionally added, glancing at Amoretta mischievously.

"Hold on there!" Brake said, taking hold of Amoretta from behind. Gathering her in his arms, he held her tightly back against him as he peered over her shoulder. "Hmmm. Looks like you tossed an S again, Amoretta."

Kizzy giggled as Brake turned Amoretta around in his arms, still holding her against him as he smiled down at her.

Amoretta giggled as Brake's eyes lit up with tomfoolery. "Don't you worry yourself one little minute about that damn S, darlin'," Brake chuckled. "We both know that ol' Sylvanus Tenney ain't here. But I am."

"Ooo! Do it, Brake! Do it!" Calliope taunted with excitement. "Kiss her right here in front of us!"

"Yes, ma'am, Miss Calliope," Brake mumbled a moment before his mouth crushed to Amoretta's. She sighed, melted against him, and let her arms go around his neck as she kissed him wholeheartedly in return.

She could hear Kizzy, Evangeline, and Calliope giggling, but she didn't care. Brake *was* there—and once again Amoretta wondered how in all the world she could ever have considered that Sylvanus Tenney were meant for her. She was amazed at how perfectly her body fit against Brake's—how perfectly their mouths blended to generate such a blissful drinking of desire. Oh, how thoroughly she loved him! How wholly, utterly, and consummately she loved him!

Amoretta could no longer imagine a day without Brake—an hour. He'd become everything to her; he'd become life to her!

All too soon for Amoretta's liking, Brake broke the seal of their kiss, gazing down at her as his handsome mouth on his handsome face smiled a handsome smile.

"Still worried about that S, honey?" he asked in a low, provocative tone.

"No," Amoretta sighed.

"And what are you doin' back here anyway, Brake?" Kizzy asked then. "I thought you were with Lawson and Shay decoratin' the Ackerman place."

"I was," Brake answered, still staring down at Amoretta for a moment. "But I was thirsty and needed myself a swig of Amoretta Ipswich," he added with a wink.

Kizzy rolled her eyes and sighed with amused exasperation. "Oh, for pity's sake, Brake."

He chuckled and looked up to his sister. "I rode back to pick up some more of them smaller pumpkins Lawson says he has down in the root cellar. Mrs. Ackerman would like to have a few more to decorate the food tables with."

Evangeline said, "Well, I best get them for you, Brake." Smiling, she added, "Heaven knows if I let you and Amoretta go down there together, alone...Mrs. Ackerman will *never* finish decorating her tables."

"That's wise thinkin' there, Evangeline," Brake agreed. "Meanwhile, I'll just have me one more swig of Miss Ipswich here."

Amoretta was breathless as he kissed her again—and again—and again.

"You best hurry, Evie," Calliope laughed, "before Brake eats Amoretta up altogether."

Late afternoon found the Ipswich girls primping in preparation for the Meadowlark Lake Halloween gathering. Fox Montrose had asked permission to escort Calliope to the event, and though she looked absolutely beautiful in her new blue and white dress, Amoretta thought Calliope didn't appear quite as excited as one might think. Still, having caught the attention of Fox Montrose—well, being on the arm of a handsome man could be very unnerving. Amoretta knew it firsthand, and even though she knew she could do no more to improve her appearance, she hoped she looked well enough in her new green dress to be a complement to Brake's good looks and not a damper.

"Ooo! I love that color on you, Evie," Amoretta exclaimed when Evangeline entered the room wearing a dark crimson dress embellished with ecru lace.

"Do you think it's all right...to wear red, I mean?" Evangeline asked, frowning as she studied herself in the mirror. Dex Longfellow had asked to escort Evangeline to the Halloween party, and Amoretta could see Evangeline was as nervous as a mouse in a mousetrap factory.

"Yes," Amoretta assured her. "And anyway...it's more crimson than just plain red."

As she and her sisters finished preparing for the evening, Amoretta tried to ignore the nagging whisper in the back of her mind—the whisper that kept reminding her that her apple parings had once again spelled out S as the first initial of her true love. Oh, she knew it was all just silly superstition—a game. Still, it bothered her. Certainly Evangeline's parings had appeared to be an M, and Calliope's were rather nondescript. But Kizzy had tossed an L for her lover's initials—L for Lawson. So why hadn't Amoretta's parings formed a B for Brake? The fact had bothered her from the moment Brake had ridden off with a burlap bag full of small pumpkins for Mrs. Ackerman's tables. She'd tried to ignore it and told herself she was being ridiculous—that all the nonsense in her mind was simply because she'd read far too much on the subject of Halloween customs.

"Oh! I-I forgot to do something," Amoretta suddenly told her sisters. Her evening would be ruined if she couldn't get the S apple parings out of her mind.

Thus, since she'd determined she would try just one more Halloween custom before she tossed the book she'd read into the fire, Amoretta quickly took the hand mirror resting on top of the chest of drawers and scurried out of the bedroom.

"You'd better hurry, Amoretta," Calliope called after her. "Brake will be here to collect you at any moment!"

"Yes, yes! I know," Amoretta answered. She paused only long enough to retrieve a candle and wood match from the kitchen. Then she hurried into the parlor, blew out the flames to the lamps lighting the dusk darkness of the room, and began.

Placing the hand mirror on the mantel above the hearth, Amoretta lit the candle she'd brought with her. *"Still, one need not possess either a crystal ball or gifts of clairvoyance to discover one's own true love,"* Amoretta quietly quoted from her book. *"All that it is required is a hand mirror and a lit candle on All Hallows' Eve,"* she whispered.

Then, with a great trepidation mingled with the excitement of hope, Amoretta reached out and retrieved the hand mirror from the mantel. Gulping the anxiety that had risen to her throat (for her imagination still feared Sylvanus Tenney's ghostly image might appear behind her in the mirror when she looked into it), Amoretta slowly raised the mirror and candle.

She gasped as she saw not Sylvanus Tenney's image in the mirror with hers but Brake McClendon's! A moment of joy—of pure elation and rapture—ricocheted through her body. Brake! Brake was meant to be her true love!

However, her hopes fell to the floor at her feet as she heard Brake ask, "What in the hell are you doin', Amoretta?" and realized that it was not his ghostly image she was seeing in the mirror but his real image—for he was standing just behind her in the darkened parlor.

Startled by his presence, and the drop of wax that the candle let loose to her hand, Amoretta squealed, dropping the candle. It clattered to the floor, extinguishing the flame.

"You scared the pudding out of me, Brake McClendon!" she scolded as she turned to face him. He strode toward her, smiling his dazzling smile, however.

"Did I?" he asked. "And what were you doin' in there with that candle and mirror, precious?" he teased. "Hopin' to see ol' Sylvan-ass Tenney hoverin' behind you?"

"Of course not," she said. "But now we'll never know *who* is meant to be my lover, will we?"

But Brake laughed, stepped forward, and placed his hands at Amoretta's waist. "Precious...you don't need a mirror and a candle to tell you that. I can give you that answer right here and now...and without all the hocus pocus."

Amoretta tossed the hand mirror to the sofa—let her arms reach up and around Brake's neck. She bit her lip with delight as she gazed up into his beautiful, smoldering, syrupy brown eyes.

"Is that so?" she playfully asked.

"Oh yes, ma'am," Brake mumbled as he kissed her.

"Oh, for Pete's sake, Amoretta," Evangeline laughingly scolded as she and Calliope entered the parlor. "Why did you blow out all the lamps? We can't see a thing in here." As one of the parlor lamps flickered to life, Evangeline smiled. "Oh. I see."

There was a knock on the front door of the Ipswich home then, and Brake released Amoretta and strode toward it. "That would be your gentlemen callers, ladies...if I'm not mistaken."

Indeed Brake opened the door to find both Dex Longfellow and Fox Montrose standing on the porch.

After exchanging friendly greetings and pleasantries, the three couples began the not-too-long walk to the Ackermans' barn.

Her arm linked with Brake's, Amoretta strolled beside him, fairly unaware of her sisters and their escorts, for the night was the most beautiful October night—the most perfect All Hallows' Eve she had ever, ever seen!

The air was cool, crisp, fresh, and yet filled with the comforting aroma of wood smoke and dry leaves. The sky was clear—not one cloud lingered overhead—and the moon tarried low in the sky, bright and autumn-yellow like a large celestial pumpkin. The stars winked and blinked as if they too were enjoying the cloudless night—as if they too were anticipating pumpkin and apple pie, cookies, cakes, bobbing for apples, friendly conversation, and laughter.

Amoretta tightened her embrace of Brake's arm, and he chuckled, kissing the top of her head affectionately. "I promise this will be a Halloween you won't soon forget, Amoretta Ipswich."

"Oh, I'm sure I'll never forget it!" Amoretta sighed with mingled contentment and happy anticipation.

"Oh, believe me, you won't," Brake added.

Amoretta looked up to him, her eyes narrowing with suspicion. "You seem a little too certain of that...as if there's something you're not telling me."

But Brake shrugged. "Nope. I'm not keepin' anything from you," he assured her. "But I should warn you that tonight...I'm gonna use my gypsy magic to make sure the bewitchin' spell I set on you is complete."

"Oh, you set a gypsy spell on me, did you?" Amoretta giggled.

"Of course! How else can you explain it?"

"Explain what?" she teased.

"Me and you," he answered. "You and me...so quick, so fast...so passionate."

Amoretta giggled, reaching up to clamp her hand over his mouth as Fox Montrose asked, "What's that, McClendon? Did you say somethin'?"

"Nope," Brake said, pushing Amoretta's hand from his mouth. "Not a thing." He looked down at her and winked as he chuckled.

"I bewitched you, Amoretta," he said, more quietly. "I began castin' my gypsy spell on you that first moment we met."

Amoretta smiled up at him. Oh, how she loved him! In that moment, she didn't even want to go to the party. She just wanted to be with Brake—alone and in his arms.

Sighing once more with happiness, Amoretta's smile broadened, for the Ackermans' barn was visible just ahead. The light in the barn glowed orange and welcoming, and Amoretta could hear laughter and merriment echoing inside it. It truly would be a night to remember forever, no matter what happened. The apple peeling S was behind her, as was the silly ritual with the mirror and the candle. Amoretta Ipswich knew she was meant for Brake McClendon—and nothing in all the world would ever convince her otherwise.

CHAPTER SIXTEEN

"It's an S," Amoretta grumbled. Frowning, she studied the S carved on the apple she'd just used her teeth to pluck from the barrel of water.

Sheriff Montrose was manning the apple bobbing game. When everyone arrived at the Ackerman barn, any as yet unmarried young men and women were given an apple and instructed to carve their first initial on the bottom. The apples were then placed in bushel baskets (one marked "Boys" and one marked "Girls"). Several rounds of apple bobbing were played, and Amoretta had been assigned to participate in the second group of girls. Nervously she'd watched as Sheriff Montrose had plopped ten apples from the boys' bushel basket into the bobbing barrel filled with water. She'd studied the apples carefully for a few moments until choosing a particularly juicy-looking one to bob for. Nimbly she'd used her teeth to catch the apple stem, glad that Sheriff Montrose had forgotten to remove the stems before dropping them into the bobbing barrel. Stemmed apples were much easier to capture, and thereby having to get all wet and mussed wasn't necessary.

Everyone had clapped with admiration once Amoretta had so daintily captured her apple. But when she turned it over and saw the all-too-familiar S carved in its skin, she was disheartened.

"I take it you're not too happy with the apple you got there, Miss Ipswich," Sheriff Montrose chuckled.

But Amoretta forced a smile, saying, "Oh, I'm delighted, Sheriff! It was fun. And after all, it's only a game, right?"

"Right," Sheriff Montrose chuckled.

Brake was chuckling as well. Playfully glaring up at him, Amoretta pushed the apple into his hand and said, "Here. You can have it, Mr. Smarty Pants."

Brake winked at her, obviously amused. "Well, it seems like Sylvan-ass is still hauntin' you, darlin'."

Amoretta rolled her eyes with mirthful exasperation, and even though Brake's pronunciation of Sylvanus's name secretly amused her, she obligatorily whispered, "You shouldn't call him that. Poor Sylvanus."

"Poor Sylvanus?" Brake laughed. "What's he got to be poor about? It's his S that keeps croppin' up every time you..." But Brake paused. "Now wait a minute." He looked around a moment.

"What is it?" Amoretta asked. But when Brake turned the apple over, studying the S carved in it once more, she understood.

"Sylvan-ass isn't even here," Brake needlessly reminded. "Someone here carved the S."

Amoretta felt a blush of embarrassment rise to her cheeks. "Oh no! What if whoever it was saw my reaction to pulling his apple out of the bobbing barrel? Oh, I feel just awful!"

Brake was still looking around, however. "S...S..." he mumbled as he studied the gathering of townsfolk. He smiled and pointed with the hand holding the apple. "I've got it...there. Right over there. Shane Finlay. His name starts with S."

Amoretta shook her head with disbelief. "He's all of twelve years old, Brake."

"Exactly," Brake agreed. "He can't give me much competition for your affections with that scrawny Sylvanus of his."

Amoretta giggled and lightly slapped his arm.

"What?" he inquired, feigning ignorance. "You told me I couldn't call him Sylvan-ass anymore...so I figure I'll just call little Shane's scrawny behind Sylvanus instead. It'll make me feel better." Brake bit into the apple marked with an S. "Yep, Shane Finlay and his scrawny

Sylvanus…he don't intimidate me too much." He frowned and looked to Amoretta. "You're not thinkin' of transferrin' your affections from me to him, are you, precious? Not just because of the whole S on the apple thing?"

Amoretta laughed. Brake was so funny sometimes. It seemed he always had her giggling over something clever he'd said or done.

Taking Brake's hand, Amoretta began pulling him in the direction of the cider table. Lawson and Kizzy were standing together near it, watching as Shay played a game of the jack-o'-lantern ring.

"Amoretta went bobbin' for an apple and came up perturbed," Brake announced as they reached Amoretta's father and Kizzy.

"And why is that?" Lawson asked, bending down to kiss Amoretta's cheek.

"She bobbed up another S," Brake said, showing the bottom of the apple to Lawson and his sister.

Naturally Lawson chuckled, and though Kizzy tried to force an expression of sympathy to Amoretta, it was clear by the quivering curves at the corners of her mouth that she was also amused.

Brake leaned forward, whispering, "She's still worried about ol' Sylvan-ass showin' up."

Lawson laughed, and Amoretta sighed with frustration. Although she'd had so much fun at the party with Brake, she longed to be alone in his company. They'd eaten pumpkin pie and caramel apples, drunk warm apple cider, and played games. They'd laughed and listened to the ghost stories Mr. Ackerman was telling in one corner of the barn. Yet now, Amoretta had grown tired of socializing. She wanted to be outside in the cool night air—hear the happy party noises and music from a distance. She wanted to gaze at the moon and stars and wonder what pranks the adolescent boys of Meadowlark Lake were up to. Brake had explained they'd spent the night stealing front gates and piling them in the middle of the street in front of the jailhouse the Halloween before.

Brake studied Amoretta a moment. He could see she was tired of the S cropping up in her Halloween evening, perhaps even tired of socializing. Thus, he smiled—for it was time.

Brake looked toward the big barn doors that stood open to beckon the citizens of Meadowlark Lake to the All Hallows' Eve festivities. He was astonished to see Rowdy Gates standing in the doorway at that very moment.

Brake raised his eyebrows in silent questioning of Rowdy, and Rowdy nodded. Brake smiled. It was in place. His well-laid plan was moving along quite nicely—and without a hitch. The lamplighter's—or, rather this night, the jack-o'-lantern lighter's—signal meant the last piece of Brake's plan was in place.

Taking hold of Amoretta's arm, he glanced up to Lawson Ipswich, nodding as he said, "Come on, Amoretta Ipswich. Let's me and you take a walk. What do you say?"

Lawson smiled, nodding with reassurance. Oh, Brake had asked Lawson's permission days before, but now that the moment was at hand, he wanted a little reiteration from his lover's father that permission was still granted.

"A walk?" Amoretta asked, suddenly lighting up like a firefly on a summer's night in Mississippi.

"Yeah," Brake said as he linked her arm through his and started escorting her toward the door. "There's nothin' like an autumn walk on a clear October night. Let's get your sweater from the coat barrel."

He felt Amoretta snuggle up against him as she giggled with delight. "Oh, I love it!" she exclaimed in a whisper.

"Love what?" Brake couldn't resist teasing. "My arm? Or an autumn walk on a clear October night?"

"Both," Amoretta admitted.

Brake smiled and exhaled a nervous breath. He was certain Amoretta would accept his proposal—at least he thought he was certain. Of course, the little devil of doubt that plucked at a man's mind had been incessantly plucking at Brake's since the moment he'd received permission from Lawson Ipswich to propose to Amoretta.

But he knew her heart; it beat in time with his own. He knew she loved him the way he loved her—singularly. Amoretta would accept him; he was sure she would. At least, that's what he silently told himself as he walked with her toward the road that ran parallel to the Ackerman fields—the road where the lamplighter had just finished lighting more than a hundred jack-o'-lanterns.

"You're taking me to the pumpkin parade you've been telling me about, aren't you?" Amoretta asked as they walked away from Mr. Ackerman's barn and toward his fields. Brake chuckled, and Amoretta was suddenly bathed in a feeling of warmth and security at the sound of it.

"I made a deal with Rowdy Gates," Brake began. "I asked him to wait half an hour before announcin' to everybody else that he'd finished lightin' the jack-o'-lanterns down here. That way you can see them first and have them all to yourself for a while."

Amoretta giggled. "Oooo! You really know how to spoil a woman," she said.

"Let's just say I know how to spoil you, darlin'," Brake answered.

It was cooler than Amoretta had expected it to be, and she shivered a bit, even for the warmth of her sweater. But she was with Brake, and nothing could keep her from him now—not even the growing cold of All Hallows' Eve.

"Are you ready, Amoretta Ipswich?" Brake asked as they began to round a curve in the road.

"I can't wait! I'm simply trembling with anticipation!" Amoretta admitted, almost breathless with excitement.

The moment they turned, Amoretta could smell it—the dreamy, wonderful, rich scent of pumpkins slowly cooking by candle flame. It was delicious! The air was so heavy with the ambrosial aroma of roasting pumpkin that it was nearly intoxicating—enchantingly intoxicating!

Yet when Amoretta saw the Meadowlark Lake pumpkin parade set out before her—when she first glimpsed the fences on either side of the road lined with jack-o'-lanterns of every shape and size—she was truly breathless with awe for long moments.

"I-I have never even imagined anything like this!" she exclaimed at last.

Brake laughed, put a strong arm around her shoulders, and pulled her to nestle against him under one arm. "Yep. I thought you might like it."

"It's awe-inspiring!" Amoretta breathed. She felt tears of admiration and joy brimming in her eyes. "I-I've never seen anything so beautiful!"

"Well then, let's take our evenin' stroll among them, shall we?" Brake asked.

Amoretta squealed with delight, allowing both her arms to encircle Brake's waist in an embrace of excitement and gratitude. "And though I know it will be fun when everyone comes out to see it…" She looked up to him and reached up, placing one palm against his whiskery cheek. "It's so much more wonderful with just you."

Brake took her hand from his face, gripping it firmly and kissing her fingers.

"Then come on, precious," he said as he started walking them down the very middle of the road. "Let's have it all to ourselves while we can." Brake rubbed her shoulder a moment, however, adding, "Though I think we shoulda brought you a warmer coat or somethin'."

Amoretta smiled up at him and shook her head. "No. You can keep me warm," she flirted.

Brake's smile broadened, and Amoretta giggled when he mumbled, "Oh, darlin'…you have no idea how warm I can keep you."

Exhaling a heavy breath, Brake began leading Amoretta farther down the road, between the fences on either side, and into a world of Halloween jack-o'-lantern wonder that she never could've imagined.

There were so many! Some were smiling with happy eyes and crooked teeth, while others frowned or grimaced in a more menacing manner. There were very large jack-o'-lanterns and very small ones, but most fell somewhere in between—and all were mesmerizing.

Amoretta found she was purely fascinated with the flickering lights, the way the candle flames seemed to leap out into the air. It was a marvelous sight, and she owned a moment of wishing she could keep all to Brake and herself. But then she thought of Shay and how deliriously excited she would be by the parade of jack-o'-lanterns, and suddenly, she was impatient for Brake's adorable little niece to see it.

Stopping in the middle of the road, Amoretta turned to face Brake. "Shay will love this! We should go get her right now and bring her out here before anyone else comes."

Brake grinned, but Amoretta thought it almost a halfhearted grin. Didn't he want to see Shay's face light up like its own little jack-o'-lantern when she caught sight of the marvel of squash and candles?

"All right," he agreed, however. "But…there's somethin' I need to tell you first, Amoretta…before we go back."

A small wave of trepidation rose in Amoretta's bosom. Brake's expression was void of any sort of smile. In fact, he looked unsettled.

"What's the matter?" she had to ask. Surely he didn't intend to break her heart—not after going to so much trouble with Rowdy Gates to find her alone with him amidst the jack-o'-lanterns. Brake paused, and Amoretta's anxiety heightened. "Brake?" she urged in a whisper.

Exhaling a heavy breath, he said, "It was my apple."

"What?" Amoretta asked. She felt simultaneously relieved and confused. "What do you mean, it was your apple?"

"Just now…in the barn," he answered. "The one you came up with when you went bobbin' in the apple barrel—it was mine. I carved the S into it."

"Why?" Amoretta asked. She was hurt at first. Why would he toy with her heart, knowing how rather obsessed she was about not wanting to find Ss any longer in Halloween apple parings or the one she'd bobbed for?

"Because it's my initial," he stated.

"What?" Amoretta asked again.

Brake sighed and confessed, "Brake is my middle name. I've always used it, ever since I was a kid because I didn't like my first name…Sager. Sager Brake McClendon. That's my full name." He grinned then, reached out, and placed his hands at Amoretta's waist. "Don't you see, baby? It wasn't ol' Sylvan-ass whose S you've been gettin' with apple peels all this time. It was mine—S for Sager. I'm the one meant to be your lover." He paused, his handsome brow puckering into a concerned frown. "Are you mad at me for not tellin' you before?"

But Amoretta was already too overwhelmed with pure, elated joy to even remember whether she'd been miffed at all! Throwing her arms around Brake's neck, she giggled, weeping tears of mingled amusement and happy relief against his shoulder.

"How could I be mad at you for that?" she asked, still laughing— still wiping tears from her eyes. "That stupid, silly S! I've spent so much time worrying over it…because all I wanted was you!"

Brake laughed then too. "You have no idea how surprised I was when you bobbed for that apple and came up with mine. I figured I better tell you before it got any worse…before you hopped on a horse and headed back to Boston to find ol' Sylvan—"

Amoretta's kiss silenced Brake in that moment. Standing on her tiptoes in order to capture his mouth, Amoretta kissed him and kissed him—over and over and over—kissed him with the kisses of a blissful heart.

"So," Brake began when she stopped to catch her breath and gaze into his eyes, "you're not too angry with me for not tellin' you right off?"

"No," Amoretta assured him with a giggle. "I think it's wonderful! I think *you're* wonderful!"

"Wonderful enough that you'd be willin' to marry me?"

Amoretta couldn't breathe. Had she heard him correctly? Was she truly understanding what he was asking?

"A-are you asking me to…to…" she stammered, still too stunned to speak well.

"To marry me? Yes," Brake affirmed. "Will you marry me, Amoretta Ipswich? I love you, and I cannot go another day without knowin' if you love me enough to be my wife…to be my lover and the mother of my children." He lowered his voice, his eyes burning with mischief as the flames of the jack-o'-lanterns were mirrored in them. "Do you love me enough to keep me as you lover? To share my house with me…to share my bed with me, darlin'?"

Amoretta blushed with delight and desire as she whispered, "Are you sure you want *me*?"

"Darlin'…you have no idea how I want you," Brake mumbled. "But you haven't given me an answer or—"

"Yes! Yes! Of course! At once! This minute!" Amoretta cried as tears streamed down over her cheeks.

Raising herself on her tiptoes again, she affixed her mouth solidly to Brake's. His arms wrapped around her, lifting her off her feet as he endeavored to quench his thirst for her kiss.

The repeat of the pistol hurt her ears. Thus it took a moment for Amoretta to feel the sharp burning sensation in her left shoulder. She opened her eyes to look at Brake—but he was staring past her as if he'd seen a ghost.

"What have you done?" he shouted.

"Well, you don't have a dog to kill, Brake," a voice answered.

CHAPTER SEVENTEEN

"Amoretta?" Brake asked, taking Amoretta's chin in one hand and searching her eyes.

But Amoretta found she was still too stunned with the growing realization she'd been shot to respond to him.

"No! Don't!" she heard Brake shout as he released her. Her knees went weak, and she crumpled to the ground as she heard another gunshot ring out.

"I have to, Brake!" a woman's voice cried. "They're drivin' me mad...the voices! I have to do it!"

Something in Amoretta called to attention once more, and she turned to see Brake gripping Prudence Mulholland's wrists. Prudence held a pistol in her left hand—fired it once more into the air.

"Prudence!" Brake growled. "Let go of that gun! What the hell is wrong with you?"

"Don't you touch her, McClendon!" Samuel Mulholland hollered, appearing from seemingly nowhere. Running at Brake, Samuel caught him around the waist, knocking him to the ground and freeing Prudence.

"Brake!" Amoretta screamed. Brake was struggling with Samuel—wrestling him there in the middle of the road. And he was bleeding. Brake's shirt at his right shoulder was soaking with bright red blood.

"Shut up, Amoretta Ipswich!" Prudence screamed, leveling her pistol at Amoretta. "Don't you even dare to say his name again!"

Amoretta watched, horrified and confused, as Prudence's expression grew strange—not just angry but strange. Looking to her left, Prudence mumbled something that was inaudible to Amoretta. She closed her eyes a moment, as if listening, and then her attention was back to Amoretta.

"Pru—" Amoretta began.

"I said shut up!" Prudence growled. She raised the pistol, firing another shot into the air.

Amoretta looked once more to where Brake was struggling with Samuel. Samuel was on his back on the road. Brake sat on his legs, landing blow after brutal blow to Sam's face with his fists.

"Dex Longfellow had a dog," Prudence said. Amoretta looked back to see Prudence looking to her right—just as if she were having a conversation with someone. "And...and so did Rowdy Gates. They both spurned me...and the voices told me to kill their dogs. I killed Winnie's cat, like you said, because she was fallin' in love with Brake." Prudence's attention turned back to Amoretta then. "But Brake doesn't have a dog, now does he, Amoretta? Brake has you instead."

"Prudence...I'm your friend," Amoretta ventured.

"You're not my friend!" Prudence shrieked. "Brake McClendon loved you the minute he laid eyes on you...and he doesn't have a dog!" Suddenly, Prudence put a hand to her nose. "Do you smell that? That dead smell? It smells like blood and rotten things."

But all Amoretta could smell was baking pumpkin.

"Prudence—" Brake panted.

Amoretta gasped when she looked up to see Brake standing nearby. His shirt was continuing to soak with blood at his shoulder, and she saw that his left forearm was also bleeding. Samuel lay nearby, beaten and bloodied and unconscious.

"Prudence," Brake said again, sidestepping toward Amoretta. "What's goin' on, Prudence? This ain't like you."

Prudence sighed as if irritated with having to explain something to a child. "Brake," she said, shaking her head in a scolding manner, "you know you and I were meant to be lovers. From the day you moved to town, *I* knew it. Didn't you?"

Before Brake had a chance to answer, however, Prudence again looked to her left and began mumbling.

"Move, Amoretta," Brake whispered. "Move now, while she's—"

"I said shut up!" Prudence shouted. She took hold of the pistol with both trembling hands, aiming it first at Brake and then at Amoretta and back. "Let me listen to them. Let me try to reason with them so I don't have to do this!"

"Who, Prudence?" Brake asked. "Who are you talkin' to?"

"The voices, Brake," Prudence answered, rolling her eyes as if Brake were asking the most asinine question in the world.

As Prudence looked to her right, continuing her conversation with whatever voices were in her head, Brake quickly moved to step in front of Amoretta.

"No!" Amoretta gasped, however. She would not let Brake be harmed—never!

"So...so you killed the dogs...the rats," Brake gently said as Prudence's attention turned back to him.

"Of course," she proudly answered. "Dex Longfellow...he kissed me, out under that old big maple just outside of town. And then...then do you know what he did?"

Brake shook his head and asked, "What did he do, Prudence?"

Amoretta was shaking; she couldn't stop. Though the bullet wound at her shoulder barely more than burned, she could feel her own warm blood soaking her blouse and sweater—and she felt colder than she had a moment before.

"He never kissed me again!" Prudence answered with distain. "So awhile back...I killed his dog. I was told to, of course. And I wasn't gonna do it at first, but the voices...they're so persistent."

"Prudence—" Brake began.

"I killed some cats too...for practice...before I killed Dex's dog," Prudence continued, however. "And a couple of foxes that day too." She shook her head with disgust and anger. "But the day I killed Rowdy Gates's dog, I killed Winnie Montrose's cat...because she's the one who took Amoretta out to the mill that first day to see you. You remember, don't you, Brake? The day you came waltzin' out of my daddy's mill wearin' nothin' but your bitches and boots…and started lookin' at Amoretta here the way a cowboy looks at harlot after a long, long cattle drive? Remember that?"

"But, Pru…I don't understand," Brake said, taking several steps toward Prudence.

"Brake! No!" Amoretta breathed, but he'd already stepped out of her reach. Amoretta glanced over at Samuel, ensuring he had not roused from unconsciousness to pose another threat.

"What did Rowdy Gates do to you, honey?" Brake asked, taking another step toward Prudence.

Prudence tossed her head back with a roaring laugh, and Brake took three quick steps toward her while she was distracted in doing so.

"Rowdy Gates?" Prudence asked. "Why, he was worse that Dex was! Because Rowdy Gates didn't ever give me the time of day…not once! Oh, I tried to get his attention…but he wouldn't have anything to do with me." She paused, sighed, and smiled at Brake. "And then you moved to town, Brake, and I knew…I knew you were meant for me. The voices told me so."

She was mad! Utterly insane! Amoretta felt weak and cold—frightened for Brake's safety. But she knew Brake was stronger than she was and owned a better chance of distracting Prudence and thereby perhaps taking the gun from her.

"But…but I know, Pru," Brake began carefully. "I know Sam wrote a note to Sheriff Montrose sayin' that he killed those animals. I know because—"

"Samuel is a liar!" Prudence interrupted. "Sam knows darn well that I was told to kill those animals." She shrugged. "Of course, the voices had me kill the rats just so Sheriff Montrose wouldn't figure out that someone was killin' certain people's pets. But when Sam found out it was me that killed them, he told me that I was as crazy as Mama is…that I should be in the lunatic asylum right along with her. But I told him he was my brother—and did he want me to be as lonesome and miserable as Mama is? I told him I was only mad when I killed those animals…that I was over it and I'd be just fine." Prudence sighed with what appeared to be almost boredom and then continued, "And then he went off and wrote that silly ol' note to the sheriff." She rolled her eyes with exasperation. "But I told him…I said, 'Samuel Mulholland, if you don't stay with me, if you don't stay and protect me…'" Prudence shrugged. "Well, the voices have been tellin' me to kill Daddy. So I told Samuel that as long as he stayed with me…Daddy would be safe. So he's been livin' out in the woods ever since."

But Brake had drawn very near to Prudence while she'd been trying to rationalize what she'd done. One more shot rang through the air as Brake lunged at Prudence, pushing her hands up and stripping the gun from her a moment after she'd pulled the trigger.

"Brake, darlin'!" Prudence cried out. "We are meant to be together!" Frowning then, she growled, "So give me that gun!"

Amoretta gasped, however, when Brake struck Prudence on the back of the head with the gun, pistol-whipping her into unconsciousness. He didn't attempt to catch Prudence as she crumpled to the ground, for he had already turned. And in another moment, Amoretta was safe in his warm, powerful embrace.

"Brake!" Amoretta wept. "You could've been killed!"

"You've been shot, Amoretta," Brake mumbled, however. Quickly he pulled back her sweater and tore her blouse at her shoulder. He sighed with relief, breathing, "Through and through. She shot you through and through. The bullet ain't in you."

But Amoretta could hardly breathe—for she realized just why Brake's shoulder was bleeding.

"That's because it's in you!" she cried. Frantically she felt his back—the place where the bullet should've exited his body. But his shirt was not bloody there or torn. The bullet that had gone through Amoretta's body was still lodged in Brake's.

"Brake!" she shrieked. "You've been shot!"

Brake smiled and chuckled a moment as he glanced at his shoulder. "Oh, don't you worry about that, darlin'. We'll just get that right out." He lifted his left arm and studied his bleeding forearm. "And this one here…it's just a graze." Taking her face in his hands, he forced her to look at him. "And you're bleedin'…but you'll be fine too, precious. Heaven's watchin' over you and me, baby." Brake pulled her to him and held her close as he kissed the top of her head and gently stroked her hair. "Heaven surely is watchin' over me and you."

Amoretta could hear her father's voice calling her. No doubt everyone at the barn had heard the gunshots and come running to see what the ruckus was. All at once, as her family, friends, and other citizens of Meadowlark Lake descended upon her and Brake with questions and concern, Amoretta simply held tighter to the man heaven and fate meant for her to have.

Slowly Amoretta's fear faded. The horror of it all would repeat itself in her mind over and over, she knew. But in that moment—safe in Brake's arms—her fear was gone. And though Amoretta's heart did ache for the further sorrow she knew Mr. Mulholland would endure—for poor Prudence and her fractured mind, and for Samuel—somehow it was joy that filled her bosom. As Brake lifted her into his arms to carry her to back to the barn the way Doctor Crane had instructed, Amoretta smiled at her handsome lover whose first name started with S.

"We've been shot together," she said, smiling at him. "Nothing can bring us any closer than that."

But Brake laughed in his throat, kissed her cheek, and said, "Darlin'…you have no idea what can bring us closer than that." Amoretta smiled and blushed—laid her head on his shoulder. "And once we get you healed up and take our vows in front of the preacher…oh, sweet Amoretta Ipswich…you can be sure I'll show you." He laughed again and mumbled, "And you can bet on that, precious."

"Doctor Crane says they're calling it hebephrenia," Amoretta explained to Evangeline. "He says it's a terrible illness, an illness of the mind…and that Prudence is just the age when most people stricken with it begin to show symptoms."

Evangeline was slowly rocking in the rocking chair as Amoretta and Brake sat on the sofa together in the parlor. "How awful," Evangeline mumbled. She stopped the rocker abruptly, looked at Amoretta with new tears in her eyes, and said, "She almost killed you!"

"But she didn't," Amoretta reminded her.

Brake yawned. "Well, I'll say this much. That was the most eventful pumpkin parade I ever attended."

Amoretta laughed a tired, breathy laugh, even though it hurt her shoulder. She was happy when she saw Evangeline shake her head, smile, and laugh too. The hours since the tragedy with Prudence had been long and painful. Of course, Amoretta knew they had been far more painful for Brake. Doctor Crane had cleaned her wounds and packed them against infection—that was all. But Brake—Doctor Crane had had to cut into his shoulder in order to remove the bullet, before he could clean and pack Brake's wound.

"She's finally back to sleep," Calliope sighed, tiptoeing into the parlor from the hallway. "That poor little girl is wound up tighter than a Christmas morning spinner top!" Plopping down into a soft chair near the hearth, Calliope frowned as she glanced around the room. "Where're Daddy and Kizzy?" she asked.

"I don't know," Evangeline answered, covering her mouth as she yawned. "They went out on the back porch or something, I think. I'm too tired to know."

Brake smiled, kissed Amoretta's cheek, and pulled her close. "I think your daddy is finally gettin' around to proposin' to my sister," he said. "He asked my permission yesterday mornin' while we were out helpin' the Ackermans at their barn."

"What? Now?" Calliope exclaimed.

Amoretta giggled at the way her sisters suddenly perked up. Fairly leaping from their chairs, where only a moment before they'd sat overwhelmed with fatigue, Evangeline and Calliope softly hurried through the kitchen.

"There they are!" Calliope called quietly. In the stillness of the first November morning of the year, Calliope's voice carried like a sweet echo, and Brake chuckled.

"She's gonna spit out everything she sees, isn't she?" Brake asked.

"Of course," Amoretta confirmed.

"Ooo! He's talking to her again," Evangeline said. "Kizzy's crying and wiping the tears from her cheeks."

"Oh! She's nodding...and hugging Daddy now! How utterly romantic!" Calliope chirped.

"And now Daddy's kissing Kizzy," Evangeline added. "And kissing Kizzy...and kissing Kizzy. Why, Daddy! Goodness sakes!"

Brake and Amoretta laughed, and Amoretta could just imagine her father and Kizzy's happiness—for her own happiness in knowing she would soon marry Brake was indescribably rapturous.

"Oh," Brake mumbled, "I almost forgot." Amoretta watched as he fumbled with something in the front pocket of his trousers. "With all the shootin' and crazy people tonight...I never got to give you this, darlin'."

Amoretta thought her body had been so drained of energy and moisture that she'd never cry another tear. Yet as she gazed at the beautiful gold band with the beautiful solitaire diamond, she did feel tears trickling down her cheeks again. Taking her left hand, Brake gently pushed the ring onto her ring finger.

"There now," he said. "It's official. You're beholden to marry me now, girl."

Leaning up to kiss Brake softly on the lips, Amoretta whispered, "It's beautiful, Brake! But...but you know you didn't need to—"

"It's not about need, Amoretta Ipswich," he interrupted. "It's about tyin' up the loose ends of my gypsy spell to bewitch you into loving me."

Amoretta smiled, shaking her head with amusement. "I do love you, you know," she told him. "I don't ever want to be apart from you again. In fact, I want to sleep right here on the sofa...safe in your arms...so I can hear your breathing and feel your touch."

"Well, darlin'...that wouldn't be at all proper," Brake teased.

Amoretta's eyes narrowed. "I'll show you what isn't proper, Brake McClendon."

"Oooo, Miss Amoretta," Brake exclaimed in a low, alluring voice. "You promise?"

"I do," Amoretta said.

As Brake gathered her into his arms, Amoretta was aware of nothing else in the house. And as his mouth captured hers in a now deliciously familiar, impassioned kiss, she was aware of nothing else in all the world. Not of Kizzy's tears of joy as she and Lawson Ipswich entered the kitchen and announced to Calliope and Evangeline that Kizzy had accepted Lawson's proposal of marriage. Not even of Shay's excited squeal as she skipped through the house giggling, "Do I get to call you Daddy now, Mr. Judge?"—having obviously not been asleep and having obviously been eavesdropping through the open bedroom window when Lawson proposed to her mother.

To Amoretta there was only Brake in that moment—only his arms around her, his ring on her finger, and his warm and wonderful kiss—his kiss that affirmed to her heart that from the moment of her birth, her soul had been searching for him.

EPILOGUE

"The wedding of Miss Amoretta Ipswich and Brake McClendon was even more memorable for the fact that Judge Lawson Ipswich and Miss Kizzy McClendon were wed in the same ceremony. Judge Ipswich's daughters Evangeline and Calliope were joined by Miss McClendon's daughter, Shay, as attendants to the brides. All lady attendants were dressed in blue, with bouquets of late-season yellow mums held at their waists," Calliope read.

"That's lovely, Calliope," Evangeline said as she slipped Shay's new blue nightdress over her head. Evangeline smiled as Shay's dark curls bounced out of the neck of the nightgown like soft, dark springs.

"It's all I have so far," Calliope sighed. "But it's something. I'll need to finish it tomorrow, however, if I mean to post it in time for it to run in the next county newspaper."

"There!" Evangeline sighed as she studied Shay a moment. "And how do you like your new nightgown, Shay-Shay?"

"Oh, I love it, Evie!" Shay squealed, throwing her arms around her stepsister and planting a wet kiss on her cheek. "It's just like yours and Calliope's! I love it! Oh, thank you, Evie!"

"You're welcome, love." Evangeline stood, studying herself in the standing looking glass. "Come here, girls," she said. "Now let's see how we look all together."

Calliope left her chair at the small desk where she'd been writing her announcement of the weddings and hurried over to the mirror.

Maneuvering Shay to stand in front of her and Calliope, Evangeline smiled. "There! Don't we three look just delicious?"

But Calliope frowned, even as Shay giggled. "It's just all so confusing," she sighed. "I really do think I need to write it down."

"What's so confusing?" Evangeline asked, smiling as she watched Shay admiring herself in the mirror.

"All of it!" Calliope answered. "I mean, Kizzy is now our stepmother."

"Yes...and?" Evangeline prodded, still not understanding what it was Calliope was worried over.

"Well...Kizzy's our stepmother and Amoretta's stepmother," Calliope began again. "But she's also Amoretta's sister-in-law. And Amoretta is Kizzy's sister-in-law, Shay's stepsister, *and* Shay's aunt. And Brake is daddy's son-in-law, daddy's brother-in-law, *and* our uncle-in-law. Shay is our stepsister, Amoretta's stepsister, *and* Amoretta's niece." Calliope sighed. "It just makes my head hurt to try and figure it all out."

"Then don't try," Evangeline suggested. She leaned over, placing an affectionate kiss on Calliope's cheek.

"Sisters," Shay began then. Evangeline and Calliope exchanged delighted, albeit amused, grins.

"Yes, darling?" Calliope answered.

"Do you know just what I'm thinkin' right now as we're all three of us standin' here in front of the mirror in our new blue nightdresses?" Shay inquired.

Calliope smiled as Evangeline began to sing, "*There were three little girls dressed in blue.*"

Shay giggled and sang, "*Then one married and left only two.*"

"*Then one fell in love with boy, who loved her and gave her much joy,*" Calliope added.

Shay took Calliope's hand in one of hers and Evangeline's in the other. Nodding to Evangeline that she should take Calliope's, they formed a circle and began softly waltzing together.

"*Then the last little girl had a dream,*" Shay sang. Evangeline and Calliope then joined her to sing the rest of the song in unison.

"*Then the last little girl had a dream*," they sang, "*and she dreamed she was saying, 'I do.' And when she awoke, it was true! Happy three little girls dressed in blue.*"

"And I'm one now, aren't I?" Shay asked as they all continued to waltz together. "One of Mr. Judge's...I mean, Daddy's three little girls dressed in blue. Because I'm your sister now, and Amoretta is already married, so that leaves me and you, Evie, and you, Calliope. Right?"

"Exactly!" Evangeline and Calliope chimed together.

Shay giggled with delight. "Can we sing it just a few more times before bed? Please?"

"Of course, angel," Evangeline said. "And then, since Daddy and Mommy are staying in the house in the woods for a few days, the three of us will just hop into Daddy's big brass bed and go to sleep together."

Shay laughed, her springy curls bouncing as she danced with evident joy.

"All right. Let's sing it again then," she giggled.

Evangeline and Calliope joined as all three of Judge Lawson Ipswich's remaining unmarried daughters waltzed together, singing the song their father loved to sing to them.

There were three little girls dressed in blue.
Then one married and left only two.
Then one fell in love with a boy,
Who loved her and gave her much joy.
Then the last little girl had a dream,
And she dreamed she was saying, "I do."
And when she awoke it was true!
Happy three little girls dressed in blue.

Kizzy studied herself in the small mirror on the wall of her bedroom. She hoped she looked her best—looked as beautiful as Lawson said she did—and as desirable. She was surprised to find herself so terribly nervous on her wedding night. Kizzy hadn't expected to be so. Lawson was ever so complimentary and affectionate that she knew she had no reason to be anxious—and yet she was.

Lawson Ipswich was a giant of a man in character. He was handsome and wise, educated. He'd had a woman—a wife before—for more than a decade. He had three grown daughters. What could he possibly want with a new and very young wife, and a new and very young daughter?

Kizzy turned from the mirror, trying not to show her nerves as Lawson strode into the room then. Yet her nervous condition only heightened when she saw that he wore only his bottom underwear drawers. He'd already removed his shirt, boots, and socks—and Kizzy's heart leapt in her bosom with mingled terror and exhilaration.

Lawson hadn't looked up at her yet, however. He held a small stack of papers in his hands and was frowning as he seemed to study them. Sitting down on the side of the bed, he mumbled, "Everything looks to be in order."

Kizzy was somewhat relieved that he was working on their wedding night, but she was disappointed as well. His being distracted had lessened her anxiety but heightened her wondering whether she were good enough to be loved by him.

"Is…is it a court case?" she ventured.

Lawson looked up at her then, and Kizzy thought the smolder of desire apparent in his eyes would find her dashing for the door and escape. What if she couldn't make him happy? What if she disappointed him in life? What if he took her to his bed and was disappointed in her?

"No," he answered. "It's the papers for…the papers to…"

Kizzy frowned. "What's the matter, Lawson?" she asked, for she could see then that he was distressed.

"I had the papers drawn up, Kizzy…and I didn't tell you," he answered. "These are the papers for you to sign…if you're willing."

"For me to sign?" Kizzy asked as trepidation crept in on her wedding night. "Papers for what?"

Lawson inhaled a deep breath—seeming as if he were searching for courage. "These papers...they will allow me to officially adopt Shay...and change her last name to Ipswich."

As hot tears filled Kizzy's eyes, Lawson asked, "Are you angry with me? You don't have to sign them, Kizzy. I should've spoken with you about it first, but—"

As she threw her arms around her husband's neck and began smothering him with kisses, Lawson chuckled and dropped the pile of papers to the floor.

Taking his wife by the waist, he ground his mouth to hers in meeting her happy and impassioned kiss.

After a long while, Lawson broke the seal of their kissing, gazed into Kizzy's eyes, and asked, "I guess you'll be willing to sign the papers then."

Kizzy giggled and nodded. "Yes, Lawson! Oh yes!" she breathed. She sighed as she gazed at her handsome husband—reached up and ran her fingers through his soft, dark hair.

Lawson's loving thoughts toward Shay had restored a measure of her confidence—for she knew he would never make such an effort if he didn't truly love both Shay and herself.

Thus, Kizzy took Lawson's whiskery face in her hands, melted against him, and asked, "But why don't we take care of that in the mornin'?"

In an instant, Lawson had taken Kizzy in his arms, pulling her down on the bed with him as he kissed her with a ravenous passion. "Yes," he said as he slipped one shoulder of her nightdress down to reveal the tender flesh of her shoulder. "I have other things to attend to tonight." He kissed her neck, her throat, and her shoulder again. "Very pressing matters to do with my wife."

Kizzy Ipswich giggled, wrapped her arms around her husband's neck, and pulled him to her. "Oh, I love you, Mr. Judge."

"And I love you...my beautiful gypsy of the woods." Then he kissed her—the first kiss of the rest of Kizzy Ipswich's very loved and very loving life.

Amoretta gulped—pretended to be reading the book she was holding as she sat in the chair in Brake's parlor.

"What're you readin' there, darlin'?" Brake asked as he strode into the parlor wearing nothing but a pair of underwear bottoms.

"Um…a book," Amoretta stammered—having no idea what book she'd picked up just before he entered.

She heard Brake chuckle and felt a hot blush rise to her cheeks as he hunkered down in front of her. "You're not nervous or anything, are you, precious?" he asked.

Amoretta gulped again, forced a smile, and lied, "Oh no. Not at all. It's j-just…well, I usually read awhile before I go to…"

"Bed?" Brake finished when she didn't.

"Yes," Amoretta agreed, nervously nodding.

"Well then, honey," Brake said, taking the book from her hand and turning it upside down, "you might want to have it right side up when you're readin'. It seems to me it would be a whole lot easier to understand that way."

"Oh…oh, of course," Amoretta breathed as he smiled at her. His eyes were warm, alluring, ablaze with desire and determination. It caused her heart to skip several beats, just looking at him—just knowing that at some point in the night she'd be in his arms—in his bed and…

"You know what, honey?" Brake said then, taking the book from her hands and laying it on the floor.

"What?" Amoretta asked as her heart began to pound so hard it was nearly painful.

"I find the best way to handle these sorts of things," he began, "well…it's like a doctor settin' a broken bone in an arm or leg."

"How?" she asked.

Brake smiled at her, brushing a strand of hair from her rosy cheek. "You don't fiddle around with it. You just take hold and straighten it out."

A quiet squeal escaped Amoretta's throat as Brake simply reached out and lifted her out of the chair, tossing her over one shoulder as he stood and strode toward the bedroom. Laying her down on the bed in exactly the same manner she'd seen him stacking sacks of flour in the mill the first day she'd set eyes on him, Brake hovered over her for a moment, trailing lingering, moist kisses over her neck.

"I love you, Amoretta," Brake breathed, pressing his mouth to hers.

At the first taste of Brake's hot, familiar kiss, Amoretta sighed—began to relax. After all, this was the man she'd loved from the moment she'd seen him! This was the man who'd saved her life, made her laugh—the man who was meant to love her.

Yet as Brake kissed Amoretta's mouth and then her neck, using his chin then to nudge down the left shoulder of her nightdress, she stiffened, remembering the ugliness of her still-healing bullet wound.

Quickly she pulled the fabric of her nightdress up to cover the wound, rendered shy and feeling far from worthy to be loved by such a handsome and physically perfect man as Brake.

"What is it, Amoretta?" he asked, frowning at her with concern.

"It's...the wound. It's horrible," she confessed, feeling tears brimming in her eyes.

But Brake pushed her hand from her shoulder, gently tugging on the fabric of her nightdress until it slipped down far enough to reveal the still red and purple wound there.

"No," he breathed, gently pressing his lips to the healing flesh that would always be scarred. "Look," he said, taking her hand and placing it over his own healing wound. "They're a pair...a couple...just like we are. They were meant to be together." Slowly Brake relaxed his arms so that his strong body lay flush with Amoretta's. "You see?" he asked her, pressing his wounded shoulder to hers. His skin was warm and exhilarating to her senses. "They're mated, your wound and mine...and nothing will ever change that." He kissed her mouth and in a low, soothing, yet provocative voice said, "Remember that night...when you said we'd been shot together and that nothin' could bring us closer than that?" He grinned and asked, "And do you remember what I told you?"

Amoretta blushed and glanced away from him.

But Brake took her chin in one hand and forced her to look at him. "What did I tell you?"

"That you'd show me what could bring us closer," she whispered shyly.

Brake grinned. "Yes, I did tell you that. And now, my beauty…" He kissed her neck, then her cheek, and then her mouth. "Now I intend to make sure my gypsy spell I bewitched you with sticks for good…by showin' you exactly how close we can be."

Amoretta smiled, quirked an eyebrow, and asked, "Two bites to a cherry?"

Brake chuckled. "Or we could go peel some apples and toss the parin's over our shoulders if you'd rather."

Amoretta sighed as her palms traveled over the warm, smooth contours of her husband's muscular shoulders. "Oh no, Mr. Gypsy," she sighed. "I'm through with apple parings…for good."

"Then tell me you love me, Amoretta," Brake breathed. "Tell me you love me as much as I love you, and I'll show you just how close we can be."

"I love you, Brake," Amoretta whispered.

Brake smiled at her, and as his mouth claimed hers with a desire and passion he no longer had to bridle, Amoretta Ipswich McClendon shed her insecurities and fears, replacing them with an unbridled passion of her own. And all through the frosty November night, as the fire smoldered warm in the hearth, a much hotter fire blazed between Brake and Amoretta as they melded their love. Thus was consummated the bewitching of Amoretta Ipswich.

AUTHOR'S NOTE

One sweet little song, sung to me by my mother when I was a babe in arms, and well, you know it doesn't take much to spark a story in my often restless mind. It also doesn't take much to cause the other threads and plots of a story to begin bouncing around in my head. This isn't news to you; I've often told you that the most random things usually inspire my imagination, stories, and writing. However, I cannot begin to express how absolutely that is the case with this book. *The Bewitching of Amoretta Ipswich* is a prime example of how the simple things in life inspire me most. For example, here's the skinny on how this kind of stuff works for me:

Let's begin with postcards. As you may or may not know, I've been intrigued with postcards since I was 'tweenager. In fact, I began sort of subconsciously collecting postcards during a trip to Disneyland with my auntie and her family when I was twelve. (You know my auntie (pronounced ON-tee)—the one who collected black widows in canning jars as a kid—see *Sudden Storms* Author's Note.) Anyway, when I was twelve, I began collecting postcards from places I visited or that people sent me. By the time I was in college, anyone close to me knew that I was a budding deltiologist (one who collects postcards), and it was shortly after college that my hobby as a deltiologist really erupted! (See *Confessions of a Postcard-Collecting Fanatic* below).

Now a natural consequence of my deltiologist-ness was that in the mid 1990s my lifelong love of all things historic and old led me to the glorious, ephemeral world of antique postcards (specifically those of the Edwardian era). And that's where my deepest postcard love began to linger. Though I delighted in all the postcards I had personally gathered—treasured and adored all the postcards my family and friends slathered me with (see Trivia Snippet #2)—I began to notice that there was something about antique postcards that just sings to my imagination and heart!

Thus, slowly I've begun to compile a collection of antique postcards. I love them! And I love them even more if they have a wonderful, personal note written on the back. One of my favorite vintage postcards isn't very pretty at all on the front. It features a man and woman standing by a waterfall with a little poem that goes something like, "Go change your name to Mrs." and "smothered her with kisses." And yes, you're right—I purchased the postcard because of the kissing poem. However, when I turned it over and read the back, it instantly became a favorite! Postmarked December 8, 1910, the postcard is addressed to *Miss Rena Andrews, New Millford, PA*, and reads: "May be I will be up if I can. What size ring do you want? What Can I get your father and mother? N.W.S." How romantic, right? Love it! I am so smitten with antique postcards that I can't even begin to describe how utterly smitten I am! (I'm sure you're more than getting the picture by now.)

Well, the fact of the matter is that some of my favorites have always been Halloween postcards. But the other fact of the matter is that antique Halloween postcards are worth their weight in gold. They are *so* expensive! So unless you have money to burn or come across one while browsing in an old drawer at some little antique store, they're hard to get. However, I do have a few, and they've always intrigued me a bit differently than the rest.

The artwork is either gorgeous or kind of weird and creepy. (I prefer the gorgeous artwork.) And most of the time it seems antique Halloween postcards depict some romantic Halloween custom or superstition. (You're starting to see it now—another thread of my inspiration for *The Bewitching of Amoretta Ipswich*—aren't you? Paring an apple and tossing the peels over one shoulder and so on.)

So it's true—a large plot thread in this book was based on the fact that I was looking through my antique Halloween postcard collection one day and thought, *Hmmm. That would be a fun pretense—that a girl is intrigued with the old Halloween customs and one day, bam! They come true for her!*

My postcards inspired not only the story of Amoretta and Brake but also of Kizzy and her daughter, Shay. I wanted Kizzy to be a—well, whatever you call a girl hermit. At first I thought of making the gossip suggest that Kizzy was a witch, but I didn't like the whole witch-in-the-woods thing for Kizzy. And then one day, postcard—wham!—struck again. There I was, adding a lovely hand-tinted photo postcard to my collection, and it hit me: Kizzy could be moonlighting as a gypsy! And that led to all kinds of wonderful possibilities.

Moreover, one of my favorite tinted photo postcards is one of a simply beautiful little girl—a little girl who is my perfect vision of

darling little Shay! Of course she's not smiling so much in the photo I have (right here), but this is just how I imagine her to be—an ethereal beauty just like her mommy and uncle Brake.

Once I'd decided the McClendons were descended of gypsies, I started doing my research. Wow! What a ton of misconceptions I had about the origins of gypsy people. It's actually quite involved and confusing. But one thing I learned was that the core of gypsy heritage is Romani. And many, many gypsies are descended from Romani peoples living in Romania. Thus, I figured out that Brake, Kizzy, and Shay have Romanian gypsy ancestry. You probably didn't give a whoot about knowing that, but there it is, just for fun. (Smiley face!)

As for Lawson, I know that some who read this book might think something like, "Lawson and Kizzy? But he's so much older than she is!" To this, I offer what is often referred to as a "mental picture": Lawson Ipswich is the same age and physical build as Hugh Jackman! That's right! Is anyone in all the world still feeling sorry for Kizzy for snagging an older man? I say unto thee, nay! Right? Of course there are others in Lawson's age group that we are familiar with: Matt Damon, Ricky Schroder, Shemar Moore—and if you're a Brad Pitt fan, Lawson is actually six years *younger* than ol' Brad! I thought that might be a fun perspective, just in case someone was worried about Kizzy. (Another smiley face!)

Oh, I wish I could learn not to babble on and on and on about stuff! Sorry. It's like once I open my mouth, people should shout, "Run for your lives!" or something. But I did want to share just some fun, however unimportant, things with you about my inspiration for this book. I hope you found *The Bewitching of Amoretta Ipswich* entertaining—that it made you feel all warm and cozy just as if you were sitting in the Ipswich parlor before a crackling autumn fire or snuggling on Kizzy's worn sofa—or filled your dreams with visions of smooching in a haystack with your own handsome hero…
~Marcia Lynn McClure

The Bewitching of Amoretta Ipswich Trivia Snippets

Snippet #1—As I said, my mom sang to us girls a lot, and not just lullabies. She sang fun ones too, such as "Pony Boy," "I'm a Lonely Little Petunia in an Onion Patch," "Cruising Down the River," "K-K-K-K Katy," "Mairzy Dotes and Desert Blues" (which I realized one day, while singing the song to my daughter, had some very questionable or, as she put it, "not very appropriate" lyrics. But her dad used to sing it to her, so she never thought about it before that moment!) One fun song with appropriate, albeit morbid, lyrics was "My Little Girl." There are many renditions, but my mom's went like this: *My little girl, you are so sleepy, and you've gone upstairs to bed. Put your glass eye on the table; put your peg leg under the bed. Put your false teeth up in the window; put your false hair on the shelf. My little girl, I'd love to love you, but you've scattered everywhere.* Fun memories!

Snippet #2—So you know my friend Sandy? The one who cracks me up so often and has been my true, cherished, and loyal friend for twenty-eight years now? Well, one year she and her husband had to attend a work thing for his job. It was held in Colorado, and while there, she picked up a postcard and mailed it to me. On the front of the postcard was the most beautiful photo of purple (even though they're termed *blue*) Colorado columbine flowers! Columbines have always been one of my mom's favorite flowers, and therefore, I've always thought they were dreamy and so beautiful. Anyway, I received the lovely postcard but forgot to mention it to Sandy. So one day, she calls me up and says, "Did you get my postcard? The one with all the *concubines?*" (Read that again, if you missed it the first time and aren't already in stitches!) Concubines? I laughed so hard my guts nearly exploded! Oh, sweet Sandy—she adds such spice to my life!

Snippet #3—A little "where'd you get that name?" trivia for you now. (I'll try to make it quick.)

- Sylvanus Tenney is the name of my great-great-great grandfather—a Civil War veteran, by the way.
- Amoretta—My son Trent knew a girl in high school named Amorette. I always thought it was a beautiful name and had jotted down in my "list of names to use someday" file. Loved it! However, Amoretta Ipswich has a more melodic feel, so I added the "a" to the end of it. I've had several people tell me that they just can't quit saying it: *Amoretta Ipswich. Amoretta Ipswich.* It has a ring, right? And then there's her surname, Ipswich. I'd always, always loved that name, from the moment I first heard it years ago. But I kept forgetting to jot it down in my "list of names to use someday" file—until one day, I was over at my son Mitch and daughter-in-law Mallory's house. I had given Mallory a really pretty clock that I just couldn't find a place for, and it was hanging near her

front door. As I was leaving one day, she asked me what the sort of colonial word on the bottom of the clock was. "Ipswich," I answered. Whew! I'm so glad Mallory asked me about it, or I might never have remembered Amoretta's maiden name!

- Dex Longfellow—Well, I'm sure you had an easy enough time figuring that one out! You know I love the poetry of Henry Wadsworth Longfellow and that I collect antique books, right? Well, I was looking for a name for Dex and glanced over to see a new Longfellow book I'd just acquired, and yes, it's that boringly simple.

- Rowdy Gates—I'll tell you about Rowdy Gates's name because it's another thing my mom contributed to the book. My dad and I always loved the old Clint Eastwood spaghetti westerns—you know, *Two Mules for Sister Sarah*, *A Fistful of Dollars*, and so on. Well, my mother always loved the old Clint Eastwood westerns too. But one day, she confessed to me in secret that her favorite Clint Eastwood role was that of Rowdy Yates on an old TV show *Rawhide*. So since Rowdy Gates is the kind of man he is (brooding, secretive, and frowning a lot), I named him after Clint Eastwood's Rowdy Yates, just because my mom thought he was handsome.

Snippet #4—I really do loathe the phrase, "You've got to bloom where you're planted." It's a personal pet peeve of mine. True or not, it just makes me clench my teeth every time I hear it.

Snippet #5—One Romanian sentence that Brake mumbles to Amoretta in the book during "Two Bites to a Cherry" (which, by the way, was also something I found on a vintage postcard) I neglected to translate to English for you. But here it is: "Daca AS fi fost un om bun, MI-ar face eforturi pentru a vă câștiga." It translates to, "If I were a good man, I would endeavor to win you."

Snippet #6—I've never included "Acknowledgments" in my books for the simple reason that it would take a book the size of Webster's dictionary to thank everyone who has ever contributed in some way to my inspiration and success as an author. However, I would never be able to get a good night's sleep again if I didn't thank Nate and Andrea Childes for their incredible contribution to *The Bewitching of Amoretta Ipswich*! Nate and Andrea are dear, dear, dear friends (along with Andrea's sister, Anjanette; Andrea and Anjanette's mother, Connie; and Nate's mom, Brenda), and as you may be wondering why in the world I'm thanking Nate and Andrea in the trivia snippets of this book—well, just take another ogle at the front and back covers. Yep! Darling Nate allowed me to use his boom-chicka-wow-wow images for *The Bewitching of Amoretta Ipswich*. (Admittedly, I didn't really tell him about the back cover; he'll find out when Andrea gets her copy in the mail. Yikes!) Nate's a good friend, a good sport, and a good cowboy actor and model. His adorable wife, Andrea, is an angel of a wonderful friend and a good sport as well in letting her husband be exploited. I love them both so very much, and they have no idea how they enrich my life with their friendships and hilarious senses of humor. Love you, Nate and Andrea!

Confessions of a Postcard-Collecting Fanatic
(a.k.a. Back to Tennessee to Find Mississippi)

The summer I was twelve—that's when it really all began: my obsession with postcards. My auntie, Uncle Ken, and three cousins took me on their family trip to California. What adventures my cousins and I had as we rode along in the camper, perched atop the old blue pickup. Yep, me and Danny and Helen and Diana—ahhhh, sweet memories! I remember my Uncle Ken wanting to drive, drive, drive—tossing our full-bladder concerns to the wind! I remember my auntie sleeping in the cab of the pickup, her head in my uncle's lap as he drove—Dan, Helen, Diana, and I holding notes up to the cab window begging for a pit stop. Tree, rock, cactus—we didn't care! I remember singing funny songs with my cousins, something about, *"Ten little angels all dressed in white, tryin' to get to heaven on the end of a kite. But the kite-string broke, and down they fell. Instead of goin' to heaven, they all went to— Nine little angels..."* Naturally, when we reached the last little angel, the song changed to, *"Ten little devils all dressed in red, tryin' to get to heaven on the end of a thread. But the thread broke, and down they fell. Instead of goin' to heaven, they all went to— Nine little devils..."* (Fear not. The last chorus of the song, just in case it is unfamiliar to you, goes like this: *"One little devil all dressed in red, tryin' to get to heaven on the end of a thread. But the thread broke, and down he fell. Instead of goin' to heaven, they all went— Now don't get excited; don't loose your head. Instead of goin' to heaven, they all went to BED!"*)

Once we reached California (bladder damage permanent but contained) we visited SeaWorld, Lion Country Safari, the San Diego Zoo, and, of course, Disneyland. What excitement! *And* postcards, postcards, postcards! In my young, dreamy mind, I thought I'd never really been anywhere too exciting, never really been anywhere with my own money burning a hole in my groovy 1970s jeans pockets, never been anywhere with such fabulous (and cheap) postcards! So I stocked up. I mean, the postcards at Disneyland were better than any photos my little 1970s camera could take. And you could buy them of everything—even the *inside* of the Haunted Mansion and the Tiki Tiki Tiki Tiki Tiki Room! It was fabulous!

Remember that old gray bear in the Bear Country Jamboree—the one with Tex Ritter's voice that sang, "Blood on the Saddle?" Remember him? He was one of my favorite things, and you could buy a postcard of him. I mean, when Julie Andrews was singing about her favorite things, she had obviously never been to Disneyland and seen that old gray bear singing, *"There was…bbbllloooood on the saddle…and bllloood on the ground…and a great big puddle…of blllood all around."* It was the comedy stuff of legend. I roared! (Sort of like a bear, I guess.)

These first postcards I loaded up on were about the size of the smaller sort of index cards I used to give my kids to draw on in church when they were little—about 3½ by 5 inches—and cheap. I bought them for myself, for my parents, for my friends—and when I got home, I mailed them to my parents and friends and kept a stash for myself. I was completely intrigued. I had been somewhere! I had seen things, lived adventures, and the postcards helped me not only remember the adventure but also prove to the skeptics in the seventh grade that I had, indeed, lived it!

Proof of adventuring is very important to a twelve-year-old—especially when one had known the agony of enduring skeptics in the past. For instance, the summer I turned six, my auntie (yes, same auntie) had taken me up to the North Pole to see Santa while I was visiting her in Colorado Springs. It was amazing! And it wasn't even very far at all. In fact, we *drove* there—in our *car*. No sleigh necessary. And it was the most magical, beautiful place I had ever seen. Dressed in my groovy, psychedelic miniskirt, I met Santa, face-to-face for the first time—even had my photo taken with him. Furthermore, my auntie bought me these beautiful little pink, plastic, glittery reindeer ornaments. They were mesmerizing—all pink and covered in white glitter and definitely the most beautiful things I'd ever owned!

Naturally, when first grade started in September, I took my beautiful little pink, plastic, glittery reindeer ornaments to show-and-tell. I mean, they were undisputable proof that I had actually been to the North Pole and seen Santa! Weren't they? Can you imagine my shock, my astonishment, when no one believed me? No one! Everyone thought I was lying. I was so bitterly disappointed, frustrated, and angry. And you know what? Years later I realized if I'd just asked my auntie to buy me a North Pole postcard too…ha! Well, we would've seen what the skeptics in first grade would've had to say then. (Any remaining skeptics can visit www.santas-colo.com.)

And so I cherished my Disneyland postcards—the ones of the innards of the Haunted Mansion, the ones of the puffy-maned lions (which I collected at the time—toy ones, not real ones) ripping animal flesh as they ate, the ones of the two-headed snake at the San Diego Zoo—fabulous pictorial treasures of adventures gone by. Yep! The first postcards I collected were those I purchased myself in California that summer when I needed a good hairstylist in my life.

And then there was Sandra. Sandra and I met when I was about fourteen. It was one of those epic meetings, the ones that change who you are. We met at a girls' camp (that was the year someone poured a bucket of guppies down my brassiere, and I thought I had gotten them all out…until I got home hours later and disrobed only to find a dead guppy stuck to my bosom!), and Sandra and I were tried-and-true friends ever after. In fact, thirty-something years later, she and I still exchange Christmas cards. We don't hear from each other much more than that, but that's all we need to confirm we still carry our friendship in our hearts.

Anyway, Sandra went to Aspen, Colorado, one year with her family and sent me the most beautiful, Christmassy-looking postcard I had ever seen! In truth, I probably hadn't really seen too many postcards except the ones I had purchased myself in California, but this one of Aspen was super-duper dreamy—the very stuff to write kissing scenes by! (And yes, by the tender age of fourteen, I had already tried my hand at writing romance.) I loved the Aspen postcard, the simple piece of flimsy cardboard. Loved it! Kept it near my bedside and looked at it at night before I went to sleep. What a brilliant idea, really—the postcard. A pretty little indication that someone thought enough of you to go to the trouble of purchasing, writing, and tracking down postage and a mailbox—all while on vacation and all on your behalf. Loved it! The idea entirely captivated my imagination. Someday I would go somewhere, and then I could send postcards to the people I cared about, letting them know just how much I cared about them. Fabulous notion!

For years the only postcards anybody ever got from me were from Colorado Springs—that being the only place I ever went, at least before I left home for college. After leaving home, however, look out! "Postcard Woman!" That's what they called me. My beautiful college roommate Sandy had this *gorgeous* hair. She became famous for it and is still known, in some social circles, as "Hair Woman!" But not me—no, sirree! I was certainly never known for my hair. But "Postcard Woman!" That's what they use to call me.

Statistically, at the height of my postcard frenzy (age eighteen to approximately age forty-five), I received about one postcard to every 250 I sent out. But no matter. I loved it! I loved the sending much more than the receiving. And 250-to-1 or not, I have some great ones in my collection. Understand that for many years, I had *two* collections—one collection of postcards I purchased myself (or that have been handed to me) and one of postcards that have been *mailed* to me (my favorite one, and the collection I ended up keeping one year when I was worried about maybe becoming a hoarder of nostalgia and began to discern my *favorite* things from my semi-favorite things and filtered out the ones I'd collected for myself). My friend Sandra (different Sandra than Sandy the Hair Woman—the Sandra who was with me during the "dead guppy in the brassier" incident) to this day will occasionally send me postcards whenever she travels. A few years ago, I received one from her via Africa! What the heck she was doing in Africa she never said, but I was thrilled all the same.

And now for a little "Marcia's Postcard Collection" trivia:

1. The only love letter still in my possession from someone other than Kevin (because I had a dingbat moment and burned all my letters from other boys when I got married) is a postcard sent to me

from a boy while he was away in the summer of 1984. (Actually, I guess he wasn't a boy, being 22 and a college man.) The last line of the postcard reads, "If you want, we can be discreet and none of our other lovers will ever know." Hmmm—I may have to provide a few more details about that story at a later date.

2. The strangest reason someone ever gave me for bringing me a particularly questionable postcard? My friend's husband brought me a postcard from Alaska with a picture of a famous "madame" in the 1930s gracing the front. When I asked him why he chose that particular postcard (a lovely, curvaceous woman, rather scantily clad), he answered, "It reminded me of you." Hmmm. I've never quite known whether I was flattered or offended by his reasoning. (I'll stick with flattered.)

3. My first internationally mailed postcard received—from Egypt! Courtesy of my bosom friend Sandy (a.k.a. Hair Woman). Imagine my excitement the day King Tut arrived. It's still one of my favorite and most prized postcards.

4. Longest I ever traveled simply to buy a postcard? So my sister and I drove from Franklin, Tennessee, to Memphis one year to visit Graceland. (Another story that must be told!) After we'd meandered through the home and gardens where Elvis had lived, breathed, and passed away, my sister pointed out to me the Mississippi boarder was only ten to twenty miles away. Now, I'd seen Mississippi postcards in all the Elvis souvenir shops in Memphis, but as my good friend, and fellow postcard-collector, Scott says, "If you buy it yourself, it doesn't count unless you step foot in the city or state it's from." Of course, airports count, but that being neither here nor there, my sister, Luanna, and I decided we couldn't come so close to Mississippi and not add a Mississippi postcard to my collection.

And so we headed for the Mississippi boarder, stopped for some Popeye's Fried Chicken, and drove to the first gas station we could find. No postcards. We tried the next one. No postcards. Thirty miles into Mississippi, we found a Walgreens drugstore—and no postcards! Ahhhhhhhhhhhh! Can you imagine our frustration? Not to mention the frustration of my little nephew, Jonathan (eighteen months old at the time, whom I'd spent all day teaching to say "Elvis").

Finally, hot, tired, and defeated, we drove back to Memphis, where I screeched to a halt before the Heartbreak Hotel Souvenir Shop and bought a dang Mississippi postcard! Scott would not approve, but I *had* stepped foot in Mississippi, so I counted it until someone sent me one a few years later.

5. Two perfect strangers became a couple of the best postcard-sending pen pals I've ever had. One I met in Wal-Mart about five years ago—a girl from Ireland. I told her if she sent me a postcard from Ireland, I'd send her one from Ferndale, Washington (which is where I lived at the time). Not a very even swap, I admit. Still, she did send me postcards from Ireland—and then from Prague and a plethora of exciting places I'll never visit. And I sent her postcards from every place I ever went too. Can you believe it? I've never saw her again and eventually lost contact with her when I left Ferndale. I only talked to her for a few minutes in Wal-Mart, and yet we wrote each other whenever we had postcard adventures to share for years to follow. Can you believe it? The same goes for a little white-haired lady from South Carolina I met on an airplane about ten years ago. We started chatting on the plane, and when I found out where she was from, I mentioned my postcard obsession and asked if she'd be willing to swap postcards. Well, she sent me postcards from wherever her journeys led her for years and years. We exchanged Christmas cards too, and the year I didn't get a Christmas card from her, I was very heartsick. She was in her late seventies when we met, and not receiving another card from her since, I can only assume she's moved onto her greatest adventure—and I'm pretty sure they don't sell postcards there.

It's amazing when I think about it—what those little pieces of cardboard represent. It's like living the adventure all over again, having a glimpse into a total stranger's world. It's receiving a little piece of an old friend's heart. I love postcards! They're disappearing, you know. The world and all its rotten technological advancements are making postcards obsolete. It's actually very difficult to find them now, probably especially at that particular stretch of the Tennessee–Mississippi boarder. Thank heaven I began an antique postcard collection about fifteen years ago—because antique postcard are still all the rage among us deltiologists of the world!

Oh! And don't worry. When my kids were little and we took them to the North Pole—well, let's just say that postcards equal proof, and I made sure they had it!

Watch for the release of Book II of the
THREE LITTLE GIRLS DRESSED IN BLUE Trilogy!

The Secret Bliss of Calliope Ipswich

My everlasting admiration, gratitude, and love…
To my husband, Kevin…
My inspiration…
My heart's desire…
The man of my every dream!

ABOUT THE AUTHOR

Marcia Lynn McClure's intoxicating succession of novels, novellas, and e-books—including *The Visions of Ransom Lake*, *A Crimson Frost*, *Untethered*, and *The Pirate Ruse*—has established her as one of the most favored and engaging authors of true romance. Her unprecedented forte in weaving captivating stories of western, medieval, regency, and contemporary amour void of brusque intimacy has earned her the title "The Queen of Kissing."

Marcia, who was born in Albuquerque, New Mexico, has spent her life intrigued with people, history, love, and romance. A wife, mother, grandmother, family historian, poet, and author, Marcia Lynn McClure spins her tales of splendor for the sake of offering respite through the beauty, mirth, and delight of a worthwhile and wonderful story.

BIBLIOGRAPHY

Beneath the Honeysuckle Vine
A Better Reason to Fall in Love
The Bewitching of Amoretta Ipswich
Born for Thorton's Sake
The Chimney Sweep Charm
A Crimson Frost
Daydreams
Desert Fire
Divine Deception
Dusty Britches
The Fragrance of her Name
The Haunting of Autumn Lake
The Heavenly Surrender
The Highwayman of Tanglewood
Kiss in the Dark
Kissing Cousins
The Light of the Lovers' Moon
Love Me
The McCall Trilogy
An Old-Fashioned Romance
The Pirate Ruse
The Prairie Prince
The Rogue Knight
Romantic Vignettes-The Anthology of Premiere Novellas
Saphyre Snow
Shackles of Honor
Sudden Storms
Sweet Cherry Ray
Take a Walk With Me
The Tide of the Mermaid Tears
The Time of Aspen Falls
To Echo the Past
The Touch of Sage

The Trove of the Passion Room
Untethered
The Visions of Ransom Lake
Weathered Too Young
The Whispered Kiss
The Windswept Flame